BY JENNIFER DUBOIS

The Spectators

Cartwheel

A Partial History of Lost Causes

the spectators

the spectators

A NOVEL

jennifer dubois

random house | new york

Copyright © 2019 by Jennifer duBois

Published in the United States by Random House, an imprint and division of Penguin Random House LLC, New York.

RANDOM HOUSE and the HOUSE colophon are registered trademarks of Penguin Random House LLC.

LIBRARY OF CONGRESS CATALOGING-IN-PUBLICATION DATA
Names: duBois, Jennifer, author.
Title: The spectators: a novel / Jennifer duBois.
Description: New York: Random House [2019]
Identifiers: LCCN 2018013007 |
ISBN 9780812995886 (hardcover: acid-free paper) |
ISBN 9780812995893 (ebook)
Classification: LCC PS3604.U258 S68 2019 | DDC 813/.6—dc23
LC record available at https://lccn.loc.gov/2018013007

Printed in the United States of America on acid-free paper

randomhousebooks.com

9 8 7 6 5 4 3 2 1

First Edition

Designed by Debbie Glasserman

To the women of my family, especially
Carolyn, Beverly, Marjory, and Kate—
In gratitude for your resilience, and
in celebration of your second acts

Beware, my body and my soul, beware above all of crossing your arms and assuming the sterile attitude of the spectator, for life is not a spectacle, a sea of griefs is not a proscenium, and a man who wails is not a dancing bear.

—Aimé Césaire, *Notebook of a Return to the Native Land*

I don't think you can be a grown-up in today's world and be shocked by anything anymore.

—Jerry Springer

the spectators

semi

1969

FOR YEARS, THIS IS HOW WE REMEMBERED THE MAN WHO WOULD BE MATTIE M: walking through Greenwich Village, hands shoved into pockets, leaving a contrail of energy in his wake. He was Matthew Miller then—Counselor M. Miller, Esq., to the courts; Mattias Milgrom to his grandparents. Matthew to a very, very few. They say he had the charisma of a Kennedy, and not without reason—though he didn't have the face of one, and doesn't now; he only appears mild and un-shockable and impossible to rouse to fury, if you didn't know better. He had an inelegant, raccoonish walk he later unlearned for the cameras. But he also radiated a subtle electricity—something slight and untraceable that kinectified the air around him—and it was easy to mistake this, then, for the particular dynamism of compassion. Because compassion took work, he always said, and anyone who told you otherwise wasn't really trying to be good at it.

This quality, whatever it was, is entirely undetectable on television.

If men can change until they disappear, then it shouldn't surprise us that worlds can, too. And yet no matter what anyone says, there is no ceiling to our capacity for surprise. Two hundred years ago Washington Square Park was a mass grave, and before that it was a marsh.

Today Christopher Street is a single diseased artery running from the Bronx drag queens all the way to the hospice under the West Side Highway. Thirty years ago you could still get arrested there for window shopping too close to another man. Fifty years ago Matthew Miller was born in a cold-water flat in Crotona Park, and twenty years ago he lived in a walk-up apartment on West Fourth Street that looked out onto a brick wall. And now he makes something like $3 million a year, according to *Variety*, and nobody knows where he lives.

If anyone in the Village says they remember Matthew Miller, the question to ask is: which one?

WE BEGAN GOING TO THE STONEWALL SOMETIME AFTER ALL-STREET CLOSED. Say what you will about the Genovese family, they were nothing if not democratic: when it came to the laundering of money, anyone's dollars would do. Night after night, they served us watery, mislabeled drinks; night after night, we paid and did not complain.

Our nights there streaked together: they were innumerate, each a whirling aleph of potential. Those evenings now are a kaleidoscopic disco ball, with lights that blink out if we look at any one too closely. Stand back a step and the spinning resumes, pixelating us to present.

We stand in the park on Christopher Street, on one or many nights. The street kids hover nearby, trying to bum cigarettes: they are a pack, with inscrutable loyalties that seem to dissolve and re-form the way schools of fish change direction. Across the street, street queens in stolen dresses strike poses for the man behind the peephole. In the park, Brookie drapes himself over the statue of General Sheridan and begins taking liberties with his waistcoat.

"Well, well, well," he says. "Not as buttoned up as you look, are you?"

Brookie turns to us and stage-whispers: "It's like *iron* down there, girls."

Stephen notes that the statue is bronze, and we head across the street.

Inside, we blink against the darkness and begin counting the almost-strangers: we know faces but not names. A porcine lawyer and a scare queen dance to the Supremes in a low, viscid light. A man in a camel-hair coat stares at the hat in his hands, half-pretending to have wandered in by accident. All around is the smell of weak, formaldehyde-tasting liquor; and piss—especially, though not exclusively, near the bathroom; and Ambush perfume, hovering above a smell of sweat that is, it must be said, undeniably masculine.

"God knows we don't come here for the ambience," says somebody, probably Paulie, on one or many nights.

In the front room, all and sundry are picking up good vibrations; in the back room, the loneliness won't leave us alone. The women's room door swings open and reveals its royalty: the queens recently exiled from the Goldbug or the One-Two-Three. Everyone here comes from somewhere else: Milano's and Omega; Westchester and West Virginia; off-Broadway callbacks and the New York Stock Exchange. Our own group hails from rich Midwestern matriarchies and poor Howard Beach Catholics, St. Paul's preparatory academy and the St. Vincent's psych ward, the United States Navy and the Tisch School of the Arts. Brookie has recently returned from a stint in San Francisco, which we will never stop hearing about. But wherever we have come from, tonight, we are here.

We dance, we drink, we lose each other. We sip from glasses streaked with grime and, it turns out later, hepatitis. We stare at boys with hip-huggers and teased hair; we stare at boys in stage makeup who do not necessarily work in the theater. A man we've known forever takes off his glasses, and we stare at him, too. Perhaps he catches us—perhaps we let him—and for a moment, the Dionysian evening stills to a single Apollonian face: even as the ephebes and catamites, concupiscent and riotous, dance all around us in the dark.

There is nothing new under the sun, one of us always said about everything: and no, maybe not even this.

We stop at the wishing well—which is sometimes filled with ice, though usually with something less poignant: empty boxes, crates of beer. It doesn't matter: we did not come here to be prissy. We toast to the wish we all share—the one that is always the same, and that almost always comes true. Then we toss our coins, and sometimes they bounce back at us, and either way Brookie declares that tonight, he can feel it, is his lucky night.

Which, in a way, they all were.

IT WOULD BE TEMPTING, IN LATER YEARS, TO IMAGINE MATTHEW MILLER WAS amongst us, even then. Perhaps he was one of those furtive, suit-wearing figures, barely visible beneath the smear of sodium lamps, lingering down by the docks until the cops came by with their night-sticks.

Perhaps he was one of the shadows stealing across the Ramble, wedding ring in pocket, telling himself he did not know who he might meet there.

Perhaps he was a slouching, behatted shape coming in late to a show at the Jewel or Metropolitan.

Perhaps we even reached out—into that extraterrestrial, annihilating darkness—and touched him: this man we believed would always be a stranger.

Perhaps this was the last time we were right about Matthew Miller, or much of anything at all.

BEFORE WE GO OUT, WE MUST GET OURSELVES READY.

We linger over drinks and records; we try to persuade Paulie not to sing. We tell Stephen he's handsome if we think he deserves it that week—it seems unjust that such British Invasion looks can harbor such continental depression. Brookie asks Stephen if he's ever considered not dressing like a narc. Stephen asks Brookie if he's ever considered not dressing like a pimp. Then Stephen tells Brookie that novelty-seeking is a classic sign of narcissistic personality disorder, and Brookie asks what's the disorder where you diagnose everyone with a disorder, and Stephen says it isn't *his* diagnosis, it's Freud's, and we groan and say oh please God not again.

Outside, maybe, it is summer. The night has scaled down the sour smell of New York City in the heat. Paulie moves ahead of us, always the best at managing cobblestones in heels. Brookie and Stephen are arm in arm now, abruptly reconciled. We pass Washington Square Park, its arch glowing golden in the darkness. Above us, maybe, is a full moon. It shimmers like an enormous backlit tooth, and we stop for a moment to stare. Then we float down Seventh Avenue, making jokes so funny we know we'll remember them forever.

In Paris the students are wresting the hands off of clocks—if only we'd had *that* idea.

WE HAD OUR BAD TIMES, TOO, OF COURSE.

There were those afternoons Stephen spent on the floor, listening to Billie Holiday and asking everyone in earshot if they felt like committing suicide.

"Not more than usual," Brookie would say. We'd laugh—or if we didn't, we'd let pass an airless, respectful beat where laughter might have gone. We would have felt differently if we'd known how many times Stephen would go on to try it—and try it, and try it—before finally getting it right in 1988 (which was, as we all agreed, not a minute too soon).

There were the nights we reopened sealed wounds, settled questions. There were the nights we became the wrong sort of drunk. There were the restless puritanical nights of going nowhere at all— though these, at least, we have forgotten. There was the night a scare queen accused Brookie of stealing the Cinzano ashtray she'd been carrying in her purse. There were the nights white lights flooded the dance floor and we raced to find properly female partners. Stephen once grabbed a startled-looking butch dyke we thought for sure was going to deck him, but who turned out in the end to be a very good dancer. This was a pretty funny story when we told it later. There was the night the cops stormed the women's bathroom and pulled down everyone's underwear. This story was never funny, and we never told it.

———

HERE'S A STORY THAT'S A DIFFERENT SORT OF FUNNY: MATTHEW MILLER, ONE-time champion of the abandoned and depraved, is now Mattie M of TV's *Mattie M Show*—ratings zenith, cultural nadir. You can catch him any weekday afternoon, ministering to a parade of unfortunates before a vampiric studio audience—as well as six million at-home viewers, enjoying the thrills of the Colosseum from the comfort of their own living rooms.

But enough of this. Enough. There is nothing more to say. Matthew Miller was here, and now he's gone. And if we don't yet believe in the permanence of disappearance, then there is nothing in this life that will convince us.

THOUGH WE'D BEEN SEMI-REGULARS AT THE STONEWALL, WE MANAGED TO miss the riots. This was not the night we were arrested, and first met Matthew Miller. That happened a week earlier, at a raid no one remembers anymore.

Afterward, we were taken to The Tombs and booked by a fat-lipped warden. Our cell smelled of cinderblock and shit. We'd managed to get roughed up a bit during the scuffle, and there was a bruise on Paulie's cheek that seemed to be blooming before our eyes (there's something strangely auroral about a hemorrhage, as we'd all come to learn later). But it was Stephen who really alarmed us: he'd hit his head weirdly, and now his eyes were waxing and dimming in a way we did not like.

Across the hall, the fat-lipped warden smirked.

After a while, we heard a clang and a silhouette appeared in the doorway—a man with a medium build, wearing a hat at an angle. This, we figured, was the lawyer. We'd all heard stories about the kinds of lawyers cops called for people like us.

"I'm Matthew Miller," said the man. He had the faintly twanging vowels one associates with Depression-era New Yorkers. "I'm your PD."

He stepped forward, into a bar of less-dark shadow. He seemed to take on substance as he moved—coiling with potential energy, like a bulldog or a boxer.

"Is anyone here hurt?"

We pointed at Stephen, whose eyes were still flickering through their lunar phases. He was restless, and had already retched twice in the corner.

"Lemme take a look," said the lawyer. He managed to sound like he was actually asking permission. From his pocket, he produced a tiny flashlight, which he waved into Stephen's eyes.

"Well, I don't think you're ready to give up the ghost quite yet." The lawyer stood and began jotting something in a notebook. On his left hand, a wedding ring glinted, with prop-ish shininess. "But we do need to get you to a hospital. What's your name?"

Stephen didn't answer, and so the lawyer turned to us. A cloud outside shifted, and in the minor light we saw him, for a moment, in more detail: a wedge of white calcium on his thumbnail, a certain asperity to his brow. His eyes a bemused, hallucinatory green. On his face an expression that could, to the untrained eye, look very much like nothing—but which turned out later to be an unsurprised acknowledgment of the world's complexities, and a fundamental disinclination to judge them.

The lawyer drummed his fingers against the pages of his notebook. His nails, we noticed, had been bitten down to the quick. We winced, imagining the nervy sparks he must feel.

"What's his name?" he asked us again.

And we waited, wondering who wanted to know.

part one

ONE
cel

1993

CEL IS IN THE GREENROOM PRE-INTERVIEWING THE DEVIL-BOY WHEN THE first reports of the shooting come in.

The devil-boy's name is Ezra Rosenzweig, though Cel has been told to address him only as Damian. He has a black odalisque neck tattoo and thumb-sized subdermal horn implants; Cel keeps expecting these to twitch expressively, somehow, like the ears of a small dog. But the devil-boy's horns do not move, and alongside his shaved eyebrows they contribute to an expression of general impassivity, so Cel doesn't quite register the extent of his surprise when he stops speaking of satanic baptismal rites and says, "Oh, shit."

Cel follows his gaze to the television, turned to a perpetually mute CNN. On the screen is a crimson-blazered anchorwoman with melancholic eyes. Below her, a BREAKING NEWS chyron declares that a shooter, or possibly two, has opened fire at a high school outside Cleveland. Cel turns up the volume.

"—*High School has over fifteen hundred students enrolled,*" the anchorwoman is saying. Below her, rolling text announces reports of multiple casualties. The anchor wears an expression of perfectly choreographed concern—Cel would never have noticed the hint of relief beneath it if she didn't work in television. *"No word yet on who the shooter, or shooters, may be, but some early reports have suggested that students themselves could be involved—"*

"Awful," says Cel, realizing that this is not the right word.

Luke appears in the door, holding a clipboard. The clipboard is with him always, whether he has need to clip anything or not.

"You saw," he says, glancing at the television.

"We saw," says Cel. "You remember Luke, right, Ezra? I mean. Damian." On the screen, chopper footage is showing a bird's-eye view of the school: red-bricked, flanked by skeins of dusty playing fields. "Luke is a producer here at the show."

Luke loathes the use of indefinite articles in reference to his job.

"Yeah," says the devil-boy, with unexpected timorousness.

"Hi," says Luke, turning his head in the devil-boy's direction. Luke has a gift for interacting with guests as though they are not entirely there; the way he addresses them somehow suggests that their speaking back would be not just impertinent, but impossible—as though he is a weatherman and they are a green-screen tornado.

On the screen, the frame has extended to reveal an army of emergency vehicles: fire trucks, ambulances, police cars, local and state. Beyond the line of cars, Cel can just make out a few figures in lime-green jackets—EMTs, she figures, though none of them seem to be doing anything but waiting. Cel's mouth goes dry as she thinks of what they are waiting for.

"So." Luke lets out a low whoosh of air.

"Awful," Cel says again, senselessly. The devil-boy is staring not at the television but at Luke, a look of respectful, nearly sycophantic curiosity on his face. Cel sincerely hopes that Luke doesn't see this, though she suspects that, all appearances to the contrary, he actually always sees everything.

Luke turns, his gaze scraping at the air.

"I'm going to borrow Cel for a minute, okay, pal?" Luke does not wait for the devil-boy's assent. "Sara here will wait with you."

Sara Ramos, the audience coordinator, has materialized in the doorway. Cel regards her with interest—however much she dislikes her own job, she cannot imagine the horrors of Sara's—then follows

Luke and his clipboard into the hall. Outside, Luke tells her that Mattie wants to cancel today's taping.

"Out of respect for the victims," he adds after a moment. From his tone, Cel can't tell whether he agrees with this decision or is just tired of fighting with Mattie. Either way, she knows he must be apoplectic about the timing.

"Of course." Cel nods at the door, where the devil-boy is waiting, unsuspecting. "So we'll tell him—tomorrow?"

Luke's grimace deepens beyond his usual default grimace.

"I mean, is this just for today, or—?"

"I don't know."

"So—Monday, then?"

"You don't have to *tell* him anything. Jesus." Luke runs his clipboard-free hand through his hair. "Tell him we'll be in touch."

"Is Mattie on *strike* now, or what?"

"We just need to be very attentive to the optics." Luke is using what Cel thinks of as his press release voice.

"After Secret Crush," says Cel.

"*Stop* mentioning it. But yes."

Cel only ever mentions it to Luke—even she isn't that stupid. "Secret Crush" technically refers to an entire category of shows—the formula is exactly what it sounds like, and Mattie has done dozens— but these days is usually used to allude to a single episode. In that show, the Secret Crush object and subject were both men—longtime co-workers, evidently—and though this was not the first time that had happened, it was the first time anyone involved seemed genuinely surprised. The Crushee had stormed off the stage and, later, badly beaten his admirer in the parking lot. Cel had heard he'd suffered permanent brain damage, though she'd also heard that the whole thing was staged, a PR stunt so ill-conceived that it was arguably better to let the world think it was an actual hate crime. Cel's predecessor had quit and/or been fired and/or, according to some accounts, been hospitalized: the show had had to replace her in a hurry that bordered on derangement, which is how they'd wound up with Cel.

"I suppose that makes sense," she says now. It does, from the standpoint of public relations—which is, she has to keep reminding herself, her job, her job, somehow her job. But what really makes sense is that behind Mattie's stated reason for canceling is another reason, and that this reason is cynical and self-serving. One of Mattie's many areas of genius is his ability to maintain a perfect streak of Cel's abysmally low regard.

"*Yes,* Cel," says Luke. "I suppose it does."

He is using his rage-patience voice—though for once, Cel doesn't blame him. Ezra Rosenzweig a.k.a. Damian a.k.a. the devil-boy represented Luke's single, modest victory in a grueling half-year battle over ritual Satanism—which, in spite of massive audience interest and wall-to-wall competitor coverage, Mattie had refused to touch. Mattie generally wasn't big on trends—he'd treaded lightly on the McMartin Preschool trial—but he wasn't generally *this* stubborn, either. Luke had spent months trying to "persuade Mattie" to "join in the national discussion"—and for months, the "discussion," or whatever, had carried on without them: ubiquitous and manic, ever metastasizing and, apparently, boundlessly lucrative. Every show competing with *Mattie M*—and plenty that would never admit they were trying to—had done at least one Satanism episode. Most had done many: examining every angle, actual and hypothetical; bringing in commentators of increasingly tangential areas of expertise; finally resorting to episodes that were, essentially, thought experiments: "Unholy Alliance: Could Satanists Be Lurking in Your Church?"; "Devil M.D.: Satanism and Pediatricians"; "Pentagram at the Pentagon: Where Are Your Tax Dollars *Really* Going?" In spite of the hyper-saturation, the ratings had stayed outrageous. The very act of sating the audience's appetite seemed to somehow sharpen it, which was a television phenomenon you didn't see every decade.

"It's not even a finite resource!" Luke had bellowed earlier that month. "It just keeps making more of itself! Cel, this is how the stock market is *supposed* to work!"

"I'm sorry, Luke," says Cel now. "The timing is unfortunate."

"Yes, Cel," says Luke, through a tightened jaw. "It *is* unfortunate."

But this seems to be meanness out of habit—he doesn't even seem to be enjoying himself—which makes Cel feel sort of bad for him.

"Don't panic," she finds herself saying.

"*No one* is panicking."

"The audience isn't going anywhere. You know our buddy Ezra isn't going anywhere."

"Just back to Coney Island," Luke says dully. He shakes his head, taps his fingers mournfully against the clipboard. "Which reminds me—we gotta call him a car."

THE DEVIL-BOY TRIES TO TAKE THE NEWS MANFULLY.

"Sorry about this," Cel says, gesturing at the TV. The chopper footage is showing another line of cars—these ones illegally parked, with their doors hanging open. Cel tries not to think about who they belong to, and what they've been abandoned to find. "I know you were really looking forward to sharing your story with us."

The devil-boy's perkily upright implants look incongruous, now, with his abject expression. The guests are never entirely what you think they'll be—Cel learned this on her first day, when she walked in on an obese woman using a spit-shiny comb to tame the cowlick of the illegitimate son she would later hurl slurs at on the air.

The devil-boy nods absently, his horns bobbing.

"We were certainly looking forward to *hearing* it," says Cel—which is both inane and another epic understatement. In recent weeks, Mattie's Satanism boycott had come to seem increasingly apocalyptic; Luke alternated between comparing it to ritual seppuku, the Jonestown suicides, and, once, memorably, the Nakba.

"Are you kidding me?" hissed Joel, the senior producer, after that last one. "I don't give a shit about your politics or your sociopathic sense of humor, but don't you *ever* let me hear you make another joke about the Middle East around here. You think we need this shit right now?"

"But nothing about the seppuku," Cel whispered, after Joel had stalked away.

"He still thinks I'm Japanese," said Luke. "He thinks I'm being *literal* with that one! And, Cel, you know, some days? It's tempting." He mimed ritual self-disembowelment.

But even Joel agreed that Mattie's position was untenable, and that some sort of compromise would have to be made. That compromise had come in the person of Ezra Rosenzweig—bona fide Satan hobbyist, whose life, though devoid of any criminal history per se, was (Luke argued) perhaps even *more* frightening when considered in terms of its pure, sinister potential. And now, already, they are calling him a car. It is more than disappointing—Cel knows that—and the devil-boy doesn't look thrilled about it, either.

"Don't worry." Cel pats the devil-boy on the arm, near a tiny pitchfork tattoo she hadn't noticed earlier. The devil-boy's skin is psoriatic and dry, and she has the urge to hand him some moisturizer from her purse. Cel is not generally prone to flickers of proto-maternal tenderness—and she understands this isn't one coming from her, but from the television, which is now showing a roof under which many teenagers presumably are dying.

"Oh, hey!" Cel says, and the devil-boy looks stricken. "I almost forgot!"

She dashes to her office and returns, triumphant, with a gift bag.

"Here you go!" she says—in someone else's voice, possibly someone else's lifetime. The devil-boy looks cheered, though he really should not; there is nothing good in the bag—just a *Mattie M* pen and beer cozy and T-shirt, always extra large. Cel cannot imagine anyone wanting it, and after six months with the show, she can imagine a lot of things.

"Thank you," says the devil-boy. According to his bio, he is from suburban Connecticut.

"Sure," says Cel. "So, Sara will be by in a minute and—"

"It's horrible."

"I'm sorry?"

"It's horrible." The devil-boy is still staring into the gift bag, and Cel wonders if he's talking about the beer cozy—or, just possibly, addressing it—but then he looks up at her, eyes shining.

"It's a *tragedy*."

Not the gift bag, then.

"It is," says Cel.

"I don't understand it." There is a flare of defiance in his voice, as though he expects someone to contradict him.

"Nobody understands it." The devil-boy stares at her, evidently dissatisfied.

"Maybe it's one of those things nobody *can* understand." This sounds right, or close to right—though Cel suspects, even as she's speaking, that it is not. "Maybe it's one of those things nobody should even *try* to understand."

The devil-boy is still staring, and Cel tries to remember how old he is. Is it possible he is only twenty? His bright eyes and lost expression magnify the puppyish effect created by his little horns, and for a moment Cel imagines him as a creature of myth—a faun or chimera or some other hybrid, condemned to straddle the terrestrial and celestial realms: at home in neither, alone in both.

"Maybe," says the devil-boy—sounding hollow, unconvinced. He drops his head to stare once more into his gift bag. "Maybe some things are like that."

OUTSIDE, IT IS RAINING—AS THOUGH THE WEATHER HAS DECIDED TO PUT ON something a little more somber, all things considered. For a moment it seems to Cel that the people around her are moving somehow differently—that they are gathered deeper into themselves, barricaded more thoroughly against the world—but then she remembers that most of them haven't seen the news yet, and that people in New York always look this way.

She walks a block before stopping underneath a Newport billboard. The rain moves in half-deflected slants; the concrete next to her is spattered in a Pollock-esque arrangement of pigeon shit. Cel takes out her pack of Camels and lights one. A woman smoking Camels underneath a Newport billboard, ha-ha. This is the kind of visual that might have struck her back when she first moved to New York, back when everything struck her. She'd walked around in those days with eyes open, head raised, face awash (she now understands) with the idiot vulnerability of a person available for two-way conversation. When people handed her fliers, she'd actually read them! She'd read absolutely everything then: billboards (McDonald's delivered!) and posted warnings (the Playing of Radios or Tape Players without Earphones was, more or less, Prohibited) and banners at rallies (there had apparently been an Armenian genocide, which Cel had never heard of) and signage at protests (there was a group of very religious-looking Jews who opposed the state of Israel, and Cel had never heard of them, either). All of it, all of it, was news to her. She studied the city the way she'd once studied the woods, the delicate eyelet of a butterfly wing. It is excruciating to think of now: how anyone watching her would have known she was astonished by the sight of a spiky-haired pig on a leash, and worried about those boys who hung off the backs of buses, and surprised, over and over, whenever homeless people emerged from shapes she'd thought were shadows or things.

The trick with the homeless was to try to regard them as hallucinatory. Cel managed this for about a week, until she nearly stepped on one of them—a woman, lying on the ground, her face sheet-white in the daylight. Cel had thought she was a pile of blankets. When Cel looked down, the woman's eyes pulsed with something—a sort of dark ferocity that sent a shiver through the membrane separating Cel from the woman. Cel hadn't meant to look at her eyes at all— they were just where her own eyes had landed—but now she had, and the woman had seen that she had, and this made Cel feel something more than seen. She rushed past the woman blindly, pretending to dredge her pockets for coins.

Cel had seen a wild turkey die in the woods once. This had been in the winter. She'd startled herself by coming upon it—it was in a tree nearly directly above her, shocking in its size and proximity. The turkey tried to fly away but fell, tangling in a branch on the ground. It was covered in something that looked like gray moss. It stayed there for a long time, struggling. Cel had nothing to kill it with and was relieved she wouldn't have to decide whether or not to try— though this seemed indecent. It also seemed indecent to stand there watching, and also indecent to leave, and so Cel stayed there paralyzed until the bird was finally quiet, its enormous yellow eye still open.

The look in the homeless woman's eyes had reminded Cel of this, obscurely. And afterward, she had felt a kind of lid within her lowering. In a way, she thinks of that woman as the last thing she had really seen in New York City.

Cel tosses her cigarette to the ground and steps on it. She rejoins the churning scrum of people and becomes, once more, invisible.

NIKKI IS ALREADY AT THE BAR, FLANKED BY THE USUAL CADRE. THEY ARE WALL Street types, mostly, wearing suits, giving off vibes that are by varying degrees restless, sexual, cocaine-y, or straightforwardly murderous.

"They canceled the taping," says Cel, emerging from Nikki's coconut-scented hug. "Because of that shooting?"

"Oh, *right*," says Nikki. "I was sort of afraid you'd been fired."

"Not yet," says Cel morosely.

Nikki turns to the guys and says, "Guys. This is my roommate Cel. Cel, this is Alec and Scott."

Cel nods. Alec and Scott are the usual: they radiate confidence, they wear ties. They will be going back to work later—they are always going back to work later, these men, and maybe this is why they tend to strike Cel as so menacingly goal-oriented. Their flirtations have the urgency of sailors on shore leave, or animals with very short mating seasons.

"Cel may look sweet," says Nikki, "but don't let that fool you." Cel can tell from how Nikki's talking that these men like her already. Men always like Nikki: her raspy voice, her tan skin—both of which seem fake but, actually, are not.

"Cel," Nikki announces, "has a secret."

"Oh?" says one of the men.

Nikki nods, and Cel sees her eyelid flinch into the smallest fraction of a wink.

"Cel," Nikki declares, "works for the bad guys."

The men look at Cel with marginally renewed interest. One of them has far, far too much hair—Teen Wolf hair, one might call it, if one were feeling uncharitable, which one isn't going to be anymore. There must be a lot of these men in the city, but Cel never sees them when she isn't out with Nikki; Cel half suspects that Nikki summons or possibly creates them—that they materialize out of the ether only to buy her drinks. Or maybe it's Cel's witnessing this process that creates them: a sort of Schrödinger's-cat scenario, but with fratty financiers.

"The bad guys, huh?" says Teen Wolf.

Cel nods—dangerously, she hopes. Nikki has recently concluded that Cel's problem with men is, broadly, her personality. After six months in New York City, Cel is willing to concede this might be true. Men tend not to notice her jokes, or if they do, find them startling—as though witnessing a pigeon using an ATM. She'd said this to one of them once, startling him further. These sorts of men seemed to grow dumbly literal with women: hewing close to introductory-language-type dialogues, veering wildly into non sequitur. After a few months of this, Cel began venturing a few non sequiturs of her own, prompting Nikki to stage the intervention and impose a whole new set of protocols.

"*Which* bad guys?" says the less lupine of the dudes.

Nikki shakes her head. "It's too shocking to say."

"Tell us," says Teen Wolf—a little rotely, Cel thinks.

Cel has agreed to a trial period of following Nikki's advice—advice that essentially boils down to: talk less—and so, instead of answering, she gives them her signature mug-apology-shrug: raised right shoulder, head cocked to left, cheek pulled into sardonic half smile. "It needs a catchphrase," Elspeth had told her when she'd been brainstorming it at Smith. "Like '*Whaddaya gonna do?*' Or something." Cel had tried bellowing this in an overwrought Italian accent—"*Whaddaya gonna do!*"—and it did seem to add something, though, for obvious reasons, she isn't about to do any of that now.

"We'll never tell," says Nikki. "You'll have to guess."

"You say this badness is shocking," says Non-Wolf. "So I guess you're probably not one of us."

He means finance, Cel figures. Muteness isn't so bad if you regard it as a game, or a sort of formal constraint—she thinks of her college creative writing seminars (write a haiku, write a paragraph using one-syllable words, write a sonnet in iambic pentameter) or the drama exercises from her improv days (*Be a walrus! Be a walrus with a limp! Be a walrus with a limp and a dark secret!*). Structural parameters can open up artistic possibilities—look at the villanelle, or the Oulipo's fussy shenanigans—so why not romantic ones, too? It is in this spirit that Cel has experimented with some creative interpretations of *talk less* over the weeks: once she'd pretended to speak very limited English, and once that she was hard of hearing, and once that she was slightly mad. For the madness, she channeled her own undergraduate performance as Ophelia—which role she had played as a "goggle-eyed, breathy-voiced schizophrenic," according to the Smith *Sophian;* reprising the part in the bar, she tried to make her voice even breathier. Nikki had refused to talk to her for a while after that. Tonight, as promised, she is keeping it simple.

"No," she says.

"Pharmaceutical company?" says Teen Wolf—he was Alec, maybe? Cel knows a person can't help having hair in abundance any more than they can help being bald. Still, there's something a little decadent, almost rapacious, about having quite as much hair as this.

"Getting closer!" chirps Nikki.

"You work for Saddam Hussein?"

"You work for Jesse Helms?"

Cel can't believe they're still asking—she is amazed by how reliably this routine inspires male curiosity. They must imagine she does something sexily ruthless—something sinful-chic, capitalist-naughty. Something that pays her lots of money to click around on stilettos and be very good in bed. People always forget that professional low-grade wrongdoing can, like anything else, be boring.

"Professional assassin?" says the non-wolf—Scott, she thinks. "Mercenary for hire?"

Cel taps her nose, and Teen Wolf looks for a second like he might almost believe her. This thrills her, childishly. He isn't sure she's kidding, and why should he be? She could, for all he knows, be anyone at all.

"Do you give up?" says Nikki.

"We give up," says Teen Wolf.

"Even our depraved imaginations have limits," says the other one, and Cel looks at him in what she hopes doesn't scan as a double take.

"Sweet little Celeste here," says Nikki, lowering her voice in conspiracy, "works for *The Mattie M Show.*"

At this, Alec makes a sound that is a cross between an "oh" and a "ha." Cel shrugs like *Guilty as charged!,* aware that her performance is veering perilously close to full-blown mime.

"You guys!" says Nikki. "I mean, *The Mattie M Show*! Come on! You can't tell me it's not crazy that she works there."

"It is crazy," says Alec.

"I am completely obsessed with this fact," says Nikki. She is; it seems to clash with some firm concept she had formed of Cel before they actually met, and she's never quite gotten over the surprise. It is true that in Cel's response to Nikki's ad for a roommate she'd introduced herself only as a Smith graduate (true) with good credit (more like no credit) who worked in public relations (technically also true, though there was more she might have said about that). And it was also true that when Nikki first met Cel—at a coffee shop on the Lower East Side one rainy afternoon—Cel was wearing a bright yellow rain slicker and too-long jeans that were soaking wet at the bottom, and had probably appeared entirely incapable of ever surprising anyone.

The first thing Nikki said to her was, "You weren't kidding. That raincoat really is *yellow.*"

The second thing—after Cel mentioned where she worked—was "Holy *shit.*" Nikki slammed both hands onto the table, her rings making a boisterous clattering. She leaned over with blazing eyes and said, "Tell me *everything.*"

"But there's more!" says Nikki now, and Cel can tell she's worried about losing the room. "You'll never guess what she does there."

"Security guard?" says Scott.

"Booking agent?"

"Morbidly obese drag-queen stylist?"

"She's the publicist!" exclaims Nikki, as though learning this herself for the very first time. She is exceptionally good at this whole act: dropping hints, throwing cues, drawing Cel out of her faux-recalcitrance and then reacting with faux-shock—which men should really find confusing, but somehow never do. Cel feels that there must be some way to monetize this skill, but every time she tries to think of something she just comes up with *pimp*.

"Tough gig," says Alec. "Were you there when that guy got tire-ironed on the set?"

"It was the parking lot," says Cel. "And no."

"*That* publicist had a breakdown," says Nikki. "And Cel's her *replacement!*"

This is usually the part of the conversation where Cel says, "Hey, it's a living!"—and just because this has become something of a catchphrase doesn't mean it isn't true. It *is* a living: she makes more than anyone in her family ever has. She makes enough to pay her rent and loans. She makes enough to stand here, in the most expensive city in the country, drinking an eight-dollar cocktail, having this stupid conversation.

Cel has the sense that someone has asked her something. "Sorry?" she says.

"I said, how do you sleep at night?" says Alec.

"Pills," she says, and decides to start counting her words.

"*The Mattie M Show*," says Scott. "Wasn't there a guy who married his sheep?"

"Goat," says Cel coolly.

"*Don't*," says Nikki, shifting into her civilian register. "The woman's only on her first drink."

"I'll have to buy her another, then," says Alec, and Nikki nods her approval. To the extent that this whole thing is a shtick, Cel finds something generous in Nikki's willingness to always play the straight man. Though then again, Nikki does tend to come away from these evenings with dates more often than Cel does—so perhaps it's really more of a symbiotic thing: something ecological, evolutionary, like the remora and the shark.

Alec points to her martini glass. "Gin?"

Cel nods.

"Olives?"

She holds up three fingers. Nikki says it's important to issue very specific drink orders to men you might sleep with, and Cel sees the logic of this. Though also she's just really cheap and loves olives.

When Alec returns, he clinks his glass against Cel's and says, "To Mattie M."

"Long may he reign," says Scott.

"Cheers," says Cel, and Nikki winks at her. A carnival barker, maybe, is what she should have been.

"So, I have to ask," says Alec, and Cel thinks she knows what's coming. He leans toward her; his breath is gingery. "The fights. Are they real?"

Cel squints at her olives. She never knows what to say to this, even on nights when she's saying anything at all. The fights are real inasmuch as they occur—chairs are really thrown, beefy security guards really intervene (Cel is always surprised that men so large, for whom sweating seems so imminent, smell as good as they do: light citral cologne, mint from the wintergreens they crush during commercials). Cel has never seen anyone get really hurt, but she doesn't imagine that they aren't getting a little hurt: having a chair thrown at you can't feel great, even a cheap one from a short distance. The Secret Crush guy got really hurt, of course—but that was unambiguously real, and also happened in the parking lot.

"They're staged," says Alec. "I knew it."

Cel shrugs and makes a *So-so* wave with her hand. *Are the fights real?* is, at the end of the day, too simple a question. The fights are preordained but not rehearsed; they aren't explicitly encouraged, but everyone knows the drill. And though the guests do amp up their reactions, they aren't inventing them, exactly. The whole thing is part playacting and part reenacting: both a pantomime of imagined feelings and a ritualized display of real ones—something between a gladiator fight and a bacchanal.

"Sorta," Cel says finally. *Are the fights real?* Is this conversation? When you get right down to it, it's all very hard to say.

"Well, I guess it doesn't matter," says Alec, looking a little disappointed. "Those people are probably gonna brawl whether you put them on TV or not."

Cel wobbles her head on a diagonal axis that communicates neither negative nor affirmative: she knows because she's practiced in the mirror. Maybe the fights are a formal constraint of the show the way Cel's silence is a formal constraint of this evening. One could argue that *Mattie M* is best understood as a subversive commentary on the talk show format; that its rigid structure is, paradoxically, precisely what enables its daring anarchy; that its careful adherence to the aesthetic it's critiquing is at the very *heart* of its vital genius. One could argue that the whole project is actually a triumph of Keats's negative capability—a masterful inhabitation of that liminal space between incompatible uncertainties. Cel doesn't actually believe any of that, but she can see how someone could.

To Alec, she says, "Yeah."

She's forgotten if she was supposed to be agreeing with something and, if so, what—but then again, it doesn't really matter. The very act of speaking to this sort of man mutes her meaning—just as another person's deafness makes you dumb, and another person's blindness renders you invisible. Alec swallows the last of his drink in a soundless glug.

"So you still haven't told me where you're from." His tone suggests that he has asked.

"New Hampshire." It is extremely unfair that this should count as two words.

"Oh yeah?" says Alec. "My family has a house on Lake Winnipesaukee. Beautiful area. Does your family live near there?"

Cel shakes her head.

"Near Dartmouth?"

"Berlin."

"Oh," Alec says, and winces. "I've been through there. Really economically depressed area."

Cel feels a familiar flash of heat; she isn't sure what kind of face she's making.

"If you ask me, I mean." Though she didn't, and anyway it is not really a matter of opinion. Cel feels her ire unfurling; she takes a sip of her martini and waits for anger to cool into resolve. She is accustomed to this process—this sort of internal annealing. Still, there is the question of how to respond. Asking Alec where *he's* from will mess up her word count. Eliding "where" and "are" won't make up for "New Hampshire," and will also probably make her sound drunk. Cel feels her ongoing low-grade desire to flee flaring into an electric sense of requirement—something like the prickling dawn of a panic attack, the first hazy aura of a seizure.

"Another drink?" says Alec. Cel nods, ordering the panicked feeling down. All that evil requires is for good women to remain polite! She laughs, and Alec looks pleased with himself.

"Be right back," he tells her.

"'Kay," says Cel. A syllable saved is a syllable earned! Should she be counting syllables? She would have to consult Nikki. Cel turns to find her, becoming aware as she does that 1) she is in fact conclusively drunk, and 2) there's been a subtle shift in the bar's background noise. The sound of conversation has become both softer and denser, and she notices a weirdly orderly bunching of people near the bar. The group seems to pulse a bit, revealing a glimpse of Nikki's velvet hat. Cel picks her way toward her, mentally preparing to argue—should Nikki object to her abandonment of Alec—that a man who is into muteness is probably *really* into invisibility.

The group, it seems, is gathered around a television. She can hear it but not see it—the broad-backed financiers are blocking her view—which means it must be small, and not for watching sports. Cel hadn't known this bar even had a TV.

Cel pokes Nikki in the back. "What's going on?"

"Shh." A financier reaches over to turn up the volume, knocking over a hillock of peanuts. The vine-tattooed bartender eyes him fretfully.

"—*In the stricken community of Glendale, Ohio, grief turns to terror tonight amidst reports that one of the two shooters responsible for today's massacre is still at large—*"

Cel can tell from the anchor's voice that this is network news: this is a voice prepared to tell the nation anything—presidential assassination, space disaster, nuclear holocaust. She maneuvers in order to see the screen: CBS.

"—*Though police have yet to release the juvenile suspect's identity, authorities have confirmed that the second assailant has died from a self-inflicted gunshot wound sustained during the incident—*"

"Awful," Cel hears herself saying again. The word's wrongness has expanded since she said it last.

"Yeah," says Alec, who is suddenly behind her, the two martinis pretzeled into one hand. Cel registers an automatic sense of envy at the male hand's capacity to hold so many things at once—an inequity so indisputable, so bloodless, that she has even managed to semi-successfully joke about it with other men, at other bars, on other days—then feels a flood of self-disgust for even noticing it. Why is she thinking about these things right now? And why is she now thinking about thinking about them?

"They said it was a student?" she says to Alec, to apologize.

"That's what they said a minute ago, yeah."

The screen is showing the same row of emergency vehicles from earlier—though either the shot is wider, or there are many more of them now. Behind the fire trucks and ambulances is an ominous cluster of black SUVs, and behind those is a line of yellow school buses. They look expectant and incongruously cheerful, like pencils in a case. Cel tries to focus on the screen, but her gaze keeps slipping to Alec—his hand, cradling its forgotten drinks; his face, utterly absorbed in what he's watching. It is a perfectly fine face, after all—the face of a man you would be glad to see your friend marry—and Cel feels a sudden, inexplicable tenderness for him. She is appalled at how she'd hated him, only moments ago, and only for mistaking her for someone else—when in fact she invites such misunderstandings, she *revels* in them. She loves being free to thrill in the secret fact of her own mind; she likes to feel aggrieved by her mask while delighting in the hideous privacy behind it. *I'm here, I'm right here and you don't even know it!* Cel knows this much about herself.

Time has gotten staticky, and after a while Cel realizes that the crowd around the TV has dispersed. She has entirely lost track of Nikki: life, after all, goes on. She taps Alec on the shoulder. From his expression she sees he's forgotten she was there, but she leans in anyway and gives him something between a hug and a shrug. *Whaddaya gonna do?* A line she'd never used onstage but uses all the time in life—usually as a way of suggesting she's forgotten something that she has, in fact, never known. She wonders if one of these days she's going to catch herself using it to apologize for her entire life.

Cel is halfway home before she realizes that the shooting might be the kind of news big enough for people to tell each other where they were when they heard of it. She already knows that if anyone asks her, she will lie.

TONIGHT, LIKE EVERY NIGHT, CEL DREAMS OF THE WOODS. ZIGGURATS OF PALE green ice on the river; frozen sap cracking like gunshots. Silver birches, shining like polished pewter under even a quarter moon. Tracks sketched on the snow: the angular calligraphy of wild turkeys, the semicolon hopscotching of rabbits. "It's like Route 66 out there," her grandfather, Hal, always said.

On good nights, Cel dreams only of the woods: tonight she is not so lucky.

The silver birches: staggering like sylphs in the wind. *The trees, Cel: are they drowning or waving?*

The silver birches gone, her mother weeping among their stumps. Her mother saying, "How? How?" Her mother saying: "I can't believe it."

And Cel saying: "I can." Her mother's eyes: rheumy and uncomprehending. The part of Cel that wants to stop is smaller than the part that wants at last to speak. "I can definitely believe it."

The silver birch trees on the ground: a glowing ossuary in the moonlight. Cel saying, finally: "You're horrible, you know. You are absolutely horrible."

TWO

semi

1969

BY THE SPRING OF 1969 WE'D MOVED INTO A WALK-UP ON FIFTEENTH STREET, and were mostly done with the taking and renouncing of each other as lovers. Our group back then was sometimes five, often six, though never less than four. There were substitutes and swings—ex-roommates who came from California; theater aspirants pretending not to be alcoholics; lovers who joined for a night or a season—and we all provided our share of extras. But it was Brookie who cast the principals: finding the ones who'd really matter, then Pied-Pipering them back to the apartment.

This is how we acquired Paulie—one Memorial Day, as he was being arrested on Riis Beach for exposing his navel.

He began singing "Sit Down, You're Rocking the Boat" while the cop issued him a ticket. He had a commanding and classically trained tenor, and we turned to see where it was coming from. We were surprised to find a delicate, curly-haired boy, with elfin features that, we learned later, turned somewhat troll-like in distress. "Midnight Confessions" had been playing on someone's radio: they turned it off. Paulie sang even more spiritedly then, and a couple of castrati joined in: *And the people all said beware (beware!)*. In that moment Paulie seemed to all of us a leading man, though he would turn out to stay a chorus boy forever.

Later, we took him out, to a restaurant on a patio overlooking the water.

"Oh, don't flatter yourself," said Stephen, who was in his usual spirits. Not that it mattered much, at first: Stephen had the sort of face you didn't want to give up on. "Everyone gets arrested on that beach. *He's* been arrested on that beach."

He was pointing at Brookie, who was sprawled over the railing, trying to feed a french fry to a seagull that would neither take it nor go away.

"Was that what you were arrested for?" said Paulie.

"It was something sorta like this," said Brookie. "The thing wasn't a french fry, but the gentleman *was* a seagull."

We laughed, especially Paulie.

"And is that where the long arm of the law caught you?" Paulie pointed to the scar on Brookie's arm: this was a raised fascicle of flesh, somewhat smaller than a hand. "You poor dear."

He trilled his fingers on Brookie's deltoid, waiting for someone to tell him the tale.

Brookie had gotten the scar a few years back while protesting all-white hiring at a White Castle. This was a very good story, which was maybe why Brookie did not tell it—perhaps he'd vowed not to spend this currency on another white boy's regard. Or maybe he was expecting one of us to tell it for him, compounding his valor with discretion; for whatever reason, valorous or otherwise, we did not.

"It wasn't about *you*," Stephen said abruptly, and we all looked at him. His moods would reorganize, but never fundamentally alter, according to circumstance: he was like a compass, spinning around and around to always point in the same direction. "It's because it's a holiday weekend. They did the same thing before the World's Fair. They did the same thing before the *Chicago* World's Fair, when they hauled out all the horse manure."

"Stephen is incredibly interested in horse manure, you'll find."

"*Furthermore* . . ." Stephen's hair was falling in his face. It was feathery and light and we told him it made him look like John Lennon—or, when we were in a certain mood, Farrah Fawcett. ". . . if the police were really trying to arrest every stereotype on that beach—"

"Stereotype!" Paulie cried. "Who's a stereotype?" He cast a wrist over his forehead and pretended to fan himself. There was something aristocratic about Paulie, in spite or maybe because of his imperfect teeth and waxy skin—perhaps they subtly suggested Britishness, hemophilia. His eyes, one had to admit, were very blue.

"—then they wouldn't do anything else, and we'd see complete societal breakdown."

"A stereotype!" Paulie's performance had veered Deep South, with notes of Scarlett O'Hara. "A stereotype! What ahn akuzaytion!"

"I'm going to need the vapors myself, if this keeps up."

"A stereotype! My word!" Paulie paused a few beats longer than any director would have allowed. "Darlings, I'm the *prototype*."

The food arrived, with excellent timing, and Paulie clasped his hands together in supplication. He then declared in an impeccable Vivien Leigh that, as God was his witness, he would never go hungry again.

YEARS LATER—WHEN WE WERE AT THE VERY BEGINNING OF THE VERY END, and had stopped speaking of our aspirations as ongoing—Brookie suggested that this whole episode had been staged.

"You *knew* everyone was looking," said Brookie. "It was the biggest audience of your life! And here I'm thinking, why are the cops bothering this little white chickadee? Do they not see they have a black man right here, just sitting on a towel like he owns the thing? Are they just gonna let me get *away* with that?"

Under his mask, Paulie smiled with his eyes.

"So this is already highly suspicious. Then, as to the lewdness—on the one hand, yes, okay, here is this gorgeous boy's exposed navel."

"Well—not *only* his navel."

"Meanwhile there are so many exposed *cocks* on that beach it's a miracle no one's put an eye out. Right next to me, mere moments ago, a soda bottle has disappeared into an asshole."

Paulie shook his head.

"Hand to God," said Brookie. "It was there, then it was gone. And that's not the only thing. All around us we've got disappearing cocks, fists, dildos—"

"Suspension bridges—"

"Someone's probably taken the cop's *gun* and put *that* into an asshole—"

"There's probably someone out in the water trying to fist a shark."

Paulie was laughing soundlessly through his oxygen mask.

"Now, *there's* a menace to society," said Brookie. "The guy out there with the shark."

"Why can't the cops arrest him?"

"Or at least one of these tired old queens who's blocking my view of the water?"

"Who *knows* where that parasol is about to go!"

"—and out of this entire den of iniquity, the police wanna go after *him?* This beautiful boy and his beautiful navel?"

We fell silent, allowing this injustice to spiral the room—while protozoa, pneumocystic and innumerate, swelled in Paulie's lungs. We stared at his hands. There was a purple umbra where the IV went in—to help him eat, the doctor said, which was how we learned he couldn't—and his nail beds, we saw, were turning the same color.

"Of all the dens of iniquity, in all the towns, in all the world—"

Paulie was shaking his head with a familiar, throwback sort of disapproval. He pulled off his mask.

"Of awl the dehns of ini-kwity." He paused, breathing shallowly. His Bogart was still pretty good: it was probably the last to go. "In awl the towns." He paused for longer, then shook his head again and put the mask back on.

"But we've got your number now," said Brookie, once he could talk again. "We know the score. You'd spotted opportunity. You were trying to get *discovered.*"

Paulie pulled off his mask again. Underneath his sores, we thought we saw the faintest pentimento of a smile—afterward, we said we were sure we did.

"Well," he said. "It worked."

———

IN JUNE, PAULIE MOVED INTO THE APARTMENT ON FIFTEENTH STREET. THE place then was all cinderblock shelves, tapestries strewn over milk crates. In the kitchen, we kept turntables on the stove burners. We had an ancient tub where we sometimes chilled champagne and where, one memorable Sunday, a corpulent lover of Stephen's was discovered taking an actual bath. There were not, were never, enough bedrooms. Paulie's had been a sewing room once: it had no heat and no closet ("Get it?" he liked to say, despite frequent assurances that we did). He slept there in a swirl of fake Twiggy lashes and Zig-Zag cigarette papers. He'd tried to put up a *Funny Girl* poster in the bathroom, but Brookie banished it after a week. "I just can't piss with Barbra Streisand staring at me," he said. "She always looks like she *knows* something."

It was a time of scheming, of radically expanding hopes. On a single afternoon in July, five hundred of us congregated in Washington Square Park—in broad daylight, on a Saturday. The Gay Liberation Front declared us at the precipice of a quantum leap forward, and Brookie liked this phrase, with its Marxist undertones. All of us liked the GLF dances, and the fresh-faced youths who came from as far away as Baltimore and Amherst College (consciousness, among other things, newly raised) to attend.

But only history moves in eras: lives are lived in days—and around the margins, our little lives were still stubbornly unspooling. We were trying to write plays and direct them; we were trying to memorize lines while demanding they be revised. We were trying to raise money for the theater company (we had taken Stephen's sarcastic suggestion of putting up a donation box at a GLF mixer, earning us a handful of Canadian coins not worth exchanging). We were trying, all of us, to have sex.

We had our feuds, with the city and each other. Stephen could not tolerate the bongo drummers that hung around Bethesda Fountain. Brookie had a habit of keeping LSD in sugar cubes, which clashed with Stephen's habit of drinking actual tea. Paulie was always huffily gathering up detritus—bank statements and LIRR timetables and copies of *One* magazine—and leaving them in reproachful puddles outside our doors. These grievances were prosecuted in a performative, sitcom-y spirit: we thought ourselves hilarious and, some of the time, probably were.

By the fall, it was agreed that Stephen was becoming a real problem. Years ago, he'd attended a lecture about homosexuality as mental illness—at the Mattachine, of all places, where the speaker received a standing ovation—and ever since, he'd conducted himself as though we were all sufferers of a disease that he alone was brave enough to acknowledge.

"It's a shame," he'd say—sounding regretful and contemptuous, in the way of older women discussing vices not their own.

He liked to keep us apprised of possible treatments, such as a British procedure in which female hormones were implanted in the leg. One of the more maddening things about Stephen was how reasonable he could sound while being completely insane. He looked like an Oxbridge man with a hangover—you wanted to ask him where Aloysius the bear had gotten off to—and he had a tendency to discuss all ideas abstractly: the virtue of suicide, the certainty of despair. This made such conversations feel oddly bloodless; he'd adopt a tone of intellectual jousting, and you'd forget he was a fanatic.

Or if you didn't entirely forget—tell yourself you did. Who is there now to dispute you?

The worst fight came in October, with the publication of *Time*'s cover story on "The Homosexual in America." It was an enduring mystery how a copy of *Time* came to be in our apartment: we all denied knowledge of its origins. The article contained a broad overview of the many lamentable traits of us "inverts," drawing heavily on some of Stephen's favorite theorizing. A doctor called Berger was quoted at length. Brookie was furious, and planned to join the protest at the Time-Life Building. The rest of us called for peace while indulging in secret provocations. One of us cut out pictures of Dr. Berger and pinned them to Stephen's lampshade in the shape of a cock. We began alluding to the article when talking about anything at all ("That's just your homosexual irrational jealousy/homosexual megalomania talking, my dear Helen"). One day in November, Stephen tried using the article's terms to explain Brookie's own anger to him—calling it a function of his innate masochistic brutality, etc.

etc.—and Brookie responded by calling Stephen supercilious and whimpering. Stephen smiled superciliously and whimpered that if he was, that only proved his point.

"You know what, Stevie?" said Brookie. "If you want to sit around drinking tea and reading *Time* and pretending your most cherished wish is to live in Levittown with some clueless fish—oh really, Paulie? *Now* you're a prude? Forgive me for disturbing the Mount Holyoke prayer group! Can one of you ladies be a dear and point me toward Greenwich Village?"

Brookie shook his head, disgusted with us all.

"Fine: Stephen can go on pretending that his most cherished wish is to live in Levittown with a liberated and highly respected capital-W Woman, excuse *me*, where he will lie back and think of the Carmine Street public pool. What's *not* going to work, however, is taking all of us down with you. Because that *is* what he wants, you know."

Brookie turned to the rest of us, a look of the purest, most well-intentioned fear-mongering on his face—remembering that moment now, it seems clear that he could have been a politician. But then, Brookie could have been a lot of things: some people are funny that way.

"That's not what I want," said Stephen quietly. "I want us to get better."

In college, Stephen and a boyfriend had gone to therapy, trying to go straight together. Brookie was not supposed to know about this, and one hoped he would not bring it up now.

"But here's the thing, Stevie." Brookie was speaking slowly now. Perhaps he felt the carnage could not be undone, only clarified; perhaps he felt that stopping now would just be lazy. "*We don't have to do that anymore. Neither do you.*"

Stephen was sitting on the radiator, looking stunned.

"What's the phrase—there's nothing novel under the three moons of Jupiter?" Brookie was breathing shallowly, in that way that meant a beginning or an end. "Choosing fear is *every* weak person's only idea. People like you are everywhere, Stevie. It's just that you never hear about them, because there is never anything to say."

Stephen moved into the theater then, to wait out the rest of the sixties.

THAT WINTER, WE SPOTTED MATTHEW MILLER ON TELEVISION.

We had a teetering black-and-white Zenith that had moved into the apartment with Paulie; we'd consented to its presence only because we swore we'd never watch it.

"Well, *well*," said Brookie, when we spotted Matthew. "If it isn't Clarence Darrow."

And so it was: the lawyer, of the mild manner and riotously green eyes.

We'd all come to like the lawyer, in the end. There was an understated choreography to the way he'd marched us out of jail—he kept maneuvering us behind him, obscuring the other prisoners' views as we proceeded down the hall. It was something like the way musk oxen protect their young, said Stephen, though that might have been the concussion talking. Matthew Miller did not invite our gratitude for this, and we found we liked that, too—how he did the things he said he would, brusquely and without ceremony, and then abruptly went away again.

But now, it seemed, he was back—on TV, giving an interview about the comic Dougie Clay, whom he was apparently representing in an obscenity case.

"*We may not like what Dougie Clay has to say,*" said Matthew Miller. We had evidently caught him at the tail end of some kind of soliloquy. Next to him stood a tiny, skittish, flat-faced woman who could not possibly be his wife. "*I, for one, find it reprehensible, and only medium-funny.*"

At this, we laughed—even Brookie. The woman next to Matthew Miller smiled, exuding the approximate charisma of a seahorse. Alice, oh poor Alice! She seemed somehow aware that the ship she was on was sinking, though it is doubtful she could have imagined the depths to which it would eventually descend.

"Dougie Clay?" said Paulie. "I don't think I know who that is."

"Yes, you do," said Brookie. "He's got that filthy joke about Jackie O."

"Who is that *woman*, though?" said Paulie, pointing.

"And I'm not going to misquote Voltaire at you gentlemen, either," Matthew Miller was saying. *"Defending to the death your right to say it, and all. I certainly hope it won't come to that."*

And we laughed, a little, again.

"Is that woman possibly his *wife?*" Paulie sounded sorry for her already. Something about Alice elicited an instinctive surge of pity even then, long before she strictly deserved it. The isotope of pity is, of course, contempt. And standing there before us—with her pale baggy blouse, her thoroughly defeated hair—she was already taking the shape of a running joke.

"And I'm not going to bring up the slippery slope song-and-dance, either," Matthew Miller was saying. *"The road to hell is paved with slippery slopes, but you could say that about anything. Instead, I'll end with paraphrasing Mill. 'Truth gains more even by the errors of one who thinks for himself than by the true opinions of those who only hold them because they do not suffer themselves to think.' "* It was clear that this was not, in fact, a paraphrase. *"We should be proud—and grateful—to live in a country that doesn't lock up our vulgarians. Even—maybe especially— Dougie Clay. Thank you."*

We stared for another long moment in silence.

"What was that woman even doing there?" said Paulie.

"Softening his image, maybe?"

"Softening his *image*, ha!" said Brookie. "I bet his image isn't the only thing she has a softening effect on."

Then he shrugged, and laughed, and changed the channel, and Matthew Miller was forgotten. Most of us remembered him only occasionally, and only when we were reminded.

BUT THERE WAS, PERHAPS, ONE EXCEPTION—ONE AMONG US WHO FELT A minor, jubilant shudder whenever Matthew Miller's name was mentioned. It was still very faint, and notable mostly for its accompanying sense of privacy: the triumphant feeling of hiding (but happily! successfully, for once!) in plain sight. For even then—in the waning months of 1969, at the brutal precipice of a strange new decade—

when, notwithstanding Stephen's exile, we were closer than we'd ever been before: even then, we had our secrets.

One of us was auditioning for other, better theater companies.

One of us had already started lying about drugs.

One of us had taken a double dose of Quaaludes and slept for twenty-seven hours: a dry run for the real thing.

And one of us had seen Matthew Miller—several times, in fact—and never told a soul.

THREE

cel

clock on her bed stand: it is nearly one, which means it is Elspeth.

"Did you see?" Even in times of calm, Elspeth never starts a conversation with hello.

"Yeah." On TV, a mute NBC is playing the usual. The coverage has expanded outward while Cel slept, though the facts, it seems, remain the same. They still haven't found the one that is missing—Ryan Muller, according to the crawling-text box. The other one, apparently, was Troy Wilson.

"It's just." Cel stops so she doesn't say "awful" again; then she just stops.

"Are you watching CNN?"

"Yes." Cel changes the channel so that this will be true. On CNN they are playing security footage she hasn't seen yet. The shooters are standing outside a classroom—only moments before bursting into it, presumably. One of them, incredibly, appears to be laughing. Cel wonders if this is the one who escaped or the one who shot himself.

"It's crazy how young they are," says Elspeth.

It is true: the shooters are dwarfed by their ammo gear; even through the grainy video, Cel can see that one of them has braces. Abruptly, the taller one kicks the door open. There's something performative about this—to kick open a door that nobody would have known to lock.

"God," she says. "It's like they're playing for the cameras."

"They probably are," says Elspeth. "They're probably copying some action movie."

"That's horrifying."

"But it wouldn't be surprising, would it? They're swimming in the same cultural sea as the rest of us."

"Oh, don't start."

"I'm not."

"Mattie canceled taping today." Cel feels this fact should be introduced, regardless of her own interpretation of its meaning. The point isn't that Elspeth *is* wrong about Mattie, but that she *could* be: the ambiguities of the situation must be acknowledged.

"Very good of him," says Elspeth. She is using the tone she reserves for when Cel is being "rhetorically elastic," which is a term she coined especially for Cel. "Rhetorical elasticity" is supposed to explain how Cel wound up convincing herself that working at *Mattie M* might be a good idea—which, she will be the first to admit, it was not. But it's also what allows Cel to tilt her head and regard even *that* sad fact from a different angle. Because what is "rhetorical elasticity" but a highly developed imagination? And what is imagination if not the very basis of empathy? And anyway, it doesn't really matter what you imagine: only what you actually do.

Cel realizes she's watching the same anchor who was on that afternoon. She can't believe they've kept her on so long. The anchor's demeanor has changed in the intervening hours; gone is the breathless, gallivanting quality that sweeps through whenever a twenty-four-hour news channel finds itself reporting news that actually warrants its format. The novelty of substance has worn off, leaving only the stark fact of facts—which this woman is doomed (for how much longer? Cel wonders) to repeat and repeat and repeat.

"Did you know that there are more people alive right now than have ever lived?" says Elspeth.

"That can't be right."

"Don't you think that's frightening?"

"I think it isn't true." Cel changes the channel. "But if it were true, I think I'd kind of like it."

"No."

"Yes."

"Why?"

"I don't know." Cel had said this mostly to be contrary, but now she sort of means it. She flips through the channels: news, news, Steven Seagal movie, news. "I like the idea that if mortality can't be beat, at least it can be outnumbered. It's, I don't know. It's optimistic."

And what is optimism, after all, but a sort of inflated denial? Cel flips—news, MTV, infomercial about the perils and possibilities of making juice at home—and finally she finds it: an episode of *Mattie M* in syndication. It's inevitable, at this or any hour.

To Elspeth she says, "Do you know what I mean, though?"

This *Mattie* episode is about co-dependent multiples: a pair of identical virgins that slept in twin beds, a set of pale middle-aged triplets still living with their parents. One of the triplets, Cel remembers, had cerebral palsy. She remembers that Joel had wanted a more dramatic set of sets—quads, quints, etc. He had yelled at Luke about it.

"What do they expect?" Luke had said afterward, ominously unfazed. "IVF is only ten years old, and most of these people don't even live to adulthood."

On the screen, the episode is nearly over. Mattie M is facing the camera for his final thought; the multiples, nonplussed, are arrayed at his side.

"Do *I* know what you mean?" Elspeth is saying. "I don't know, Cel. Do you?"

Cel is always struck by how aggressively dorky Mattie looks on TV—pleated khakis, novelty socks; he doesn't necessarily pull these off in real life, but he's formidable enough that you do sort of forget he's wearing them. On-screen, he exudes an aura of beleaguered middle management. The audience likes the juxtaposition between the guests and Mattie, which makes the show feel like the jubilantly anarchic crashing of a very square person's party—more than once Mattie has reminded Cel of the rule-conscious fish in *The Cat in the Hat*. Cel clicks up the volume. The final segment music is playing.

"That's our show for today," Mattie says. Even with the sound down, Cel can hear the tired wryness in his voice, which tends to ratchet up toward the end of the taping. It's hard to reconcile Mattie's on-screen persona with his reputation around the studio—where ever since the Satanism strike he has been regarded as a mercurial, irrational figure: an Old Testament–type deity who might, at any moment, subject you to arbitrary sacrifices and trials.

"Join us next time," he says, *"when we'll be exploring the darker side of Jazzercise."*

Cel braces herself for Mattie's sign-off, which she hates. She has caught her hatred from Luke, who communicates his displeasure every time he hears it—usually verbally, though sometimes through elaborate sighs and eye rolls, and once by thumping his foot in a way that reminded Cel very much of a cartoon rabbit.

"Until next time, take care of yourselves," says Mattie, *"and let's all try to understand as much as we want to be understood."*

"God, I wish he'd change that," says Cel automatically, in her best Luke voice (pedantic, baritone).

"What?" says Elspeth.

"Nothing." Cel had forgotten she was still on the phone.

"Are you watching *Mattie M* right now?" Elspeth is using her Concerned Clinician voice; her *Do you have a plan to hurt yourself?* voice.

"It's just on. I changed it." Cel changes it, to make this true.

There is a dense, evaluative pause. Cel glances behind her. The television casts a flickering blue cuboid on the wall.

"Was that—I mean—were you *talking* to it?"

"No—well." Cel exhales raggedly. "It's just—you know Mattie's sign-off? *'Try to understand as much as we want to be understood'*? Well, Luke—the producer, you know, he's sort of my boss? I complain about him all the time? Anyway, he thinks it's really terrible, and he says so every day. So I was sort of doing an impression of him? Because at this point I hear it so much that it's sort of auto-matic?"

Elspeth says nothing. Cel is pretty sure there would've been a beep if she'd hung up.

"It's sort of a Pavlovian response," she says, trying an Elspeth word.

"Okay, Cel." Elspeth is now using her *indulging harmless delusions* voice. "Listen—it's really late. I'm going to bed."

"Me too."

"You should."

"I *am*."

She doesn't. Instead, she watches the credits and waits to see her name—which, in spite of everything, is still a little bit exciting.

Let's all try to understand each other as much as we want to be under-stood.

"It's terrible," Luke had declared on Cel's first day. "It's moraliz-ing and clunky."

Cel had asked then if they could make Mattie change it—was anyone ever so innocent? She has since listened to Luke expound on his objections ad nauseam—*It's sentimental pseudo-religious pablum! I can't stand that impulse to reify the self-serving! It's like that Christian capitalism shit. Like, just admit you're sociopathically greedy like every-one else—no one's gonna blink, this is America!—but don't try to erect some grand mythology around it.* Cel knows now that the sign-off is one of the many topics on which Luke is best left unengaged.

But Mattie used to be such a *good* boss, people tell her over and over. She hears this from Joel and Donald Kliegerman, from Sara Ramos the audience coordinator, from Jessica and Sanjith and once, very drunkenly, from Luke—and, even now, Cel can sort of see what they mean. Mattie is undramatic, civil, notably lacking in ego. His bad moods take the form of remoteness rather than tantrums; he is afflicted with the sort of self-loathing that tends to mind its own business. But ever since the Satanism debacle—as the months stretch on and the network's ire mounts and Mattie's refusal morphs from mystifying to infuriating to frightening—the consensus on Mattie has shifted. Opinions are split on the principle of his stance, or whether there even is one—where some see a meaningful distinction, others see only an inscrutable, very expensive hypocrisy. But everyone is united in the understanding that only Mattie can afford to do what he is doing, and if this is the direction fame is taking him they'd be better off working for a diva who throws plates at the wall.

Another thing people like to tell Cel: how different the show had been, once. Cel hears this from everyone: from cameramen and producers, key grips and catering staff, security guards and chauffeurs. People who'd been at the show since the beginning spoke of its early years in tones of wonder, like the aged considering the baffling obsolescence of their own childhoods. Others described Mattie's transformation with a sort of awed curiosity, as though discussing a discovery of science. It seems impossible that the universe is expanding and giant sloths once roamed Atlanta and there's an African fish that breathes with a mammalian lung. And it seems impossible that *The Mattie M Show* was once nothing like its current incarnation—with its lurid carnie shit, its rubbernecking and mayhem—that its stories were once uncynical, anchored in substantive policy discussion, undergirded by a potent bleeding-heart agenda. And yet somehow all of it, all of it, is true.

Over the months, this conversation came to seem a sort of Inquisition, a torment that would cease only with a credible profession of faith. Cel grew weary of trying to reassure people that she believed them—that deep down, she didn't even find the show's progression all that surprising. In a way, in fact, it was inevitable. There were only so many social dysfunctions, and only so many angles from which to explore them; once you'd run through your standard-issue welfare recipients and pregnant drug addicts and unmedicated schizophrenics, once you'd responsibly highlighted the relevant societal blind spots or institutional failures or governmental indifference they represented—then, sooner or later, you were going to have to go looking for something new. You were going to have to find people with issues too extreme to be widespread: exotic familial arrangements, startling degeneracies, vices and depravities the average viewer didn't even know existed.

And was it surprising that the more marginalized people tended to have the weirder problems, and a disproportionate willingness to discuss them on TV for one thousand dollars and a gift bag?

And was it surprising that the weirder problems attracted the wider audience, or that the wider audience attracted the network's attention?

The rest was just centrifugal acceleration. *Mattie M* shot out in a new direction—going as far as the competition, then parodically further, until it landed in a place of high camp, or high kitsch, or maybe just low irony. Or maybe something else that Cel hasn't thought of yet.

It makes sense that the show's veterans are defensive about it. Never do something for money that wouldn't be a favor if you did it for free, Cel's grandfather Hal had often said—and what he meant was not that you should be willing to work for no pay (Cel had once tried to explain the idea of an internship and was met with bottomless conceptual estrangement), nor that you should hold out for work you were (good Christ!) *passionate* about. Though his was a life spent in near-constant labor while slipping rung-by-rung down the economic ladder, he remained a committed capitalist to the bitter end. But he was suspicious of work without evident utility—he viewed this as the basis for many global iniquities—and he probably would have thought that there was something ugly about what the *Mattie M* staff was paid to do. And so Cel gets why the old guard endlessly invokes their standing defense—they hadn't signed on for *this*—and maybe there had been something valuable about the show back in the good old days, when it was still a lot like *Comment.* Cel could even believe this, too, though she had to take everyone's word for it. By the time she had a real TV, *The Mattie M Show* was already well on its way to what it would become—and the early episodes, for obvious reasons, never show up in syndication.

THE NEXT MORNING, CEL KNOCKS ON THE DOOR OF LUKE'S OFFICE. INSIDE, he's watching television: coffee mug in one hand, remote clutched in the other. Out the window, the light is clear; the sky has a polished, marmoreal look, like the heavens on a chapel ceiling. Cel loves the view from Luke's office—which, combined with his personality, makes her feel like she's inside the aerie of some enormous bird of prey.

"Shh," says Luke, though Cel hasn't said anything yet.

On the screen, yesterday's murderers are still wearing ammo gear, still kicking down doors. Still? Still, again, eternally. Luke changes the channel. NBC is showing a shot of the White House flag at half-mast; on CBS, a newscaster is diagramming a map of the school, with bathroom-door stick figures denoting the victims. On Channel 5, Pete Streetman is listening as a frizzy-haired woman lambastes the usual. "Mortal Kombat," she says. "And Marilyn Manson, and the breakdown of the two-parent family—" ABC is showing a still of the president, gray-haired and ruddy-faced, flanked by a retinue of solemn advisers. On CNN, two pundits are speculating on the question of sociopathy versus suicidality in the killers. Luke flips back to Channel 5.

"—video games," the frizzy-haired woman is saying. "Violent movies, kids going to school dressed made up like corpses, *The Mattie M Show*—which these shooters, apparently, watched regularly."

Luke puts down his coffee cup. Cel has the impression he's been holding it precisely for this moment.

"Half the country watches *The Mattie M Show* regularly," says Pete.

"Well, that's precisely my point," says the woman. She is wearing a black blazer, and jewelry too sedate to be at all visible on-camera: this might mean she hasn't been on TV before, though for a local channel that doesn't tell you much. "Did you know that every *Mattie M* fight winds up viewed by eleven million people—often over the course of many years? And with syndication, an encounter that may only last a moment in real life can be an eternity on television."

Cel wishes Luke would turn up the volume. She can hear the woman fine, but she has the sense that there might be something more to understand than what is actually being said—the way a sound's menace can seem to depend on the quality of silence surrounding it.

"Who is this woman?" says Cel.

"Please let her be far-right," says Luke. "Preferably stridently evangelical."

"Did you know, Pete, that during a twenty-four-hour period a person could watch an average of nine *Mattie M* fights across six different stations?"

Rhetorical questions are insufferable, statistics even worse—but this woman manages to deploy them with humility, as though she's only just discovered this information herself and is as surprised about it as you are. Cel inches closer to the TV—gingerly, as though she might have to disarm it.

"I did not, Suzanne, but I'll certainly take your word for it." Pete is speaking deliberately, which probably means he's exhausted—Cel wonders how long he's been on. She writes down the woman's name: *Suzanne Bryanson*. What kind of name is that? It sounds made up. "But I think some of our viewers will say, 'Hey, *The Mattie M Show*— you know, it may not be to everyone's taste, it may be crass, but really, how much does that matter?'"

Suzanne Bryanson is shaking her head without interrupting him—the sort of deference which might indicate something (political professionalism?) in a man, but in a woman just comes standard.

"Even if *Mattie M* is trashy," Pete says, "isn't it a little much to be framing it for murder? At the end of the day, isn't it really pretty harmless?"

"It isn't harmless if it inculcates indifference." Cel wishes Pete had made her answer the first question before asking another. "It isn't harmless if it contributes to our collective moral *deadening*."

"Jesus fuck," says Luke. "Who *is* this person?"

"Could she be a candidate for something?" This seems an innocuous possibility. Republican politicians bring up *Mattie* fairly regularly—the line between conservative voters and *Mattie M* viewers being an uncontested fact of rhetoric, if not reality—although it's possible the cultural left hates him even more. But this woman is obviously not from *The New Yorker*—and, in spite of "moral deadening," something about her is starting to seem not-quite-Bible-thumper, either. It's the barely subdued hair and less-than-demure voice, combined with the fact that whatever case she's making has permitted a woman to go on TV and make it in the first place. It's all adding up to more Silent than Moral Majority—which would make Suzanne Bryanson something more along the lines of Concerned Mom: just an average American woman (wife, mother, saint of homestead and hearth) driven by circumstances to speak common sense to power. And though Suzanne Bryanson may indeed be concerned, and she may even (who knows?) be a mom, she is also clearly a professional *something*. She just used the word "inculcate" on a local-access cable show! Cel is sure she had her reasons.

"*The Mattie M Show* is callous and corrosive," she is saying. "It's demeaning to women—"

"Co-opting the enemy's catchphrase!" says Luke. "Smart."

"—the chair-throwing, and the hair-pulling, and the fights, as I've mentioned—"

"But the fights aren't real," says Pete, perking up. "Are they?"

"You know, I don't know, Pete." Another thing you don't see every day: on-air admissions of agnosticism. "But I do know this. If *we* can't tell whether the fights are real, then the kids watching can't, either. And that's the point."

Cel had been ready to disdain whatever expression of simple-person horse sense Suzanne Bryanson was about to say here—*I may not know much, Pete, but I do know this one thing that renders all other knowledge moot!*—but instead, she finds herself agreeing. *Are the fights real?* One might point out that the chairs are light as coat hangers, that nobody is ever really hurt. But this isn't just the wrong rebuttal, it's also the wrong critique: the real point is sneaking around in the background, unnoticed.

"I think some people would say that fighting—violence—is a part of life," says Pete. "So you can't really blame movies or TV for depicting it."

"Violence exists in the world, of course," says Suzanne Bryanson. "I would never accuse Mattie M of inventing that—"

"Unless there's a *lot* we don't know about him!" says Pete punchily.

"Has he forgotten what show he's on right now?" says Cel.

"I think he's forgotten he's on *TV* right now."

"—but we do get to decide how to regard that violence," says Suzanne Bryanson. "And every time we watch *Mattie M,* we are choosing to regard it as entertainment."

"But Mattie M didn't invent that either, did he? I mean, take boxing, take pro wrestling. Look at monster truck rallies. Look at the NFL! Isn't a fascination with this stuff just a part of human nature? Why single out *Mattie M?*"

"To some extent, yes, it must be a part of human nature," says Suzanne Bryanson: Cel cannot believe Pete keeps letting her pick between the questions. "Though it certainly isn't my idea of a good time."

Pete raises his eyebrows like he's about to ask her what is.

"Could he be flirting with her?" says Cel.

"They can't be running *that* short."

"But you're right, Pete, that violence as spectacle has probably been with us as long as violence itself. The Romans who fed the Christians to the lions didn't invent it, and neither did the people who went to watch, and neither did Mattie M. This is something atavistic."

Atavistic. Cel shivers, unreasonably. But this is something she has felt while watching *Mattie M* herself: a sense of witnessing something that—though constrained by legal documents, obscured by Mature Audience warnings, complicated by self-ironizing, and beamed out to an audience larger than the total population of ancient Europe—is, in fact, very old. Or maybe beyond time entirely: some echo of the first thing, some presentiment of the last. She feels this even though yes, of *course,* the fights are staged. That seems a part of it, somehow.

"So yes, there is brutality in our nature," Suzanne Bryanson is saying. "But this is why we have civilization. To restrain those impulses. To animate our positive potential."

There's no way she isn't losing people with this stuff. Cel is fairly sure viewers register lamentations about the modern age as a sort of cultural white noise. And it's possible this conversation has veered so far into the weeds that people at home won't notice they are, in fact, hearing something new—that Suzanne Bryanson is linking Mattie to something far darker than usual, something that isn't about modernity at all.

"You know, Pete, pundits like to talk a lot about the 'culture wars,'" says Suzanne Bryanson. "But we rarely step back and ask: What is culture? Is it some unstoppable force outside of us? Or is it something we all create, bit by bit, together?"

"Is she a fucking *sociologist*?" says Luke. "Did the electric fences go out up at Columbia?"

"She's pretentious enough," says Cel. Although this would be too good to be true. Academics are not relevant, which is why they are never on TV, which is why this woman probably is not one, QED.

"Well, you'd know," says Luke.

"Oh, not this."

"As a high WASP princess of the Seven Sisters."

"Luke, I have told you repeatedly I am *French*."

"You and Marie Antoinette! Don't you know there's a whole army of hoi polloi out there, armed to the teeth with pitchforks? The country at this point is mostly just mole people and *Mattie M* guests and immigrants. Landed elites like you and Suzie Q here need to stick together!"

"Oh, Christ, Luke. Tell me again about inventing written language by candlelight?"

Whatever: Cel doesn't care. Maybe Luke will do them both a favor and actually fire her for once. She closes her eyes.

"Shh."

Instead of firing her, Luke is going to—shush her? Cel opens her eyes.

"Some people's parents shell out twenty thousand dollars a year to hear this kind of bullshit, and here we're getting it *for free*." Luke is leaned in toward the television. So this, then, is what is called for: okay. She blinks. "These are the kinds of opportunities you've got to take, Cel, if you ever hope to achieve model minority status."

"—and anyway," Suzanne Bryanson is saying. "Everyone loves to speculate about whether the fights are 'real,' without asking ourselves what this ambiguity *means*. Whether or not the fights are real, the show goes to some lengths to present them as such—and everyone understands that's because we want them to be."

They must be running over by now, but Pete makes no move to wrap up: Cel has the sense that he's become so absorbed in the speech that he's lost track of the segment. So they're up against an orator with the power to stop time on live TV: fantastic.

"So what is undeniably real is the moral damage they inflict on our children, and on us, every single day. Regardless of what is happening in Mattie M's studio, this is what is happening in the world. Does that answer your question, Pete?"

Luke moves his hand in a short little air-punch that seems nearly celebratory. His overall mood seems to have returned to status quo ante. Cel should have been a diplomat! She turns off the TV.

"Well." Cel feels a little stunned, as though she's just witnessed an abrupt medical event—birth in a taxicab, heart attack on an airplane, emergency tracheotomy at a Denny's. Luke takes off his glasses and pulls a handkerchief from his pocket. He rubs his eyes, then his glasses, then his eyes again, and Cel begins to worry he means this as a kind of drumroll.

"I don't understand those," says Cel, waving at the handkerchief. She doesn't know what she's saying: Luke does not tolerate inanities from anyone. From Cel, he barely tolerates nonessential communication.

"The cloth thing, I mean." She feels skittish and non-sequiturish. "I get the glasses."

Luke manages an expression that is somehow unsurprised and also murderous; he holds it for a moment without looking at her. Then he puts his glasses back on.

"You know what this means, right?" He is using only about 60 percent of his capacity for tonal contempt.

Cel says nothing.

Luke says nothing.

The suspense is hideous; she folds.

"What does it mean?" she says. "Does it mean you're going to tell me what it means?"

"Well—and I'm really very sorry to say this—" He almost does sound sorry: Cel didn't know he had that one up his sleeve. He sighs, pretending to steady himself. "What it means, Cel, is that, unfortunately? You are going to have to start doing your job."

semi

1969–1970

THE SECOND TIME I MET MATTHEW MILLER, I WAS ALONE.

The comic Dougie Clay was making a triumphant return to the Village after his imprisonment on obscenity charges. I tried to get the boys to go with me.

"I don't even know who that is," said Paulie.

"Yes, you do," said Brookie. "He's that comic? The one who's always sweating?"

"That could be any comic."

"He's got that *filthy* joke that goes—wait, how does it go? It's got LBJ and Jackie and the second shooter—"

"Come along and find out," I said.

"I don't like the guy," said Brookie. "For one thing, he dresses too loud."

He fluffed his marabou boa at us.

"Anyway, it's freezing out," said Paulie.

Brookie looked contemplative. "I'm pretty sure the punch line is 'grassy hole.'"

Stephen was still gone, his bike hanging forlornly from the ceiling. And so I found myself walking to the club alone. Around me, mist bloomed through the sodium lamps; red stoplights turned the snowflakes into rose petals. Abandoned Christmas trees slumped against the stoops like drunks. I dodged a mountain of trash—Chock Full o'Nuts cups and Sabrett wrappers and discarded copies of the *Daily News*, a single slick condom glinting atop it all like a diadem. It seemed there was more garbage around these days, that it was beginning to amass worrisomely. But then I thought of the piles of trash beneath Pompeii: *nothing new under the sun.*

"You know who said that first?" my grandmother asked me once.

"The Bible," I replied automatically.

"The Vedas," she said. "But then the Bible said it, too, of course."

By the time I got to the club, an experimental poet was on; I'd missed the performance artist with the pigeon and guitar. I maneuvered my way inside, trying to find an acceptable equidistance between the stage and freezing-cold doorway. Jerry-rigged lights cast polychrome lozenges on the floor; I smelled cigarette smoke and Canoe aftershave and the jubilantly human odor of the politically underwashed. And then, somehow, Matthew Miller was beside me.

He was already unmistakable—black hair, mild face, witchily green eyes. He had skin so pale it'd make you worry for the health of a national candidate; he was made to appear tanner somehow later, for the cameras. I could not understand, as a physical matter, how he'd gotten so close. It was impossible that he'd been standing there all along; equally impossible that he'd purposefully approached. I was pondering these dueling impossibilities when he looked at me, and caught me looking.

"Excuse me." I looked away, and back, and found him still staring. His expression was tired, and not discernibly appraising.

I said apologetically, "It's just—we've met before."

His tongue bulged below the line of his lip—this, I later learned, was his single tell: for skepticism. His jaw, I noticed, was a little crooked.

"I don't think so," he said finally.

"Okay," I said. I could tell he thought I was going to insist. "My mistake, then."

There was a flash of tension just above his left eye: an effort not to raise a brow.

"Hey," I said, waving my hands in an airy, expansive little motion.

I was dimly aware of having gone off a script I hadn't even known existed. "You say we didn't meet. Fine, okay. I make a point not to tell anyone their own story."

He looked at me again—without judgment, or even obvious interest, but with, just possibly, a bit more intensity—and flicked his eyes to the stage. "You're a performer?"

"Why? You scouting for talent?" I struck a pose, then dropped it, and his expression withdrew. I could feel the exertion of a psychic talus within him: not like a drawbridge pulling up or a helmet slamming shut—more like whatever force of physics sends you sliding backwards before you even realize you're moving.

"Well, you're outta luck," I muttered miserably. "I'm not a performer."

"I don't know about that," he said.

"*You're* a performer," I told him. "You're a lawyer."

"Yes, right," he said. "Clowns and circus animals, all of us."

I was pleased to have offered some concrete evidence that we had met before, but he seemed to have somehow already conceded that point.

"You misunderstand me." I sounded like an aristocrat impertinently addressed by a subordinate—a tone I was almost certainly copying from Grandmother. From her I'd inherited all manner of detritus: an abhorrence of solecisms ("It's 'octopodes,'" she'd say severely. "'Octopi' is pedantic"); a love of metaphorically inflected facts (of early Israeli Zionists: "They wanted to cultivate the original strain of wild wheat from biblical times—they thought it could sustain two nations. And that, exactly that, is where idealism will get you."). But then, I'd also inherited her cheekbones, and her Dunhill cigarette holder, and—at the price of much mutual misery—her manners, when I wanted them.

"I don't mean performers in the sense of pratfalls and trapdoors and such." I took a long, regal puff of my cigarette. "I suppose I mean performers as in performance artists."

"I'm not sure I appreciate the distinction."

"Performance art is an interrogation of the act of performance." I shrugged, exhaling over my shoulder. "Convincing *you* is beside the point."

"How is that different from bad acting?"

"They're not mutually exclusive."

"You sound like you've studied the field some."

I turned my head to the side. "I was a theater major."

"Ah. Bryn Mawr?"

"Oh. So you're a *wit*." On the stage, an elderly man was drumming on the side of a saw.

"So what are you, then?" he said. "If you're not a performer."

"I'm a playwright." A lie I'd been telling for years that now, finally, was true.

"I keep hearing the theater is dead."

"People always say everything is dead," I said. "But they usually aren't. I have a show up at the Roundhouse right now, actually."

Six weekend nights so far before a dozen restless audience members, each dozen more restless than the last. I was avoiding it tonight, in fact, along with the rest of New York City.

"Congratulations," said Matthew. "I'll have to come see it."

"Oh, I doubt it can compare to this," I said. "I hear the opening act abuses the audience."

"I think he's already started." Matthew Miller looked at his watch. "Did you know that in Roman times they actually killed the gladiators along with the shows?"

"Oh, I don't think there'll be any of that tonight," I said. "The avant-garde isn't quite *that* avant, even in the Village. I hope that isn't why you came all the way from, what—Ossining?"

I didn't know yet that he lived around the corner.

He smiled a little. "It isn't."

"Well, it's brave of you, all the same," I said. "One hears scandalous rumors about MacDougal Street. The most lurid characters lurking there, apparently. Mothers afraid to take their children to the park, and all that."

"Terrible."

"Though in a way, isn't the whole world their park?"

I could tell he thought this was funny, even though he didn't laugh.

"So why are you here?" I said, though I knew already. I hoped I didn't sound too interested.

"I'm here in a professional capacity, believe it or not." Matthew Miller eyed the stage, where a woman with a balalaika was reading passages from the *DSM*. She'd taken off her shirt at some point; neither of us, it seemed, had noticed. "I represent Dougie Clay."

"That comic?" I said. "I thought he was in jail."

"He's out on furlough."

"Isn't he the one who made that awful joke about Jackie?"

"Yes," he said. "But that isn't really what they're after."

I raised my eyebrows. "No?"

He raised his eyebrows right back at me. "You think things are ever actually about litigating prudishness?" he said. "Now I *know* you're too young."

"Well, what are they after, then?" I said. Which was better than asking, *Too young for what, for what, for what?*

"Pick up a paper, maybe." Matthew Miller rolled his eyes, then lowered them. "You're too gorgeous to be uninformed."

I felt a bolt then—a rheostatic fluttering so intense it seemed it had to have been audible—and some part of me, I am sure, fell right over. Yet out beyond the electrical storm, another version of me was staying upright, and placing a haughty hand on hip, and leaning against a stanchion, and saying, "Well, it sounds like a thankless job."

I needed a cigarette. As if sensing this, Matthew Miller tapped two out of his pack.

"It isn't thankless, exactly," he said. "But I hope I'm not going to be doing it for much longer."

"Retirement already? Now I know you're too old."

He shook his head. "I'm not ready to give up the ghost quite yet."

"You just have other ambitions."

I leaned in toward him for a light.

He cocked his head. "You might say that."

"What comes after lawyer?" The cigarette was making me feel flushed and a little manic; I had to force myself to pause between sentences. "Judge in powdered wig?"

"No."

"Jumping straight to executioner, then?"

There was a long pause, and I started to think he wasn't going to answer. I busied myself with the mental isometrics required to keep from asking another question. But then the room crackled into clapping, and Matthew Miller shook his head, as though rousing himself from something.

"Not that either, no," he said, raising his voice over the crowd. "I want to be something else."

AS SOON AS STEPHEN LEFT, BROOKIE BEGAN HUNTING REPLACEMENTS.

He found Nick and Peter at 17 Barrow Street, where they were extremely hard to miss: they worked on Wall Street and dressed like Andover, and Brookie introduced himself by asking whether they were lost. Peter was older than us, with a pale leonine face and nascent muttonchops and a swinging, single-beaded necklace that appeared only during his off-hours. Nick was, by universal consensus, an Adonis. We awaited their relationship's demise with jackal-like enthusiasm, though we all liked Peter very much.

"That face," Paulie would say mournfully. "What a waste on *that* face."

Nick and Peter were attentive to the point of retentive about their things, fearing professional downfall via blackmail via document theft. They said it happened all the time, to bankers and lawyers and stockbrokers (the rumors about the NYSE bathroom, they said, hardly did it justice). They even knew someone this had happened to—a disgraced finance guy named Anders who worked the door at one of our clubs. He was extremely handsome, with pale Nordic eyes and a knotty wolverinish musculature—but Nick and Peter dragged us away whenever he was working the door. In a strange way, they were terrified of him, as though he had something they could catch.

IT WAS A TIME OF VANITY.

We chiseled ourselves at the McBurney Y. We adopted diets of ritualized weekday asceticism, imagining these might offset our less wholesome enthusiasms. Stonewall had survived for three months, and only as a juice bar. But in those days there was always a new sex club south of Fourteenth Street.

It was a time of intrigue, of fleeting drama and disaster. Stephen moved back into the apartment in February, following a reconciliation with Brookie the terms of which neither would discuss.

"Face-saving measures," Peter whispered knowingly. "Real Cuban Missile Crisis–type stuff."

It was a time of affectation. Nick took to smoking cigarillos. Paulie hijacked a corner of the apartment and created an "industrial chic" quarter: minimalist and hatefully clean, with a single backlit orchid on the mantel. Brookie, who had almost no patience for the actual theater, had lately developed a taste for its political variety. He attended a meeting of a Young Republicans' Club—a hundred tuxedoed men drinking scotch out of snifters, Court of Versailles drapes, the whole deal—in order to shout things about gay militancy during the cocktail hour. I began conspicuously reading Baudelaire.

Paulie had purchased a Pentax camera and was forever trying to take our pictures: we called him Diane Arbus or occasionally Lois Lane. ("Lois Lane was a journalist, you philistines!" said Brookie.)

These pictures—some of them still exist. This is how we know that once, or maybe more than once, we sat beneath a patchy-barked plane tree in Bryant Park, eating a wedge of Brie.

This is how we know we shared a spoon.

This is how we know there was an ant on the spoon, though we don't know whether we knew that at the time, or exactly what happened to the ant if we did not.

It turns out to be the most banal questions that make death real— the hazy half-anecdote, the minutiae on the tip of one's tongue, the climactic punch line that triumphed at countless parties just a decade ago. And was it really only a decade? And was that a memory or a dream? Time goes on, and these questions crop up perennially— reminding us by their stubborn stupidity that death really is permanent, and that strictly no exceptions will be made.

From the pictures, we know that we once spent a day at Jones Beach—this was because Fire Island was closed due to raw sewage— and by the trip back we'd turned crimson from sand and sun. From the pictures, we know that we once biked to Prospect Park with Stephen in the pouring rain. How did we ever convince him? The pictures do not say.

The past is a forgotten language, and every photograph a glyph: the only meaning is in the suggestion that there was once any meaning at all.

IN MARCH, MATTHEW MILLER ANNOUNCED HIS CANDIDACY FOR NEW YORK State Assembly.

Brookie and Stephen had been searching for *Medical Center*—a sense of ghoulish curiosity was one of the few things they ever had in common—and they stopped when they caught sight of him, giving a press conference in the rain on Channel 5. Next to him, Alice clutched ineffectually at an umbrella: what little there was of her seemed to be always in the process of melting.

"Alice!" cried Paulie merrily. "Alice!"

From the first time we'd seen her, we'd cast Alice as a sort of folk figure of convention: we imagined Rigaud candles, vermeil forks.

"Don't get rowdy!" we'd hiss at each other at restaurants, if we already had. "Alice will alert the manager."

Then: "She'd alert the *authorities* if she wasn't already out of dimes."

Though we did not, in fact, know anything about Alice, besides how she looked from a distance. Nevertheless, we felt certain that she represented something demanding our derision—fustiness, squarishness, all the obsolescent values against which we were righteously forging ourselves, and the future. Brookie tried to put this feeling into Marxist terms once.

"It's one of the most fundamental foundations of the system!" he declared. "The male worker is given the illusion of participating in the power of the ruling class through economic control of his wife, who is his sexual object and household slave."

We nodded wisely. Why this view of marriage should have explained our collective hostility toward Alice—theoretical household slave in question—was not something we considered.

On Channel 5, it was still drizzling; Matthew Miller's hair was darkened slightly by the rain.

"*Cynicism is easy,*" he was saying. "*It's everything else that's hard.*

*Progress is hard. Compassion is hard. Anyone who says it's easy isn't ac-
tually trying to be good at it."*

He seemed to be suggesting he might be the man for the job.
And perhaps it was forgivable—in that moment, for a moment—to
believe that he would.

"New York State Assembly!" said Brookie, shaking his head.
"Well, if we know one thing, it's that that man has an attachment to
perversity."

"Shh," said Paulie, and turned up the volume.

"But I am going to try," Matthew Miller was saying. *"I promise you,
I am going to try. Because anything is possible. And that means this is,
too."*

A hush had fallen in the apartment—not at all common for us, in
those days.

"Ha," said Brookie, finally. "Not bad. If you didn't know any better, he could almost make you believe it."

I CANNOT REMEMBER GIVING MATTHEW MILLER MY NUMBER, AND YET THESE
are the facts: one month later, he called me.

"Who is *this?*" said Paulie, as he handed me the phone.

I took it warily: I had absolutely no idea.

"Hello?" I said.

He sounds old, Paulie mouthed, and I swatted him away.

"Hello," said a voice. "How's the theater?"

"Grand." I had no idea who I was speaking to. "How's the, ah,
wife?"

The man laughed, and I felt something like fear piston down my
spine.

"I'm sorry," he said. "This is Matthew Miller. I thought your
friend told you."

"Of course." I switched the phone to the other ear and mouthed
Fuck you at Paulie.

"I'm calling because I have an idea I'd like to run by you," said
Matthew. "I very much enjoyed your play—"

"You went?"

"I said I would," he said, as though that explained anything at all. I'd tried to avoid thinking about exactly what I'd said to Matthew Miller, having learned that revisiting such moments tended to lead to lacerating spears of embarrassment, which led to random wincing, which led to looking insane and, of greater concern, to the incipient wrinkle I thought might be growing on my forehead. "Anyway, I have a municipal issue I'm dealing with that I'd like your perspective on. I'm wondering if we could meet. It's a little complicated to explain over the phone."

I'm wondering if we could meet must have overridden *municipal issue* on my face, because Paulie stood up and launched into a jig. In response, I flung a checkbook at his head.

"*My* perspective?" I said. "Now I'm sure you have the wrong number."

"I guess I'll just have to see who shows up."

Paulie picked up the checkbook and began flipping through it sadly; it must have been his own. I turned to the wall and twisted the phone cord around my wrist.

"When?" I said.

"Tomorrow? Only if you're up for it."

Up for what? I didn't ask. Matthew was giving me the name of a restaurant on Fifty-fourth; he was telling me it served food until four. Paulie, thank God, had at last retreated to his bedroom.

"All right," I said, a little coldly. I wanted to retroactively insert some aloofness into the conversation before I took the subway forty blocks uptown on a day's notice. I stared down Paulie's plants in the fireplace.

"You know," I said finally, "I can't seem to recall giving you my number."

I was picturing him tearing through the phone book, I suppose—asking around everywhere, giving frantic descriptions. *Who was that enchantress and how can I see him again?*

"It was in your arrest file," he said, sounding suddenly in a hurry. "See you tomorrow."

And then, not for the last time, Matthew Miller hung up on me.

FIVE
cel

ON WEDNESDAY, THE *MATTIE M* STAFF ASSEMBLES TO WATCH DONALD KLIEG-erman try to run a meeting.

This is not a production meeting; until further notice, *Mattie M* is in reruns. They are here today to talk about Going Forward. The real subject of the meeting, everyone knows, is Suzanne Bryanson—who a day's worth of research has revealed as the spokeswoman of a nonprofit pressure group called Concerned Parents of America, which seems largely composed of same. (Suzanne Bryanson herself does appear to be the parent of at least two children; Luke had even found a picture of them in a profile from the *Minneapolis Star,* a pair of towheaded boys straight out of central casting.) Exactly what these Parents of America are Concerned about remains hazy, but as far as the money has been so far followed, it leads nowhere useful—no fundamentalist cabal, no vast right-wing conspiracy. All of this makes CPA seem more mysterious, and in some ways more threat-ening. ("Any group with an acronym that boring is clearly up to something," Luke intoned before the meeting.)

Their challenge today, Donald Kliegerman is proclaiming, is to brainstorm strategies for how—and, to be completely candid? whether—to address the current *situation.* Strategies that are sensitive to that situation's gravity, he is saying, while also true to the ir-reverent, provocative *Mattie M* sensibility. The feeling in the room is tense and proto-mutinous. There is the sound of bodies shifting in chairs, the sense of gazes being affixed to clocks.

"In the past, we've sometimes had the luxury of deciding which national news stories we wanted to engage with," Donald Klieg-erman is saying. He is visibly resisting the impulse to crack his knuckles. "But in this case our decision is complicated by the fact that *The Mattie M Show* is already a part of the discussion, as I'm sure you're all aware."

This lands as a sort of dare—certainly, *yes,* they are aware. Dis-cussion of the shooters' *Mattie M* fandom has grown more pointed over the most recent news cycle; at least two television reports have made reference to some sort of *Mattie M Show*–inspired skit occur-ring at the school in the days before the shooting. Exactly when this happened and who might have participated in it remains unclear—Cel is given to understand that the students who might know are unavailable for comment—and it hasn't been reported in print media, so it might not even be true. Even if it is, Cel thinks the connection is a stretch. No, it can't be *good* for impressionable youths to watch *Mattie M:* the luridly troubled and theatrically un-hinged, the booing of the audience—the sound of an entire civili-zational aquifer sputtering dry, according to *The New Yorker.* But after watching all that, Cel thinks, the only person you want to kill is yourself.

Though then, she reminds herself, one of them did that, too.

Donohue and Oprah have already acknowledged the incident, Donald Kliegerman is saying; Ricki and Jenny have episodes in the works. He pauses for response, but there is nothing—only effortful silence; the strained, algebra-class feeling of everybody willing the teacher not to call on them to speak. The pause expands into a creepy, lunar silence. Donald Kliegerman uncaps his pen encourag-ingly.

"Well, I'll venture the obvious," Luke says finally. "What about a themed show? Children who kill, or something."

"We've done it," says Jessica VanDeMark.

"We've done the *parents'* perspective," says Luke. " 'My Child Is a Murderer!' was more about the fallout for the family. In this episode, we'd be looking at the murderers themselves. We'd be exploring motivations, searching for warning signs."

Luke is good at coming up with these things—slogans and blurbs and catchphrases. Cel sometimes wonders if he actually thinks this way: his inner life unfurling in an endless series of conclusive-sounding parallel constructions.

"But who's gonna appear for this?" says Jessica. "We're probably not gonna land Ryan Muller."

At this, light laughter. Cel makes a mental note: if you jump in to shoot down an idea, nobody will remember you haven't ventured one yourself.

"We'd have to bring in families with similar experiences," says Luke. "Probably not *exactly* similar. Assaults, smaller-scale homicides. Because the point is really about the capacity, you know, in a child. We talk to parents of kids currently in juvie. Maybe a reformed kid or two. We ask them everything we'd like to ask the Ohio parents, invite them to speculate on some things. Then we bring in the psych panel to connect the dots and offer the takeaway. Things to watch out for in your own child, ways to get help. Et cetera."

Donald Kliegerman is nodding, either jotting or pretending to jot notes. "Other thoughts?" he says, without looking up.

"Well," says Sanjith. His voice has a note of determined apology— like a person gearing up to collect an overdue debt. "There is a risk of appearing callous."

This strikes Cel not as a risk, but a certainty.

"But not addressing it looks callous, too," says Luke. "And it *also* looks guilty."

The word "guilty" rings in the air—and though there is no way Donald Kliegerman is going to acknowledge it, Cel senses he is grateful it's been said.

"Maybe we can't win no matter what we say," says Sanjith. "I mean, yes, the pundits are linking Mattie to this, and that makes not responding feel—uncomfortable. But why should we let this accusation dictate what we do? Give me any unfortunate thing going on in this country, and I'll give you five people who want to blame it on *Mattie M.* That impulse is just gonna have to run its course. And maybe that means our voice is inevitably gonna backfire. I mean, what's the NRA saying right now? Not a whole lot."

"Well, that's different, though, isn't it?" says Cel.

The room turns to look at her. Donald Kliegerman seems a little startled—as though he's been addressed by a statue he didn't realize was animatronic.

"Well." Cel's voice sounds off—possibly she is speaking too quietly? "I just mean." Now her voice sounds alarmingly, catastrophically loud. "The NRA can't get around the fact that guns are involved, right?"

The room is still staring intently; Cel can nearly *hear* their syncopated, underwhelmed blinks. Donald Kliegerman steals a glance at his watch.

"I mean, say what you will about *The Mattie M Show*—you can't write it on an autopsy report."

She knows no one will laugh at this, and indeed, no one does.

"So what then?" says Luke. "Just keep running the goat fuckers?"

"I do wonder if the nation's appetite for goat-fucking might be pretty limited right now," says Sanjith.

The room laughs again, gratefully.

"Right, and that's the dilemma," says Luke. "The choice isn't between a *Mattie M* episode and dignified silence. It's between this particular *Mattie M* episode and the usual. And if we ignore it, we're saying it's okay to be curious about why a man fucks his goat, but not about why a kid shoots up his school. But people *are* curious—not because they aren't horrified, but because they are. The question is genuine. It's a time of national soul-searching—maybe even our viewers are looking for heartier fare."

"But are they looking to us for that?" says Cel. In for a penny, in for a pound, was something Hal used to say. When she'd parroted this at work, Luke had asked if she was familiar with the concept of a *sunk cost*. "I mean, this show has always been a guilty pleasure, right? Okay, okay—not always. But it is now, right? It's escapism."

The room is staring goggle-eyed once more—as though she's

said something shocking. It galls Cel, if she's honest, this chivalric fealty to Mattie's vanished better self. Everyone was someone else once—for everyone besides Mattie, this is a liability.

"And, like Luke said, people have been shocked by a national trauma. And they want to follow it, yes, but maybe they also want to forget it—at least sometimes. At least for a while. Maybe *Mattie M* gives them permission to do that. And maybe that's the way the show can be most helpful—by letting people off the hook for an hour. When they're ready, they can tune back in to 20/20."

Cel sees a flicker of approval run across Luke's face; he likes snappy conclusions, even when they're attached to arguments he doesn't personally endorse.

"Conveniently," he says, "letting viewers off the hook lets us off the hook as well." He says it acidly, but Cel knows that *off the hook* is precisely where Luke would like to be; he has articulated this critique so adroitly that no one else will be tempted to try. "But if we don't address it on the show, then how do we address it? Should Mattie author an op-ed in the *Times*? Should he canvass the nation door-to-door?"

"We could issue a statement," says Jessica, exactly as Sanjith says, "*Anything* but a statement."

"So we're saying he needs to talk about it, but we're not going to let him talk about it on his own, you know, talk show?" says Jessica.

"Well, what if we sent him somewhere else?" says Cel. "That'll cast him as, like, a pundit. It'll give Mattie a chance to switch into his Donahue mode, which we all know he loves. And whoever hosts him will probably be happy, because they've already overplayed this thing so badly that getting *anyone's* opinion for the first time is gonna seem like a scoop."

"Where would we be looking at for that?" says Donald Kliegerman. This must mean he likes the idea: Mattie loves specifics.

"I'd start with the morning news shows."

"There's *Wake Up Tristate!*"

"There's *Tod Browning in the Morning*."

"He has a good relationship with Abe Rosen at PBS," says Sanjith.

"You're funny," says Luke.

"We could try for *Lee and Lisa*," says Jessica.

This elicits several groans and one Bronx cheer from the assembled. *Lee and Lisa*, though undeniably in the morning, is only very questionably newsy. Its framework is nominally point-counterpoint—Lee is supposed to be slightly right of center, Lisa slightly left—though their conversations tend to seem less like debates than bad, very mandatory flirting.

"All right," says Luke. "*Wake Up TriState!, Lee and Lisa, Tod Browning*. Give him three options, let him think he's doing the deciding. Choice within constraints." Luke draws a line underneath the list, then glances at Cel. "I had little brothers."

Donald Kliegerman declares these "good thoughts," and ends with an anemic pep talk about commitment and community. Poor Donald Kliegerman. His job is irrelevant as well as impossible, and Cel imagines this is the reason for the gravity with which he tends to deliver corporate jargon, even when well beyond the hearing of anyone who might be impressed by it. She once heard him discuss intermodulation distortion at a karaoke bar. His continued employment here, like Cel's own, is an enduring mystery of the show.

Though not, of course, the only one.

NOVEMBER

ON THE DAY OF CEL'S JOB INTERVIEW, IT RAINS. BY THE TIME SHE ARRIVES AT the studio, her glasses are terminally befogged; everything around her is rimmed with a watery opacity. In the lobby, professional people sweep by all around her—impeccable, imperturbable, untouched by subway or city or sky.

She rides the elevator to the appointed floor and offers her name at reception. The door opens, and a bespectacled Asian man emerges; he is wearing a tie and sneakers, and his haircut looks very expensive. This, Cel figures, is Luke Nguyen—though the man does not confirm this, only nods and juts his jaw in a way that suggests Cel should follow him. He does this all without seeming to actually look at her, and she wonders how he knows who she is. Though really, who else could she be?

In his office, Luke produces a piece of paper and begins scanning it with a pained expression. Behind him, an enormous picture window looks out onto a smeared Seventh Avenue. Cel wishes she hadn't worn the glasses. She does need them—her perpetually neglected right eye is now legally blind, her depth perception eternally askew—but it is Manhattan, and she doesn't have to drive, and so she wears them only sporadically, and often for effect. She'd worn them today to look commanding, and now feels too committed to take them off.

Luke glances up after a moment.

"Please have a seat," he says, and Cel realizes she is standing directly in front of a chair. She sits.

"You can take off that raincoat, you know."

"Oh, sure," says Cel, unzipping.

"What *is* that color, anyway?" Luke is still scanning the paper—which, from the back, appears to be Cel's resume. "Would we call that . . . turmeric?"

Cel tries not to panic. She looks passably normal on a glance, she thinks, but there are a hundred tells if someone looks at her too closely: her slightly large skirt; her slightly wrong shoes. Her teeth, if she smiles—which certainly she won't, but this guy seems like he might be able to somehow see them anyway.

There is a knock on the door, and Cel jumps unprofessionally.

"Luke?" A man appears in the doorway. He has enormous headphones and also an enormous head.

"Yep."

"Can I grab you for a sec?"

"We're sort of in the middle of something," says Luke. Although it hadn't felt like they were. On Luke's face is an expression of extreme impatience—a dismay that might actually prove terminal.

"Sorry." The man bobs his majestic head. "But we've got kind of a situation."

On "got," Cel can hear he's from Boston. A seizure of association commences, a hybrid of archetype and memory. Santa-sweatered teacher in New Hampshire. Red-nosed lobsterman in a squall. Ruth's worst brother eating a plate of mashed potatoes at her funeral.

"Can you come down for a minute?"

Luke looks at Cel.

"Go ahead," she tells him. If he is gone long enough, maybe she can even steal a glance at her resume—she wouldn't mind revisiting some of its claims.

Luke regards her for a moment. Is that suspicion on his face— does he not want to leave her alone in his office? Or maybe it's only her. It's only her either way, she supposes.

"No," he says slowly. "Come along with me."

Had she sounded overeager to be left? Cel wonders as she squeaks her way down the hall. Or had he somehow seen her teeth already? She runs her tongue along the top row—a habit she must quit, she knows, before it becomes unconscious. Growing up, the only thing she felt about her teeth was a dim gratitude they weren't worse; all things considered, it seemed a pretty good deal to have average teeth—default teeth!—for free. But it turns out that in New York, default isn't average; here, it seems, only perfect teeth are invisible. *Average* teeth are like Southern accents or pregnant midsections or yarmulkes or track marks or Kaposi's sarcoma bruises—data that flagged you for further consideration, if not necessarily judgment. And because Luke had noted Cel's teeth, he'd decided it was best not to leave her unsupervised in his office—with its computer and fax machine, its press strategies and market research, its incriminating documents that any number of tabloids might buy and that Cel, for all he knows, might peddle. He doesn't know anything about her, after all, except for all the things he thinks he does.

The squeaking of Cel's shoes has turned to squelching. She has the sense someone has addressed her. It's the large-headed man, suddenly beside her.

"I'm sorry?" says Cel. Is it possible she's forgotten his name? His head is even larger up close.

"I said, you're really wandering behind the curtain today."

"Oh. Yes." Cel is aware that the man must be taking stupidly short strides to keep pace with her; Luke is six feet ahead of them, walking with a harassed-looking gait.

"Wrong way, Eli," he says to what seems to be no one but turns out to be a tiny, incredibly well-muscled man in a tube top. Eli turns without a word and heads back in the other direction.

"He hands out roses to the audience at commercials," says the headphone man. "They always vote him Most Sexy."

"Oh. Huh." Cel glances at her waterlogged shoes, ponders the incredible length of this hallway. "So have you been working here long?"

"Well, this show is only five years old. Though I bet that seems like a long time to you." He laughs. "I know I'm not supposed to ask how old you are."

Cel wishes he would ask something else, then, so she'd have something to reply to.

"I worked on *Comment* before this, though," the man is saying. "So I've been with Mattie a while. Or Matthew, as he was back then. You never could have convinced me he'd put up with such a stupid nickname, but there you are. You never can tell about people."

"That's true." Cel is becoming incrementally aware that someone down the hall is shouting, and that this has been going on for a while. "You never can."

Luke hastens his pace; Cel quickens her squelching. They round a corner, and Cel sees that the shouting is coming from a diminutive blond man in a white denim jacket. He is yelling at an impassive-looking black woman. Cel feels obscurely deflated.

"What seems to be the problem here?" says Luke, in a different voice than Cel's heard so far.

"This psycho here thinks I stole his pager," says the woman. Cel wonders what landed her on the show—a reflexive question that in the months ahead will come to seem less like curiosity than camaraderie. *What're you in for?*: the question of one inmate to another.

"So you admit it!" shrieks the man, and Cel is almost disappointed that things may resolve so quickly. She really had expected to see her first melee.

"And what am I gonna do with your skanky-ass pager?"

"There was a chain of events that took place." The man raises a finger—quaveringly, with a sense of grave import—then launches into a monologue. It begins with a motorcycle and his own unlikely survival and subsequent special relationship with God and includes—alongside several claims Elspeth might call "delusions of grandeur"—a pretty interesting theory about Scientology. Celebrities are attracted to the idea of a hierarchical structuring of humanity, he says, because they think they are higher persons already. Cel finds this part marginally persuasive.

"That guy is coked up to the *tits*," mutters someone behind her. But Cel doesn't think so; there is something familiar in the syncopated restlessness of the man's speech. She has the sense she should not be seeing this moment, and she wishes she could somehow keep this man away from everyone: the cameras, the audience, the assembled crew. Though this, she realizes, is not exactly the idea around here.

"All right, all right," says Luke, clapping his hands like a high school teacher who knows he's outgunned. "Sir, I'm going to have to ask you to calm down."

I'm going to have to ask you—what a strange phrase: meant to sound authoritative, yet almost goofily deferential. Issued like a command, when really it's only the most timid gear-up to a request.

"He is clearly very nuts," adds the woman. Her tone suggests she thinks that that should settle it. And, after all, it should! They should all declare this man off-limits—beyond the parameters of sportsmanship, or whatever governs things around here. And yes, Cel understands, of *course* she understands, that gawking is the point—that *The Mattie M Show* offers not only the lurid thrills of spectacle ("I Refuse to Wear Clothes!" "You're Too Fat for Porn!"), but also the darker satisfactions of judgment. How *dare* these people live such lives—how dare they let us *know* they do? And certainly, communal judgment has its virtues: where would civilization have gotten without it? One could argue that participating in such a ritual is, in fact, an ancient, sacred duty, linking tribal council to Greek chorus to jury box to studio audience—on and on and on, throughout all of human history. But nothing one might argue seems to have anything to do with the man shouting on this soundstage. Watching this man on a talk show would be less like seeing a circus performer swallow a sword and more like watching a trapped moth beat itself to death against a screen. Cel cannot imagine it would make for very good TV.

"Nuts," says the woman again. Now she just sounds bored.

"Security is on the way," announces Luke.

"And who the fuck are you?" shouts the man.

He is standing up on arched, nearly tiptoed feet and is staring right at Cel.

"Sir." A security guard is behind him, finally, placing a pancake-sized hand on his shoulder.

"Not *you!*" the man bellows. He points at Cel. "Her! You!"

Cel can feel the entire room's attention turn toward her.

"Are you deaf?" The man grimaces in a way that's nearly lupine, and Cel can see that his teeth are like hers. "Can you talk? I am asking you a question, and the question is this." He pauses—he knows he has the room—and then explodes: "What the fuck are you looking at?"

"Hey, there," says the security guard. His grip looks firm, but his tone is gentle, which makes Cel trust him.

"I'm not leaving till I get some answers," adds the man, almost apologetically.

Cel waits for someone else to do something for as long as she can stand, which maybe isn't all that long.

"Well," she says—either finally or immediately. All eyes are upon her: she longs for death. "I was looking at you, I suppose."

"Me?" The man sounds indignant.

"Yes," says Cel, in a voice quite unlike her own. "I was looking at you and wondering about you."

"You were wondering"—the man is still shouting, technically, but some portion of his anger is gone. Instead, there is a tentative, hollowed-out surprise—as though he has never known someone to *wonder* about him, and is going to be mad about it just as soon as he finds an angle. "And *what* were you wondering?"

"I was wondering if you were okay." Which is a lie and also, somehow, the right thing to say. But before Cel can find out what she'll say next, there's a shift in the background noise and a familiar voice behind her says, "Aha."

She turns, and there, somehow, is Mattie M. She has never seen someone so famous so close before. The immediate effect is a blend of creepy surrealism and even creepier intimacy, combined with a dreamlike sense that—though she has never had any conscious opinion about Mattie M's height before—he is almost certainly too short.

"What's the big idea around here?" says Mattie. "Having a secret rehearsal without me again?"

At this, light laughter—though no one, deranged or otherwise, could possibly find this sort of gee-whiz lame-dad thing funny. What Cel wants to know is how Mattie M got so close without her noticing: his stealth, alongside the adrenalizing jolt of his celebrity, makes her feel like she's only just noticed a jaguar hanging over her in a tree.

"I'm Mattie," says Mattie, turning to the guests. Cel hates when celebrities act like people don't know who they are—though it's true that the alternatives are worse. Mattie shakes the hand of the man and then the woman; calm has been restored, it seems, though Cel can't quite see how. All Mattie did was appear. He doesn't seem especially tyrannical, though perhaps everyone is so terrified of him that his presence is enough to shut everyone up preemptively. Cel thinks of all those countries where authoritarian despots suppress long-simmering internecine wars.

"Are you Meredith?" says Mattie, turning to Cel.

"No." Meredith, it turns out later, is a giggly dominatrix with cystic acne.

"She's interviewing," says Luke, from somewhere else.

"And it's so great to meet you!" Cel shoves out her hand, helplessly. "Big fan."

Mattie pauses, and a ripple goes through his eyes. Cel is fairly sure that "big fan" is SOP: it doesn't mean you actually *are* a fan, or even that you necessarily know exactly why you should be—only that you are aware that other people do know, and are. It's a primarily symbolic exchange—one dog offering another its neck—and Cel thought it was customary. But the flash in Mattie M's eyes makes Cel wonder if she's miscalculated this. Maybe she sounded too much like she was trying to make him believe her.

He didn't, as it turns out, and Cel will learn later that this worked in her favor: Mattie, as a general matter, despises his own fans. And so it is this moment of uncharacteristically graceless lying that will wind up landing Cel her job: a triskelion of karmic confusion she just about deserves.

Back at the office, Luke tells Cel he'll be in touch. It seems he's forgotten they haven't actually done the interview. When she's halfway down the hall, Luke calls her back to collect her raincoat; he holds it at some distance from his own body, as though the color itself might be hazardous. The way he is holding it, it does look very yellow.

The huge-headed man is in the elevator on the way back down.

"Hi again," he says, and Cel nods at him. The digits above her flash silently downward; there are, of course, a preposterous number of floors. Cel stares, trying to summon another question for this man: in New York City, even the height of the buildings presents social excruciations heretofore unimaginable.

"Mattie—does he—I mean." Cel gives up: he's not going to be *her* boss, anyway. "Does he always sneak up like that?"

"He does!" The man seems entirely too pleased, she's noticed. "No one knows how he does it, but you do sort of get used to it."

"He sort of materializes at will," Luke will tell her later. "The trick is never to let him see you jump."

"And you know, I didn't mean to say that Mattie isn't a good boss, even now," says the man a moment later. Can he possibly believe Cel is still at risk of being hired? "It's really more that he's—different."

Cel nods: she is done saying things for the day. She is thinking dully of what lies ahead—the lobby with its bustling, adamantine professionals; the farcical rigmarole of the subway; an evening of circling classifieds while enduring gales of optimism from Nikki. She could try to sneak out to the Comedy Cellar, maybe, though she probably shouldn't be spending so much money. They have a two-drink minimum, which Cel objects to, deeply.

"I realized that when you asked if I'd worked with him awhile," the large-headed man is saying. "The answer is yes. But I really wanted to say—well: yes and no. Because it's like he kept changing when I wasn't looking."

He shrugs, and Cel shrugs back: she really, really doesn't care.

"But the weird thing is, I've been looking the whole time."

semi

1970

I WAS LATE TO MY DINNER WITH MATTHEW MILLER. THE ALCHEMY OF STRATE-gic lateness is tricky, though I typically liked to time things so that the man didn't realize he'd been worrying I wouldn't show until the very moment that I did. This usually meant fifteen minutes. For Matthew Miller, I made it twenty.

The place turned out to be a Japanese restaurant and also in a hotel—odd, potentially promising details to omit. Matthew Miller was sitting at a table near the back, poring over a sheaf of papers, one hand cradling the base of a nearly full martini glass. When I saw him, I fell through the floor.

Oh, I thought. *Oh.*

Walking toward him was an ordeal. When I finally reached him, he said, "Hi, there," and flipped closed his legal pad. "I appreciate your coming out."

I could still feel the *Oh* echoing within me, as from the bottom of a well. He took my hand, and I could feel his pulse—or no, that was my own.

"Are you staying here?" I said.

"No," he said, and dropped my hand. "I just keep continental hours."

I nodded as though these statements were causally linked.

"I would have invited you to my office, but—" His eyes were insistently, parodically green. The only conclusion to that sentence was: *but I didn't*.

"But it's too—small?" I said. "But it's too—messy?"

"Both, actually. And there's nowhere to sit because the sofa is covered with paperwork."

He laughed, and then I laughed, too, with a merriment completely disproportionate to the wit of what was being said.

"I'm not even sure I believe you *have* a couch," I said, accusingly and for no reason.

He eyed me for a moment, then said, firmly, "There really is a couch. And it really does have papers."

I suddenly had no idea what we were talking about. Had I really just been laughing coquettishly about a messy sofa? Matthew picked up his legal pad. The couch-papers exchange hung in the air, the silence compounding its original stupidity.

In desperation, I said, "So is it the Nixon joke?"

Matthew Miller looked up from his pad. "I'm sorry?"

The wariness on his face confirmed my worst fears about the way I'd just been laughing. "That's why they're really after Dougie Clay. Right?"

He touched his nose like, *bingo*.

"Seems like sort of a lot of paperwork for such a mediocre joke."

"It isn't really about the joke," he said.

"Well, that joke isn't really about Nixon," I said. "So maybe *that's* the joke."

He looked at me again, then shook his head as though trying to clear a cloud of déjà vu.

"You artists get away with anything, don't you?" he murmured.

"I beg your pardon?"

"Nothing." He uncapped his pen with a conclusive-sounding pop. "So, as I mentioned on the phone, I've got a municipal issue I'd like your advice about."

"About New York?" He shrugged. "Aren't you from here?"

"Anything truly worth knowing is impossible to completely know." He leaned back. There was a martini in front of me, I realized, so I took a sip.

"That's—abstract," I said finally.

"What I'm looking for is fairly concrete—fairly narrow, actually. Background about your community. That sort of thing."

"The *theater* community, I'm assuming?"

Matthew Miller's eyes cut at an angle, but he did not quite roll them.

"What you want is an informant," I said.

"Who doesn't?" He took a long swallow of his drink. "But no, this is all very aboveboard, I'm afraid. All you get is a sense of civic pride, and a small stipend for your time."

"A stipend?" This offer was beginning to sound unseemly—though really, what did I expect? "What stipend?"

"I have some discretionary funds—'lulus,' they're called." He cringed. "As in, 'in lieu of,' you know, whatever. Petty cash for miscellany. I'm using mine on policy analysts."

I looked at him blankly. "Are you—is that *me,* in this scenario?"

"Or communications consultant. Whatever. You handle your own business cards."

My attention had snagged a moment ago and I was now scrambling to catch up. The bottom line, it seemed, was this: Matthew Miller wanted to buy my time. Whether this was more or less than I'd hoped, I couldn't say.

"But the money." I lowered my voice. "I mean—in lieu of what, exactly? I mean, is this something you're allowed to do?"

"You do realize I'm a lawyer."

"You're *my* lawyer," I said. "And I'm sure we'd both agree I should know what I'm getting into."

"I wouldn't get the wrong idea," said Matthew. This buoyed my optimism—since, in my experience, people usually only tell you you've got the wrong idea when they're very afraid you've got the right one. But there was nothing on his face now: he looked unimpeachably practical, implacably benign—a man with many plans and many ideas and zero, absolutely zero, desires.

I leaned back. "Can I ask you a question?"

He nodded, I thought, a bit too vigorously.

"Did you actually believe that stuff you said about Dougie Clay?" I said. "The John Stuart Mill, and all."

I said it sort of feverishly; I could tell that I was blushing. I hadn't meant to be so specific.

"Of course," he said. "Why?"

I took a drink, and daubed my mouth.

"I sometimes wonder how much people mean the things they say in public," I said.

He looked at me searchingly. The phrase *quizzical brow* jumped out at me from somewhere—from Austen, I understood, with a horror.

"Does this conversation count as public?" he said.

"Sort of," I said. Then: "Not really." Then finally, "Yes."

He looked, in some obscure way, satisfied, which I wasn't at all sure I liked.

"So what exactly is my area of expertise supposed to be in this arrangement?" I said. "The unsightly spread of the counterculture out of the Village?" I mimed clutching at some pearls. "Just turn Sixth Avenue into a moat and be done with it, I say."

"We're in a budget crisis." Matthew Miller had an incredible, nearly undetectable deadpan. "In any case, there are these hearings coming up at the Assembly. I'd like your help with drafting a statement. As I said, I very much admired your play."

I was flooded with a wholly uncharacteristic sense of goodwill toward men—the kind people usually only get from religion or decent drugs.

"I realize your time is much in demand," he was saying. "But do you think you might spare some anyway?"

I swallowed and dropped the phantom necklace I'd been holding. I suppose Matthew took this as an affirmative.

"For you, honey," I said, hoping I didn't sound as sincere as I already, fatally, was, "I've got all the time in the world."

THUS BEGAN A PERIOD OF MY UNLIKELY AND DUBIOUS EMPLOYMENT BY THE City of New York. Like any good government employee, I was, from the start, a modest waste of revenue.

The hearings in question turned out to be The Hearings on

Homosexuality—which were, it seemed, more or less what they sounded like. Though he'd pitched my role as something like consulting, what Matthew Miller really wanted, it seemed, was a speechwriter—a ghost-speech-writer, really, who flickered in for syntactical summits and then out again into the night. And hey, I asked myself—why not? I had a way with words—on this, everybody (St. Paul's, my grandmother, even Brookie) agreed—and my play, secretly, was going nowhere. It was meant to be a meditation on the theme of transformation; it featured David Bowie, Duessa from *The Faerie Queene,* and the French Foreign Legion, and was hideously encumbered by an awareness of its own thematics.

In fact what Matthew and I were doing was not much: I helped with the rephrasing of phrasings that were already pretty good, sharpened the articulation of arguments that were nearly as elegant as I'd ever heard them made. It must be a part of Matthew Miller's job, I figured: that ability to convincingly channel other people's passions.

"Is that even possible?" I asked him more than once, when hearing of his hopes for the civil rights of the queers of New York City. Nondiscrimination in employment and housing. Public accommodation, even! He'd look at me strangely and say, "Anything is possible. Don't you believe that?" And for a moment, I'd feel that perhaps I did.

Matthew and I met at odd hours. He always seemed to have just come from somewhere else—he'd been inspecting an illegal chop-shop dump, attending a meeting at the UN Plaza, hanging around with Red Hook longshoremen at four-thirty in the morning. I'd often recently returned from somewhere else myself: a dinner on Bank Street; a party in SoHo; some green bathhouse cistern, where I'd soaked beneath frolicsome male nude mosaics. The era of insomniac cocaine use was only just beginning; it was never the wrong time to be headed out somewhere else. If anyone asked, I'd say I was off to see a show at the Permanent or—less convincingly—that I was going home to write. I seemed to regard this deceit as a matter of civic duty. I was not at the time so much as registered to vote in the state of New York.

Matthew and I met at bars, in late-night diners, in cafes. We never, never went to his apartment. His energy was outrageous, no matter what the hour, and he had an encyclopedic knowledge of the city. Did I know that the streets in Greenwich Village were twisted because in 1811 a group of residents got the city to exempt their quarter from the grid? Did I know that Nelson Rockefeller had hired Diego Rivera to paint a mural in Rockefeller Center, then had had to hire workmen to tear down the resultant Leninist imagery? Did I know that they only began arresting people for singing in Washington Square Park when black people started doing it? Matthew Miller represented two such accused back in 1969.

What sort of rejoinder was there to these questions? No, I had not known—but now, it seemed, I did. I do, still, to this day. Just as I know that New York City's law against cross-dressing stemmed from an old anti-labor statute aimed at preventing protesting farmers from obscuring their identities, and that when Grand Central Terminal first opened there was a Russian bath in the Men's Waiting Room.

"Do you want me to put that in the speech?" I said, after that last one.

"No." I wasn't even mostly serious, but Matthew Miller cocked his head as though I might have been. "I just thought you might be interested."

He thought everybody was interested—in everything, all the time—and being with him could make you want to be. He was familiar with every disagreement in that singularly fractious city. He knew these things because he talked to absolutely everyone; I was far from the only questionable character he fraternized with. The newspapers loved to run photos of Matthew speaking with such people: Matthew chatting with a homeless man standing on an actual soapbox on MacDougal and Third; Matthew taking notes on a legal pad while talking with a scare queen, a second pen tucked behind his ear. Matthew stationing himself outside a subway station—listening voraciously, democratically, to anyone who had something to say to him.

And then he'd be off again—off to listen to the little boys pushing sailboats in Central Park. ("I'm not sure they're going to grow up to be your voters," I told him. "I was talking to the *nannies*," he said.) Or to Rikers, where he apparently had many correspondents. He told me once that he answered all his letters from prisons—all his letters, in fact, from anywhere.

Though who knows if that, or anything else, was true.

IF ASKED WHAT I KNOW ABOUT MATTHEW MILLER—IN A COURT OF LAW, SAY, OR on a talk show—I could only swear to what he told me.

He said he was born in Crotona Park, that he grew up in Kew Gardens. His mother was a devoted Catholic; his father, a Jew from Galicia.

Matthew's grandfather's name (he *said*) had been changed from Milgrom at Ellis Island—though perhaps really he changed it himself, in the same spirit of shape-shifting that Matthew would prove to have in abundance.

Matthew Miller loved wrestlers as a child. As an adult, he still remembered their names—which means I'm condemned to remember them, too: Gorgeous George, Antonino Rocca, Haystacks Calhoun. So this much, probably, is true.

When Matthew Miller was ten, he said, the family moved to Newark. They told everyone in Crotona they were going to Coney Island.

In Newark, Matthew Miller delivered newspapers—getting up in fierce dark winter mornings, blowing on gloveless hands, balancing his bicycle through the deluges of spring and trying not to get the papers wet. He worked as a hatcheck boy for tips at the local movie house. He said his mother never let him miss a day of school.

Now, it all seems a little much—a little prefab-American-wet-dream. But every political genius must have his origin story: Lincoln his log cabin, Clinton his prophetic photo with JFK, Cuomo his grocer father saving crusts of bread for those hungrier than he. By those standards, Matthew's ferrying smeared newspapers through unlovely, industrial-scented predawns is only modestly inspirational. Perhaps we should have known he would never advance beyond local politics.

His success owed much to timing, he always said—he'd bene-fited from the expansion of NYU's law program under the GI Bill; he'd never had to go to war. He'd known Alice from Newark, from forever—every summer morning she would be sitting on her porch with a Popsicle, and after a while she started appearing with two—and this was an anecdote you couldn't have invented for a politician, even if you'd had the stomach to try. He married her right after com-pleting the New York State bar exam, immediately before submit-ting to the "character committee"—no minor ordeal, he said, for an immigrant boy without connections.

I listened to all of this throughout the city. I listened beneath flap-ping Puerto Rican flags; I listened under blossoming apple trees. I listened at Tiffany's coffee shop in Sheridan Square, right under-neath the gym. At just the right angle you could catch glimpses of the weight lifters on their breaks: I was too busy not-watching Mat-thew not-watch them to watch them myself. I listened beneath an enormous spray-painted whale; it was gray and saturnine and nearly life-sized, it seemed, though really I had no idea. I listened in parks decaying into mud. I listened on a mostly looted bench one day when the light did something strange to the mansard roofs in the distance—turning them nacreous, subaquatic, in a way I'd never seen before in New York City and never would again.

When I got home from these excursions, Brookie would say some variation of: "Must have been some experimental theater!" Then he'd smirk.

I don't know why I felt the need to be so secretive; Matthew Miller had never made me sign anything. And yet still I found myself (al-ready!) willing to lie—to Brookie, of all people, which was a lot like lying to myself. Together we'd been boarding school untouchables and terrified first lovers; we'd been on-and-off-again everything and more or less permanent roommates; we'd been voracious consum-ers of each other's business and opinionated keepers of each other's secrets. I'd visited Brookie at St. Vincent's after he'd been dishonor-ably discharged from his brief, ludicrous stint in the navy, and I knew that for all he bragged about his time in San Francisco, he'd in fact been very lonely there. I knew his navy release papers had been marked with not one but *two* of the three military codes for deviancy, and I knew that any time this came up in conversation he'd say, "Should have pissed the bed to make it a hat trick!"

He knew things about me, too, things I'd managed to keep from everyone else in New York. Brookie knew that I was not only from the Midwest but also—even worse—from *money*. New Yorkers cannot easily conceive of any sort of overclass west of the Mississippi; when people heard I was from Iowa, they imagined straw hats, some tragic lower-middle-class living room, maybe a collection of porcelain rabbits or something. I never corrected this impression. Brookie knew all that. He knew that my mortification, while vast, was also completely unprincipled; he knew I'd inherited money when my parents died, and that instead of nobly refusing it or using it to underwrite the revolution, I'd spent it on the production of my first, truly dreadful play. Brookie never said anything about this, not even after he went full-blown Marxist and became totally insufferable at parties. And while many people knew I'd ruptured with my grandmother, and several people knew I feared her, only Brookie knew I still respected her, somehow, and gave her quiet credit for much of who I was. Once, during a St. Paul's Family Weekend, she had tried to give him her drink order.

Brookie even knew my real first name. He never said it—not even during fights, not even after he began to hate me a little.

And now I was lying to him—to Brookie, who had circumnavigated me many times over; who had known me more completely than anyone should have the misfortune to be known.

Though maybe, by that summer, we were beginning to know each other a little less.

WHEN I FINALLY DID TELL THE BOYS, THEY THOUGHT IT WAS HILARIOUS.

"Why is this ridiculous to you?" I said. "I am a *writer*. I have a grant from the fucking NEA!"

Thereafter, they'd often ask if I was off to see His Highness, the G-Man, the Sultan. They called me Cyrano de Bergerac and Svengali. Sometimes Matthew was the Professor and I was College Boy—

which *really* made no sense, since almost all of us had been to college, more or less as boys. In response, I quoted Matthew's resume at them.

"Did you know he campaigned to get the American Bar Association to accept black members?" I was using a brightly curious, teacher's pet sort of voice, and Brookie laughed right in my face.

"Glad to hear you found yourself such an enlightened boss," he said, wiping his eyes.

Another time I mentioned that Matthew had gone to Mississippi to register voters in '64.

"Nineteen sixty-four! Well then, the man deserves a vacation!" said Brookie. "Forget the vacation: how about a medal?"

"Come on."

"You mean to tell me he once sort of helped some people who once sort of helped some black people?"

"Okay, okay."

"How was I not apprised of this? How did this not make it into the Negro newsletter?" His expression snapped into a mask of goggle-eyed worry: he was doing an impression of Paulie's impression of Alice. "Don't mention the newsletter, though, okay? I wasn't supposed to say. And it's a real powerful outfit now. All us Negroes are very powerful as a group now, actually. Ever since this one white guy filed some paperwork ten years ago. Pretty much been smooth sailing ever since."

"Okay. Enough. I get it."

"Do you?"

"Okay," I said, getting that I didn't. "Okay."

The lesson: never propagandize a propagandist.

But I couldn't stop threading Matthew into conversation, if only by reporting on all the things he'd told me—historical trivia and municipal news items that were, at best, of dubious general interest.

"Did you know that there are people who can tell the sex of a chicken without knowing how they do it?"

The boys stared at me blearily.

"Isn't that incredible?" I pressed my hands against my clavicle. "Truly, this world never ceases to amaze me."

And in that moment, I felt it might be true. Repeating something Matthew Miller had told me was to reify the link between us; even without saying his name, I felt the nova of his presence pulse momentarily in the room—I was powerless to stop it.

Brookie glared. He could tell, I think, already: I was powerless to stop that, too.

ONE THING I LIKED TO TELL MYSELF: I WAS A CONSTITUENT, FIRST AND FORE-most.

"You want my vote?" I liked to ask Matthew. I was always stalling; I must have already known that the current moment would never really be enough. I wanted all the time with Matthew all at once; I wanted the seconds all lined up and amassed into something concrete that I could hold and hold and hold. That I couldn't have this seemed a sort of foreshadowing. I didn't understand yet that life is only foreshadowing: the foreshadowing is all we get.

"I want everyone's vote," he'd say. He'd have just come from talking to constituents in Hell's Kitchen, maybe. The next day, the paper would run a photo of him in front of some luridly bright mural— cartoon primary colors, etc. I'd taken to clipping out such articles, for reference.

"So then, tell me," I'd say, and bring up some unimaginative everyman complaint. The trash, the crime, the subway. I don't know that these were terribly convincing—in fact I always loved New York, even at its worst—but Matthew Miller didn't seem to mind. He was indulging me, maybe. But also, of course, he was practicing.

I'd conclude my rants with a huffy little flourish. "And *don't* tell me to blame City Council!" I said once.

He scoffed. "City Council isn't worth your blame. The real issue is that the city is broke. Have you been in a patrol car lately?"

"I wouldn't say lately, no. Rest assured you would have been my first call."

"Well, they're falling apart. The stations are literally leaking."

"And you're going to fix that?"

"I have a few ideas."

"I'll bet you do," I said. "I'm beginning to get the sense that you're a man with a whole bunch of ideas."

In his eyes, a subaquatic flash of something?—no: only the reflection of a passing cop car's headlights.

Afterward, I'd walk back dumbstruck, dreamy, bumping into lampposts, getting myself screamed at by taxi drivers and once by a woman with a tiny pouting dog who looked like it would have liked to scream at me, too. I didn't care. I couldn't muster it. I'd be too full of a starry generosity that extended outward in all directions: toward the trash and the taxi drivers; the witchy old lady and her little dog, too; the grimacing statues in Washington Square Park and the censorious owls on Fourth Street and the glowing sugar refinery across the water the night I found I'd somehow, without noticing, walked all the way to the East River.

SEVEN
cel

"QUIT," SAYS ELSPETH ON THE PHONE ON WEDNESDAY. "YOU JUST REALLY need to quit."

Cel is staring out the living room window—she is always staring out some window or other. On the street below her, a frizzy-bearded man with a shiny purse is eating what appears to be a corn dog.

"You say that like it's so simple," she says.

"It is! You walk in, you say, 'I quit.'"

Cel is glad Nikki isn't here. The apartment is too small for another opinion, and Cel has more or less given up trying to keep anything to herself around here. They have noisy floors and high, eastern windows that admit relentless amounts of light; the walls are so thin they're essentially decorative. Their bathroom has a sink so tiny they've taken to brushing their teeth in the kitchen, and its door closes in a way that never inspires full confidence. The apartment is like an architectural version of *The Mattie M Show*: the keeping of secrets a structural impossibility.

"Do you want me to do it for you?" says Elspeth. "Because I would, you know. I'll call them up right now. I'll say I'm the publicist's publicist, and that unfortunately?—she quits."

Cel leans back from the window. There is a little semicircle on the glass, a faint intaglio of forehead. She wipes it away with her fist.

"I'll say I'm the publicist's lover and see if they fire you," says Elspeth. "Then we can sue."

"Great." Cel begins stalking down the hall, the phone cord pulling behind her. "The only thing better than working for Mattie would be staring him down in court."

Nikki's door, Cel sees, is slightly open. As a child, she'd been a hideous snoop, on those rare occasions she found herself in other people's houses. She'd invariably be shocked by their cleanliness, their sense of order, the matching plates and napkins she somehow associated with dollhouses. It seemed a sort of witchcraft was afoot. How else would the mothers know that Cel would not have brought a sleeping bag? How else would they know to give her a toothbrush they said she could keep?

"Well then, I don't know, Cel," says Elspeth. "I mean, I'd call in a sexual harassment complaint against you—I'm just that good of a friend, you know? But I have a feeling you'll shoot that down, too."

"The paperwork alone," Cel says weakly. She taps open Nikki's door with her foot. Inside, she sees a wedge of bright purple comforter, neatly tucked at its corners; she sees a spangly-looking lamp on a desk. As a child, she'd learned that too much marveling over other people's things elicited uncomfortable reactions—queasy frowns from other children, sad little smiles from their moms—so after a while, Cel learned to confine her investigations to the bathrooms. She'd pull back shower curtains to sniff at bleach-smelling air, open linen closets to fondle impossibly soft towels. Later, in her own bed, she'd lie awake thinking about the towels, fussy with a feeling that wasn't quite covetousness—more a sense of indignation that such things could exist without her knowing. She deserved to at least know about them, she felt.

"I don't get it." Elspeth sighs, as though Mattie M is her problem. Cel would never admit how much she cherishes Elspeth's familial, nearly uxorial, presumption. "I mean—you can *afford* to quit, can't you?"

Cel stares into Nikki's room. All of Nikki's things always look so new, and Cel had been impressed by this at first, and wondered how she was managing it. Cel's mistake had been assuming that—

because she and Nikki shared the same rent and the same militant cockroaches and the same warped bathroom door—they were subject to the same arithmetic. It was months before Cel realized that money in New York was almost never a question of arithmetic, but algebra; for Nikki—for a lot of people—the entire equation was determined by a set of offstage variables. Their values might be minimal, or even hypothetical—a co-signing of a loan, the promise of a bailout, a little help with an apartment deposit or an interview outfit—but they were there, creating an invisible protective buoy, magically squaring the circles for all the people whose lives, when you got right down to it, simply were not possible on paper.

"Cel: seriously?" says Elspeth. "You make like fifty thousand dollars a year!"

A frantic feeling kicks up inside Cel; she closes Nikki's door with her toe.

"I know it sounds like a lot," she says. She is trying to sound knowledgeable, steadying. She does have a bit of savings in her checking account, a miracle now dwarfed by her sense of its terminal inadequacy. Part of the reason it took her so long to figure out that everyone in New York was secretly rich was that everyone talked so much about being poor—and after a while, Cel came to understand that this wasn't exactly pretense. In New York, both luck and deprivation turned out to be gauged in relation to a whole other stratum of wealth—an overclass so remote they were invisible to Cel entirely, possessed of treasures and shortcuts beyond imagination or envy. Money, it turns out, is extremely complicated—governed by unspoken protocols Cel can never hope to predict, or expect anyone to explain. The idea of quitting her job makes her dizzy with fear.

"I mean, in Northampton, it would be a fortune," says Cel. "But here I live in a coffin with Tupperware. You'll see for yourself when you come."

"New York, good *God*. You wildly overpay to live in squalor, and all you get is the chance to correct some poor tourist's pronunciation of 'Houston.'" This had happened to Elspeth once, and she'd never forgiven the city for it. "I'd like to know who does New York's publicity."

"New York doesn't need publicity."

"They had those pins."

"Oh. Right. Well, I'll buy you one when you come." Cel retreats to the kitchen. "You are still coming, aren't you?"

"Yes." Elspeth is quiet for a moment. Cel stares at Nikki's juicer—more evidence that was there all along, hidden in plain sight, threatening her daily with subdural hematoma. "Is it possible, Cel, that you actually like this job?"

Cel says nothing: on this subject, this is the most that she's ever said.

"You know you don't have to pretend that you hate it, right?"

"I do hate it!" Cel is very, very sure she hates it. She just isn't sure she doesn't somehow like it, too. She can hear the faint tapping of Elspeth's earring against the phone.

"Cel, to be honest, more and more? I just don't understand you."

"Elspeth, you claim to understand *cannibalism*."

"I do understand cannibalism. It's a ritual of grieving or conquest."

"Exactly! Understanding the inexplicable is sort of your area. So shouldn't my life intrigue you? Just, I mean, academically?" Cel is trying to make her voice sound less chilly, but this seems to be making things worse.

"That's—well, no. Not exactly."

"Come on! You're telling me you wouldn't be excited to find a specimen like me out in the field? Someone so far beyond the pale that I have the potential to give us all a new understanding of the human family?"

"You certainly are one of a kind."

"Well, here I am, only a bus ride away! You don't even have to get any shots!" Cel is aware of laboring at the spirit of things; she smiles to make her voice sound warmer. "I mean, it's good you're coming to do some research before anyone else gets wind of this."

"No research this time," says Elspeth coolly. "This is my vacation. Any observations about your life will be regarded as pure entertainment."

"Fantastic!" says Cel. "You won't even need tickets to the show."

———

ON THURSDAY, CEL IS SUMMONED VIA PAGE TO THE CONFERENCE ROOM.

"Why didn't you just call?" she asks.

Luke shrugs. "I wanted to see if it would work."

Jessica and Sanjith are already seated at the table, looking grim. They have been gathered, Luke explains, to hash out the details for a possible Mattie TV appearance. He sounds as though he thinks they should be flattered by this, though Sanjith and Jessica seem more or less indifferent; in the current context, all careerism seems meaningless.

"How does Mattie respond to reports that the shooters were fans of the show?" says Sanjith, in what Cel takes to be a very half-assed Tod Browning impersonation.

"Well, it wouldn't surprise me if they were, Tod," says Luke. "Ten percent of the country are fans of the show."

He throws a Koosh ball in the air.

"You want to take responsibility for ten percent of the country?" says Jessica. "Don't you think two sociopathic kids are enough?"

"Two sociopathic—two *troubled*—kids, out of literally millions of people." Sanjith is trying to do a Mattie impression now, though Mattie is notoriously unsatisfying to imitate—they almost never bother with him on *Saturday Night Live,* though the *Mattie M* format would obviously be the perfect template for all kinds of sketches. "These kids probably did things millions of people do—drive cars, skip school, go on dates—well, maybe not *dates*—"

"The point is, they did things," says Luke flatly. "Isolating *Mattie M* as the variable doesn't make any sense."

"Say that again in English?"

"*Post hoc, ergo propter hoc.*" Cel can't tell if Luke is angry. Sanjith is already up at the whiteboard, adding "10%!!" to their bulleted list. Their other ideas so far are (a) Acknowledge! (meaning the tragedy) and (b) Trivialize! (meaning the show; this was Luke's contribution: "Essentially: this is serious, the show is silly. The show is trash, right? And trash may be gross, but it's *inconsequential*.").

"How'd you come up with ten percent, anyway?" says Sanjith. He sniffs the marker before capping it.

"Long division," says Luke. "There is an average of five million viewers per show, thirty million discrete viewers per year—"

"Thirty million is maybe better than ten percent," says Cel.

"They're the same, apparently," says Sanjith. "Don't tell me you're challenging HAL's numbers? Cel, he'll short-circuit!"

"I mean—when you say ten percent of the country watch *The Mattie M Show*, people start thinking about the ninety percent of the country that *doesn't* watch. Especially if they're in the ninety percent, which, statistically, they probably are."

"And they say girls can't do math."

"So if we're saying it makes no sense to link the show to the killers because ten percent of the country can't be monsters—well, I think a lot of people are going to think, *Maybe they are.* I bet most people think at least ten percent of the people they know *personally* are monsters."

There's a pause in which calculations are made.

"That's probably a conservative estimate," Jessica says finally.

Sanjith goes to the whiteboard and wipes out "10%!!" with the side of his fist, replacing it with "Ten million!"

"Your hand is blue," says Cel.

"It's metastasized from his balls," says Luke, standing up—which is how Cel knows that the meeting is over, and that Luke was never angry at all.

AFTER THE MEETING, CEL DRIFTS HOMEWARD. SHE REGISTERS THE CITY PE-ripherally: cracked-marble sky, mottled seagull pecking at condom wrapper, woman with faintly bugspray-smelling perfume. Clouds of cool air billow out from stores, bearing the scents of synthetic fabrics. If she never really looks at New York, will she ever remember it later? Her memories from Smith are vivid and hyper-articulated: the spade-shaped leaves from the ginkgo trees imported from Japan; the mural of women's accomplishments in downtown Northampton—done in swirls of blue, socialist-realist decisiveness. The lanterns on Illumination Night, like pale jellyfish against the black sea. Her first year, they'd reminded her of the mountain laurel at home; her second year they'd reminded her of her first year. The bready smell of wine at those endlessly replicated wine-and-cheese parties. She remembers the food at these parties, as humorless as the ideologies under discussion. She remembers trying to banter with an Amherst boy while masticating some incomprehensibly resurrected biblical grain—some desiccated fiber that, for good reason, had been unable to survive the competition of early agriculture. *"If there's one thing you want to trust the free market on, it might be this"*: her first laugh in a crowded room.

She remembers her first bus ride to Massachusetts. She was struck by the similarities in the landscape—the same vigorous green hills, same scoured-looking sky. Same sort of silver flashing river, bending deep at the Oxbow like a genuflecting knee. Northampton was another story: a beautiful little music box of a town. Brick apartments over storefronts, fire escapes zigzagged with batik. White women swooping around in great ethnic capes. There were pianos in the dormitory common areas, fireplaces in the bedrooms. In one, a girl Cel's age was unpacking. Her shirt rolled up to reveal a complexly impressive midriff; the tiny whelk of a perfect navel. Next to her were two people who must be her parents—two entire parents, summoned from their lives for this occasion. Around them, the dusty-sweet smell of cardboard filling up the air.

"Hi, sweetheart," said the mother to Cel. "Are you lost?"

Cel remembers her first day of Marxism class, when the girl who turned out to be Elspeth leaned over to her and said, "Hey." The girl's hair, in addition to being green, was very dirty. She smelled clean in the way of dirt; the utilitarian, no-nonsense part of a plant.

"Hey," said the girl again. "Why did Karl Marx's toilet play music every time he flushed?"

"I don't know," said Cel. "Why?"

"Because of the violins inherent in the cistern!"

Cel stared. The girl's feet were muddy and be-Birkenstocked; her ankles ostentatiously hairy; her teeth, when she smiled, were perfectly, expensively straight. Whatever this girl's idea was about herself, it was clear that someone, at some point, had had others.

"You know?" The girl was staring at Cel right back. "From *The Communist Manifesto*?"

"I *don't* know," said Cel, with a depraved panic. "That's exactly why I'm taking this class."

But miraculously, the girl was laughing.

"You're funny," she said. "You know that?"

Cel said she supposed she did, and Elspeth laughed again. And Cel caught the first glimpse of her next life, and the person who would be living it.

BACK AT THE APARTMENT, CEL IS WATCHING *MATTIE M* AGAIN, SOMEHOW.

This week's reruns are *Best of Mattie M: Forbidden Passions:* the five-hundred-pound woman and the dwarf, the eighty-year-old woman and the podiatrist, the pantsuited couples' therapist who joined her married clients in a polyamorous arrangement. ("She's good with conflict," says the man.) The crowd always hates at least one of the lovers on *Forbidden Passions*—they hated the podiatrist, and they *despised* the dwarf's pachydermal lover (who got jeers and exactly the kinds of questions you'd expect). Tonight's episode is the goat bride—technically a Forbidden Passion, though they've also used it for *Odd Couple Roommates, My Co-Worker Did* What?!, and *Believe It or Not!: Freaks Edition*. Its versatility is part of what makes it a "*Mattie M* Classic"—which, according to Luke, means that it will play on a loop at all their funerals.

On the screen, Mattie waves at the crowd over the bouncy closing chords of the intro music. Cel is usually never home during *Mattie M*'s regular time slot, and something about watching it during the day makes her anxious—as though she should be there right now, seeing this from the studio.

"Thanks, guys!" says Mattie. "Welcome to the show!"

He sits, exposing argyle but—mercifully—no ankle.

"In today's episode, we'll be exploring the wacky, wild—and sometimes even woolly!—side of romance." Mattie's delivery is deadpan enough to be a little funny, though it's hard to tell how he means it. Cel finds this ambiguity compounded through the screen; on TV, *Mattie M* almost feels like two shows at once—like one of those reversible images that some people see as faces and other people see as a vase.

"When we think of star-crossed lovers, we think of Romeo and Juliet, Pyramus and Thisbe—but man and *goat?*"

Pyramus and Thisbe? Luke must have hated that. The audience doesn't laugh, of course. Cel can't imagine who Mattie thinks he's winking at with that one; intellectuals despise him as much as evangelicals. Cel has read countless leftish articles condemning the show: editorials excoriating its craven pandering to the lowest common denominator; point-counterpoints pondering whether it has created or merely exposed America's basest cultural instincts; a twenty-thousand-word *New Yorker* piece casting it as the culmination of a civilizational erosion—under way for at least the twentieth century, and probably the entire millennium. Cel had read that one so many times she wound up memorizing the conclusion: "Having inherited the legacy of Western civilization, we have clung only to its tricks and technologies, and forgotten the animating force which created them. We find ourselves stranded in a socio-cultural tide pool at historic low ebb, with nothing to do but watch the waters retreat across the horizon—and *The Mattie M Show,* five nights a week in syndication."

It's all a little much, but Cel doesn't really dispute the general thrust. *The Mattie M Show is* insipid and base, graceless and lewd, a sound and fury signifying nothing; she understands how you can watch it and think: *The Renaissance was for this?*

The phone rings and she jumps; for a vertiginous moment she has the sense it's Mattie, somehow calling her through the television—but she answers and it's only Luke, saying that it's official: Mattie is booked on *Lee and Lisa* for Monday morning, congratulations!

"What?" says Cel. "How?"

"Well, Cel, he'll go in a car to a studio—you remember the one we work in? With all the lights on the ceiling?"

"I mean—already?"

"And then a man in a suit will ask him some softball questions— 'softball' being an idiomatic term, in this case—"

"Jesus, that was fast."

"These are fast times we're living in. Also? They had a cancellation. And also? Kliegerman wants you to prep Mattie."

"What?"

"No one is more surprised than I am. Apparently the Kliegs thinks Mattie has gotten a little too hip to my tricks."

"What the hell am *I* supposed to do?"

"You do what Mattie does," says Luke. "You do what the fucking Muppets do. You read the cue cards."

So this is what she gets for competence: yesterday's outline, Cel sees, contains the seeds of her undoing. They'd made bulleted lists of talking points and preferred euphemisms; they'd drafted plausible rebuttals to anticipated accusations, as well as snappy rejoinders to anticipated rephrasings of same. They'd noted lines of argument that are discouraged, and those expressly forbidden—blaming guns, parenting, other media (accepts the premise). They'd collated notes, compiled over the course of Mattie's previous non-*Mattie* appearances, on the stylistic tics and rhetorical maneuvers they'd prefer he not repeat. They'd collected reams of background research on Suzanne Bryanson. Cel was personally party to all this thoroughness, and now it has ensnared her. It is becoming increasingly clear to her that professionalism is a self-reinforcing trap, like pyramid schemes and drug addiction.

"I mean—you can *read*, can't you, Cel?"

"No."

"Well, you've functioned admirably well in that case."

"Luke, I've barely ever talked to the guy. And aren't you always telling me how this is all so hard?"

It certainly doesn't look easy, trying to wrangle Mattie M ahead of a public appearance. Each category of instruction requires a slightly different mode of delivery. On the big points, they can usually be fairly straightforward; it's the areas of medium importance where he's likely to act out—disputing, or simply ignoring, their suggestions. Whether this is out of a desire to feel he's participating in the process, or a childishly low tolerance for accepting advice, no one knows. The trick with this category is to impress instructions upon Mattie without ever articulating them directly. Then there are the "wish list" details—specific phrasings that are preferred, but not crucial enough to warrant squandering any of Mattie's finite cooperation; these must be imparted nearly subliminally, through frequent repetition. Cel knows all this because she's watched Luke do it several times, and heard him explain it many more.

"Look, Cel," says Luke. "Even you understand the overarching triage. The really essential points are just a matter of basic human communication—and literacy aside, we have satisfactorily established that you are at least minimally verbal."

Oh yeah? thinks Cel, and says nothing.

"And who knows, you know? Maybe you'll scramble his radar."

"Scramble his radar? I'll be lucky if he doesn't call security. He doesn't even know who I am."

"Of course he does. He made me hire you, remember?"

Luke says this all the time. Cel has no idea whether it is true, though she knows better than to let Luke know she doesn't know.

"I've been trying ever since to figure out why, and all I can come up with is that you struck him as some kind of idiot savant. We're all still waiting for the savant part to kick in—but in the meantime, it's just possible the idiot part can be useful."

"This is inspiring stuff, Luke, truly. Have you considered motivational speaking?"

"Because Mattie's resistant to messages in code. But the medium is the message, and if you're the medium, maybe he thinks there is no message. Because incompetence seems guileless, right?"

So now her *in*competence is the reason she must do more work. This is something like karma, or maybe video games? Cel's knowledge of both is limited.

"So who knows?" says Luke. He exhales sharply. "And also, at this point? What the hell."

semi

1971

THE HEARINGS CAME IN JANUARY.

I arrived at the courthouse early. I'd told myself I'd have to hunt for Matthew—though in fact I always spotted him right away, no matter where we were. Today he was standing in the westernmost doorway of the courthouse, wearing an ill-advised beige suit, talking to a man I'd never seen before. This man had blond hair and a princely demeanor; he turned out later to be the dauphin of some great packaging fortune. I hated him immediately.

Brookie was at the courthouse, too, with the GLF. He was standing right outside the doorway, dressed as Little Orphan Annie.

"Well, how lovely to see *you* again," he said to Matthew, and curtsied. I was aware of wishing to hurry Matthew past this; equally aware of being unable to publicly direct, or acknowledge, him at all. My understanding of this feeling was settling from quiet thrill into quiet misery; the shock of it was gone, and I'd be left forever with whatever came next.

I could barely hear what Matthew Miller said during the testimony, though I do believe—and the public record attests—that it was, more or less, what we'd drafted.

Afterward, he found me in the hallway.

"Congratulations," he said.

"Congratulations to you!" I said, giving an awkward little salute. I expected him to turn away again—he was usually emphatically Irish in his exits—but instead he stayed there, looking at me, even as the clerks and reporters and secretaries and witnesses swept in and out of doors.

"We should celebrate," he said, or maybe I only thought he said. I could hear the squeak of snowy shoes, the steam of overly aggressive radiators. Why couldn't I hear anything else? On the window high above us, frost pressed into the glass like the palm of a hand.

"What?" I said.

"I'm saying we should celebrate." This time, I heard him, even though he seemed to have lowered his voice. "I'm saying: come over for a drink?"

HIS APARTMENT WAS DIM, DARK, TRAGIC-BACHELOR—OH, WHO KNOWS: IT was very hard to pay attention. Across the street, the glowing eyes of some sort of creature stared out from a neon bar sign.

"I think it's supposed to be a cat," he said when he saw me looking.

I do remember books: *The Other America, The Death and Life of Great American Cities*—along with some Jefferson, Debs, Trotsky, Fromm. I asked him where was Freud, and he said he despised Freud, and I said what would Freud say about that? And unbelievably, he laughed.

I was aware that there was no visible bed—he turned out to have a Murphy folded up into the wall. In the corner, a telex crouched precariously on a file cabinet.

"Nice escritoire," I said, though luckily Matthew did not hear me; he'd retreated to the kitchen. I followed him. On the counter, a desiccated meat loaf was escaping from its foil.

"Don't touch that," he said, emerging from the refrigerator and handing me a beer. "It came out of a vending machine."

"Well, now I've seen it all." My mouth was dry.

"Are you shocked?" His eyes were full of laughter. "I thought there was nothing new under the sun."

I wasn't sure if he was making fun of me or not.

"Maybe only this," I said.

"What would the formidable Lady Sinclair have to say about that?"

He meant my grandmother. He remembered everything about everybody, I reminded myself.

"I'm sure she'd be speechless," I said.

"To her," he said, clinking my glass.

"To her."

We drank.

"Do you think you'll ever see her again?" said Matthew after a moment. I was sure I'd never told him I hadn't.

"I don't know," I said, which was the truth. I did not long for some loving, tearful reunion. Still, there was a formal grace in the acknowledgment of a family: something like the record of your birth in the town register, the correct spelling of the name on your gravestone. I'd tried explaining this to Brookie once, and he'd stared at me, agog.

"You know what happens to fags whose names get written down?" he said.

And another time: "So an old lady doesn't like her homo grand-kid? This is the oldest story in the book! I've heard this one a million times!"

"Not from me," I told him.

"You writers never understand that just because *you're* telling something for the first time doesn't mean we're hearing it for the first time."

A sentiment my grandmother would have surely appreciated.

Matthew Miller seemed to be listening very intently, even though I was not speaking. I blushed and shook myself.

"Maybe I'd go back." I took a sip of beer, though I hated beer and came to learn that Matthew did, as well: he kept it around for when politicos stopped by. "For a long time I thought I would go back, if I could ever know what I was retrieving."

"Whether it'd be worth it, you mean."

"Or what 'it' even *is*." For a long time, I'd wanted to know what my return would mean—I wanted to understand its shape, shift its slight weight in my hands. Over the years, I'd watched its hypothetical mass grow smaller, until I was almost sure I had my answer—if I didn't know the precise dimensions, I knew what they rounded down to. "I was waiting to understand that, I think, for a while."

"And now?" said Matthew.

"I think now I'm just waiting not to be waiting anymore." But then there was always that desire to know something permanently: orthogonal rays of curiosity angling to a vanishing point. Because when could we say with certainty that what had not yet happened never would? "Obviously, I should not care."

"But of course you do," said Matthew. "Because nothing is ever that simple."

Out the window, a girl in a green plaid skirt stepped daintily over a pile of trash.

"My grandmother had this friend," I found myself saying abruptly. "Confirmed bachelor, you know. He'd come over wearing Patek Philippe ties and make enormous vats of martinis and show us slides of his travels in Europe. I was riveted. Well, you can imagine."

Could he?

"In retrospect, I'm almost sure she knew about him." I once saw them talking intently in the kitchen, her hand pressed sisterishly to his wrist. Surely she had known, and surely he had not told her—and surely this was why she'd loved him, in her way. This went without saying. It all—always—went without saying. "On some level, I think she was a pretty hard woman to faze."

"Yet you managed it."

It seemed Matthew had gotten a little closer, somehow. I shook my head.

"Her objection to me wasn't moral so much as aesthetic," I said. "What she really couldn't bear was histrionics. *Theater* people." As she'd said meaningfully and more than once. "There was a whole lot of *Brideshead*-type stuff at St. Paul's—much clutching of hands, reciting of poetry in the woods. You know."

Did he? He was undeniably much closer. I could see the silver hairs in his beard, the fingerprint-sized birthmark on his neck. The tiny scar slicing out from the edge of his left eye. It deepened, which is how I knew he was smiling: I could not bring myself to look at his mouth.

"She admired people who revealed nothing," I said. "She would have liked you, probably."

"Why is that?"

His eyes had a nervy alertness that made me feel like I'd been shocked every time I met them. Now, my courage failed me. My hands were trembling; I squeezed them into fists.

"*Res ipsa loquitur,* was another thing she often said."

His hand was on my hand; my hand was somehow unfurling. I stared at the divot in his wrist, the gap between bone and everything else.

"Why do you care, anyway?" Now my voice was trembling, too. "She isn't even registered in New York."

We were turning to each other, somehow, finally.

"I care," he said. And in that moment, for a moment, it seemed certain that he did.

OH, THAT APARTMENT: HOW I MISS THAT APARTMENT. ITS HIGH CEILINGS; ITS creaking cedar-smelling floors; its whistling radiator pipes, sounding vaguely like sirens—which half the time they turned out to be. I walk past it sometimes, still; from across the street, that neon cat still stares into its living room. The back window looked out directly onto a brick wall. We were reckless in front of that window—that first night and many after. The six inches to the bricks, the thirty-some-odd feet to the alleyway below, the unknowable volume they comprised—these might have been the dimensions of the entire city, the entire world. It might have been the entire galaxy we traversed, safe in our ship, witnessed only by stars, gazing indifferently from the past.

We double-locked the door against intrusions we never spoke of. Beyond us, roaches rampaged in the hallway; shadows zebra-ed down the fire escape. Inside, Matthew Miller told me many ludicrous things, and I believed them.

What more is there to say? In that outlandish, inscrutable season, I would have believed anything at all.

cel

1988

CEL'S UNINVENTING BEGINS IN THE FALL, WHEN A MAN ON A BUS SNARLS AT her to *move the fuck over, princess.*

She is wearing an ironed skirt and conventional makeup. The man has a matted beard; his feet are black and bare. He hates Cel categorically, which still feels like a triumph. As Cel moves over she feels the fluttery recklessness, the sense of suspended rules and expanded possibility, of a masquerade ball.

Because this, *this,* has been the project of her life. She spent all of high school trying to make herself into the others; she parroted their talk, scouring her speech of Hal's obsolescent expressions, Ruth's loopy malapropisms. She tried copying the spirit of their clothes until ninth grade; after that, she stuck to army boots and wore her coat indoors nine months out of the year. This was deemed weird, but the boring sort of weird that didn't particularly excite aggression. In conversation, Cel was mostly laconic, occasionally extremely foul-mouthed, which somehow never stopped surprising people. Her pop-cultural awareness never remotely approached normal levels, but she was good at absorbing tidbits and savvy at deploying them. She organized these expenditures on the same syncopated cycle Hal used with the bills—deferred until the very last moment, right before the lights were shut off, the car repossessed. Cel knew her performance was effortful and basically unconvincing, to anyone looking too closely. But she also knew that nobody was really looking at all.

But at Smith, it seems, her acceptability is presumed. It becomes quickly clear that this brings certain liabilities. The excision of her former life was supposed to make a surface; instead, it seems she's created a vacuum. In October, a man on the street calls her a WAR PIG and asks how much money her dad makes. On Halloween, an Amherst boy dressed as Che lectures her on the class struggle. In Marxism class, there are scoffs over her halting analysis of systemic inequality. She is lectured on the Vietnam War and the plight of the mentally ill; she is lectured on bourgeois signifiers and the unacknowledged troubles of the rural poor.

"You could tell them a little about yourself," says Elspeth, after Cel tells her exactly that much.

But Cel has not spent a lifetime building a sort of privacy only so she can throw it in some stranger's face at a party. Elspeth says she might at least try Birkenstocks. Cel's slight overdressing, she says, seems precious; a sign that she is in need of special instruction. If Cel is no longer invisible, it's because the background behind her has changed.

And so she buys a mustard-yellow collared shirt, brown pants that flare at the hem. She stops wearing shoes in the summer. She throws out her lipstick, her drugstore curling iron—faster and faster, she rids herself of these things, these treasures from a sinking ship, though with more regret than she'll ever care to admit.

It is clear that she will have to start all over. She mourns a little while, then begins again.

part two

The nightingales are sobbing in
The orchards of our mothers,
And hearts that we broke long ago
Have long been breaking others. . . .

—W. H. AUDEN

This ghost that runs after you,
my brother, is more beautiful than you;
why do you not give him your
flesh and your bones?

—FRIEDRICH NIETZSCHE

TEN

semi

1971–1976

IT CAME SLOWLY, THEN ALL AT ONCE: A DELUSIONAL, FIENDISH LOVE.

How many nights, how many calls, how many pennies cast up at his window? How many keys dropped down to the sidewalk—and who could say from which apartment they fell? And yet it seems to have only been one night, eternally recurring—it seems that it is happening somewhere, even now, without me.

The margins are easier to access: hours before, hours after. Images limned with a feeling they cannot possibly have inspired on their own. Dodging the junkies on Clinton Street. Dodging the anal-retentive NYPD German shepherds on the A train. Listening to the call to prayer on Atlantic Avenue in some gorgeous miscreant dawn. Wandering the warehouse district, gazing up at the cast-iron buildings, looking for a party that was never found. Standing atop the Empire State Building, the skyline before us like a sideways key. Calling Matthew from a pay phone outside Tracks or the Gaiety, ELO spilling out into the street. *Do ya do ya want my love, do ya do ya want my face, do ya do ya want my mind?* The smell of poppers acrid in my nostrils. I'd tell myself that this was why my knees sometimes shook when the phone rang, why they broke (once! only once!) when he answered.

I don't mean to make it sound simpler than it was. I did not yearn for Matthew when I admired a man lifting weights at a Nautilus, or floated in a Quaalude haze past the Ice Palace, the air around me thick with sassafras and pine. I did not long for him when I went prowling around the Gansevoort Street pier, watching the dawn break over the container ships. They were yellow and blue and had been around the world: oh, the things they'd seen! And when I fucked other men, it wasn't purely out of principle. Yet I found I could never entirely banish Matthew, either. He was simply *there*, within me—he seemed to have moved in somehow and taken up a phantasmal, stridently permanent, residence. This alarmed me, though not as much as it should have: like many early symptoms, its significance was clear only in retrospect.

ONE MAN'S RAPTURE IS ANOTHER MAN'S PUBLIC SERVICE ANNOUNCEMENT: mine was the joy of the junkie in the gutter.

The boys, of course, did not approve. A cold peace descended in the apartment: the boys united in some judgment of Matthew I could never quite define. One did not bow helplessly before one's vices; drugs were consumed on the weekends, according to schedules. There were the usual objections to monogamy—it was an anachronism, an opportunity cost. The serial monogamists were all kidding themselves; we called theirs the Elizabeth Taylor approach. Now, we agreed, was not the time for restraint.

I'd point out that Matthew and I were not monogamous, and made a whole big point of showing it off. But certainly it was becoming clear—as months stretched unbelievably into seasons—that I was in the thrall of a profound and unseemly attachment. This was embarrassing in a square, sentimental way—like coming down with a case of midlife Christianity. We found this sort of thing contemptible in part, I think, because we thought it feminine—stilettos and machismo: odd bedfellows, indeed.

I understood all of this, and did not care. Like the twitching addict, like the serenely saved, I knew the happiness of a different, better dimension.

And even now, who can be certain I did not?

———

WE WERE NOT, AS A GROUP, GENERALLY GIVEN TO MORALISM. ONE OF BROOK-
ie's regulars had spent a year on Rikers for stabbing a man over, I
believe, a slice of pizza. The notion that there was something *unseemly* about my relationship with Matthew was a hilarious attitude
coming from them, and I would have said so if they'd ever had the
courtesy to articulate any of this out loud.

But they didn't. And so, in those days, we did not fight about Matthew Miller: we fought about everything else instead. We fought
about civil rights, women's lib, economic equality, and what order
they should go in. We fought—Brookie and I did—about the Pan-
thers. We fought about whether Larry Kramer was a visionary or a
traitor; we fought about whether Andy Kaufman was a genius or a
gimmick. We fought about the Joan Baez album Nick played for an
entire summer—that hollow alto of hers sounding increasingly aggrieved as the months wore on.

*"As I remember your eyes were bluer than robin's eggs . . . My poetry
was lousy you said—"*

—and Stephen would say, "Case in point."

We fought about whether the new vibe at the sex clubs was sociopathic or interesting. We fought about whether the hippies were really only hedonists, then fought over whether *we* were in any position
to judge. On matters of consensus, we sought hairline fractures. We
all hated Ronald Reagan, but managed to generate some real hostility over whether "Dutch" would have made a good drag name.

One night on Fire Island the boys dragged me out to see the
moon. We'd spent the month in a swirl of tea dances and theme
balls, tambourines and ethyl chloride. I'd thought "full moon" was a
euphemism, though it turned out to be the thing itself—and it did
indeed seem startlingly close, like an asteroid hovering just before
impact.

"Makes you feel like it could crash right into us if it wanted to,"
said Paulie.

"Would you blame it?" I said. "We crashed right into *it*."

"That's what they want you to believe," said Brookie, so that we
might argue about that, too.

———

"ALL YOUNG PEOPLE TAKE THEIR OPINIONS TOO SERIOUSLY," SAID MATTHEW when I told him all this. "They think they're going to be stopped on the street at any moment and asked to justify all their life's conclusions."

"Young people think that?" I said. "Then what's your excuse?"

But, in fact, I knew the answer already: in Albany, Matthew's career was in something like ascendance. He'd been assigned to some important committee, and people were beginning to recognize him around town. He still did a lot of traversing, even though he wasn't technically campaigning—he went to the Bronx, crumbling like the ruins of Petra; he went to visit squatters, shivering amidst falling plaster. He went to many places beyond his district, which should have been the first clue.

We could not, of course, go anywhere together. And yet never has New York felt denser or more dizzying as there in that little apartment, that glowing-eyed cat staring us down, listening to Matthew Miller narrate the city.

He was obsessively well informed. He was addicted to data, to complicating information—and all this was thrilling, cerebrally erotic, at first. He could seem *maddeningly* without agenda, beyond a commitment to reality—and, I suppose, a militant insistence that reality existed (not an entirely uncontroversial idea, then or now). He liked to say that if you were sure of more than three things, then you probably didn't have all your facts straight. Though he always did, and he never let you forget it—not to keep the peace, not to support his own policies—which made him a very hard man to agree with. He had a reflexive need to volunteer mitigating information. Lambaste the union busters in the transit strike—their elitism, their blind pursuit of profit, their callousness toward the common man— and Matthew, who was about as pro-union as anyone could get, would note that his opponents' position wasn't exactly an *elite* one, since it was shared by the majority of the city, which was particularly hostile to a fare hike at the moment because service was the worst in living memory; and furthermore, while he had no opinion on whether they cared only for profit, it was undeniable that theirs were hardly the only profits at issue, since the strike would be likely to affect *many* people's profits, the common man's included.

Matthew liked to say this impulse was a holdover from his years as a lawyer, when he learned to expect exculpatory evidence—though there were times I suspected its real source was his years as a Catholic, when he had learned to volunteer confession.

And yet. We never, never spoke of Alice.

Matthew knew a lot about the gay world, too—though it remained rather an abstraction, in those moments when we weren't fucking each other's brains out. He told me about taverns in eighteenth-century London where men performed marriage ceremonies; he told me about the drag shows of Weimar Berlin. He told me how Greenwich Village and the Castro became gay neighborhoods after World War II, when a certain set of small-town soldiers just never went back home.

"I'll have to take your word for that," I'd say, and kiss him. Then I'd kiss his cock through whatever stupid suit he was wearing, then his State Assembly lapel pin, to be a little funny. And then we'd be at it all over again.

I was amazed at the intensity of the thing. I told myself it was because we couldn't go anywhere together, and because Matthew was away so much. I told myself it was because it wasn't *real*—or anyway, not completely. Because really: who was this man? I wondered as I clutched his back, kissed his neck, pushed myself inside him.

Who are you? And are you here? And are you this?

Please be this.

ONCE, I SAID, "THE BOYS DON'T APPROVE OF YOU, YOU KNOW." I WAS, AS Brookie might have put it, "heightening the contradictions."

"Is that right?" Matthew Miller said, and kissed me. "Tell the boys I'm sorry."

"You don't seem *terribly* sorry."

He turned over and began stroking my eyebrow.

"What can I say?" he said after a moment. "Tell them we love each other anyway."

DID HE EVER REALLY LOVE ME?

This is all I can say for certain: he often seemed to, when pretending would have gained him nothing.

IN THE APARTMENT, WE PLAYED MOVIES ON THE WALLS. WE TOOK LSD THREE times with a liquid eyedropper; we took DMT once and vowed we never would again. I was working on a new play—a retelling of *The Possessed,* set in modern-day New York, with fags and queens cast as the conspirators. Suicidal Kirillov was based on Stephen; Paulie was the aspiring revolutionary Verkhovensky; Brookie the highly philosophical Shigalev. This made me the bitterly misunderstood Stavrogin, and I gave him the very best jokes. Its working title was *The Dispossessed,* which I simultaneously despised and felt helplessly committed to. This seemed like a very big problem, at the time.

We had a lot of these, then. The great disaster of the fall was a particularly hearty troop of crabs—these could usually be treated with A-200, though in this case one of us (it seems crass to say now who) required multiple rounds of Kwell and, ultimately, shaving. We all complained wretchedly. Everything is relative.

Then there were the other kinds of problems—the ones that have taken on heft with the passing years, revealing their natures only in retrospect. For Nick, it was a night at St. Mark's, when he was strangled by a man we'd never seen before and never would again. For Brookie, it was a bad trip at the Mineshaft, when he watched himself turn into a mouse in the bathroom mirror. He'd punched his reflection, adding a helical scar to his collection. It turned out later that the acid tab he'd taken had had Mickey Mouse's face on it. We laughed about this, though not because it wasn't horrifying: the bald murine face, the enormous black eyes . . . once more, we'd dissolve. Things had turned out fine. And though we knew we were supposed to believe that they might not have, we never lingered long in any worry.

At the time, these were only the best stories to tell at certain kinds of parties.

ONE NIGHT I WAS HEADED OUT TO SEE MATTHEW AND THE BOYS WANTED ME to come to some party instead.

"Come, dahling!" said Paulie, clicking into a Boston Brahmin accent and pulling me into a waltz. "Let us prepeah for a night of meah-re-ad pleasheahs."

"Good luck with *that*," said Brookie, when he saw us. "Who needs fun when you're fucking a fascist?"

For a long time, Brookie had kept his commentary about Matthew restrained, and relatively oblique. "Well, you know what they say," he'd said once, when a piece of our subway car fell directly onto the tracks. "You can't fuck City Hall."

"He's in the State Assembly," I hissed. "Read a paper, why don't you."

"Love has pitched its mansion in the place of excrement," he said another time—which was a line from Yeats, and also the door above the VD clinic on Ninth Avenue.

Brookie's remarks had lately taken an anti-colonialist bent; more than once, he'd hinted that my relationship with Matthew was a form of appeasement—as though Matthew were a conquering imperial force and I a cringing collaborator. "Fascist," though, was new.

"Oh, so Matthew's a fascist now?" I turned, and Paulie dropped my hand. "He'll like that. He's gotten so bored of being called a Communist."

The apartment was strewn with people who did not live there: a rotund boy who always wore a purse; Stephen, who'd moved into a former barbershop in Chelsea; Cherry Cerise, a cruel-tongued drag-and-*style* queen who had shown up during a blackout and then had stayed and stayed.

"Who said he was a Communist?" asked the nameless boy with the purse.

"The National Lawyers Guild," I said.

"Well, okay then!" said Brookie. "As long as we're slightly to the left of the National Lawyers Guild. Yeah, that's good. That's spectacular. I am definitely comfortable with those politics."

"*What* politics?" I said.

"Exactly! No sense rocking the boat now! Wouldn't want to spook the market. Wouldn't want to alarm the PTA!"

What did the PTA ever do to you?, I almost asked, but I was afraid he might actually have an answer.

Instead, I turned toward Paulie. "How do I look?" I said.

"You sure you were *tryna* look like something?" said Cherry Cerise. She had hated me instantly. Brookie enjoyed pretending this bothered me a great deal.

"I think what my esteahemed cawleague here means to say," said Paulie, "is that you, my deah, look rahvishing."

"Is that—is he trying to do *Kennedy?*" said Brookie.

"I think he just veered Jimmy Stewart," said Stephen.

"Ravishing!" said Cherry Cerise. She issued an unfeminine little snort and waved her hands. "I'm so bored I can't even see you."

"Anyway, Semi, it doesn't really matter how you look," said Brookie. "You're not that young anymore, doll, but to Matthew Miller you are *literal* jailbait."

"Rah-vishing!" Paulie said again. "Why, if I weren't awlready mahried—"

Brookie shook his head. "The 'National Lawyers Guild,' man." He sounded tired, which annoyed me. "That is one phrase I never imagined would get thrown around in this apartment."

"Well, I'm thrilled to have had the honor of surprising you." I said it snappishly, wanting to goose that tiredness out of his voice. What I really wanted to say was this: *Matthew Miller is a good man, though he is very different from you, especially in the ways that he is good.*

"Surprise me." Brookie laughed emptily. "Yeah. You have done that, all right. You have definitely, definitely done that."

BROOKIE'S VIEW OF MATTHEW AS APPEASEMENT: IT HURT ME THEN, IT HAUNTS me now. Because he was right, in a way, though his prophecy operated through an ironic, queered mechanics. In the end, it was indeed my proximity to Matthew—that striving boy from Crotona Park, careful by nature and necessity; that blood-tested husband, pinned by expectation, then scrutiny, into a more conventional life than he might have led; that known philanderer who, either through inclination or circumstance, remained reasonably faithful to two people during the whole ignominious span of his adultery; this man who was my first and, as it turned out, only love, and whose departure left me gripped by a lethally unattractive sadness that didn't lift until it was subsumed into a much darker one—in the end this, all of this, saved my life.

The genocide was coming for my people. And because I'd loved Matthew Miller as I had, I would be condemned to live through it.

IN THE END, I DIDN'T GO TO THE PARTY, OR ANYWHERE ELSE, THAT NIGHT. IN-stead, I hid out in my bedroom, waiting for the boys to leave. They seemed to take forever to get ready—had we always taken quite so long? It never used to feel like any time at all.

When they were finally gone, I crept into the living room and opened the window. A chlorinated smell came blasting in from nowhere; the ferry schedules rattled on the counter behind me. Above me, the sky had the density of velour; across the street, someone's geraniums or whatever seemed to bob in their window box. On the sidewalk below, an old lady locked eyes with her Chihuahua while it took a shit. The boys, of course, were long gone.

It was quiet, I remember, so construction must have been suspended for the night: everything was in a state of tearing down or building up back then. This lends to the eeriness of still living here, or at all. Talking about this sort of thing is one of the most efficient ways to make yourself sound old, I've discovered—good luck finding someone who cares about who you are in this life, let alone your last one! But again and again, it stops me short; this sense that the years are only different plays shown in the same aging theater. I turn a corner or run up a subway stop or walk into a building and think:

But wasn't this something else once?

And wasn't I?

And what life was that then?

And whose life is this now?

THIS WAS A THOUGHT THAT CAME BACK TO ME RECENTLY, WHEN I RECEIVED A message from a journalist wanting to talk about Matthew Miller.

Matthew Miller, from what I try not to gather, has been in more PR trouble than usual lately. His show is already routinely described as one of the fundamental pathologies of our age; one hears it spoken of in the same breath as video games, and this comparison has become particularly relentless since the shooting in Ohio. Although this parallel seems to invert the issue, when you really try to think about it—which, clearly, no one ever should. The concern with video games seems to be that their simulated violence might somehow alchemize into reality. But what's potent about Matthew's show—the few dire times I've caught it—isn't that it makes fake things seem real, it's that it makes real things seem outlandish. The true meaninglessness of this whole discussion can only truly be grasped when experienced from a rollaway cot in a hospital room where the TV is bolted to the wall and the remote is wedged impossibly underneath a dying man who is finally, finally sleeping.

One must submit to many outrages in a hospital, and cable television is not the least of them.

I doubt this analysis would interest the journalist, however. He's from a tabloid, most likely, and I decide not to return his call. Not that Matthew Miller doesn't deserve it. But these days, the idea of justice strikes me as straightforwardly perverse; my appetite for that particular futility is, at the moment, exhausted.

But then, tomorrow is another day. And I suppose it is just possible that the journalist will try me back.

ELEVEN
cel

ON FRIDAY, CEL SITS IN MATTIE'S DRESSING ROOM, LISTENING TO LUKE CON-duct the handoff.

The whole thing feels overly elaborate, like a changing of the guard. Cel's eyes keep flicking between her knees, which seem to be jiggling of their own volition, and the back of Mattie's head in the mirror, where the vanity lights offer an unprecedented view of an incipient bald spot.

That morning, Cel and Luke had received a special lecture from Joel on the importance of prepping Mattie "within an inch of his life."

"I don't want him to *blink* in a way that surprises me," said Joel. "You got that?"

Cel and Luke had nodded solemn nods, blinked what Cel hoped were unsurprising blinks.

Now Cel stares at Mattie's mini-fridge—she wonders what he keeps in there. Maybe it's serial-killer empty, or filled with rows of only one strange thing. She glances at the CCTV monitor, casting its Orwellian stare on the empty soundstage. In the corner she can make out Theo, doing something inscrutable with the cables; they are filming promos later. *What the hell*, Luke had said on the phone: well, what the hell, indeed.

"Is that so?" says Mattie, and Cel snaps to attention.

"Oh," she says. "Well."

"She's being modest," says Luke. He knows she wasn't listening. "You're in good hands."

He stands and offers Mattie his hand; Mattie shakes it without standing, making the exchange look like an ingénue dismissing her unsuccessful suitor. Then the door closes and Cel is left alone with Mattie—who is staring at her now with real curiosity.

"So!" Cel coughs irrelevantly into her sleeve. *Echoing what Luke said* would be a spectacular way to start—echoing what anyone said was generally a good way to start anything—and this is what she would say, obviously, if she had been remotely listening earlier.

"So as Luke indicated"—which probably he did—"we need to be really, really clear in our messaging."

"Yes."

Mattie already looks far too entertained by this.

"We just need to really be on the same page."

"Naturally."

"Given the situation. So, the approach we're taking, as you know—wait, let me back up." Cel inhales a short puff of breath. "The *very* first thing you should say on the air—after thanking them for having you on, of course—"

"Of course."

"Right—so actually the second thing, I guess, should be to express your sorrow at this tragedy. Your bewilderment and outrage."

"Sorrow. Bewilderment. Outrage."

"You want to offer your condolences to the families—well, actually maybe you should offer the condolences *before* the outrage, but you know."

Mattie takes a sip of water. "I don't want him to take a sip of water you haven't discussed ahead of time," Joel had bellowed that morning. Cel watches Mattie swallow, searching for unforeseen publicity dimensions.

"And actually the word 'condolences' might be—might imply

more ownership than we want to, you know?" Mattie is giving her an odd look, but it's too late to know why—there are already too many disastrous variables in play to hope to isolate just one. "It's a little stiff, maybe, too? It sort of sounds like you're issuing a press release."

Mattie gives her a look like *Am I not?*

"You may want to say something like 'My heart goes out to the families' or 'I can hardly imagine the pain these families are experiencing.' Something that basically conveys that you are just a person trying to wrap your head around this tragedy."

"Identify basically as a person. Gotcha."

"But so, okay, *then*—" says Cel, breathing wheezily. She seems to be developing some sort of late-onset asthma—could she actually be allergic to Mattie? She's never been this close to him for this long, so it's very possible she wouldn't know. "Before they even get to their questions, they're going to present a sort of sketch of the show."

"The goat," Mattie offers dully.

"The goat, sure! Stuff like that, *exactly*. Things that have nothing to do with the issue at hand, but that, you know—"

"Frame the discussion."

"Right." Cel swallows stickily.

"Do you want some water?"

"Oh *no*." This comes out far too emphatic—she sounds like she's declining a priceless family heirloom, a nip of black tar heroin. "But *then* after all of that, they're going to launch into their questions. And their questions are really going to be statements."

"Roger that."

"And the statements that we really, really need you to resist are the ones linking the show to *any* sort of, you know, sweeping cultural analyses."

Mattie blinks. "That sounds, you know. A bit sweep—"

"And this is where you need to be sort of trivializing!" If Cel can step on the end of his sentences, maybe it won't seem as though she's improvising her own. "Well, not trivializing of the event, obviously! Or even the suggestion per se."

"Which suggestion?"

"Well, whatever one they're making. That's the thing, actually—you have to act like the conclusion is ridiculous but that the question itself is not."

Cel can see Mattie's tongue bulging in the corner of his jaw.

"But so then, they're probably going to want you to speculate." Cel looks at his water glass longingly—it's half-full, the objective correlative of all of Mattie Miller's unwarranted luck in this life. "Like in court cases, where defense lawyers have to come up with someone else who did it, you know? Well, I mean, of course you do."

"I do."

"Like, if it's not *The Mattie M Show,* then what?"

"What?"

"What?"

"Well, what?" Mattie's lips are contorting into an ambiguous tilde, part smile, part sneer. "Or is that not in your notes?"

"Um." Cel shuffles her papers around as though it actually might be. "Well, what *you* think isn't the point, exactly."

"Oh no?" Mattie's eyebrows have now gone the way of his lips. Cel closes her good eye, and for a moment his face appears as a riot of squiggles, as resistant to interpretation as a work of modern art. She opens it again.

"I mean, viewers don't expect you to have the entire answer," she says.

"That's certainly a relief."

"But if you could venture something that most people agree is *a* problem, even if it isn't the reason for this problem, then they'll hear you out. And then even if they disagree with you—at least, at that point, the conversation everyone is having is about that other thing you're wrong about. And not about, you know, you."

Mattie leans back into the couch. On his face is an expression that Cel might once have hazarded a guess at naming, but that now she is hesitant to confidently deem an expression at all.

"Conversations about me are my least favorite conversations," he says.

"That's the spirit!" says Cel. "And the way to get out of them is to downplay the show's significance. And that's where your kind of self-deprecating attitude can really work for you, I think? You can maybe say sure, it's maybe crass, maybe it's not to everyone's taste, but ultimately it's harmless and stupid. Not 'stupid.' I mean." She riffles through her notes. Any minute now, she tells herself—yes, any minute!—an intern will come to escort Mattie to the soundstage, delivering them all from this hell they've created together. " 'Silly.' You want to say it's a silly, sexy show."

The pause that follows seems to contain not only this but all the-oretical worlds—Cel feels the entirety of human history, the ghosts of all possible string-theory pasts and presents, slide silently through her own.

"There is nothing about the show that is either of those things," says Mattie finally, in a flat, profoundly non-television voice.

There's a tap on the door then and the intern enters, holding hair gel and a towel.

"You ready, Mattie?"

"Eternally." He stands. "This has been illuminating," he says—probably to Cel, though he doesn't turn around to look at her again before walking out the door.

THE NIGHT BEFORE *LEE AND LISA*, CEL IS BACK AT SLIGO'S.

"You're not going to sleep, so you may as well drink," said Nikki. This seemed like a good idea—had seemed, in fact, like the only one—but now, waiting for her second gin and tonic, Cel thinks it might have been a mistake. It is still early; a caul of grimy light filters in through the windows, illuminating the usual vista of flirtation and maneuver, naked ambition and brute-force advertising. Cel hasn't been to Sligo's since the day of the shooting, and she'd like to believe this is the reason for her sodden jitteriness—rising flutter of anxiety, sinking sensation of doom. Really, she knows, she's just ner-vous about the show.

"Hey," says Nikki, emerging from the crowd and handing Cel a cocktail. "Do we *know* that guy?"

Cel looks where Nikki is pointing.

"I don't know," she says.

"Well, it looks like he maybe knows you? Hi."

The man is upon them. He has brown-gray hair and wintry eyes; up close, Cel feels a decided recognition.

"Hi," he says.

"Hi," Cel adds, because this seems to be what's being said.

"We met the other day," says the man.

"Of course." He could be a lawyer for the show, maybe; she never can place those people out of context.

"Here," he clarifies. "On the day of the shooting?"

"Oh, *right*." This does seem right, though ultimately she'll have to take his word for it. She's pretty sure he isn't the one she spent the whole night talking to.

"Sorry," Cel says. "That was such a weird day."

"It was," says the man, swallowing an ice cube.

"I'm sorry," she says, "but can you—"

"Scott. You're Cel." His face clouds with an ironic sympathy. "Some week you guys are having."

"I'm sorry?"

"At the show?" She'd forgotten he knew that part already. "Bad luck about the shooters being fans."

"Well, a lot of people are," she says.

"And that skit, or whatever."

"I don't think we really have the details on all that."

"Can I ask you something you probably get all the time?"

"You can try!" chirps Nikki. Scott smiles at Nikki—does Cel dare to think: a little indulgently?—and leans toward her.

"What's Mattie like in person?"

"Oh, don't bother," says Nikki. "She's getting paid not to say."

"You know, it kind of doesn't look great if your publicist won't even tell people what a good guy you are."

"Trust me," says Nikki. "I've tried."

"No, I mean, Mattie *is* a good guy," says Cel. "He's a really great boss—everyone always says so."

"Really?"

"And—that's about it." Cel begins to apology-shrug, but something about Scott's squint makes her smother this. It comes out instead as a little spasm.

"But *really*?"

"I don't know, I mean—" Cel is talking quickly now, trying to outrace the purplish heat she can feel heading to her ears. "I mean, he's not really *like* anything, per se. He sort of lights up when the camera's on—he's like a Teddy Ruxpin doll or something. He's not like that the rest of the time, but he's not really like anything else, either."

"This is literally the most she's ever said about this," breathes Nikki.

"I wonder what he does in his free time," says Scott. "How he unwinds after all the, you know, Ruxpinning."

"I don't know," says Cel. It's strange she's never wondered.

"He must have oodles of money," says Nikki contemplatively. "Just *piles*."

"I know he gives some of it away." Cel should have said this part up front, probably.

"Oh yeah?" says Scott. "FCC bribes or—?"

"Charity, believe it or not. He gives a lot to AIDS." Cel gnaws at her lip. "He's kind of a progressive, actually. Or he was, anyway."

"And I thought *Clinton* was damaging the party's image," says Scott. "I mean, Troopergate, *The Mattie M Show*—who knew the apocalypse would be such a circus?"

He taps Cel's glass and raises an eyebrow.

"Better not," says Cel.

"Mattie's on *Lee and Lisa* tomorrow," says Nikki. "Cel has to chaperone."

"Yikes." Scott leans forward again, and Cel smells something dimly oceanic—she pictures a vast, empty apartment, with a cold glittering skyline outside a picture window, though she doesn't know whether this is a genuine thought or something imported from cologne advertising. "I guess they'll probably run with this whole fanshooter thing, huh?"

"I guess they'll probably try," says Cel.

"It's a pretty cheap shot, if you ask me." Although she hadn't. "But I see why people are making the connection."

"I'm not sure I do."

"I just mean, it sort of seems of a piece with the fighting, the wife-beating—"

"The wives—the women—they don't fight," says Cel. "They don't get hit, I mean."

Scott is giving her exactly the look she deserves for this.

"Okay, so." Scott pauses, then adopts an avuncular, Brokaw-esque voice. "How do you respond to concerns that *The Mattie M Show* is contributing to a coarsening of the culture? What do you say to parents who are concerned about *its* influence on their children?"

Cel takes a sip of her melted ice. "First of all, *Scott,* let me just say that *The Mattie M Show* is pure entertainment." She has put on her own fake voice—her Job Voice, Elspeth calls it, though Cel thinks of it as Please Let Me Explain. Its tone is one of confidence tinged with diffuse exasperation; it conveys a sense of: *I* know this, and *you* know this, but certain exigencies demand we pretend we *don't* know this, and so we both must try to be patient—though it is true that we are, all of us, very busy people.

"And *The Mattie M Show is* entertaining, which is why millions of Americans tune in each day to watch." Cel knows this wording so well that her inflection becomes a little singsongy, like a child reciting the Pledge of Allegiance. "It isn't a PBS documentary, but not everyone wants to watch one—and if you do, you can certainly change the channel. By the same token, *The Mattie M Show* is not for children, as its Viewer Discretion warning indicates. I would remind concerned parents that, the last time I checked, all televisions come with an off switch."

Nikki golf-claps, as per usual.

Cel leans her head to the side, squeezing the rest of her lime into her empty glass. "Do I sound convincing?"

"Were you trying to?" says Scott.

"I don't know!" Cel laughs, which surprises her. "Imagine Mattie saying it."

Scott looks, for a moment, as though he is actually trying to do this. "You know what's weird?" he says. "The guy's all over, but I can barely remember what his voice sounds like."

"Yeah," says Cel. "He sort of has one of those voices. What do *you* think, anyhow?"

Scott blinks. "You mean—in general?"

"Do you think the show is totally reprehensible, or what? Seriously. You can be honest." This happens sometimes—these hapless opinion polls of alarmed strangers. You could call it rogue market research—which is what Cel will call it, if anyone asks why she's asking, though luckily no one ever does.

"I just mean—" Cel takes a breath and wishes for the trillionth time she knew a way to show when she was actually serious. Sincerity should be something you could externally indicate, like a turn signal. "The show—it's exploitive, right? But so are most things. So do you think it's, like—like, unconscionably exploitive? Is it unforgivable, is what I'm saying. No, scratch that, of course it's unforgivable—what I mean is: is it beyond the pale of other unforgivable things?"

Scott looks amazed.

"You'll have to excuse her," says Nikki. "She was an only child."

"Well," says Cel. "Sort of."

Nikki gives Scott a look like: *Case in point.*

"What does that mean?" says Scott. "You *sort* of had siblings?"

"Technically, I mean, no," says Cel, now peevish. *Sort of* is perhaps not the best answer to give to a yes-or-no question, but it's not the worst answer, either; worse would have been to try to explain what she actually meant.

"So what's the verdict?" Cel can feel Nikki's disapproval boring into her back. "Are *Mattie M*'s sins mortal or venial?"

Scott opens his mouth, then closes it again. "I guess I'm wondering why you're asking. You realize I'm not exactly a regular viewer?"

"I gathered, yeah, but that's not the point. I'm interested in what people think, in general. And you seem like you'd have an opinion."

"I've got plenty." Without asking, Scott pours half of his remaining drink into Cel's empty glass. "On this, I guess what I think is that this whole thing has been going on for a really, really long time."

"When you say 'thing,' you mean—?"

"I mean all of it. Exploitation, sure, and callousness, yes. But also the sense that something uniquely apocalyptic is occurring. I mean, that's never *not* going on."

Cel likes that he's willing to assert something without assuming she agrees with him: with most people, it's one or the other.

"Maybe that can be a new ad campaign," says Nikki. " 'Watching *Mattie M:* It's Not the End of the World.' "

"Oh, I didn't say *that*," says Scott. "But if I had to talk about it on television—which, thank God, I don't—"

"Are you kidding?" says Cel. "Can we hire you? I'll have them fax over the contract tomorrow!"

"But if I did, you know—that's what I'd say. This new thing is the death of us? That is a very old complaint. It's probably the first complaint. *Other* things have changed, of course. The *gadgetry's* changed." Cel knows where this is going; she feels senselessly deflated. "Teenagers with semiautomatic weapons, *that's* new. God, what a face! I know, I know—you can't talk about *that* on television."

"Forty-one percent of our viewers own firearms," Cel says sadly.

"How is that possible?" says Nikki. "I don't think I know anyone who's ever even touched a gun."

She does, in fact: Hal had one that lived year-round in the shed. Cel had mentioned this once at a party at Smith and learned it was not a thing to discuss at college. It was certainly not a thing to discuss in a bar in lower Manhattan. And yet for a teetering moment, she feels this disclosure on the very tip of her tongue.

Instead, she says, "Are you sure?"

A shadow crosses Nikki's face before she laughs. "Woman of mystery," she says. "Like I said."

"Cheers to that," says Scott to Cel, and clinks his glass against her own.

———

BECAUSE CEL ABSOLUTELY MUST SLEEP, OF COURSE SHE CANNOT.

She'd had the most outrageous insomnia her first week in New York. Her second week, she began going to the Comedy Cellar—always alone, a fact that still feels like a secret even though she doesn't know who she's keeping it from. Sometimes Nikki thinks she's with men, and sometimes Cel allows this. Lately she's been going more often. But tonight it's too late for the Comedy Cellar, and Cel is on her own.

She lies awake, thinking of all the ill-advised things she's said to Mattie, the many more she almost said to Scott. *"You sort of had siblings?"* he'd asked—and for a moment, she'd nearly told him how she and Ruth had torn through the hills, through the woods, through the stream. How she cannot remember ever being lonely.

"What on earth are you two doing?" said Hal when he'd come upon them once, casting his shadow over their stream.

We're smelling the water, they told him.

"I see." His voice full of its characteristic weariness. Hal never seemed to finish working in the summers, only taking breaks to drink cans of root beer, to flip through his books on World War II ("Why?" went Cel's standard comment later. "He already knows how it ends.").

"Does water even *have* a smell?" Hal had sawdust in his hair, as per usual, and he smelled sharply sweaty.

"Yes!" they shrieked, and he looked at them like they were both crazy—which maybe (Cel thought giddily, frantically) they both were. Because she *could* smell the water: it was complicated and loamy and much more assertive than you'd think.

Afterward they'd run inside, giggling, to play something on their ruined old piano. Once, a million years ago, Ruth had taken lessons. The piano as Cel knew it produced notes only tenuously tethered to their moorings; each key contained an echoey, multidimensional sound—a hint of a chord within a pitch, like a voice gone hoarse. Even Hal agreed there was no point in trying to sell it. Ruth taught Cel to play "Elfin Dance," their piano conjuring elves that were strange and wise and unpredictable in ways that were not always benign: figures worthy of respect, as well as caution.

Cel had almost wanted to explain that to Scott, too.

The last time she'd tried explaining anything to anyone was at the Smith College Counseling Center. Her therapist nodded, sweet-faced, while Cel tried to describe the moments of pure magic: Ruth sitting on the white-and-yellow checkered dresser, next to the curtains with the parrots, telling sagas of their tragic heroism. The airy, gray morning when the wind made Cel feel somehow close to the sea, and she crept downstairs to find Ruth staring at their Christmas cactus.

"It's been growing since 1930," she said, blinking at Cel through her tortoiseshell glasses. "Isn't that astonishing?"

And wasn't it?

Or the treasures Cel was forever finding in the stream—a paper-clip bent into a heart; a little ceramic fish, bright indigo against the mud; an unfathomably shiny penny, glowing like a tiny copper moon, that never looked the same once Cel pulled it from the water. For many years Cel took these as coincidence: Ruth's denials were disarmingly convincing. And perhaps this was because they were true—perhaps it was not Ruth who put things in the stream, or any-way not quite.

"It must be terribly hard to think of her as a bad mother," the counselor had said. "So maybe it's easier not to think of her as your mother at all."

You don't have to believe me, Cel had wanted to say, but neverthe-less it is true: it was a supernatural childhood, but not all of its sor-cery was dark. Ruth was like the elves made by that teetering piano: wild and singular and nothing like what you saw in the story-books—an analysis the therapist might have encouraged if Cel had ever gone back for a second appointment.

Because she hadn't, Cel had never told the therapist about the time she'd finally heard "Elfin Dance" played correctly—by a chubby child in a yellow-brick community theater building in Northampton. She'd never told the therapist, or anyone, how dis-oriented she'd been by the elves' cutesiness, how (momentarily!) tempted she had been to pinch the chubby child playing it. And yet she'd almost said all this to Scott, at the bar, for no reason. It seemed

only a kind of luck that she had not: Nikki should count her bless-
ings.

Cel begins to drift off twenty minutes before her wake-up call. As
she does it occurs to her that Scott already knows where she was on
the day of the shooting, so she'll never be able to tell him she was
somewhere else.

TWELVE
semi

1977–1978

WHEN DID MATTHEW'S TALK BECOME CAMPAIGNING? THAT ASSUMES IT EVER was not. But sometime in the winter of '76, it seems, there was a shift to broader, more ambitious themes. He began to speak of a re-vamped liberalism—rhetorically syncretic, ideologically modern, merging the humane instincts of the Old Left with the idealism of the new. All this interested me about as much as Brookie's Marxism.

But alongside the abstractions, unnerving specifics were emerg-ing. Matthew seemed abruptly alert to the political frailties of Ed Koch. He respected Koch's background as a tenant lawyer—he al-ways made a point of saying so, even before his opinions had calci-fied into stump speech. But Koch didn't understand real poverty, he said, and his policy on integration was "magical thinking." Accord-ingly, Matthew believed him vulnerable on race. Matthew, it turned out, had his own ideas about how best to negotiate the rivalry be-tween the Harlem and Brooklyn black leadership—this is the revela-tion that made me roll over, one night in the spring of '77, and say, "Don't tell me you're thinking what I think you're thinking."

Beneath the sheets our legs were interdigitated, our pulses were still racing.

He said: "There's no law against thinking."

"There are laws against a few things I know you don't just *think* about."

"Not in the state of New York," he said.

"Oh, you should be all set then. Just tell voters your sexual perversions do not run afoul of current law, and that you know because not only are you a homo, you are also a lawyer."

"What voters?"

"Exactly."

I could not believe he was serious. There were whispers about him already—I knew because he'd told me—and during his run for State Assembly, someone had distributed a smattering of fliers with the phrase "Vote for Barry, Not the Fairy." The Barry campaign denied involvement, and at any rate, they'd lost. But it was obvious that, in this regard, Matthew had already been extremely lucky; the idea of him trying to get away with anything more than he already had seemed out of the question—and running for mayor, even only in the primary, would involve getting away with a whole lot more than that. He was too much of a realist not to understand this.

"The conventional political logic of anarchic times—" he was saying.

"Oh, *Christ.*"

"—prophesies conservatism among the populace."

"Are you—is that Edmund fucking Burke?"

"Never mind."

"No, I was seriously wondering."

He was silent.

"I'm listening," I said, after a moment.

"I'm thinking that that thinking is wrong." He'd turned his back to me by then, disentangled his leg from my own. "Revolutions begin with tearing things down, right? And historically, most never get farther than that."

"Due to the mass beheadings, and all."

"Right. The beheadings, and the crucifixions, and the people being made to wear red-hot iron crowns, as in the Slovenian Peasant Revolt."

I didn't know where he got this stuff.

"Throughout history, people have taken the most outrageous risks just for the chance of tearing things down," he was saying. "And here we are." He gestured vaguely toward the city. "Already sitting in the ruins."

"Well, lucky us."

"People are walking around just—dazed—by the crumbling bridges, the water main breaks, the gas explosions—"

"The blackouts."

"Yes, and—"

"The crime."

"Right."

"You get mugged and it's not even worth reporting. It's gonna take the police an age to get there and they'll probably lose a tire on the way. It'll take forever to schedule your court date, then it'll take forever to get there, and if you even survive the trip without getting mugged *again*, you'll find that the courtroom is filthy and the hearing's postponed and no one thought to tell you."

I was parroting Matthew precisely; we must have both been surprised by how carefully I'd been listening, all along, to this ludicrous catalogue of all the things he thought he'd fix.

"On the way back, you'll be grievously injured in a mass transit mishap," I said. "By then you won't even have the wherewithal to litigate!"

We were quiet; I expect he was allowing me to listen to myself.

"You're right," he said after a moment—which meant, essentially, *I'm right*. "The question is, what do we do?"

"What *do* we do?" I said: echolalia more than inquiry.

"I'm saying maybe caution isn't inevitable. I'm saying maybe chaos can produce other appetites."

"That's good," I said. "Are you saving that for your concession speech? Because I'm probably not going to be writing that one."

He rolled over and gave me a hard, multivalent look.

"I resign," I said. "Effective noon tomorrow."

"You make a terrible Nixon."

"Well, so did Nixon."

"The thing about right now is that it's a time of conclusions not yet foregone," he said. This line sounded both awkward and re-hearsed. Was it then that I first felt him talking beyond me—to an audience that I could not see, that I hadn't even known existed?

"Do you know how rare an opportunity that is?"

No: it was there—in that "you," which wasn't really *me,* but a direct address to some demographic amalgamation. Not only were we not having the same conversation, he seemed to be having his with someone else entirely.

"I'm sure it's not entirely without precedent," I said. I turned over so that we were finally back-to-back.

"If you're not careful, that thought is going to start to seem like a slogan."

"Oh, I don't know," I said. "Maybe we'll just call it a talking point."

WHEN I GOT BACK TO THE APARTMENT, THEY WERE WATCHING *MARY HARTMAN, Mary Hartman.* The room had a bready, hungover smell.

"Well, well, well!" said Brookie, squinting. "If it isn't—Semi, right?"

On his lap was the rotund boy, whose name I either still did not know or else kept forgetting. Cherry Cerise perched beside them on the armrest, filing her nails and looking nonplussed.

"So good of you to drop by, what with your many civic commitments," said Brookie. He launched into a tuneless rendition of "If I Knew You Were Comin' I'd've Baked a Cake."

"Shh," said Paulie. "They're finding out that Wild Child was raised by Bigfoot!"

"I can't believe you take this show seriously," said Stephen.

"Is this the one where the guy drowns in his soup?" I said.

"We should all be so lucky," said Brookie. "I'm starving."

As if on cue, his stomach made a sound like a plucked guitar string.

"I take it completely seriously," said Paulie. "I take it post-seriously."

"We're *all* terribly hungry!" Brookie was using his protest voice now.

"I'm not," said the boy in his lap. "I just had a sandwich."

"You are a marvel of literalism," said Stephen.

"Shh," said Brookie, leaning forward and stroking the boy's ears. "Can't you see the child's delirious?"

"I think I saw an orange peel in the hallway," I said.

"Save Our Children!" Brookie shrieked. "Where *is* Anita Bryant when you need her?"

"I give up," said Paulie, turning off the television. "There you go, Brookie. You win. Activism works."

Brookie was staring at me with moist, charity-pamphlet eyes. *Hungry,* he mouthed again, and I lost it.

"What do you want me to do—breastfeed you? Because I've got some bad news on that front."

Cherry Cerise laughed at this, which surprised us all.

"Doesn't your rich boyfriend give you an allowance?" said Brookie.

"No, actually." I was trying to channel my grandmother's most frigid, Plasticine rage. "And he makes eighty dollars a week. By *working.*"

"I see." Brookie waved a hand grandly. "So you're viewing this whole thing as an investment. How very *prudent* of you."

"This is better than *Mary Hartman,*" whispered Paulie.

"No, it isn't," said Brookie's boy matter-of-factly, and for a moment I nearly liked him.

"Say what you will about the bourgeois," Brookie said. He hadn't taken his eyes off me, though he spoke as though to the entire room. "They can't be beat for sheer financial literacy."

I felt a dark, lacerating anger coming loose inside of me. I grabbed my mail from the counter to explain why I'd come back in the first place. Then I left again, and stayed away for longer.

THAT SUMMER, IT SEEMED, I DID NOT SLEEP.

Night after night, I lay beside Matthew, miserably awake. Occasionally I snuck up to the roof to stare at the skyline—at the offices where hundreds of closet cases no doubt still were working, no matter what the hour. Everyone was an amateur arsonist in those days: landlords setting fires to get insurance, residents setting fires to get public housing. Addicts vulturing through afterward to steal metal from the fixtures. There'd be upwards of twelve thousand fires that year, Matthew would tell me later—but you could feel it even then, that impulse toward mass self-annihilation. I thought of it as I listened to the alarms going off around the city: the alarms that sent everyone running, the alarms that everyone ignored, the alarms that brought the red caps racing up the stairs into the buildings. I thought of it when I crept back down to pretend to sleep beside Matthew—to watch him dream unknowable dreams and wonder if, underneath all the noise, some new silence was growing between us. I listened for this silence intently, the way the rest of the city listened for the step of Son of Sam. I tried to hear it beneath the sound of David Byrne blasting from car radios. I tried to sniff it underneath the smoke—the smoke that smelled like camping, the smoke that smelled like the apocalypse. I tried to glimpse it somewhere in those strange summer darknesses: the blackouts that were listless and perfunctory, the ones that were urgent and anarchic. The one when the air outside the window became a rotating constellation of blue glow sticks. They waved and vanished, like electric eels cartwheeling into the abyss, and in the morning it turned out that most of Bushwick had been destroyed.

BY THE NEW YEAR, MATTHEW HAD EITHER DEVELOPED OR REVEALED AN ENtire political idiom, full of slogans and shorthand. He railed against "poverty pimps" and something called the "mandate millstone." He lambasted Cuomo's position on abortion. He was skeptical of the value of corruption as a campaign issue; he believed the *real* issue was low- and middle-income housing. Voters wanted a candidate who'd address the problem at its fundamentals, rather than eternally fussing about with rent control. Crime was an issue, undeniably, he said, but much more so for the poor than the wealthy. In view of the state's inability to exercise its basic function of locking up criminals, the rich were finding ways to lock up *themselves:* hiring private security apparatuses, buying top-shelf locks and security devices, encircling themselves with iron gates through their block associations.

"People are literally erecting barricades!" he shouted at me once. "Retreating into castles, digging moats. Filling them with water and bears."

"Bears?"

He told me they used to do this in Czechoslovakia.

It was like listening to a physics lecture in an unstudied language—though I wasn't so much bored as incredulous. A recent *Times* profile of Matthew had mentioned the copy of *City of Night* he kept in his downtown office—where, it was further noted, he spent many evenings working late. Since then, the *sotto voce* speculations about him had become marginally less *sotto*. It was true that he was not a *Greenwich Village bachelor,* as my grandmother might have put it; Alice was some alibi, anyway. But Matthew would never be able to run the sort of emphatically heterosexual ads people liked to see. He had barely invoked Alice at all when he ran for State Assembly. Maybe he knew that they were never completely convincing as a couple—she had a damp small-minded look about her that would cast doubt on any man's heterosexuality—and there were, of course, no children, which was what was really meant by "family." It didn't take a political savant to figure all of this out, and I wasn't the person who was supposed to be one.

He would, I thought, make a very good mayor. And I knew that if Matthew were anyone else, I'd tell him to fuck prudence and fuck discretion and hey, while we're at it, fuck Alice; I'd tell him to put on a dress and run for fucking *president.* I'd tell him I'd take the bus up to New Hampshire to register voters myself! But Matthew wasn't anyone else: he was only himself, and there was only one of him, and the fact of his stubborn singularity scrambled my principles in a way that made me hateful.

Was I asking him to choose? I didn't want to think so. But neither did I imagine myself by his side, in pearls and pillbox hat, beaming as the results came in at the Limelight. The whole thing was impossible. I pondered this impossibility on bracing walks that winter, watching the whitecaps bob in Long Island Sound. I pondered it while tramping around the Lower East Side that summer, the wind rattling across the Manhattan Bridge like an oncoming train, feeling wretched in a way I somehow associated with my own misbehavior as a child. I pondered it as I lay in Matthew's bed that autumn, while the random smell of toast fluttered up from someone's apartment.

"This is impossible," I said. I think I thought he was asleep.

He turned over. "Nothing's impossible." He cradled himself around me.

"Aren't some things, though?" I said.

He kissed me. He smelled of Tide and city and late-night coffee. He seemed to think this settled the question.

THE BOYS AND I WERE UPTOWN, IN NOVEMBER, WHEN WE HEARD THAT HARVEY Milk had been killed. Without discussion, we turned back toward Sheridan Square. We shivered while waiting for the subway: we were underdressed for the weather, overdressed for the N train. We'd been planning to go dancing. Instead, we watched as an extremely shiny rat dragged a muffin across the tracks.

"This city won't ever have a Harvey to murder," said Brookie loudly, and an MTA policeman gave us a sour look.

"Shh," said Nick. "Don't make him use his *walkie-talkie.*"

"They don't work underground," I said, and they all looked at me.

Our train pulled into the station. It was bombed with unreadable black snarls, like the scribbling of a psychotic child.

"Mesdames," said Brookie. "Your hearse awaits."

In the park, everyone had candles. We hugged each other gingerly, around the flames. Then Brookie went off to talk to someone, and Nick and Peter went off to smoke with someone else, and I was left standing with Stephen near the statue of the general, watching two dowdy teenagers weep. Paulie was away in Italy that fall—he'd been cast in some sort of touring commedia dell'arte and sent us elated postcards every single week. The whole thing sounded awful. Things were much quieter without him.

"He was such a brave man," I said abruptly.

I meant Harvey. I was glad Matthew was not so brave.

"Those who live by the sword," said Stephen.

"Well, not only them." I watched the teenagers, wondering how old they were, what they were sneaking away from to be here.

"I don't think that horse is even real." Stephen was pointing across the street, where a couple of boys in bell-bottoms were clustered around a mounted policeman.

"Of course it's *real*," I said. "I mean, they're petting it, aren't they?"

It was very clear I needed to start going out more.

But in fact the boys were losing interest already, and dispersing. I watched to see where the prettiest one would go; my line of vision tilted to follow him across the park, until it slammed directly into Matthew Miller.

My mouth went dry—just as it had the first time I'd seen him on television, or the night he'd materialized at the club, or any of the other times when his appearance had seemed a miracle too hopelessly complete to be real—and for a moment I was seized by that old wrenching tenderness, that doomed euphoria, of love not worth the naming. Any other politician in Matthew's position would have been too afraid to show up here; any politician not in his position wouldn't have thought of it at all. But this was Matthew Miller, world-class hypocrite and true progressive, and he was unafraid of courting the gay vote.

I had to get out of there. But then, as though moved by some predatory instinct, Brookie was upon me.

"Look who's here!" he said, poking me in the ribs. "It's our patron saint. But who's this *friend* he's with?"

Next to Matthew stood a very blond man in a very puce scarf.

"Is this the competition? Because if it is, honey, I can't say I like your odds. Let's say hello."

"Let's not."

"Why not? I never get to talk to liberal closet cases. And that little friend of his is just a peach."

"Brookie."

"And isn't Saint Matthew technically my lawyer, too? Are you trying to strip me of my constitutional right to representation?"

"Brookie."

"This is one step short of disenfranchisement! Don't make me alert the NAACP!"

"Brookie, *please.*"

He laughed harshly. He could hear there was real desperation in my voice, I think—that in this moment I was actually afraid of him, as small and shitty white people so often were.

"You know what happened to you?" He shook his head. "Never mind. I don't care. But don't worry. I won't embarrass you. You are *massively* overestimating my interest in this."

And he went marching off toward Matthew Miller. What could I possibly do but follow?

I suppose I couldn't have expected Matthew to seem visibly surprised to see me; I certainly didn't expect him to bend me into a deep embrace. Perhaps I wanted the opposite, then—some contrived coldness that would acknowledge the potential danger of warmth. At the very least, I wanted him to be too afraid to touch me.

Instead, he waved, smiling with a recognition so limited, and so unfeigned, that for a moment I felt my own sanity waver.

"Semi," he said, and shook my hand—which was one of the few physical encounters we'd not had before. "It's good to see you."

Why did Matthew say my name? Because he always, always said voters' names.

Now he was turning toward the blond man. The social polish bounced off that guy in every direction; he was practically chrome-plated. I loathed him conclusively.

"Semi," said Matthew. "This is Eddie."

"I'm Sid," said Brookie. "This is Nancy."

"Semi is one of my Village constituents."

The "Village" explaining why I was the way I was, I guess, and the "constituent" explaining why Matthew Miller was speaking to me at all. All those schizoids and trannies and gray-footed homeless, all those addicts and ingrates and weirdos and fags—like it or not, Matthew Miller *worked* for these people! Such was the nature of representative democracy!

Matthew and Eddie had begun tag-teaming their condolences.

They'd admired Harvey Milk tremendously, they were saying, as both a politician and a man. There were other people waiting to speak to Matthew, I saw—other people he'd want to deliver this speech to, in case he'd need their votes one day. I guess he figured he could count on mine. The eulogy was wrapping down now; the hand-shaking recommencing. Matthew shook hands with Brookie, who bent to kiss his class ring, and then with me—again managing to convey the exact quality of warmth one might extend toward an inconsequential speechwriter from eight years earlier. I stared at the hand manipulating my own. Matthew Miller: a man without secrets.

Then Eddie Marcus was upon me again. Years later, he'd be fired from the water commissioner's office over an extravagant cocaine habit; there were suspicions he'd been accepting kickbacks to finance it, though this part was never proved. His coke thing was beginning even then, in fact, which may have explained some of his irrational optimism about Matthew's career. I wish I could say that I'd intuited this: that my hatred stemmed from insight, and not a cramped and lunatic resentment. I wish I could say I saw right through him. But I wasn't kidding myself—or not as much, anymore. Even as I stood there, I was realizing I might not be able to see through anyone at all.

THAT NIGHT, MATTHEW SHOWED UP AT MY DOOR—UNANNOUNCED, HAT IN hands. This was a scene I'd longed for, once. In the bedroom, I pretended I still did.

Afterward, Matthew rolled over and said: "Eddie thinks I can take it."

"What?"

And with that, he began officially campaigning.

According to Eddie, he had compassion, energy, consistency; if he presented himself as the tough-talking leftist alternative to Koch, he could be a plausible candidate. Eddie Marcus, evidently, didn't know the half of it, and I was surprised Matthew would let himself be swayed by such an uninformed opinion. But he kept on talking, his back smooth and warm against my chest, and it occurred to me that in this moment he was *happy*.

"This is a strange way to commit suicide," I said, to shut him up. I felt him freeze in my arms.

"I'm not the only politician with a private life," he said quietly.

"Have you considered that yours might be a bit more private than most?"

"If the only people who went into public service were people with lives that couldn't raise an eyebrow, then there wouldn't be any public servants, and the city would be even more Hobbesian than it is." He was speaking patiently, pedantically. Practicing for the provocations of televised debate, I suppose.

"So *this*"—I gestured to myself, to the bedsheets, to him and then the rest of him, then back to myself for good measure—"is all irrelevant. You should have run for Pope while you had the chance!"

"Calm down."

"What, am I being hysterical?" I said. "Hysterical girls—they just can't be escaped! I mean, look at the lengths you've gone to to do something really original with your personal life, and still it all boils down to the same thing. But hey, maybe you can use that in your speeches! To relate to the average voter. *We've all been there, right, fellas? See, we ain't so different, you and me.*"

He had rolled far away from me and was curled toward the wall.

"I know I'm not on the payroll anymore, but you can have that one for free."

I could feel him trying to manage his breathing, which made me want to start again, which made me even angrier.

"I am not saying it's irrelevant," he said. "I'm saying that, at the end of the day, everyone has interests. Everyone has liabilities. Everyone understands this."

"The voice of the progressive insurrection, comrades!" I sounded exactly like Brookie. "You're talking about mutually assured destruction."

"I'm talking about whatever it is that keeps people from shoving each other in front of the subway, yeah."

"They do do that sometimes, you know. You should probably know that if you're going to be mayor."

"This isn't because I don't love you," he said.

"Are you—is that you trying to say you *do* love me? God, you sure *talk* like a politician."

"But I love this city, too."

"You mean you love your fucking voters? You don't even know them!"

"Not all of them. Not yet."

"Are you kidding?"

"I don't think so, no."

Matthew sighed into the wall.

"You're going to get taken down, you know," I told him. "I mean, I hope you know that, right?"

"I'm not saying something couldn't happen." He sounded like he was talking to a constituent, or a child. "I'm saying it's not a good use of anyone's time."

"You might be right it's not a *good* use of time," I said. "But I don't think you realize the sorts of things people these days do for fun."

NOW, OF COURSE, MY CONCERNS ABOUT EXPOSURE SEEM ALMOST QUAINT. *Times* flurry aside, by modern standards there'd been vanishingly little media interest in what Matthew then regarded as his "private life." It was pre–Gary Hart: a much subtler time.

I almost say this to the journalist the second time he calls.

I've been back from the hospital fifteen minutes and am already a little drunk; I answered the phone somewhat by accident. The journalist wants to know how I'd known Matthew Miller. I tell him Matthew Miller was my state assemblyman.

"But he wasn't only your assemblyman," says the journalist—whose name, he has made an elaborate show of revealing, is Scott. I suppose he thinks this puts us on some equal footing.

"That's right, Scott," I say. "He was also my lawyer. So if you have any questions for me, you should really be talking to him."

I hang up.

On the sofa, I straddle my wine bottle and begin flipping through the channels. It isn't a coincidence that Matthew's show is on—statistically it seems to always be on—and I usually make a whole big point of not watching it. But I'd spent the better part of the evening watching Brookie get de-intubated: perhaps I am beyond the point of making points.

The episode concerns a brother and a sister who—one assumes—are fucking. And sure enough, before you know it they are clutching hands, speaking of their love with an earnestness one never hears from people whose earnestness in love is presumed. Matthew leans forward with an expression of mild, nearly tender bemusement; the tableau puts one in mind of supplicants before an especially lenient confessor. An engaged couple who've strayed from the sexual guidelines of a reasonably progressive church. I've seen glimpses of the show before, of course—enough to note that Matthew appears to be aging well, though I attribute this mostly to stage makeup. That dogged realism of his appears intact—he's unfazed by the incest, at any rate—and I can see how a more sympathetic viewer could see this as a salutary attitude, in this age of the terminally self-righteous. But I am not a sympathetic viewer, and I don't tell myself stories about Matthew Miller anymore.

I turn off the TV. Its dying starburst sears electric shapes into my eyelids; I watch these for a while instead.

THIRTEEN
cel

AT 5 A.M. ON MONDAY, CEL IS SITTING NEXT TO MATTIE MILLER IN A TOWN CAR, skimming its silent way along Eighth Avenue. Even at this hour, he'd refused to go up Sixth.

Cel rubs her eyes. She spent most of the night churning; she found herself inexplicably vexed by the matter of where her ears should go. Where did other people put them? At three, she gave up and took a shower. She'd tried to be quiet leaving, but as she tiptoed out the door Nikki had called "Break a leg!" in a voice that sounded very wide awake.

"Sir?" Cel says, when they are almost halfway to the studio.

"*Sir.*" This time, he turns. There's an uninvolved expression on his face; Cel stifles the impulse to reintroduce herself.

"If you don't mind, there are a few things I'd like us to go over before we arrive."

"Okay," says Mattie. "Shoot."

Cel can't tell if this is a joke. She sends out a silent plea that the universe not let him say anything like this on television.

"So as we discussed, where things may get tricky is when they try to posit some cultural basis for this incident." One of the downsides of trying to do this in the car is that Cel can't see her notes; one of the upsides is that Mattie M can't see that her hands are shaking. "And that's where they might try to draw the show into that. *'We're losing our way,'* you know—"

"I know," says Mattie quietly.

"*'And the show is a symptom.'* That sort of thing." Cel detects the slightest bulge beneath Mattie's lower lip—this is, presumably, his tongue. What such a gesture might indicate, she couldn't say. Luke would know, most likely. "I mean, okay—maybe it's all right to grant that we're losing our way generally? Or that we're all losing our way together? I mean, *overarchingly.* But what you really want to challenge is any suggestion that the show has some key role in this."

Mattie remains silent, which Cel takes as dissent.

"This is where you're really going to want to play up the show's— well, playfulness, I guess. It's, you know. It's tongue-in-cheek."

Mattie's head snaps toward her. "It's *what?*"

In her mind's eye, Cel can see herself physically backpedaling, as on a bicycle.

"Well, I mean—clearly, the show isn't completely, um, serious." She isn't sure what made the phrase "tongue-in-cheek" come to mind, unless it was the fact that Mattie's tongue was, at the time, literally in his cheek. "There's a degree of the, ah, parodic under way. There's a degree of satire afoot."

"Ah." Mattie's eyes are unmoving, yet there is a feeling of some faint, subvisible shifting beneath them; Cel has the sense that she is staring at ice about to buckle. "And who, precisely, do you imagine this show to be satirizing?"

For all the many times Cel has described the show as "satire," she has never directly been asked this question. She shuffles her notes.

"Well." Cel feels sweat breaking out on her back, and only then does she become aware of the chill from her previous sweating. "Well. You'd put it in your own words, of course."

"I don't envy you, you know," says Mattie.

I don't envy you: this is simultaneously ruder and, somehow, much kinder than Cel expects. It is also, surely, some kind of trap. Cel is shivering: should she ask the driver to turn down the AC? But she won't, of course she won't.

"I mean it," says Mattie. "It's a tough gig, telling people things they don't want to hear *and* already know. Usually it's one or the other."

The car is slowing down; they are arriving, somehow, already.

"Did you know that in Roman times, if they were dramatizing a myth with a murder in it, they would actually kill the gladiator during the performance?"

"I—no, I didn't know that."

"Now *that's* reality programming."

"I think that might just be reality," says Cel—but they are stopped, and Mattie is halfway out of the car, and Cel is gathering up her papers and following him into the studio.

LEE AND LISA IS STAFFED BY A CAST OF *MATTIE M* ANALOGS: A WHITE, MUCH friendlier Luke; an older Joel in a V-neck; a woman about Cel's age, with more expensive clothes and a significantly better handle on her professional duties.

Inside, a guest-greeter ushers them into the makeup room. Luke is already there, hovering near a cornucopia of enormous pastries. Cel is sure that the *Mattie M* pastries are not remotely so large—though *Mattie M* guests are notoriously easy to please. They are all already so thrilled to be in New York City, and the ones who are supposed to present as sympathetic get a free outfit from Old Navy, too.

Lee stops by at a quarter past six. On-screen, he and Lisa are both peppy and anodyne and dumb-seeming—Cel is almost certain Lisa is being paid to seem slightly dumber. In real life, Lee is a sleek bulldog of a man, professionally slick and notoriously pugilistic. Lisa is still in makeup, Lee explains to Mattie. He laughs like *You know how women are!* and Mattie laughs like *Yes, yes, certainly, of course I do!* This is all so fake and gross that Cel actually begins to feel better. Because really, what's the worst that can happen?

At six forty-five, the sound guy comes in. Cel watches as he unbuttons Mattie's shirt—he *is* wearing an undershirt, thank God—and mics him out.

"Love the show, by the way," he says as he adjusts Mattie's ear-piece. "So good to meet you. Big fan."

A buzzy silence fills the room, or maybe just Cel's ears.

"Don't be nervous," Mattie tells her.

"I'm not." Though she is. "*You* don't be nervous!" Though certainly, he should be. "Do you want a scone or something, Mattie?" She gestures at the pastry pile. "There's enough for the whole Russian army."

"The whole—Russian—army?" says Luke. The sound guy looks a little alarmed.

"Oh, ha," says Cel. "Sorry. It was an expression of my grandfather's. It just meant that we had, you know, a lot of food? As you might gather from context."

This seems to concern the sound guy even further. Now, of all times, good *God*. When Cel was a kid, these used to pop out all the time—"Pass the salt, will ya?" she'd say, like a 1920s newsboy; "Pride goeth before a fall," she'd intone, like a minister from the Second Great Awakening. These archaisms had contributed to Cel's image as not only odd, but somehow haunted: a child who'd been left in a closet for a half century, never aging, acquiring strange superstitions and an outdated wardrobe and a faint mothball smell.

"I guess he thought the Russian army was really well fed? Or just big, or . . ." Cel can't fathom why she's still speaking.

"It's from the World's Fair," says Mattie. "Chicago. Eighteen-ninety-whatever-it-was."

A producer appears in the doorway.

"Mattie, hi? It's time to plug in. So good to meet you, by the way. Love the show. Big fan."

Mattie nods and stands. Cel can hear his knees crack. If the producer knows the first thing about Mattie, she'd know he isn't a fan of his fans, and Cel wonders if she's actually trying to piss him off—wrong-footing him by making him feel irked before he even gets onstage. But no, she tells herself: she is being paranoid. This show is extremely simple. Lee and Lisa are here to look like they're having a great time. Mattie is here to be seen making a humanizing effort at tolerating this. Cel is here to speak like a contemporary human, or else not at all. She takes another bite of her scone.

"The World's Fair?" says Luke. "How do you even know that?"

"I used to know a lot of things," says Mattie. "Believe it or not." He studies himself in the mirror, but doesn't make any adjustments. Then he shrugs.

"Or maybe it's just that Cel and I are both ghosts." He makes a spooky woo-woo gesture with his hands. "Good thing Lee and Lisa haven't got wind of *that*."

THEY PLAY HIM OUT TO THE OPENING CHORDS OF "SYMPATHY FOR THE DEVIL." Mattie laughs when he understands what song it is; he even tries to dance, a little, as he makes his way across the stage.

"Thanks for having me," he says, sitting down.

"Thanks for being on the show," says Lee, in a tone that says *Don't thank me yet.*

"It's my pleasure," says Mattie. "And may you never be on mine."

"First of all, Mattie," says Lisa, "I have got to say—I am *such* a fan of yours. I know the Leebster here has a whole big list of questions"— Lisa rolls her eyes affectionately—"but I just have to ask you something first."

"Shoot," says Mattie. Cel winces, but no one else seems to notice.

"The question is this—" Lisa leans forward again: the skin of her décolletage is brown and speckled like an egg. "Do you like to watch your own show?"

"Do I watch my own show?" says Mattie. "I mean, do you watch yours?"

"No! I just can't stand to!" Lisa swats him on the arm and giggles. She has a laugh like a toy piano—what were those things called? It's something like Cel's own name, which must be why she remembers it. "Would you believe me if I said I've never seen it? The Leebster makes so much fun of me."

"Never?" says Mattie politely.

"Never!"

"Well, I can't say I've *never* seen my show," says Mattie. "I am an occasional viewer. But I don't need to watch regularly. For one thing, I already know what happens."

Lisa laughs like this is a remark of real comic genius—a celesta: that was what those little pianos were called—and Cel realizes she's throwing to Lee.

"You may not watch your show, Mattie, but you're certainly one of the only ones who doesn't," says Lee. "And this week, we did learn of two people who weren't only occasional viewers. I'm talking, of course, about Ryan Muller and Troy Wilson, the shooters in this week's horrific attack that left twelve high school students and one teacher dead."

Behind him, the screen begins a slow-fade montage of already-familiar photos: boy on fishing trip, girl in karate suit, corsaged couple at prom—Cel can't remember which one of them was killed. Mattie is nodding somberly. Beside her, Cel can feel Luke torquing himself into indignation.

"And the question on everyone's minds is: Who were the shooters? What could have motivated them? Because when something so heinous happens, I think we *all* feel a little bit guilty."

The background shifts to pictures of the shooters: Troy Wilson is vampirically pale, with elegant, sharply canted eyebrows; Ryan Muller is gray-faced and bloated, like a beached, possibly decaying porpoise. Mattie, Cel notices, has stopped nodding.

"Last week, reports surfaced that Ryan Muller and Troy Wilson were fans of your show, Mattie," says Lee. "As a host myself, I have to ask: what did you feel when you heard that?"

"Well, it doesn't surprise me too much," says Mattie. "A lot of people are fans of the show." *Millions and millions of people,* Cel chants in her mind. "Even sweet Lisa here, if what she says is true."

"Oh, it's true!"

Lee laughs good-naturedly. "Well, nobody is going to argue about your popularity, Mattie. I've seen your ratings and *I'm* jealous. But what I think a lot of people are wondering is—what kind of effect is your show having on viewers? Young viewers, especially—young viewers like the killers. Is *The Mattie M Show* really good for them?"

"Well, that's tricky," says Mattie. He takes a sip of water: Cel has never before realized what a fatal show of weakness this is. "Is the show good for people? Well, relative to what? Is it better than reading Tolstoy? Running a marathon? Volunteering at one's place of worship?"

Mattie is on thin ice, but the mention of religion means that he at least wants to grope back toward solid ground.

"No. It isn't. So if you're watching my show instead of doing those things, or voting, or spending time with your kids, or flossing"—he turns to camera, Final Thought–style—"then I will be the first to tell you: turn it off!"

Cel is light-headed with gratitude.

"But if, like most of us mortals, you're watching for entertainment, or to unwind after a long day—well, then, is my show worse than watching sports? Than watching wrestling? Is it worse than having a few beers or a couple of cigarettes? Probably not. *The Mattie M Show* is a pleasure, sure—you might even call it a vice. But as vices go, you could do a whole lot worse. If you don't believe me, you should check out my show. Weekdays at two on Channel 6."

Lee laughs, then cuts it with the artificial precision of an END APPLAUSE sign. "Well, fair enough, Mattie. But what do you say to the wider argument—the idea that exposure to TV violence can be damaging? Should we be concerned about that as citizens? As parents?"

"You know the first person to call television a quote vast wasteland unquote?" Mattie mimes the quotes as well as quoting them. "The first head of the FCC."

Lee's eyebrows pop upward with jack-in-the-box springiness. "Okay," he says. "Well, that's certainly some interesting trivia, but I don't see—"

"The last time people weren't concerned about TV was before it was invented," says Mattie. "And then? They were concerned about radio." He sounds slightly exasperated, a little bit pedantic. The schism between Mattie's on- and offscreen personae runs along a different axis than most celebrities': people always expect Mattie to be dumber than he is, and their surprise at his forceful intelligence makes it seem like a negative—as though it's a sinister secret he's been keeping all along. Which, in a way, it is.

"Is television a good thing?" says Mattie. He is speaking a bit too loudly, considering the diligence of his microphone. "I don't know—is gravity? Is consciousness? Is capitalism?"

WHAT THE SHIT, Cel thinks. Did he just besmirch capitalism on live TV? What's next—a defection to the Soviets? She has to suppress the impulse to chew on her knuckles. She thinks of her *Lee and Lisa* counterpart, poker-faced and polished. Would she chew on her knuckles at work? No. Probably not on her own time, either.

"So you're saying it doesn't matter whether your show is doing something dangerous because it's—inevitable?" Lee shakes his head. "Mattie, I think that might strike even *your* viewers as cynical."

"I'm saying my show is fulfilling the legacy of television. Of human entertainment, generally," says Mattie. "I'm saying there's nothing new under the sun."

"So you see no connection between the shooters being followers of your show and your being here today?"

Cel squirms at "followers"; it makes Mattie sound like David Koresh.

"Look," says Mattie. "I'm sure there were many, many things these kids were into. Countless things they saw and read and did, most of which we'll never know about. We've heard they liked Mortal Kombat, and that they had a poster of the Cleveland Cavaliers, and that they had a copy of *Mein Kampf*—"

"So you're saying—don't blame you, blame Hitler?"

"Holy shit," says Luke. "I have never in my entire life heard someone Hitler *himself*."

Cel closes her eyes. Maybe this isn't real—maybe she's delirious from stress, or maybe this is the first symptom of the psychosis she's long thought was never coming for her. Or maybe she's just having a stroke! She thinks of this possibility with happiness.

"No," says Mattie. "I am saying we didn't know these kids, and now we never will."

Cel resists the urge to cup her head in her palms; she settles for cradling her cheekbone in her fingers, where she can discreetly dig them into her face.

"Sounds like a job for *The Mattie M Show*," says Lee. "Any chance you'll do an episode?"

"The rest of you seem to have it covered," says Mattie.

"There *has* been a lot of coverage," says Lisa. "And there's *also* been a lot of blame. Blame flying every which way!" She flaps her hands at the air, as though to disperse a circling bat. "But before we get to all of that, I want to ask you, Mattie: who do *you* blame?"

"Who do I blame for the shooting?"

Lisa nods.

"Would it be too obvious to say the shooters?"

He manages not to sound sarcastic here, which is good; they've warned him of the risks of coming across as condescending, *especially* with Lisa.

"The shooters, yes, of *course*." Lisa laughs again—the exact same triad of notes—though it seems a little sinister in repetition: the laugh of a talking doll in a horror film, right before it comes to life. "But if we had to look beyond the shooters. Which I think a lot of people think we do? And when people do that, what an awful lot of people see is you." There's an icky intimacy in her voice now: the tone of a much more private performance. "I mean, not *only* you, obviously! Also video games, movies, music—violence in pop culture, generally. But because of the shooters' relationship to your show—"

"Relationship?" says Luke.

"—there's been a lot of focus on you. When people look beyond the shooters, you are what they see. So I'm wondering—what do *you* see?"

"What do I see when I look beyond the shooters?" says Mattie. "Well, I suppose I see their guns."

"What?" shouts Luke, and Cel drops her scone.

"Well, that can't be all that surprising, can it?" says Mattie, and Cel wonders if he's mocking them a little, his handlers, watching impotently from the greenroom. Because they have drafted him a bulleted list of topics not to venture, and guns are decidedly on that list. Guns, they have told him, are a losing game—even on a show like *Lee and Lisa* where the point, sort of, is to argue. It's that rare issue that manages to make everybody look bad all at once, and bringing it up can do no one any favors. They have discussed this with Mattie at some length.

"I mean, what actually killed those kids?"

"Fuck!" says Luke, kicking the file cabinet.

"Well, *people* killed these kids, would, I think, be the counterargument." Lisa blushes, presumably for sounding smarter than she's contractually obligated to be. Cel read somewhere that she has a degree from the London School of Economics.

"Well, that's an interesting perspective, Mattie," Lee is saying. "Though I know at least one person who'd like to disagree with you. He's actually here today, as a special Surprise Guest."

They play the *Mattie M* Surprise Guest air horn, and the opening bars of the theme music.

"Oh?" says Mattie, in a faltering, good-humored sort of voice.

"I'd like to welcome Blair McKinney," says Lee. "A sophomore at Circle Valley High School and a survivor of last week's shootings."

A spiky-haired teen with an underbite appears on the second monitor. Across from him sits an identically styled Lee—same tie, same gelatinously coiffed hair, same look of just and bottomless concern. The interview is pretaped, evidently, though it will seem live to viewers. Luke has become slack-jawed and silent, agape with the dawning dimensions of this new horror.

"So we understand, Blair, that you'd rather not talk about what you experienced during the shooting," says Lee. His voice conveys a gentleness Cel would not have believed fakeable before she began working in television. "We completely respect that, and I know our viewers will, too."

He says this as though this is a point of personal honor, not a contractually mandated condition of the kid's appearance; the idea must be to emphasize that *some* talk shows have boundaries.

"But I understand you've agreed to talk with us a little about the days leading up to the shooting, and specifically about this *Mattie M* skit we've all been hearing about. You say it was actually a class assignment, is that right?"

The kid nods shakily. "Yeah," he says. "For English class."

"And what was the idea of this assignment?"

"Well, we had this media studies unit? Where we were learning to, like, interrogate the media."

"And what did that involve?"

"Well, we'd talk about, like, advertising, and how nobody thinks it works on them but then really it actually does? Or about, like, why the ratings system thinks violence isn't as bad as, um, some other stuff. But mostly we talked about TV."

"And you watched TV, too, is that right?"

"Sometimes."

"Sounds like a pretty fun class."

"It was," says Blair. "Ms. Stinson was awesome."

"And Ms. Stinson, your teacher—can you tell us what happened to her?"

"She, um. She died." There's a brief roiling across the kid's face, like he's trying to suppress a sneeze, but he gets it under control. "Yeah, she was in a coma at first, and then she unfortunately passed away on Thursday."

"I'm so sorry," says Lee. "She sounds like a really special teacher." He waits an obnoxious, respectful beat. "So the *Mattie M* skit was an assignment from Ms. Stinson?"

"Well, she was always encouraging us to do, like, projects and sh—and stuff. Skits and interactive stuff. Like, a couple people read only really left- or right-wing newspapers for two weeks and then tried to have a debate about the issues but they couldn't because they couldn't agree on any of the actual facts? Which I guess was kind of the point. So our idea had been to do like a *Mattie M*–style show."

"You talked about *The Mattie M Show* a lot in your class, is that right?"

"We did, yeah. It was really easy to talk about because everybody watched it. I think even Ms. Stinson did, a little, but she never liked to tell you what she actually watched at home."

Lee laughs—fondly, a little proprietarily, Cel thinks, as though this were a shared memory.

"And what happened in your *Mattie M* skit?"

"Well, we'd thought we'd do, like, a Surprise Guest thing."

"Based on Mattie's Surprise Guest episodes."

"Right."

"And who was it you were surprising in the skit?"

"Well, Ryan and Troy."

"Ryan Muller and Troy Wilson?" says Lee. "The shooters in last week's attack?"

"Yes," says the kid. He is speaking very quickly now, and Cel can see the sheen of sweat break out above his upper lip. "The surprise was that they were actually the guests on the show in the first place, so it was kind of, um, subverting the *Mattie M* paradigm, I guess? The idea was that in an era of trash TV, and in the age of, um, irony—aren't we all sort of the potential stars of a *Mattie M* episode? We were trying to be, like, critical."

"Sounds like you put a lot of thought into it."

The kid shrugs. "We did, I guess."

"And how did Troy and Ryan react to the skit?"

"I mean, they weren't *happy* about it," says Blair, and bites his lip. "Honestly, Ms. Stinson wasn't too happy about it, either, once she found out they hadn't been in on it."

"Had you thought about how Troy and Ryan would react?"

"Well, I mean, they sort of reacted negatively to everything, so."

"It sounds like they weren't very well liked."

At this, Blair hesitates. "Well—no." He gaze flicks off-camera, and Cel wonders who is coaching him. A lawyer, she hopes, for his own sake. "But that wasn't why we did the skit."

"No?"

"Well, what I mean is, that was sort of part of it. Because they were, as you say, not well liked, but the bigger thing was that *we* were not well liked by *them*. And by 'we' I mean everybody. I mean, I never thought they'd do anything like what happened. But they did just sort of seem to basically hate people and they didn't make any big secret about it. It was sort of like this joke, actually."

"What was the joke?"

"Just how, like, antisocial they were. It was like a joke they were in on. Like this one time, Ryan went as Freddy Krueger for Halloween? He could be pretty funny, actually, sometimes."

"So you thought they wouldn't mind?"

Blair flicks his eyes in the other direction; he's looking away from whoever's there in the room with him. "We thought they might not mind it," he says quietly.

"So tell me what happened after the *Mattie M* skit."

"Well, Ms. Stinson wasn't happy, like I said. I mean, she thought it was really original and interesting and that my impression of Mattie—I was playing Mattie—was really good, and she said she would have given us an A if we'd asked Ryan and Troy's permission first."

"What grade did she give you, may I ask?"

"She hadn't yet," says Blair. "She said she'd have to think about it. I guess she was still thinking."

"Okay," says Lee. "Now I'm just going to ask you one last question—not about the shooting, but about right before. Is that still okay with you?"

Oh, Christ, thinks Cel. Blair nods grimly.

"What did you think when you first saw Troy and Ryan enter the classroom with guns?"

"Well, at first I thought it was their project."

"Their project?"

"Well, we all did, for a second. Because we'd talked a lot about violence in media and we knew that's what their presentation was on. And so we thought they were doing, like, Mortal Kombat. We thought the guns were fake. A lot of people still think Ryan thought the gun was fake, but I don't know about that. I mean, how could you not know?"

This is an interesting question. Cel can tell Lee hasn't heard this part before, but that he doesn't want to disrupt the careful crescendo he's constructing in order to pursue it now.

"When we talked earlier," says Lee, "you said that this moment made you realize something about *The Mattie M Show*. Can you share that realization with us now?"

"Well, I didn't realize anything right then. I was just trying not to—trying not to get killed." Cel can feel him wanting to glance left again, but he manages to keep his gaze on the camera. "But then later, in the hospital, I realized that the shooting might have been, like, revenge for the whole *Mattie M* thing."

"And how did that make you feel?"

"Bad," says the kid. "Kind of guilty. Like a part of this is my fault."

"Blair, I don't think anyone would ever say any of this is your fault," says Lee. "You're an exceptionally brave young man who has been through a terrible thing. There's been a lot of debate this week about who or what besides Ryan and Troy is responsible, but I think we can all agree you're not responsible. You're a sixteen-year-old kid who did a school project, imitating one of the most popular television shows in history, and this is absolutely not your fault."

"Maybe not," says the kid. "But I still wish I'd never done the skit. I wish I'd never even seen *The Mattie M Show*."

"Well, you're certainly not alone there," says Lee, and the kid smiles a little. "There's nothing we can do about that, unfortunately. But what we can do, Blair, is give you the chance to say whatever you want to Mattie M right now. We can promise you he'll get the message. Does that sound like something you'd like to do?"

The kid nods.

"So tell us, Blair: if you could say anything to Mattie M right now—if you knew that he'd be listening—what would you say?"

"I'd say that maybe if I hadn't watched his show, then none of this would have happened. Or maybe it would have happened anyway. I don't know. But I also know I wish I hadn't done what we did, and that I wish he didn't do what he did, either." He's becoming more animated now: Cel can tell he's rehearsed this part not because it's scripted, but because he means it. "I'd say to Mattie that I'm only sixteen, but I can deal with wishing I'd done things differently. I'm only sixteen, and I'll be dealing with that for the rest of my life. I'm a high school student and not a celebrity and I've never been on TV before today, and I can deal with admitting I was wrong. I'd like to say to Mattie that if I can say I'm sorry, then maybe he should, too."

And Mattie almost looks like he might, when they cut back to him, but the thing's been choreographed so that there isn't time: Lisa is declaring *That's our show!* and leaning over to thank Mattie for coming. He says something back, but neither Cel nor the audience can hear it. They're playing him out to "It's the End of the World as We Know It."

FOURTEEN
semi

1979

All around us was the feel of a city past its prime: a too-ripe fruit, a fading party, a starlet aging into tragedy. Junkies passed out in the parks amongst their lemon rinds and needles. The smell of citrus undercut with shit. The sixties hadn't smelled great, either, yet this filth seemed more abject—the stink not of rebellion, but defeat. The revolution had come and gone, leaving nothing more than the detritus of a weather event.

All of this seemed to energize Matthew, perversely. He spoke endlessly of strategy: of issue voters and voting blocs and ethnic groups. He was bullish about the immigrant working class, in whose midst, he believed, lurked many potential voters. Not among the *Hungarians*, of course, since they preferred a harder line on communism ("Of course," I echoed faintly); on the Greeks, he was agnostic. But he was hoping to chip away at some of Koch's other bases—the Italians, the Poles, the Jews—especially the doves, and especially the young. You didn't have to feel like an American to feel like a New Yorker, he said, and these second-generation voters were New Yorkers through and through—no matter what language they spoke at home, no matter who they rooted for in the Olympics or the more ambiguous wars. He didn't expect them to go canvassing the city, or to argue with their families about him over dinner. But he believed in the quiet power of double lives—and that all immigrant children were, to some extent, living them—and he believed in the possibility of anonymous votes, unprophesied by polls, that might deliver him the election.

He was quoting Blondie again, I figured; I was coming to blame a lot of things on Eddie Marcus's lunatic confidence. He was one of those dangerous people whose expectations in life had actually been fulfilled. Coming from him, a jaunty Panglossian worldview could seem nearly credible—you'd start to wonder if it *wasn't* all just a matter of attitude, in the end. And Matthew's charisma was such that a career of national prominence would not have seemed outlandish, if one didn't have all the details—which Eddie Marcus, it seemed, still did not.

Matthew's own doubts about the campaign were frightfully utilitarian. He fretted over how the "straphangers"—I guess he meant commuters—might react to a transit strike; he thought it might play well for Koch. Though deeply committed to the unions, he worried about the potency of the TWU; its history of militancy would compound the political liabilities of a fare hike ("obviously," he said)—which were already considerable, since deterioration of the subways was New Yorkers' top concern, after crime and dirt and education. And there wasn't even enough money in the budget to repair defective undercarriages, let alone buy new subway cars!

"But if *you're* elected," I said once, listlessly.

"The mayor doesn't control the budget," he snapped. "That's one of New York's biggest structural problems of governance!"

Though he could also sound quite inspiring, at times. He could almost make you believe that an acknowledgment of reality's ambiguities was not a useless dithering, but a righteous first step toward action. He could nearly persuade you we were on the brink of a renaissance; that Times Square—with its strip joints and cheesy massage parlors and movie theaters catering to the most unoriginal perversions—was in fact the very center of the universe.

"Anything is possible," he liked to tell me. And also: "If it's true there's nothing new under the sun, that's because everything has happened once already."

Real estate agents were beginning to sell people on the idea of returning to New York, a fact he found senselessly promising.

"You can *sell* people on anything," I said one time. He was stroking a phantom line above my eyebrow to which he had some long-standing attachment. "And if they buy it, then that's politics."

"If they buy it, then that's reality."

"If they buy it, then that's theater."

"Cynical is easy, you know," he said. "It's everything else that's hard."

"Oh yeah?" I brushed his hand away. "I hadn't heard that one before."

"Don't be petulant," he said after a moment.

Petulantly I said: "I'm not."

AT A LOSS, I FUCKED A PAINTER. HE LIVED IN THE ANSONIA. WHEN I RODE UP TO see him, I'd push all the buttons in the elevator. There was a different scene on every floor: flamenco dancers, barefoot violinists, pinched-faced ancients in New Deal garb, ensconced amongst the turrets. Everyone in that building was either on the way up or on the way down. And in that elevator it was easy to believe my life might still be in its rising action—arcing up toward artistic triumph and personal fulfillment and spectacular, climactic nights with many men I did not love.

ON TV, JIMMY CARTER NAGGED US ABOUT OUR CONFIDENCE.

"He actually looks like a peanut if you think about it long enough," said Brookie.

We were stoned. We were always stoned.

"Anyone looks like anything if you think about it long enough," said Paulie. He was dressed as a werewolf. He'd recently been cast as an extra in a movie about marauding Native American spirits; it was shooting in the Bronx, where disaster tourists roamed the afternoons, clutching their cameras and wandering into all the shots. Down the street, another studio was making a movie about the firebombing of Dresden. Paulie didn't get a callback for that one.

The soundtrack of that summer was breaking windowpanes; sidewalks glittered with chevronels of storefront. There were bank robberies every day. We heard about a Puerto Rican bank that got robbed so often they'd posted a sign asking robbers to be patient while English interpreters were summoned. We laughed about that, though not as much as we used to laugh about other things. We spent our nights at the Serpentine or the Mineshaft or lying on pillows at St. Mark's. We were somehow doing more drugs and having less fun. Brookie kept threatening to move back to California.

"Do you really have to come home like this?" said Brookie to Paulie. "Do they really not give you a sink?"

"Not really," said Paulie, swallowing a bite of sandwich through his makeup. "The other night I growled at some tourists."

"If you don't want those people coming, maybe you should stop making those movies."

"Hey, all publicity is, you know, whatever." Paulie frowned into his sandwich.

"No sense of civic engagement," said Brookie, shaking his head. "Not like Citizen Semi over here."

"Are you suggesting that Paulie only choose projects that cater to suburbanite sensibilities?" I said. "Maybe it *is* time for you to leave New York."

"You'll see," Brookie muttered. "One of these days, I'm outta here. And then you're all going to have to start finding your own friends and making your own jokes."

"I make jokes," I said.

"One day you're gonna wake up and, poof, I'll be gone. And *then* won't you be surprised!"

"Not if you keep talking about it," I said. "Anyway, this city isn't without its opportunities. Just look at Paulie here! Dreams *do* come true."

Paulie bared his teeth at us.

"And see?" I said. "A joke!"

"You'd miss me, though," said Brookie, looking up at me. "Wouldn't you?"

"Please."

"Wouldn't you?"

"Oh, Christ," I said. And then: "Yes, of course I'd miss you. I'd miss you if you ever gave me half a chance."

NOT LONG AFTER THAT, I HEARD THAT MY GRANDMOTHER WAS DYING.

"Finally," said Brookie. I suppose he could see I wasn't entirely undone.

I told him that I thought I might go see her.

"What?" Brookie scoffed. "Do you think she'd come see *you* if you were dying?"

I said I didn't know. This was before I'd had the opportunity to witness countless surprise appearances at deathbeds; Paulie and Nick would have been touched, I think, by the many cameos at theirs. Though almost nobody behaves well at the end, more people than you might imagine do turn up.

But it all seemed very abstract then, this idea of a grandmother burying a grandson—it was theoretical to the point of self-indulgence, which was a mode of thinking my grandmother particularly despised.

"What does it matter what would happen if what *wouldn't* happen *did*?" she'd said more than once, often just before exiting a room. I'd be left trying to parse this sentence enough to dispute it, forgetting whatever question had initiated the exchange—which may, it occurs to me now, have been the entire point.

In the end, I decided I would go. The boys weren't overly aggrieved—though they'd all inveighed on the issue, ultimately they weren't terribly invested. There was a show at Escuelita that weekend. And perhaps they were growing used to my capitulations.

And so I went, to stare down my grandmother at last. Her friends from the athenaeum were there, already eyeing her book collection. They cleared out when I arrived, either from delicacy or terror. And then I was at last alone with her, shaking in her serge-curtained bed.

"Hello, Grandmother," I said.

She did not reply. The doctors had said she wouldn't recognize me. I'd told them I was used to that. Above her was a framed picture of Prague's astronomical clock, glowering like an evil eye. I had no idea what it meant to her—asking would have once been impertinent, and now was impossible. When everything's unsaid, it becomes difficult to regret any specific silences.

These days, such regrets have become my life—waking me from sweaty nightmares with the electric emergency of things too late to say, or do, or know—and in such moments, my grandmother's approach can start to look a lot like wisdom. Which is another thing too late to say, only further proving her point.

But the silence between my grandmother and me then: it had a sort of peace.

I sat with her awhile, and when I left I took the clock off the wall.

MATTHEW HADN'T ANSWERED WHEN I CALLED FROM IOWA, AND HE DIDN'T ANswer when I was back in New York. But this happened sometimes. And so it was ten days before I realized what was going on.

A few hours after that, he called me—intuiting, with the impeccable sixth sense of the cowardly, that the hardest part was over.

He said: "I need to see you."

"Oh?" I said. "You gonna send a helicopter, or what?"

On the other end, his breathing sounded ragged and shallow. I pressed my ear into the receiver so I could hear it better.

"Because the subway's down, you know," I said. "That's the kind of thing people are going to expect the mayor to be aware of."

And you're too gorgeous to be uninformed, I might have said, but I didn't want him to know that I remembered.

"I'll send a car," he said.

"You better believe this is the last favor I'm ever doing for you."

I hung up before I could hear him tell me it was the last one he'd ever ask.

THE RIDE TOOK FOREVER, THE CAR FINALLY DEPOSITING ME BEFORE A RESTAU-rant on the Upper East Side. Inside, the place was empty—maybe good old Eddie had rented it out for the occasion. Matthew was sitting at the bar, cheek cupped in his fingers, poring over some papers—engaged in the hideously dull calculations of governance even then, no doubt. When he saw me, he shook his head ferociously, as though trying to concuss himself back to reality.

We sat, and I watched Matthew stare into the tablecloth. I could have gone ahead and gotten things started (*Let's get this over with,* I might have said. *We both know how this goes: nothing new under the sun!*), but the longer he stayed silent, the more determined I was to wait him out. I could afford to be stubborn: I'd already lost what I had to lose, which quite possibly was nothing.

"Well," he said after a long while. "They caught us."

There was a buzzing in my ears, a smell of camphor in my nostrils.

"And 'caught' meaning—?"

"They have pictures."

"Oh." The sun shifted, casting a fretwork of shadows on his face. "Well, how do I look?"

"I haven't seen them."

"How do you know?"

"They were quite—specific. In their descriptions."

" 'They' being . . . ?"

"The *Post.*" He drummed his fingers on the table; he had bitten his nails down so far that it was uncomfortable to watch this. "Well. Most proximately."

"And by 'proximately,' you mean . . ."

"I am given to understand there's more."

"More what?"

"Doctored forms. Well, stolen first, doctored second, to make it appear as though you were being compensated for nothing, out of state funds." He winced. "That's a felony, if we were going to get into it. But we aren't."

"Why not? Don't know any decent lawyers?"

He shut his eyes.

"Did they at least have a good pun for the caption?"

He opened them again. "I can't see you anymore."

I laughed, too loud for the room. "*That's* why you sent a car? So I could hear *that* line in person? I guess you really did need a writer."

His eyes were asking me to understand, but I was not going to—was never, never going to, if he wasn't even going to try to make me.

"Sooner or later—"

"Yes," I said. "Well, that's an excuse for anything, isn't it?"

The waitress came to pour coffee; her gestures had a Stanislavskian crispness that for some reason exhausted me. I was a player with a small Act I part, staring down the interminable second half—I was sweating under the stage lights, the collodion melting into my eyes. And still, and still, the show must go on!

Somewhere in the distance, Matthew Miller was explaining some things to me. He was saying that he'd agreed to admit to infidelity and withdraw from the race. He was saying there would be a press conference. He was saying they'd agreed not to release the pictures, nor describe what manner of man was in them. A possibility was occurring to me, or so I thought. Now, I know that I wasn't considering an idea so much as crafting a plot point—a deus ex machina so saccharine I would have been mortified to catch myself buying, let alone contriving, it. But still, for a moment, it seized me—the thought that Matthew had ulterior, possibly honorable, possibly *chivalric* motives.

"Why would the *Post* agree to that?"

He said quietly: "I suspect it isn't their terms."

He's doing this for me!, I thought wildly: the sort of piercing realization that seems to hint at the true order of things, and sometimes even does. You somehow know a man loves you, and then somehow, for a while, it is true.

"You don't have to do this to protect me," I said.

Matthew looked at me oddly. "I'm not protecting you."

I felt a spiky laugh grow in my throat, and when Matthew leaned forward and said, "I'm protecting Alice," it burst out onto the table.

"*Don't,*" I said, "bring poor Alice into this."

I was still speaking rather loudly. To his credit, Matthew did not look around to see who might have heard.

"Did you notice that the *one* time you take me out in public is the one time it's the cowardly thing to do?" I was retroactively developing an intense interest in the protocol of this conversation. "Did you notice that? Is that kind of funny? Is that kind of a coincidence?"

On Matthew's face was nothing—not performance but deletion. A canceled check, a trick mirror. The light changed—the room flooding with the flat brightness of an approaching meteor—but it turned out to only be a truck blocking the window. It rumbled away, the world restored.

"I guess it probably isn't a coincidence," I said.

"There is the question," said Matthew carefully, "of what good I could still do."

Though seconds earlier I'd been conjuring my own noble intentions for Matthew, it was unendurable that he would try it himself. This is probably when I first hated him.

"I'm sorry," he said. I wanted to laugh in his face, but was afraid what else might come out if I tried. I knew even then that nothing could capture the feeling of this moment—anything I did could only distort it, mock it, make it into a piece of high camp. In the end, I decided on a homicidal civility.

"Well," I said, proffering my hand and flashing a bright, savaging smile. "I wish you all the best in your future endeavors."

And then it was over, and I was somehow out the door. I stumbled along the street—Matthew had known better than to try to get me back into the car—though I don't know where I went, and probably didn't then, either. All I knew was that I would never love like that again—I knew, I knew, I knew that I would not.

And in this, and only this, I would be right.

FIFTEEN
cel

ON THE WAY BACK TO THE STUDIO, MATTIE IS SILENT. HE'D REFUSED TO SPEAK
to anyone after the interview—he'd stormed back through the greenroom, sending several pastries falling to the floor, and then made a
beeline to the limousine, hitting the locks when Luke tried to get in
behind him. Cel, alas, was already inside. She shot Luke a look like
What the hell am I supposed to do? and he responded with a flail like
You think it even matters? She watched him watch them for a moment before turning to hail a taxi.

The way back to the studio is along Seventh, but Mattie tells the
driver to take the FDR. The day is softening into broad midmorning
light; Cel can't believe it's still so early. She tries to calculate exactly
what percentage of this debacle can be said to be her fault. Blair
McKinney, she decides, is not. They'd baited Mattie with an abstract
question only to entrap him with the irrefutable concrete: *you* think
the problem's guns, Mattie, but the kid that got shot with one thinks
the problem is you. The whole thing would have been bad enough
even if the kid hadn't shown up—even if Mattie had only managed
to pick a pointless fight with half his viewers, as well as one of the
most vociferously well-funded lobbying groups in the country. Like
Mattie, the gun rights people had been on the defensive since the

shooting. They certainly weren't natural allies of the CPA, with its whiff of nanny-state presumptions. But now Mattie had just given them a powerful incentive to join in attacking him, and Blair McKinney had given them an elegant way to do it.

Above them the sun is winking manically, spinning murderous spokes of light.

Hal had had a .30-06 hunting rifle. He'd taught Cel to use it in the stealthy way he taught her many things: by enlisting her help until she'd learned enough to know how to begin to learn more. He must have believed she would have, if she had to, and Cel likes the idea that Hal had bet on her in this way: it links her in a nebulous, posthumous sort of love, and the gun made this literal. She almost wishes she still had it—though as a child, she hadn't liked to touch it. She regarded it as necessary and private in a way just short of ugly. Maybe Ruth had felt this, too; maybe that was why she didn't use it. Cel and Hal had said this to each other, consolingly, a few times right after. But even then, Cel had had her doubts. Most likely Ruth had forgotten about the gun, or else never known it was there. One thing Cel does not doubt is her mother's determination.

"I know how that went," says Mattie abruptly, and Cel jumps. "So you don't have to tell me."

He is staring out the window away from her; beyond him, the river is a flat silver annelid.

"Not that you would, anyway," he says.

"I'm sorry?"

"Your job is to never quite tell anyone anything, right? So in a situation like this your job is to *not* tell me how I did."

"I think it's my job to tell you how to do better?"

"Yeah, well, you don't have to do that, either."

Cel nods, and Mattie tells the driver to turn down Houston. They are on the lam now, apparently, just like Ryan Muller.

"So why don't you tell me something else," Mattie says, when he leans back.

"What?"

"Tell me something else," he says. "Tell me something I don't know about you."

"I really don't know what you—"

"One thing."

"You don't know anything about me."

"So it shouldn't be hard to pick."

"Okay." Cel scans her life for fun facts; facts of any sort seem scarce. Behind Mattie, she catches fractional snatches of scurfing water. "Okay," she says. "I was voted Most Changed in high school."

"Most changed?" says Mattie. "From what to what?"

"From who knows what to you tell me, I guess."

Mattie nods at this, but doesn't laugh.

On Houston, they encounter a parade. Or maybe not a parade—there are people wearing leather jackets and diapers and Bush masks—though Cel doesn't put anything past New York City. At their center, a clot of emaciated men hold up something that looks very much like a coffin.

"I think it's a funeral," says the driver doubtfully—and yet it seems clear that whatever this is is not *only* a funeral. Men shout and wave banners around the coffin; a short, sibylline person walks behind it, shaking with an oracular fury. Cel can't even tell whether the coffin is real: some real things are like that.

"I think it's a protest," she says. It comes out in a horrible, hushed, schoolgirl sort of voice, and she winces at the sound of herself. She is grateful for the tinted windows.

The driver mutters something, and Mattie barks at him to turn down Essex. This is startling, as Mattie is not generally a barker. The driver shakes his head; it is obvious they're not going anywhere for a while, and Cel can feel him wishing this drive were metered. Mattie's gaze is locked on the driver's headrest; Cel can't tell if he's even noticed the funeral at all. Maybe he is the clinical egomaniac Luke always says he is, though Cel has little use for diagnoses. They are just one way of describing things, which cannot save you from the exhausting crush of all the other ways.

Cel stares at the coffin; it sways slightly, like a bassinet, and she wonders if this is done for effect or if the men don't have the strength to hold it steady.

All funerals remind Cel of her first, for the birches. Her mother weeping, tracing her finger along the ring of a stump, while Cel told her she was horrible, horrible, *horrible*. Her mother saying she hadn't meant to cut them down—she hadn't been the one to cut them down at all! The wind kicking up all around them—or did she invent that part later? Cel can only imagine what Hal would say about this, her deranged attachment to those fucking trees persisting through the years. In comparison Ruth's funeral had seemed a wan, senseless thing. It was early November—a dull, liminal stretch of season that felt unmoored from memory; Cel couldn't remember anything else ever happening around that time of year, and maybe this was why Ruth chose it. That was another thing she and Hal said to each other, for a while. Cel gave the eulogy, saying kind things cheapened by the unseemly length of time she'd been preparing herself to say them. Afterward, they ate a casserole at a folding table in the church cafeteria.

The car begins to move, finally, and Cel turns to look at Mattie.

"I forgot to ask you for a secret." She says this only because there is no risk of him telling her one; it strikes Cel that she actually doesn't want to know anything more about Mattie than she already does.

"I don't have any secrets," says Mattie.

"If that was true, you wouldn't need a publicist."

"Well, in that case, you're fired." Mattie is deadpan enough that Cel flinches a little. "Because believe it or not, it is true: you are looking at a man without secrets."

He turns to stare out the window; he seems to be scanning the streets for something, though they are now far past the funeral.

"Well. Not my own secrets, anyway," he says after a time. "Only other people's."

IT *WAS* WINDY THE NIGHT OF THE BIRCHES—OF THIS, CEL IS ALMOST SURE. She can almost see the hemlocks' balletic swaying, a minor prelude to every storm. *Horrible, horrible, horrible,* she chanted—and was it the weather that made her wild? Did she feel a sort of heathen saturnalia—a sense of the world arranging itself to perform its heresies (lightning, thunder, rain), creating a chasm where unspeakable things might be shouted? She was only nine, and she *was* very sorry about the trees. Yet it isn't the grief she remembers most, but the rage: that rage that was a funnel cloud within her, with no landscape to destroy. On whom might she exact her vengeance? Certainly not Ruth, who listened to the litany of her own outrages with an infuriating, impersonal patience. This is how she listened to the news about the trees, at first: radiating a subtle incuriosity that made Cel crazy, frenzied with an anger that was as deep as anything she's ever known (and sometimes, she fears, far deeper).

"Horrible," Cel said again and again, and then: "I *hate* you sometimes."

At this, her mother buried her head on the stump and began to weep soundlessly.

Later, Cel crept into her mother's room and threw her face in her hair.

"Mom?" she whispered.

After what seemed a long while, Ruth said, "Yes?"

"Could you ever teach me how to cut a tree like that?"

"What?"

"Not a special tree, I mean. I mean, like maybe just a little hemlock."

Saying this hurt Cel, which made her feel brave.

Ruth sighed and turned to the wall. "I can't teach you that," she said. "Maybe your grandfather."

Cel disentangled herself from Ruth and went to the window. Below, the birch trees lay where they fell. Something in their glint seemed to take a skeletal character—a pile of femurs after a genocide—and she shivered.

"Why can't you teach me?" she said.

"Because I don't know how to do it, Cel." Her mother sounded wondering. "Because it really wasn't *me* that did it. It was someone else."

semi

1980

"FUCK THOSE WALL STREET CLOSET CASES," SAID BROOKIE WHEN I FINALLY
told him about Matthew.

We were on the train, forcing down execrable coffee. The graffiti
in our car was strangely shaky, like a barely mastered alphabet.

"He wasn't Wall Street," I whispered. The car was filling with a
watery yellow light; it must have been the morning. I have no idea
where either of us was going. We rode there for a while in silence.

"Well, fuck 'em, anyway," said Brookie after a while. And then:
"Don't cry, don't cry, don't cry."

I'D WATCHED MATTHEW'S PRESS CONFERENCE BY ACCIDENT—I WAS STUM-
bling through the channels and there he was, reading from notes,
blinking too rapidly, and because I was not yet accustomed to this
particular taunt from the universe, I watched. Matthew had evidently
already confessed to something, his *indiscretion* or however he was
going to put it, and one could hear light jeering from the crowd.
Though "crowd" is perhaps overstating the case—the spectacle of
Matthew's public surrender to character assassination turned out to
be lightly attended, compounding its pitifulness. Eddie Marcus

never would have allowed this during the campaign—*don't let them take photos of empty rooms at events!* being one of his more astute insights.

"And so," Mattie was saying, "in order to avoid being a distraction to the Democratic Party and to avoid causing further pain to my family, I have decided to suspend my campaign at this time."

His voice was uncertain, as though he weren't used to public speaking—as though he hadn't already made one career out of it, and wouldn't go on to make another. Next to him stood a pale, besieged Alice, looking about as miserable as she always had. It was impossible to guess what she knew.

On TV, Matthew thanked his supporters, then apologized to them, then said something I missed that elicited a smattering of mean-spirited laughter. Say what you will about Alice, she had a poker face that couldn't be beat—except, of course, by Matthew. His was so good you didn't even know he had one; you didn't even know he was playing any sort of game at all. The phrase *ghost bet* floated up from somewhere as I watched him speak. He really was a talented politician, I thought. What a loss, what a terrible loss, for New York City!

Other people thought so, too; for a while, Matthew was an object of no small amount of progressive nostalgia. The specter of his lost career flickered around reality—when Koch made his hideous compromises, when Dukakis got in that preposterous tank, when Bush demanded that we read his thin, hectoring lips and the nation, unbelievably, complied. Matthew stayed pure, throughout it all, and continued to be spoken of wistfully in certain lefty circles. And even when his show made this absurd, Matthew himself was never quite viewed as a joke—more as a baffling waste, like a genius rock star dead at twenty-seven.

Though this is likely not why the journalist is calling me again.

"I want to know what ended Matthew Miller's political career," he says in his second voicemail. *"I think maybe it was you."*

"That's some crackerjack investigative reporting, Scotty!" I tell the answering machine. I've been talking to myself quite a bit in recent months.

I want to know what ended Matthew Miller's political career: for a while, I had wanted to know this, too. It might have really been the tabloid, of course, likely in conjunction with some seedier Barry campaign underling. It could have been a story Matthew Miller erected to disown a decision he'd already made—a way to dodge his darkest fear by pretending it was already real (this theory was volunteered by Stephen, formulated by his psychiatrist). I even entertained the notion that it could have been Eddie Marcus, casting Matthew as both a scapegoat and a stepping-stone—though he'd sabotage his own career soon enough, that blond fuck.

It could have been any one of these things, or none, or something else I might never think to think of. It would never have occurred to me to take *all* the credit for Matthew's downfall, however. Listening to the reporter's voicemail, I almost feel a little flattered.

I listen to the message again for spite, then applaud into the darkness. I am perhaps not well suited to living alone.

I ENTERED AN ERA OF COMPULSIVE, BRUTALIZING WALKS.

I stalked the ruins of the Lower East Side; I floated up to the dreamy realms near the park, hoping to cause a scandal. On Division Street, I gave thirty dollars to a man playing the French horn. He smiled at the money, then looked at me and frowned. On Orchard Street, I watched a procession of Chinese men bearing tall cloth banners, and began crying before I understood it was a funeral.

I threw myself into writing, which I undertook in the same spirit as the walking—savagely, joylessly, with no sense of actually trying to get anywhere. I took some solace in thoughts of the work I'd be doing if I'd never met Matthew—the great art that he was personally denying the entire world! I erected elaborate fantasies in which future historians discovered the tragedy of my lost oeuvre (the mechanics of this part were unclear), inspiring global mourning for my brilliance. I liked to imagine Matthew becoming known as a great cultural criminal of history, along the lines of whoever torched the library at Alexandria. I spent entire walks thinking about this.

I was dimly aware, even then, that I was being histrionic. And yet the knowledge that my misery was in some sense inescapably *theatrical* (as Grandmother would say) only made it worse. I felt myself entombed within a carapace of clownishness; inside it, I was echoingly, vertiginously alone.

I walked to the East River, to watch the crimsonish sheen fall over the water. I walked to Forty-sixth Street, to watch Afroed, scorpion-spined boys play Frisbee without their shirts. I stared so long that a kid in a Ramones T-shirt stopped to ask if I was okay. Was there someone he could call for me? Was there anything he could do? In another life I might have had some ideas. But I had entered a stretch of celibacy—which, like the walking, I approached with a militancy out of all proportion to circumstance.

We need to get you *out*, the boys kept telling me—I'd say that I was *always* out, and they'd say I knew that wasn't what they meant. They proposed the Spike, the Eagle, the Man's Country baths; they reminded me how much I'd liked Tenth Floor's tiny dance floor. I couldn't really imagine that: the lethal boredom of my present was beginning to lacquer over the past. From my new vantage point, all possible ways of being, all potential courses of action, looked more or less the same. When you truly can't remember why anyone bothers with anything, hedonism just seems exhausting.

Though the boys must have succeeded once or twice: I recall Donna Summer; excited discussion of whether the best new anti-parasite treatment was carcinogenic. But after a while, the boys' obsession with joy—and their relentless insistence that I had experienced it, once—began to seem suspicious. Could their claims really hold up under scrutiny? I began to study my life as a skeptic, then a full-blown conspiracy theorist, scrutinizing my memories for signs of the *real* story. Wasn't that the glint of a second shooter just off beyond the edge of the frame? And why, in that supposedly lunar nothingness, did the flag seem to ripple in the wind? And wasn't it true—wasn't it, in fact, *undeniable*—that I had been fooling myself all along?

I went to cruising sites and clubs, though not for any normal reasons. I went to the Metropolitan bathroom and eyed the men eyeing me through the stalls. I invited sex only in order to reject it—though this was a cheap thrill, as they go. The only person I think I ever really disappointed was a flasher on Clinton Street; he opened his coat with a sudden *voilà* gesture, and I looked so unsurprised that he closed it again, very quickly, and went off muttering into the night.

I went down to the West Side Highway, for old times' sake. I walked the Lower East Side, scowling at the peace signs. I sneered at pigeons, at colorful laundry waving in the early morning light. I went to the Rambles, to the exact spot where a rat had once scurried over my foot while I gave a blowjob to a man in a beret. I wondered what had happened to the man; I wondered what had happened to the rat.

Out of gratuitous, impotent spite, I wished bad things for them both.

part three

But seasons must be challenged or they totter

Into a chiming quarter

Where, punctual as death, we ring the stars. . . .

—DYLAN THOMAS

Every silence quotes a greater silence.

—ALICE FULTON

SEVENTEEN
semi

1980–1985

A HUNDRED THOUSAND STORIES, ALL WITH THE SAME ENDING. A TRIUMPH OF plotting the Greeks would envy. So when, exactly, do we raise the curtain? Which narrative thread shall we pull to unravel a generation?

SAY IT BEGAN WITH THE THING IN PAULIE'S MOUTH.

What *sort* of thing? we asked three times. Paulie was in the living room, practicing for an audition. This is when we heard it first: an odd, slurring distortion in his speech.

This was in the spring of '82. Paulie was in a foul mood, due to the public boycott of his werewolf movie. City Council claimed it unfairly stereotyped the Forty-first Precinct.

"Too bad we don't know anybody there anymore," Brookie said, and winked at me.

"He was in the State *Assembly.* Hey, Paulie. Say that line again, will you?"

Paulie obliged, and we heard it once more—a strange sort of curl, like he was playing deaf, which we immediately accused him of doing.

"Because if you are, then it isn't very good."

"I'm not."

"It's also very offensive."

"I'm *not*," he said, and we noticed that he'd answered. "It's this cold sore."

A cold sore?

"Or something. There's this spot."

We marched him to the kitchen and bent him over the sink. A flashlight was suggested and produced; batteries were sought and found. Then, one by one, we stared at it—this knurl of dark matter, crouching at the back of Paulie's throat. *Now, how did that get there?* we thought and must have said out loud. The thing in Paulie's mouth wasn't large or particularly gruesome—yet it was so unlike anything we'd ever seen in a mouth. Something about it seemed both comical and ominous—a goose outside your airplane window, right before it's sucked into the engine.

"This is bad timing," said Paulie when we finally let him up. "I have to sing tomorrow."

"You have to go to the doctor tomorrow," we told him.

And miraculously, he agreed.

Perhaps in that moment we saw the plot run straight through to its ending—perhaps this was how it began for us.

OR PERHAPS IT WASN'T THEN, BUT A FEW MOMENTS BEFORE. PERHAPS IT began as we were leading Paulie to the kitchen, as we were watching him open his mouth.

The Angel of Death was swooping low over the houses. Between the sound of wingbeats in the distance and the sound of feathers settling on the roof, there comes a silence. This is the final echo of a certain kind of hope, the downbeat of a new sort of fear.

Perhaps *this*, then, was the beginning.

OR SAY IT BEGAN WITH THE RUMORS. WE'D BEEN HEARING THEM FOR A while—though we could never quite agree on what we'd heard, or when, or whether, in those early days, we were hearing about the same thing at all. In the grand tradition of epic villains, ours went by many names.

Some of us remembered being handed a pamphlet on Fire Island sometime around Labor Day. Was this in '81? Though we were vaguely aware of it even then, we supposed, this new affliction affecting the astoundingly slutty—sailors, hustlers, anyone whose sex life was a full-time job. Who had that kind of time? We should only be so lucky! We threw away the flier; we'd thought it was about a party.

Some of us heard about something coming from Los Angeles—a scourge of the jet-setters and out-of-sight-wealthy—and this version sounded vaguely faddish, like something you might want to get in on early. But promiscuity, like class, is a spectrum on which everybody claims the middle: we did not worry about it much.

Then there was the thing called "the Saint's Disease," which you caught at the Saint and was the reason Stephen never wanted to go there anymore. This was just the club bug of the month, we figured—a new critter to add to the menagerie, alongside the crabs, the amoebas, the enteric parasites (shigellosis, amebiasis, giardiasis). These would tear through like mono at summer camp, and the Health Department would send people out to test the water. Then we'd all wash up at the pharmacy to get a shot; they made you stand in line holding a ticket, as at the deli, and we made a big show of pretending to be embarrassed. This routine was just the cost of doing business; if you were squeamish about it, then maybe you needed to look into a different kind of business.

Nevertheless, we decided to indulge Stephen's paranoia, and avoided the Saint for a while.

Perhaps *these* were the beginnings—misty, choral, understated, for a storyteller with some subtlety.

A MORE CONVENTIONAL VERSION MIGHT BEGIN THE DAY WE RAN INTO NICK ON St. Mark's Place. It was a Sunday, late in the fall of '81. Paulie had forced us out—who can remember why? Nick was standing over a blanket piled with back issues of *Honcho,* looking horrible. We hadn't seen him in a while. Perhaps he'd finally broken up with Peter, we thought, though we wouldn't have expected *Nick* to be the one looking so undone—and these are the thoughts we were indulging when we heard that Peter was in the hospital. He'd been there for three weeks. The doctors said he had the gay pneumonia.

"At least it's not *regular* pneumonia," said one of us, who would regret this line forever.

The doctors were ordering a second course of pentamidine, Nick told us; Peter's mother was flying out tomorrow. We never considered that Peter had a mother: we'd thought maybe she was dead? But no: we hadn't actually thought of it at all.

Nick blinked at us as from a strange distance. He'd come out to buy books for Peter, he told us, and did we have any suggestions? They weren't either of them big readers, normally.

We stood with him awhile, debating his purchases. It was one of those excruciatingly perfect late autumn days, we noticed, the kind that used to make us sad as children. But what had we ever had to be sad about as children? We turned in circles for no reason—west to Astor Place, south to Seventh Street—and maybe Paulie gave us a look. The wind was kicking up a little—scattering detritus, riffling the fraying pages of *Honcho,* introducing an alterity to the moment that made us uneasy. Then the clouds moved, and down came little éclats of light; we felt reassured, somehow, and yet somehow sure we shouldn't.

We decided on a Penguin edition of *The Magic Mountain* for Peter; for his newly discovered mother, a jar of lavender oil from a Senegalese man. We insisted on paying, though Nick never let us pay. He did this time, however: maybe this was the beginning.

SAY IT BEGAN WITH THE THEORIES.

The word was only bottoms got it.

The word was only black people got it.

The word was it came from poppers. Maybe something they were mixing in the drinks. Barroom iodizers, conceivably.

The word was it came from Haitians. Or possibly Hispanics?

The word was it came from nowhere, because it didn't really exist, and was a conspiracy to sabotage our liberation.

The word was it came from drugs. Maybe nitrate inhalants, or maybe only butyl. Maybe don't take Rush. Maybe don't take Bolt. Maybe play it really safe and don't take anything, for a while.

WE WENT TO CLUBS, TO DANCE RELUCTANTLY TO DISCO. WE WENT TO CENtral Park, to mourn John Lennon. This turned out to be the last time we saw Anders—shivering close to the bandshell, while "Imagine" played over the speakers. Five weeks later, Reagan was inaugurated. And then, all of a sudden, we began going to hospitals.

We came prepared, in the beginning. We armed ourselves with magazines and flowers. Inside, we donned robes and masks and plastic caps; we walked through doors marked WARNING.

There is nothing new under the sun—but nothing new to whom? It's the sun that can never be surprised; the same cannot be said for people.

Inside, we braced ourselves against the smell of offal; the venous arms we tried not to look at, vowed never to remember. For the most part, we did not cry. We made bad jokes instead, then went ahead and made them again anyway. We read aloud from paperbacks. We left earlier than we'd meant to.

In our apartments, we read fliers from the Gay Men's Health Crisis. We drafted care schedules—Nick organized Peter's with trading-floor efficiency. We found ourselves making redundant copies in the middle of the night. We stood next to the copier thinking about Peter, and how little we'd ever thought of him before. We remembered how, through all the years of our raucous libidinousness toward Nick, he was never once afraid of us. We remembered that he'd been a veteran. We allowed ourselves to be comforted by this fact.

We sent away for vitamins advertised in the back of magazines. They cost a fortune—but an ounce of prevention, etc. etc., and that was when there *was* a cure. What we had were treatments. There was co-trimoxazole and Compound Q and pentamidine, supplied through a special arrangement with the government. There were vitamin "perfusions"—neologism-zero, perhaps, in what would become a secondary epidemic—and there were strategies and schemes, for those who could afford them. We knew a man who went to Sloan-Kettering every other day. We knew a man who went on disability and lived off the interest from his trust fund. We knew Peter, who'd enrolled in studies run by two doctors who each would have disqualified him if they'd known of the other. A period of subterfuge commenced—chaotic taking of cabs, slightly hysterical fear of discovery—all of it reminiscent, perversely, of a French farce. We laughed about this—with Peter before he died, and then among ourselves afterward. This was the last, best thing that Peter's money ever bought him.

In January, he gave up, and abruptly quit both studies. Later we heard that Nick had taken him to Switzerland to have his blood recycled. We liked to imagine Peter sitting on a mountaintop, feverish and red-cheeked and straight out of Thomas Mann, which we further liked to imagine he had read. We liked to imagine him breathing the crystalline air; we liked to imagine him laughing. We liked to imagine him eyeing the youths on the ski slopes to the very last. We liked to imagine he hadn't yet gone blind.

WE WENT TO GMHC STUDY GROUPS. WE WENT TO MEETUPS. WE WENT TO SEE *Tootsie*.

Arguments were advanced and rebutted, mischaracterized and willfully misunderstood.

It was said that closing bathhouses was a slippery slope. Today the tubs, tomorrow your bedroom!

It was said that you were more likely to die in a car crash than of AIDS. (Brookie said: "In *Manhattan*?")

It was said that an obsession with promiscuity was blaming the victim.

It was said that the newfound devotion to monogamist handwringing was a form of complicity in a sexual fascism masquerading as public health concern—which was all the more threatening precisely *because* it deployed the vocabulary of reason. This was one of the most efficient ways to affect widespread evil, as the Nazis knew too well.

It was said, by Stephen: "Here we go again with the Nazis."

It was said, by Brookie: "You'll see."

CERTAIN SYMPTOMS WERE SEMAPHORES.

KS bumps behind the ears. White fungi blooming around fingernails. Weight loss so violent it could only be the first phase of decomposition. These were suddenly everywhere—on the subway, at the parties. On the body of a man you'd fucked, when you flipped on the lights.

But there were subtler, more ambiguous tells, if you knew where to look.

There was the riddle of swollen lymph nodes. (But if your immune system is fighting, doesn't it mean you still have one?) There was the question of small, seemingly inconsequential maladies—a bad tooth, an anal fissure. There was the epistemological conundrum posed by fucking *psoriasis*—which could be caused by stress, meaning you could actually give yourself some of the symptoms just by worrying about whether or not you had them.

And what if this extended to the whole thing? What if we were in a panic—a mass hysteria, a run on the banks? What if we were fleeing a phantom, and dying in the terrified stampede?

It was said that underneath the hospitals, there were bodies unclaimed in the morgues.

THE DYING BEGAN AT THE MARGINS. THE VERY FIRST FUNERAL MIGHT HAVE been for someone we'd never even met. The deceased was a man who'd been casually fucking someone we used to casually fuck, perhaps, back when anybody did anything casually. We were still innocent enough to be impressed by the awkwardness of this: our friend had been fucking this guy, and then he fucking *died*. It was still novel, that musical-chairs quality of death—the time comes up and we must sit where we stand, with all our contingencies reified (date on headstone, photo in obituary, cause of death on autopsy). There is no guarantee that this freeze-frame will happen to capture the most *conclusive* version of one's life.

This is how our friend came to be sitting in a dingy funeral parlor on the Lower East Side, making terrorized small talk with the maiden aunts of a man he'd never loved—had perhaps not even particularly liked, we considered now with some horror. The boy in the coffin, we saw, was very young—a little *too* young for our friend, we thought, even if he was apparently not too young to die. We wondered what the thing between them had been; we wondered if, after all, it hadn't been a little predatory. We glanced nervously at the dead boy—at his criminal, newly permanent fragility—and then at our friend, still talking to the aunts. We'd never known this man to be cruel—really, we'd hardly known him at all. But then, here was this boy, dead in the box, while our friend remained blatantly, almost tastelessly alive. It was hard not to have suspicions.

But this, we knew, was unfair. We could not blame our friend for being alive; were we not alive ourselves? Theirs had probably been a typical sort of thing, uncomplicatedly carnal, maybe getting just a bit embarrassing in its final lap. Maybe our friend had already been looking forward to forgetting the details. But then the boy went and died, and there was no forgetting anything. Because what could any of it matter—love or lust or searing indifference or destructively in-choate desire? When you had been alive with someone for a time, all other distinctions became negligible.

We were realizing that we did not really belong at this funeral. We'd gone out of curiosity—we knew that even then—and then got bored, and began telling ourselves a story. It was disrespectful; we understood that. Our punishment is to be able to recall the whole thing now with idiotic precision, when there are other funerals we'd rather remember better. Due to sheer volume, this eventually be-came impossible; the memories melted down and averaged out, the specifics collapsed into prototype, and recalling them feels as lonely as visiting a mass grave.

But we had no idea how many funerals we'd go to in the end. We didn't know they'd wind up blurring into an endless sensory loop—cloying smell of lilies, cheap hum of dirge—like the most tedious of recurring nightmares. We didn't know that, while we were coming up with some interesting new ways to die, there are really only so many ways to grieve. We couldn't have imagined that, before long, we'd know them all.

IT WAS DURING THE BLACK PLAGUE THAT THEY FIRST STARTED MARKING THE dead. We'd heard this from somebody once, and maybe it was true. For a time, we kept a running tally of our own. There was Peter, his ashes scattered off in Switzerland. The guy who worked at the video store on University Place; we'd been taking his recommendations for years. A kid we'd nicknamed the Butterfly, though no one remembered why: once, we'd seen him everywhere. His real name, we read in the paper, was Martin. One actor from the company, then another—by the end there would be four, two of them quite good, as well as the sour-faced stage manager we'd never even dreamed was gay.

"And all along I thought I was shocking *him,*" said Paulie, and this was one of the last things he ever said.

AND YET LET IT BE SAID THAT WE STILL WENT TO PARTIES! There were never any AIDS "patients" in attendance; we spoke with a new, final enlightenment of "People with AIDS." We were living in an era of acronym—GRID, A-I-D-S, AIDS, PWAs, FUO, PCP, KS, OI, ARC—and dense, ever-evolving jargon. Conversation was euphemism without subtext. We embraced all updates to the dialectic, believing in the progress soon to follow.

Though this was not the only theoretical model on offer; from other corners, stranger voices whispered.

It was said to be an invention of the government—something conjured in a lab by the right wing, or maybe the Pentagon.

It was said to be a Cold War initiative. It was said the Russians thought so, too.

It was said to be real, but mystical in its origins. It was said to be a curse from King Tut's tomb.

It was said to have been spread by a French flight attendant who traveled the world, sleeping with men under cover of darkness, announcing when the lights came on that he was dying of the gay cancer and that now they would, too.

"Oh please," said Paulie. "Does he wear a cape?"

"And does he slash teenage lovers with a hook?"

"And does he tie damsels to the tracks while twirling his mustache?"

"And is he calling from *inside the house*?"

It was said to be real, but metaphorical—conjured by the sheer force of American puritanism. It was said that when Foucault received his diagnosis, he laughed.

It was said that the flight attendant was not French, but French Canadian. Or French Guianan? French something, anyway. This seemed right, which did not make it true.

"Who's gonna make their sexy folk devil *German*?" said Brookie, tapping his head. "I mean, think about it."

It was said that the media weren't talking about it enough, and where the hell was *The New York Times*?

It was said that the media were talking about it too much, and where the hell were they for the good news?

It was said that the media had actually invented it, when you really thought about it. Because illness was a universal human problem; the special specter we called AIDS was nothing but moralism and yellow journalism and tabloid paranoia—a form of highly literal blood libel. It was said that to accept the prevailing narrative was to participate in this.

It was said (by Stephen) to be real, but psychological: a somatic manifestation of the death wish. It was said that those who died were the ones who'd hated themselves the most.

It was said by Brookie—once, and only once—"Then why the hell are you still here?"

———

CAUSES OF DEATH, PROXIMATE:

Suicide, in ones or twos.

Homicide, like the man in Italy who shot his family because they'd come down with what turned out to be the flu.

Failure of the pancreas.

Aspiration of mucus into the lungs.

Organ failure, complete.

CAUSES OF DEATH, STATED:

Sleeping sickness (Perry Ellis).

Liver cancer (Roy Cohn).

Encephalitis (on our death certificates).

A long illness (in our obituaries: this was the single ailment almost no one ever got).

CAUSE OF DEATH, ULTIMATE: HUMAN IMMUNODEFICIENCY VIRUS (HIV).

We knew our enemy's name now; we had even given it an acronym.

THE WORD WAS THAT HOPE, LIKE LIFE, WAS ELSEWHERE.

As ever, optimism centered on Europe. It was said that the American government expected a cure from France; it was said the Germans expected it from America. (*And only thirty years after the Marshall Plan!* sniffed the ghost of someone's grandmother from somewhere.) Auden went to Oxford. Santayana went to see some Roman nuns. There was a feeling that if Europe could not cure you, it could at least let you die reasonably. It was said that in France, you got psych counseling with your diagnosis.

San Francisco was spoken of with new reverence. They had a community, an organized political presence; they had the gestures of an improvisational, pre-apocalyptic culture. It wasn't all bingo and Gay AA and canasta clubs, either; we'd heard of themed J.O. nights, inspired by the sexual ordeals of youth (we imagined Boy Scouts, summer camp, that outdoor theater where we had to play opposite Maximilian Snyder in a toga every night for three weeks, trying to deliver lines while suppressing onstage erection). Yes, out in San Francisco, they were making the best of things. Everyone was threatening to move there, which is maybe why Brookie finally stopped.

Yes, we told ourselves: this was why.

IT WAS SAID BY LARRY KRAMER THAT WE SHOULD STOP SCREWING.

It was said by the CDC that we should limit our screwing.

It was said that we could keep screwing, just as long our partners were healthy.

It was said that we could keep screwing, just as long as what we did did not cause bleeding.

It was said that celibacy was unhealthy.

It was said that giving advice about safe sex was to collaborate with the death regime.

It was said a star had it. Someone you wouldn't think of, someone kind of butch.

It was said interferon might be the new best hope.

It was said the incubation period might be up to eighteen months.

It was said that Liberace was suffering complications from a watermelon diet.

It was said the star might be Burt Reynolds.

It was said that airtight seals should be placed on our coffins.

It was said by the New York State Funeral Directors Association that its members should not embalm our bodies.

It was said by Pat Buchanan that gay teachers should be fired.

It was said by bathroom graffiti: STOP NIGGERS SPREADING AIDS.

It was said by William F. Buckley, Jr., that we should have our HIV statuses tattooed on our arms.

It was said you could still get a drink at the Lion's Head, even if they could tell you were sick.

It was said by Ronald Reagan: nothing.

It was said by Brookie: "See?"

———

IT WAS A TIME OF SECRET ICONOGRAPHIES. WE CARRIED LINGAMS AND ROSA-ries, rabbits' feet and crystals. We sent away for mail-order injections, for megadoses of vitamin C. Paulie wore worry beads, though he mostly kept them under his shirt; he adopted a macrobiotic diet and spoke mistily of "going to the other side." Peter began to polish his war medals, and then display them. Toward the end he produced his uniform, and displayed that, too, on a hanger. ("And now he wants 'Taps' at his memorial," Nick had whispered, mystified.)

We ate health food; we wore earth tones. We watched wellness visualization tapes. We may have prayed a couple times, but you'll never get us to admit it.

We will admit to calling sex lines. We'll admit we omed into white lights.

BUT THEN, THERE WERE THE UNFORESEEN ADVANTAGES!

Announcing you had AIDS was like pulling out a loaded weapon. Some guy actually robbed a bank this way. Paulie, inspired, used it to chase away a mugger.

And then, there were the extra police at the pride parade.

And then, there were the reconciliations: ones we'd thought would never come, ones we'd thought were coming long ago, ones that never actually materialized but did, until the very end, seem possible. Because anything at all was possible: we understood that now.

IT WAS SAID THAT YOU SHOULD GO TO THE ER IF YOU GOT TURNED AWAY AT ST. Vincent's. It was said the law said they had to take you.

It was said that Rock Hudson had gone to Paris. It was said he might be cured!

It was said that this was a mistake.

It was said there might be promising drugs in Mexico.

It was said the Mexican drugs were not effective.

It was said they *were* effective, and the powers-that-be knew it, and that this is why they were illegal: because they might put the medical establishment out of business.

It was said that you could sell them at a considerable markup in San Francisco either way.

It was said there was a house on Fire Island whose every last tenant had died.

It was said that homophobia was the greatest threat to gay health.

It was said there was a Buddhist abbey north of Bangkok where monks tended to the unclaimed ashes of the dead.

It was said you were lucky if it didn't go to your lungs.

AIDS WAS A STORY THAT STARTED WITHOUT YOU, LONG BEFORE YOU REALIZED you were in a story at all. We scoured our pasts for points of entry; we scanned obituaries for names. We thought of our trips to California, to the bathhouses in San Francisco. We thought of the gorgeous muscle-shirted Puerto Rican. But then, this disease didn't get where it was by being obvious. And so we considered the inverse—men and moments that seemed counterintuitive, if not straightforwardly benign. What about the aging hippie we'd met at the Palladium? It had been a "Golden Oldies Night" and we'd gone as sort of a joke. Maybe *that* was the beginning.

Or perhaps a sleeker sort of irony was afoot here. Perhaps we *had* gotten it in San Francisco, but maybe not from the men—maybe it was from the shot of methedrine we'd been persuaded to try there. A pretty Chinese boy had wrapped surgical tubing around our bicep until the vein bulged; maybe this had been the fatal penetration.

We were beginning to understand the Aristotelian anomaly at work here. AIDS was both a fatal flaw and a rising action—leading inexorably to the cathartic crisis called death—yet there was no discerning its inciting event. But half of us were going blind like Oedipus, and didn't we deserve to know why? Habeas corpus, we bellowed! This is America.

PAULIE LINGERED LONGER THAN ANYONE HAD EXPECTED—DESCENDING WITH exquisite, almost imperceptible slowness, like a predator after its prey. Just when we thought we'd come to terms with some new phase of his absence (*What terms?* we wondered manically. *Define them, define them!*)—just when we thought we'd jettisoned inappropriate hope and superstition—he'd wake up just enough to show us we were wrong. We were always surprised, though never surprised enough; we saw that we had, on some level, been awaiting his resurrection.

Sometimes they're waiting for something, murmured one of the nurses. We worried that he might be waiting for us to give up. And so we tried, and vowed we had, and then he'd stir and show us that we had not, and we'd weep and promise to do better. And so, in the end, he must have given up on us.

When it finally happened, we shouted insanely at the nurse. She'd been a saint throughout; we thought that we might hit her. We had a wild urge to pull the fire alarm. The nurse brought us water in a plastic pitcher. Brookie wept until he actually spit up, which was one of the few emissions we'd not yet seen in a hospital.

When the stethoscoped man finally came to do the time of death, Paulie had been gone for at least a half an hour. We kept asking the stethoscoped man if this mattered. Very kindly, he told us it did not.

And even then, we could not be entirely convinced. We stole glances at Paulie's chest; we caught each other doing it. And so what if we were! At this point, we were beyond taking anyone's word for anything. If Paulie was so sure he was dead, then he was going to have to prove it.

AND HE DID, EVERY DAY, FOR YEARS AND YEARS, UNTIL FINALLY WE BELIEVED, and required proof no longer. Enough is enough, we'd think—when finding his curling Streisand poster in a box of tax returns, when hearing some awful show tune and inexplicably knowing all the words. Okay, we'd think, we get it. You're gone and we'll miss you forever. Now, enough. Show's over. Off the stage!

The lesson is, never encourage a ham.

The other lesson is, never issue a dare to a dead person. They've got all the time in the world.

IT WAS SAID, AT LAST, THERE WAS A TEST.

It was said the test yielded no new information: the single-virus theory was, after all, just a theory.

It was said: "Like gravity is a theory? Or like Freudian theory is a theory?"

It was said the test yielded inaccurate information: it issued false positives for liver damage, LSD use, vaccines.

It was said the test yielded irrelevant information: HIV did not cause AIDS. Do your homework, it was said! It was said, follow the money.

It was said the people who said this were denialists and idiots, lunatics and murderers—though who *wasn't* being called a murderer in those days?

It was said the test yielded redundant information: because what, fundamentally, did it tell you? All it told you was that you would die someday; all it told you was the single thing that could be said with certainty about everyone. The test flipped a trick coin and called its prediction prophecy; to submit to its verdict was to participate in an epistemological con.

It was said the test yielded too much information: it was a biological aleph, revealing not only what you had, but who you were. ("The thing in the tube literally turns purple," said Brookie.) It was said this information was likely to be of interest to insurers, to employers—maybe even prosecutors, in the twenty-five states where it was still illegal to exist. And sure, maybe *San Francisco* would get around to passing some reasonable protections—but we should be clear by now that New York, being half run by closet cases, was not going to be getting its shit together in that or any regard. And *anyway,* if your paranoia stopped at criminal prosecution, then you needed to reacquaint yourself with the twentieth century. It was said that medical concentration camps could be next.

It was said, by Stephen: "Not a chance. People wouldn't stand for it."

It was said, by Brookie: "What people? You're telling me *Reagan* wouldn't?"

"Koch wouldn't."

"You're sure about that?"

"Well, forget Koch. New Yorkers wouldn't. And how would they pull that one over anyway? Just every fag in Greenwich Village disappears without anyone noticing?"

It was said that this was literally what was happening right now.

DID MATTHEW MILLER TAKE THE TEST RIGHT AWAY? HE HAD A SHOW ON WNYC by then, where he discussed the issues of the day. He still lived on West Fourth Street, as far as anyone knew, and he must have seen many of us by then: young people with peeling-off skin and highly visible chest IVs, their canes tapping tentatively over West Village cobblestones. And when he saw them, had he been afraid? Had he worried over moles, lingering colds, bruises he couldn't remember acquiring? Would he have known to worry that flying might trigger latent pneumonia, and the next week obsess over the possibility that last summer's sunburn might—even now—be fatally depressing his immune system? Had he been glad for another reason to avoid having sex with Alice? And had he thought back to that writer—the one he'd hired and then forgot to fire for a decade—and found himself wondering, for the very first time, how deep his sad, annoying loyalty had gone? His love had been a pleasure, and then a liability, and now maybe it would save Matthew Miller's life. Did he recognize the irony of this? Did it make him wretched with terror and regret? And is it wicked to hope that, at least for a time, it did?

BECAUSE THE RELIEF MATTHEW MILLER WOULD FEEL WHEN HE FINALLY TOOK the test—oh, for him, it would be so easy. In other quarters, things were not so simple.

The mostly unspoken corollary of *Why me?* is: *Why not you?*

Why not you?

Why the fuck not you?

Survival is a gruesome sort of blessing: one not to be trifled with, nor entirely longed for. It is not an easy fate to wish on anyone—not even Matthew Miller, not even yourself.

MANY OF OUR FINAL ILLNESSES CAME FROM THE ANIMALS: IN THE END, THEY claimed us for their kingdom.

On our bodies, warts mosaicked into scales; on our tongues, fur sprouted, rendering us dumb as beasts. Thorny corollas of herpes scabs made faces reptilian. There were the chameleon-like chromatics: blood leaking from capillaries, flushing skin to plum. The blue ichthyic hands of end-stage pneumonia. Backs speckled from thrombocytopenic purpura, making human men look venomous—like snakes or lizards or those strange little octopuses in Thailand you can step on without noticing and then die from four hours later.

These were the final insults, our last dismissals from the human family. We died of bird tuberculosis, pigeon-toed and flightless, hobbling on forked passerine feet. We died of toxoplasmosis, foaming at the mouth like rabid dogs. Perhaps it is universal—this sense of chimerical morphing. We are all made creaturely in death. And yet it is a very particular loneliness to die from a disease meant for sheep or cats, from a parasite that was never even after you in the first place. It was something like dying in outer space, your body condemned to float out beyond the carbon cycle, through eternities not our own.

TO THE END, THERE WERE THE PERVERSE BEAUTIES. NOT ONLY THE MORAL kind—the kindnesses, the sacrifices, the depths of human bravery and goodness, all the abstractions we either found or pretended to find inspiring (*inspiring:* such a terrifying concept, implying similar feats might one day be expected of us all). There were also those moments of concrete prettiness; images that appealed, almost reflexively, to our vestigial sense of the aesthetic. Paulie's limpid, hollowed-out face in the moonlight, a couple days before he died. The perfect symmetry of the wen on Brookie's shoulder, like a coin pressed into skin. The fearful elegance of the lentivirus itself: its shape, its strategy of haunting.

All this wreckage and suffering, all this otherworldly ugliness and waste—amidst all of this, we were denied even the purity of our horror. In those moments of loveliness, we'd remember that this apocalypse was not complete, and thus not inevitable.

And this was a violence of another order.

EIGHTEEN
cel

"LUKE, IT WAS AN AMBUSH," SAYS CEL ON TUESDAY MORNING. SHE IS IN HIS office again. She cannot remember showing up, or knocking, but here she is; the facts must speak for themselves.

Cel's voicemail had been completely full that morning. There were messages from journalists of every variety of credibility and decency; some were left at odd hours, from reporters with heavy accents. The Ohio shooting itself hadn't registered much beyond American media—the global press seeming to regard American gun violence as a bewildering, highly niche concern—but the story of Mattie's opinions about it is, apparently, of worldwide interest. The European journalists had a lot of questions about the *Mein Kampf* comment; the Americans were mostly interested in Mattie's gun remarks. The NRA has issued a statement about the comments, and many of the reporters wanted Cel to comment about that. She'd listened to the messages fretfully, with a dim, half-guilty sense of excitement.

"It was completely unacceptable," she says. "*Beyond* a cheap shot. But really? In the long run? It's their fuckup." Cel tries to say this in the authoritative voice that rich people say such things—as though her personal displeasure implies significant fallout. "And in the long run? It's gonna cost *them*."

Cel has expected Luke to yell, but he says nothing, only pores serenely over a stack of photos. His silence compounds the eerie quiet of the building: this is normally the time of day when the lights are tested, the guests are prepped. Tomorrow, filming will resume with a drag queen beauty contest—an anodyne throwback that makes Cel think snobbishly of Mattie M's competitors.

"There will be consequences," she adds randomly, in a severe, vaguely Old Testament sort of voice. Still Luke says nothing. Cel does not like this newly passive, inert Luke; it has the feel of something worse than the calm before the storm—the desiccated beach before the tsunami, perhaps.

"I mean, Luke, I'm not going to bullshit you." Luke likes when people say this sort of thing. "We'll be playing defense for days."

"What do you think of her for wronged wife?" Luke is holding up a picture of a woman with teased hair and bifocals. "Too confusing?"

"What?" says Cel. "Oh. I think so, yeah. What are those *glasses?*"

"I know." Luke considers the photo sadly, then puts it down. "How about her?" He holds up another. "Too sexy?"

"What? I mean, yes, probably. Wait, why are *you* doing this?"

"I've given myself a demotion."

"Oh." Cel hadn't realized this was an option. "Does Mattie know?"

Luke issues a snort like a teakettle. "Does Mattie *know.*" He says it decisively, as though this comment explains itself. "*Mattie,* thank God, is not my problem anymore."

"Did you quit?" says Cel. This comes out sounding alarmed, which makes less than zero sense.

"Ha, no," he says. "You aren't that lucky. They're bringing in someone external."

"Oh." Cel has heard of this sort of thing—studios hiring someone to echo the prevailing views more stridently than anyone in-house would dare.

"Which doesn't mean you're fired, necessarily," says Luke. "Though it doesn't necessarily mean you're not."

"Ah," says Cel. She hadn't thought to care.

"But he's not listening to us," says Luke. "So let's see if he listens to someone else."

"Sort of a wait-till-your-father-gets-home scenario."

"Well, I wouldn't know, but sure."

"Who is it?"

"Eddie Marcus. From Advantage Consulting. Mattie wanted him. Apparently they go way back."

"Back to what?"

"The less we know about that, the better. But, Cel, to be completely honest?"

Cel gestures *By all means,* even though he isn't looking.

"To be honest, I can't see it mattering. From what I've heard, this Marcus guy isn't very credible. Maybe Mattie really is just bringing him in to Kevorkian this whole thing. Which honestly? Is fine by me. Just as long as it's humane and I don't have to know the details." Luke spins around in his chair. The back of his neck is paler than the rest of him, and his exposing it feels like a strange form of vulnerability—as though he's a beta predator admitting defeat. "Although I have to say if that's the plan, then you were doing a pretty good job of it already."

He spins back around, and gives Cel a look like he's caught her giving *him* a look. Which maybe she was? These days, almost anything seems possible.

"You know, I haven't been entirely fair to you, Cel," he says. This sarcasm is cross-cutting in so many directions that it might not even be sarcasm at all. "All this time I've been thinking you were terrible at your job. But that depends entirely on what your job actually is! As a publicist, it is true, you are extraordinarily incompetent. But I look at this kamikaze mission Mattie's on now, and I wonder if maybe I've got it all backwards. Maybe he hired you to help him crash this thing. In which case, I'll be the first to say, well done!"

Luke pulls out another photo. He regards it for a long while, his fingers drumming against his chin. Outside, volute-shaped clouds drift through a painfully blue sky.

"Is that—are you playing a *sonata* or something?" says Cel.

He stops.

"Why did I even come in here?"

"I don't know," says Luke. "All I know is that today I'm judging beauty contests." He flutters the photographs. "If you want to help out, we're still short on tiaras."

———

CEL DECIDES TO WALK, SINCE IT SEEMS THAT NO ONE WILL CARE. SHE HEADS south, past tourists in culottes, girls in Bettie Page bangs. A woman led by an army of officious dachshunds. Old men playing chess in the park, using bottle caps as pawns. An economy old Hal would have liked. One of them, with gray-matted hair and a bright red nose, winks at her.

In front of the Sunshine Hotel, she's almost run over by a taxi. "Watch where you're going!" the cabbie shouts, and Cel is nearly touched by the depth of his anger. Once in Times Square she saw a man scream *Look the fuck out!* just before a bus nearly barreled through another man in a crosswalk. Afterward the shouting man's terror had morphed into a sort of trembling apoplexy; he could barely bring himself to shake the other man's hand.

Cel becomes aware of an umber cast to the light; across the street, men are packing up their drums. She scurries underneath an awning promising BABES GO-GO GIRLS BEAUTIFUL LADIES, moments before the rain hits. She waits. When the rain downshifts, Cel makes a dash to the sidewalk, almost slamming into a woman walking her dog. The woman, Cel sees, is crying. Cel scrambles away before fully registering the other details (leash wrapped three times around wrist of one hand, half-smoked cigarette in the other), muttering apologies she knows will be drowned out by the dopplering honks of what seems—but cannot really be?—a single spectacularly outraged taxi.

CEL IS HOME EARLY ENOUGH TO DO LAUNDRY—WHICH, BY GOD, SHE DOES! BY the time she gets back to the apartment again, she is panting, her legs like aspic: six months in New York and she still hasn't managed to master her own stairs. She leans against the wall, thigh muscles twitching, before fishing out her key. The key is strictly a formality: their lock is so easily picked that Cel had taken to using her Smith ID for a while until Nikki proclaimed this bad for morale.

Inside, the floorboards croak boisterously—Cel always feels a bit reproached by them—and today, this feeling is compounded by the sight of Elspeth, sitting primly on the sofa.

"Well, well," she says.

"Oh, hi!" says Cel, dropping her laundry basket.

"You forgot about me," says Elspeth. "Why are you *wet*?"

"I was at the Laundromat and my clothes didn't dry. I didn't *forget*." Cel hangs these statements together as though one supports the other: no one can say she has learned nothing from working in television.

"Did you use the dryer I told you?" says Nikki, emerging from her room.

"Yes," says Cel, dropping onto the sofa. "I even took someone else's stuff out. I had to touch so much whimsical underwear, and it still didn't work."

"You're, like, *leaking* cold water," says Elspeth.

Cel throws her a blanket and pats her on the head. Elspeth is wearing the usual—flowered skirt, clunky glasses, bafflingly large sneakers. Her green skunkish-striped hair is arranged into stalagmitic points.

"Nice hair," says Cel. "You look like the Statue of Liberty. I guess you've met Nikki."

"I have *indeed* met Nikki," says Elspeth. "She was just telling me about her, um, pants?"

"It's a skort," says Nikki. "Like, it looks like a skirt? But underneath it are shorts."

"The wonders of New York."

"Oh, I'm sure you can get them everywhere," says Nikki. "Even Massachusetts."

Elspeth kicks Cel under the blanket.

"I thought you were supposed to be here later," says Cel.

"I was *supposed* to be here at noon," says Elspeth. "I left you a message and everything."

"Sorry. It's been kind of—hectic around here."

"I can imagine. Well, no, actually, I can't. Anyway, I had so much time to kill I wound up waiting for student rush tickets to *Phantom*. Then I actually *got* them, and I called and you *still* weren't home, so I had no choice but to actually *go*."

"You did?"

"My God, the daddy issues in that thing! It's like Freudianism set to song! Have you seen it?"

"I have," says Nikki. "A couple times."

"Isn't it hilarious?" says Elspeth. "And I mean, disturbing, obviously."

"I think it's romantic," says Nikki.

Elspeth looks at Cel with an expression of blunt disorientation, as though she's gotten off at the wrong bus stop. Cel pats her foot reassuringly.

"I'm sorry I forgot," she says.

"You said you didn't forget."

"I know," says Cel. "I'm sorry about that, too."

ON WEDNESDAY, THE CPA CALLS FOR A BOYCOTT OF *THE MATTIE M SHOW.*

"A boycott!" says Luke on the phone. "Well, why not, right? First apartheid South Africa, now us!"

The boycott makes the first hour of the *Today* show: already it is clear that offscreen, something real is beginning. The CPA's targeting seems reasonably savvy—pitched at companies conservative enough to be sympathetic to the cause, successful enough to consider withdrawing their business, and big enough to hurt the show badly if they did. These are the companies that have never been thrilled to be advertising on *Mattie* to begin with, but for whom, until now, the calculations have been relatively straightforward—not only because the ads reliably move sales, but also because *Mattie's* viewership is wide enough to serve as a proxy for public opinion. *Mattie* is just too popular to be a branding liability, no matter what any of the advertisers think privately; for this reason *Mattie* regularly wins business from "family-friendly" companies who shun considerably milder shows with somewhat smaller audiences. But now, it seems, the calculus is shifting.

On her way to Luke's office, Cel nearly trips over the new publicist.

"Excuse me," she says, and the man nods magnanimously. His hair is cicatrized with something she can only hope is gel, and Cel can tell from just looking at him that he has absolutely always been rich. What is it, the way a person with money seems the host of every room he enters?

By way of greeting, Luke hands Cel a Coke with a straw. She's been a straw fanatic ever since reading an article about pull tabs and rat urine. She keeps accidentally bringing this up at parties. Suzanne Bryanson is on TV again, looking marginally more polished—she's invested in some decent makeup, at least a bit of eyebrow intervention. Ominous upgrades, she thinks, implying a commitment to the long haul.

"I can't imagine what Mattie meant with that comment," Suzanne Bryanson is saying. They must be talking about Mattie's *Mein Kampf* remarks. *"But I do know it is ultimately a distraction. That conversation is the same as the endless debate about the authenticity of Mattie's fights. But that's not really the point, is it? The point is that we want those people to have been hurt. We feel entitled to the reality of that violence."*

It's obvious that much of this is memorized, though Cel doubts many people will notice, and she truly can't imagine who will care.

"We are disappointed as consumers if it is fake," says Suzanne Bryanson. *"And over time, this deadens us to pain. It contributes to a sort of latent mass sociopathy in the culture."*

Cel has never seem someone attempt such Gettysburg-ian loftiness on television, let alone pull it off.

"I cannot listen to this shit," says Luke, turning off the TV.

"I met the publicist," says Cel.

"Well, allow me to kiss your ring." He stares into the hallway, where aerial hoop performers twirl sedately. They're here to entertain the audience during commercials, but the juvenile delinquent episode has been canceled yet again—and so once again there is no audience, and the twirlers twirl for no one.

"Will it shock you if I'm not overly optimistic about that guy?" says Luke.

"I think I'm pretty much beyond shock at this point."

"Ha!" says Luke. "Don't let Mattie hear you say that. He'll take it as some kind of dare."

———

THE BOYCOTT MAKES THE NIGHTLY NEWS, THEN THE ELEVEN O'CLOCK, THEN— weirdly—the *Tonight Show* monologue.

"Turn that off," says Elspeth. "Go to bed."

"I am," says Cel. "I will."

She doesn't. Instead, she watches the midnight rerun of *Mattie M* on the NBC affiliate. Tonight's *Forbidden Passion* is about the brother and sister. They're actually sort of sweet, those two: young and reasonably attractive, by *Mattie M* guest standards: their resemblance faint enough to register only as looking good together. They'd held hands even when the camera was off, Cel remembers.

She watches until the booing starts, then turns it off and tries to sleep.

semi

IN JANUARY, WE GATHERED BLANKETS AND MEDS AND WENT OUT TO SEE THE comet. In the park, they'd turned off all the lights. Stephen said it didn't do that much for the stars.

"So, what?" said Brookie. "You want to catch this thing the next time?"

We huddled together, shivering for our various reasons. We stood amongst bond traders and dark-lipsticked lesbians and young men with skin flaking off their faces, men who did not go out much anymore in the daytime. We stood amongst the drunken longtime homeless; the bewildered newer homeless, recently sprung from the hospitals. And then, there it was, baldly visible through the weft of branches: exactly as prophesied, and right on time.

"They can figure *that* out," said Brookie. "They can figure out how to put a man on the fucking moon!"

"I thought you didn't believe in that."

He sighed. "I believe in everything nowadays."

Above us, the comet was a glowing goetic arrow, streaking over its spectators and beyond: over the apartment in Chelsea and the little theater in the Village, over the hospital room where Paulie had died and the beach where we'd first met him. It sailed over the firelit oil drums in the Bronx and the nude dancers tonguing Plexiglas in Times Square; it sailed over newsstands selling I ❤ NY crack pipes and that monstrous new dormitory they were putting up on Third Avenue. It streaked over our newly transfigured haunts—the Everard Baths were now a shopping center, the Saint subsumed by NYU—as well as the city's many mad renovations. They had replaced every single china mosaic at the entrance to Bethesda Terrace; they had redone the Crotona Park Pool—where, in another alleged lifetime, a young Matthew Miller had played. For let it not be said that our government was doing nothing for us! Let us render unto Caesar all the credit he deserves!

Yes, in the world beyond our hospital rooms, New York was lurching itself back to life. The comet streaked over the new boutiques in Park Slope, the skyscrapers distorting the long-static skyline, the bistros winking along Columbus Avenue. Columbus Avenue used to be a slum where servants lived with their carriage horses: Matthew Miller told me this once, and for all I knew, it could be true. There have, of course, been stranger resurrections.

"It's nice to see something no one else will see again, either," said Brookie.

IT WAS A TIME OF PROPHECIES AND PILGRIMAGES.

We flocked to the faiths of our childhoods, or else invented our own. We spoke of deities and demiurges, undines and alchemy. We marveled at the second law of thermodynamics; at the fact that, on a different day each year, all the ginkgo trees in New York City bloom quietly, synchronically, in the night.

It was a time of cultic initiation—of underground studies and buyers' clubs. It was a time of Hail Marys. There was peptide T, albendazole, oral amphotericin B, dextran sulfate—drugs that almost certainly wouldn't save you, but that probably wouldn't kill you, which was more than you could say for most things, those days.

It was a time of mass conversion. Young people's sense of immortality is widely thought incorrigible, but this doesn't match with my notes—another footnote for the anthropologists, who are, after all, our eulogists. The young may be skeptical of mortality, but they can be persuaded—it only takes a generation watching itself go extinct.

Beyond this, transformations varied. Some of us were seized by serenity heretofore unthinkable. Bitchy cynics beamed from underneath their covers, speaking in slogans and sincerity. The chronically conflicted were finally certain, radiating the sort of deep ataraxia they'd never found in Valium. There were the reifying effects of illness, compounded by the body's vanishing. By the end, our people were so skeletal they could only be martyrs—prisoners of conscience; wild-eyed prophets wandering the desert; victims of the sorts of evils that always shock the world, though only, of course, in retrospect.

THE OTHER SYMPTOMS WERE THE SIDE EFFECTS.

Paulie: nearly comatose from antibiotics, which anyway were failing. Bright purple tumors clustered in his gums. His breath scraping its Sisyphean way to the surface—which was, we kept telling ourselves, a sound we wanted to keep hearing.

Nick's chest, still vaguely gorgeous, puckered where they'd lasered off his lesions. His abdomen stapled where they'd removed part of his liver. He was glad it wasn't his stomach; other people, he said, were not so lucky.

Brookie, shaking from interferon. Stripes tigering his arms, for what reason we may have never asked. We were coming to accept these sorts of things; we were learning.

IT WAS SAID THE DOUBLE-BLIND STUDIES WERE SOMETHING TO CONSIDER. AN even-odds shot at a placebo: oh, what the hell, at this point.

It was said that the double-blind studies were sadistic. It was said that it was *perverse* to let your life become a controlled variable, your suffering a sunk cost, your death the foregone conclusion against which other, more surprising outcomes might be gauged. And then to spend eternity as a data point in some ambitious creep's paper!

It was said that all of this was a necessary constituent of publishable medical data. It was said one might as well be useful.

It was said that we would make ourselves useful to science just as soon as science made itself useful to us.

It was said that dying usefully was a last chance to live meaningfully, for anyone who hadn't gotten around to it yet.

It was said that what had just been said was unforgivable, and that the sanctimonious *fuck* who said it deserved the goddamned sugar pill.

It was said that nobody had meant any of this—not a word, not a word, not a single useless word.

THERE WAS STILL SEX, OF A KIND.

Sex was Clorox and nonoxynol-9; mutual masturbation at great distances. Sex was hydrogen peroxide and coming into the air. Sex was inspectors from the Department of Consumer Affairs flooding the bathhouses, hectoring everyone about voluntary compliance.

Brookie: "That's when you have a safe word, right?"

Sex was jack-off clubs and safe sex signage, safe sex pledges, safe sex lit. Sex for some of us was still just sex: Stephen went to the bathhouses until they closed and then went other places instead. "Bernie Goetz," we called him fondly: our very own Death Wish Vigilante.

Or maybe sex was somewhere else entirely, in the other profane sacraments. Kneading the skin of a hyper-articulated spine. Whisking iodine along a nipple. Sex was in the wishbone silhouette of jutting ilia, the phallic morphology of a keloidal scar. Sex was in the lytic cycle itself—its penetration, its intimacy. Sex was a hand cupped lightly around a single bony finger, a calyx of supplication: as futile and fleeting as love itself.

WE CALLED TO HEAR THE SOUND OF THE PHONE RINGING. WE CALLED TO SEE who would still pick up. We called for hospital room numbers and funeral arrangements and hometown mailing addresses. Cherry Cerise was from West Virginia! How had we never known that? She was going to get shit for that, all right, when she came back to New York.

We called to try to speak of other things. What did other people talk about? Well, the economy was tanking, for one thing. The murder rate was doubling, even if you didn't take our deaths into account, which nobody did. Other people worried about tainted Tylenol and Legionnaires' disease; they worried about leaking Freon gas from the skating rink in Central Park. They worried flagrantly over the little boy who fell into the polar bear cage at the Prospect Park Zoo, the lone jogger assaulted in the park.

"None of Us Is Safe," intoned the *New York Post*.

"Oh?" said Brookie mildly. "I hadn't heard."

We called to learn if we could stop by with a sandwich, and if not a sandwich, then with soup, and if not soup, then flowers, and if not flowers, then could we maybe just stop to say hello, and if not today, then tomorrow, or the next day, or the next?

We called to find out what we could do, and we called to be let off the hook.

We called to be told we might be needed; we called to be told we weren't, anymore.

THE FUNERALS CYCLED EVER FASTER; ON THE WEEKENDS, WE JUGGLED THEM like lovers. By now we were used to military-shiny coffins, to their sickeningly quilted interiors—we were beginning to have opinions on these things! We were familiar with the newest technological upgrades: the deceased appearing on video, in living color. We were used to the people who actually seemed surprised to be there—every funeral had one: a clueless parent, a well-intentioned boss, a teenage niece. Dramatic tension comes from the sense that events might unfold differently than they do: we watched tiredly as they grieved.

By the end there were funerals for so many people who were dead that you could hardly believe that once you'd known so many people who were alive. There was the painter from the Ansonia. There was Cherry Cerise. There was the stony-faced bouncer who'd once tormented us outside the Electric Circus—that one was drugs, we assumed (though we were trying not to assume things). Nick, his beautiful features distorted by steroids, whose family was poorer and much less afraid of us than we'd been expecting (though we were trying not to expect things, either).

Loss of this magnitude does not only remove; it subsumes, retroactively obliterates. If all this death was not a nightmare, then these lives, it would seem, had been our delusion. Had there really been so many of us, once? We did not think it could be true.

ONE SOMETIMES HEARS THAT THE DEAD APPEAR TO BE SLEEPING. THIS WAS not the case with ours. Our dead were so dead they were uncanny; they made death into works of high camp. Next to our dead, objects seemed animate.

Take, for example, a postcard of the *David*—saved for years for the very witticisms that you will shortly be reading to a room of assembled mourners. Your hands are shaking slightly, and the postcard along with it; you stare at the *David* accusingly. Paulie had loved this statue, loved that city. You've been there once yourself, to Florence, and marveled over the *David*'s aliveness. There is some impossible kinesis in his stillness—the sense of a flickering basilic vein, a still-twitching muscle, a ruddy, pulpy heart, caught just now between beats. This statue breathes—you can't believe he doesn't—every time you blink.

Consider this image—this representation of a representation of a man—and then consider the thing in the coffin before you. Look at its scarecrow arms, its putty skin; at its crude, uncanny shape— primitive and only dimly anthropoid, like a cave drawing or a voodoo doll. (*I look awful. You don't. I'm horrifying. I look like a thing that was never even supposed to be a person. You're not horrifying, and it doesn't matter how you look. Yes, I am, and yes, it does.*) Stare at this object for a moment, and then try to imagine it singing "I Just Called to Say I Love You" in a loud, morning-radio voice, sporting a pageboy haircut that doesn't quite work with its jawline. It had done this once, the shape, but recalling this now seems monstrous, nearly blasphemous: as though the person is an insult to the thing, and not the other way around.

Witness enough dying, and it's life that begins to seem like the heresy. Let the dead bury the dead, you think, and leave whatever's in the coffin alone.

IT WAS A TIME OF EXODUS.

We went to the Philippines for psychic surgery.

We went to Mexico to see holistic healers.

We went to Paris, to beg.

We went to Beth Israel, to beg.

We went to our parents, to beg.

We never left home and still never came back.

IT WAS SAID THAT AZT WAS A POISON.

It was said that AZT cost ten thousand dollars a year.

It was said that the virus had developed a resistance to AZT, though this was not reflected in the price.

It was said, by Brookie: "Not an inefficiency in the free market!"

It was said that our terror was *useful* to these people. And couldn't we see that? And couldn't we think what that *meant*? They are making fortunes selling us these poisons, which we gulp in unthinking gratitude. And then we wonder why we're dead!

PERHAPS THE POLITICAL IS ALWAYS PERSONAL; ONLY OCCASIONALLY IS IT terminal.

It was a time of collective action. It was a time of chanting.

ACT UP, Fight Back, Fight AIDS.

ACT UP, stand tall, tomorrow morning at City Hall.

AZT is not enough, give us all the other stuff.

It was a time of insurrection.

It was a time of throwing caution to the wind.

It was a time of empowerment.

It was a time of backs against the wall.

It was a time of militant pragmatism.

It was a time of radical concessions.

It was a time of war.

It was a time of when in Rome.

It was a time to ask politely.

It was a time to ask again.

It was a time to beg, if it came to it, but then it had been that time for a while.

It was a time of agitprop and spectacle: kiss-ins in hospital lobbies, pharmaceutical executives ambushed at their homes. Bodies in open coffins paraded past City Hall, supplicants dying-in at St. Patrick's Cathedral.

It was a time of actions speaking louder than words.

It was a time of silence speaking louder than words.

It was a time of anything speaking louder than words, because words were always cheap and anyway we were out of them.

It was becoming a time of imagery. A pink-eyed, rabid-looking Reagan on a poster. Bloody handprints on a sign. Over a hundred red balloons bobbing at the AZT pricing protest, and no Paulies anywhere to break into song.

THERE WERE, TO THE VERY END, THE PUNCH LINES.

Did you hear they officially discovered the cause of AIDS? It turned out to be track lighting on industrial gray carpet.

The guy who'd played Verkhovensky in *The Dispossessed:* "I'm not gonna take this lying down." He had to sit upright for a full twelve days before he died because of a lesion blocking his windpipe.

Paulie, purple from internal bleeding, the CMV running helter-skelter: "You should see the other guy."

How does Anita Bryant spell relief? A-I-D-S.

Another one from Verkhovensky: "When I'm gone, throw a party. I've already sat the shiva."

IT WAS SAID BY THE CATHOLIC CHURCH THAT CONDOMS ENCOURAGED IMMO-rality.

It was said by the bathroom graffiti: USE RUBBERS AND LIVE!

It was said by the CDC that AIDS was the leading cause of death of men under the age of forty-four.

It was said by Ed Koch: "How'm I Doin'?"

It was said by Stephen: "Keep your powder dry." This was said in his suicide note, so nobody could ask him what he meant.

SOME FATES ARE GENERATIONAL; DODGING THEM FEELS HISTORICALLY MORTI-fying. To keep showing up at funerals became a special sort of shame—like being an able-bodied British man strolling around the cricket pitch at the height of World War I.

But perhaps it was not too late for us! Test results told you what the body made known to the test: but bodies have a lot of tricks up their sleeves. Could we ever be completely sure we had been spared? Over time, this terror became a sort of hope. We'd compulsively re-visit the possibilities, the places where fate might have come to meet us. We'd long ago memorized the usual suspects—the slut, the sailor, the candlestick maker—though deep down, it was our happi-est nights we regarded with the most suspicion: first times with cherished lovers, best times with dearest friends. Over time, how-ever, this came to seem crudely childish—this crypto-capitalist su-perstition that whatever we valued most would cost us highly. Young people do not want to die for anything—but if we must, then let it be for *love*! No, we thought: that would be too easy. In later years, we thought instead of smaller moments—those accidental evenings we'd be ashamed to say we treasured.

The Halloween—this must have been in '81?—when we'd slept with a man dressed as Reagan: if AIDS had any sense of humor whatsoever, it'd be then. Greenwich Village flickered with lanterns and gleeful mischief, and we forgot we were supposed to be un-happy.

Or the night we'd taken a tab of MDA and danced to "Gloria" with a tubby little character actor, strictly off-off-Broadway.

Or laughing with a man in horn-rimmed glasses over something truly disgusting in the Bloomingdale's bathroom. We'd fucked in a stall a minute earlier. Now we were laughing so hard that the boys fucking in the *other* stall threatened to call the manager, which made us laugh even harder.

TO THE END, THERE WERE THE EXCEPTIONS: THE MIRACLES AND ANTI-miracles, the outliers and loopholes.

The diagnosed were dead within a year, except that Brookie wasn't.

People everywhere were monsters, except at that one spaghetteria in the Village where the staff were always kind to the dying, even when the dying were not at their best.

The dying were angels, except that once in a while, they were not.

The entire world had ended, except that here, still, was New York City.

ONE DAY IN '88 WE RETURN FROM CAFÉ ORLIN TO FIND STEPHEN SITTING BY AN open window. He's wearing a wet T-shirt, looking etiolated and strange. He's recently grown a mustache, which we find questionable. He's begun working out, wearing plaid shirts, the whole bit—it doesn't suit him, and is anyway about a decade too late.

We stare at him questioningly, and he shrugs. Maybe this is not really the beginning of anything. Stephen has known the ending to his story all along; we have, too, if we were ever really listening.

"It's a relief, in a way," he says at last—and I, at any rate, believe him.

TWENTY
cel

THEY FIND THE SECOND SHOOTER'S BODY IN A RIVER UP IN OREGON, WEDGED against a dam. He'd shot himself some miles upstream—he must have done it in the water, hoping to anonymize his corpse—and Cel thinks this is pretty smart, before she thinks about how fucked up it is to think this way. They find his suicide note folded in a ziplock bag in his pocket—another smart move, Cel reminds herself not to think—but its contents aren't immediately released.

"You *must* stop watching that," says Nikki, as coverage enters its fourth hour. She unplugs the TV with a flourish, and declares that the whole apartment is going out.

Cel stares at her blearily. One of her eyes is closed, and it feels like it might be stuck that way.

"Out," Nikki says again, pulling Cel to her feet.

"I'll pass," says Elspeth. She is coloring on her nails with a green Magic Marker.

"Oh, come on!" says Nikki. "It will be fun! There'll be men there."

"That's okay," says Elspeth. "I already know a few."

"Ooh. Anyone special?"

"Yes, actually." Elspeth begins to fill in her thumb. "There's this man I've known for years. Handsome and smart, but tragically short."

"That's too bad!"

"Twice a year we get blindingly drunk and he spends four hours complaining that no one's ever loved him, until I sort of try to tell him I do. Then we both forget about it and do the whole thing again in six months." She blows on her nails. "It's perfect."

"A woman needs a man like a whatever needs a whatever," says Cel.

"*Exactly*," says Elspeth, and begins on her other hand.

"We can get you a real manicure, you know!" says Nikki.

"We *can*?" squeals Elspeth, and Cel gives her a look like *Cool it*.

Cel tells Elspeth she'll be home early, though in fact she intends to stay out very late. At the bar, she keeps catching herself scanning the crowd for Scott, and when someone taps her on the shoulder at a quarter past two, she turns around with a pointless smile. But it's only one of the bartenders, looking harassed, shouting something Cel can't hear three times before handing her a slip with Luke's phone number on it. Cel glances at the bartender with a questioning *can-I-use-your-phone?* kind of face, but he's already looking at her in a *do-not-even-try* sort of way, so she jostles her way outside to find a pay phone.

Luke answers after a half a ring. He tells her to meet him at the studio at 6 A.M., which is in three and a half hours.

"Well, Christ, Luke, why six? I mean, why not *now*, since we're all up?"

He tells her the ferries aren't running yet and she asks him what ferries and he tells her not to worry about it.

"Six o'clock," he says. "It's an emergency."

"Do you live on *Staten Island*, Luke? Because that's also sort of an emergency."

"Six o'clock," he says, and hangs up before she can ask how he knew where she was.

WHEN CEL ARRIVES AT THE STUDIOS, LUKE IS LYING IN WAIT. HE IS SPECTRAL and wavery down the darkened hallway, but unmistakable even in silhouette—Cel can almost see his coiled nerves, his radiating impatience that something that should have happened already has not. It isn't even six yet.

"Jesus, Luke, you scared me."

"No, I didn't," he says. Then: "You walk really slow, you know that?"

In his office, Cel watches as Luke flips on the lights, then hovers fretfully in a corner.

"Cel," he says, in an odd, abraded sort of voice. If he were about to fire her, she is sure he would be in a better mood.

"Luke, I know things have been terrible," says Cel. "I *know*. But whatever it is, we will deal with it."

"You don't."

"I don't—what?" Cel blinks. "I don't know?"

Luke finally sits, so Cel does, too. She hadn't realized she'd been waiting for him, the way Mattie does for his guests.

"Cel, listen." Luke's voice is husky with a weird out-of-character sincerity, as though he's about to make some kind of declaration—of love, or something even worse that Cel is too scared to imagine.

"I'm listening?"

Luke buries his head in his hands and begins shaking it—manually, abnormally.

"Christ," says Cel. *"What?"*

"It gets worse." Cel can hear from Luke's voice that his jaw is set.

"It—gets—worse?" The present tense makes this feel less like information and more like prophecy. "What gets worse? And worse than what?"

Luke issues a strange, half-crazed little laugh.

"Luke!" Because this is an emergency, Cel allows herself to snap her fingers in front of his face. "Please speak normally."

At this, Luke finally raises his head and plants his gaze on Cel's. As soon as he does, she wishes he hadn't.

"Cel." He looks amazed at what he's saying. "They were writing *letters*."

"What?" Cel's relief that Luke is finally talking seems to be swamping her comprehension. "Who was?"

"Mattie and the kid."

"The kid." This comes out in a tone of senseless innocence. "Which kid?"

Luke stares at her miserably; his eyes look almost moist, which is certainly impossible. There is a blank beat between them.

"You mean the shooter?"

He nods, and Cel feels her mouth fall open. She hears herself gasp "No!"—actually gasp it, like an overacting member of the studio audience.

"Yes," says Luke. "The shooter. That kid."

Cel's mouth is still open; she closes it. Her shock has overridden her standing policy against letting Luke ever see her surprised, though he hasn't seemed to notice.

"*Why* was he writing Mattie letters?"

"The answer to that, I'm afraid, is in the letter."

"No."

"Who knows? It might turn out to be a sort of epistolary mentoring relationship. There's a grand tradition of that, you know! Perhaps we've got a *Letters to a Young Poet* for the modern age."

"I didn't know Mattie wrote anyone back," says Cel.

"*Chicken Soup for the Homicidal Teen!*" says Luke, and cackles worryingly. He has begun contracting back into his usual attitude for disaster—harassed, half-amused, self-martyring: *It figures, it figures, it just really, really does.* This is one of Cel's most despised of Luke's many despised modalities—this tone that implies that the universe has arranged this specific catastrophe in order to persecute him specifically; that all calamities have him as their intended target, and any other harm is purely collateral. But it's nearly comforting to hear it now—if the problem is only Luke's, then it can't be only hers.

Cel heads for the window. Outside, the wind is picking up: spumes of cloud moving swiftly over the city.

"Those don't open, unfortunately. In case you were thinking of jumping."

"I didn't know Mattie even read his own *mail*."

"Well, I suppose every celebrity has a soft spot." Luke's voice is too bright now, shiny like a fake coin. "I mean, with some celebrities, it's Make-a-Wish. Or sometimes it's dogs, you know? So this is kind of like that, except that instead of dogs or little bald cancer children, Mattie decided to mentor a mass-murderer-in-training."

Above Seventh Avenue, the clouds are beginning to hump in a way that reminds Cel of a picture of burial grounds she'd once seen in *National Geographic*. What were they called? For a long time, she'd made a whole big point of remembering.

"Christ," she says.

"You know, I'm not sure He'll be much help at the moment. But who *can* you call in a pickle like this?" Cel can hear Luke tapping his foot. "What was the name of Eichmann's defense attorney? He might have a few ideas."

The burial mounds were kurgans, Cel remembers. She feels an idiotic relief, trailed by a baseless optimism—if this letter thing seems unbelievable, maybe it shouldn't be believed. Really, it's too crudely absurd to be true—a steroidal hyperextension of reality's logic, like the paranoia of a schizophrenic or the punch line of a joke. *Mattie M is terrible: how terrible* is *he?* With this, Cel feels a fizz of hope.

"Luke, are we sure this isn't something the kid made up?" She turns around. "Or like . . . I mean, the Son of Sam took direction from his dog! John Hinckley shot Reagan for Jodie Foster!"

"I was hoping the same thing," he says. "But no, unfortunately. Apparently this is all very literal. I'm sorry, Cel."

A peppery smell fills Cel's nostrils; she feels her heart begin to slow, and realizes for the first time it's been racing.

"I mean, I know we've had our differences," says Luke. "But I am sorry."

"Sorry for what?"

"Sorry for you. Because now you have to go talk to him about this."

"Oh, come on."

"Well, we have to deal with this, don't we?" Luke is using his assistant-professor voice. "We have to address it, do we not?"

Cel says nothing. At least these questions are rhetorical, not Socratic.

"And that starts with talking to Mattie."

"And you think I'm the man for the job."

Luke shrugs; his unwillingness to take this opening for insult frightens Cel more than she understands. "All I know is that he let you in the car."

"I was already in it!"

"But he didn't kick you *out*."

"I'm not sure he noticed I was there."

Cel leans her forehead against the glass, peering down until her sense of physical vertigo nearly matches her inner one. On the sidewalk below her, a dab of bright green bobs against the wash of concrete. She closes her bad eye and the dab becomes a black man in a lime-green shirt, bending over to pick something up.

"So you want me to what—interrogate him about this? Argue with him? Luke, he was a fucking lawyer!"

"He was a public defender! I'm not asking you to beat him in a paperwork race. I'm just asking you to go talk to him."

"I thought that's why we hired Little Lord Fauntleroy."

"Network is dubious about that guy."

"And they're not dubious about me?"

"I think the word I would use is 'unaware.' They are largely unaware of you, and this, for now, will have to do."

Slowly, the man in the polo shirt stands up with whatever he is holding. Could it be a feather, an engagement ring, a crack vial? The care in his movements suggests something not dropped, but discovered. Cel opens her bad eye and the man disappears back into the sidewalk.

"The only helpful thing I can say, Cel? Mattie will understand why you're doing it. He knows you have to, and you know why?"

Cel knows it's better to quote Luke than to let him quote himself. "Because it is my job."

"Yes. I'm afraid that it is."

Outside, the light is turning sepulchral and stormy. This is the kind of weather Cel usually likes: choppy Van Gogh skies, the sense of changing wind and altered possibility. Cel can sense Luke lingering in the doorway—beset by uncharacteristic remorse, or merely dissatisfied with having given Cel his final line?

"What?" Cel says into the window. Her breath fogs the glass.

"Just—" Luke says quietly. "I mean. Nobody's expecting a miracle. But you know, a lot of people work here."

"I know."

Outside, the storm is starting. She'd loved storms as a child: roiling skies gave her a dangerous, promising feeling—a sense of revolution, or a shipwreck from which you just might emerge into a new life. But this storm only feels like what it is: another thing to get through. Cel squints through the rain, looking for the bright green shirt of the man. But he is gone, vanished into Manhattan along with whatever he was holding—Cel will never know what it was, and she feels a stupid grief at this. That something so small can still be permanent. This is not the sort of thing worth saying to Luke, or anyone. She turns around to say it anyway, and finds that he is gone now, too.

TWENTY-ONE
semi

1991

EVENTUALLY THERE CAME A TIME WHEN IT SEEMED THE WAR HAD REACHED A stalemate. The best men had gone to their graves, with only cowards left to count them. Like other survivors before us, we were ashamed, and fled.

I went to Iceland. I wanted not to see the Northern Lights.

For years, I'd longed to see them. Now, I could hardly bear that they existed. I certainly couldn't stand their wheeling across the sky—for me and only me, alone in the foreign snow. But the thing about bearing things is that it isn't ever up to you; there is nothing elective in endurance. And so, of course, there they were: a green, electric seizure, spectacular beyond imagining. A miracle, sure, and what's one more? I shivered and thought: *Why me?*—but this was only out of habit.

I was standing in a field of volcanic stones—tarry and anthropomorphic: you could see why the locals thought them trolls. Above me was a churning chaos, the sky glowing malachite, turning the snow to colors that have no name. I was accidentally quoting Chekhov, I realized, which is about what I deserved for trying to do something original with my grief.

Hallucinatory light rotated above me—seeming to work some

deeper transformation on everything it touched, as heat turns sand to glass. The ice was pyrite, the air vitrified; the stones around me were not stones at all, but trolls, and then not trolls, but fossils—ancient creatures calcified by comets. I blinked, and they were the running mummies of Pompeii; I blinked again, and they were skeletons in the ossuaries of the Plague. They were the seared shadows at Hiroshima, forever fleeing into the walls. They were the righteous anointed by the Rapture, standing in permanent reproach of us all.

What perversity of fate is it to be forgotten by the apocalypse?

But then, there is no reason to think we get just one. This was as good a place as any to wait for the next one.

I lay back in the snow and closed my eyes. I thought about tsunamis, about millennial earthquakes. I thought of Krakatoa, of the asteroid that irradiated Siberia. I summoned imperialist extraterrestrials, I summoned horsemen.

I whispered to the universe: *Take me with you. Take me with you.*

part four

In the dark, a flame goes out. And then

The afterimage of the flame goes out.

—FREDERICK SEIDEL

A second chance—*that's* the delusion.
There never was to be but one.

—HENRY JAMES

TWENTY-TWO
semi

1993

THE JOURNALIST IS FIGURING ME OUT, I'M AFRAID. HE HAS TAKEN TO CALLING me in the evenings, after I've come back from the theater or the hospital and it is very hard not to answer the phone.

The fourth time he calls, I tell him I'm not interested in blackmail.

"This isn't blackmail," he says. "It's not going to be that kind of story."

"Not *what* kind of story?" Though surely this is submitting to his tactics; his very first goal, before anything else, is to engage me.

"This would be more like a character study," he says, and I laugh at him.

"Well, you certainly picked a character," I say. "I'll be interested to see what you find out."

Then I hang up, and am alone again, and still.

"CAN'T WE TURN THAT OFF?" I SAY TO BROOKIE, THE THIRD TIME THE NEWS OF Ryan Muller's fan letter plays on CNN.

There's no answer. I know he isn't really sleeping.

"Hey." I tap his foot. Under the sheets, his yellowed toenails have probably grown out again. The nurses are good at remembering most things, but they do forget about that. "Let's change the channel, okay?"

He swallows. His throat makes a childlike, glutinous sound. I reach for the little sponge and swab his mouth. When I'm through, he looks at me and says, "I lost the remote."

"I don't believe you," I say, swizzling the sponge in its jar. There's something about this ritual that reminds me of dyeing Easter eggs, though who would have ever sat with me through such a process?

Brookie swallows again and says, "Where the hell would I be hiding it?"

He has a point. He's wearing a johnny—pocketless, ass-less—underneath three papery blankets, the kind you get on airplanes. Even though it's the middle of July, he is always freezing—teeth chattering audibly, body juddering with the weird energy of a person mid-coke-comedown. Meanwhile, the rest of us are roasting. The nurses walk around with globes of sweat beneath their arms; when they turn off lights or hoist bedpans, you can see dark hemispheres of Pooh Bears and carousels, dogs with little bones and cats with flamboyant umbrellas—as though all their cloying universes have fallen under eclipse. Even Ashley has them, and we love Ashley: she is tiny and unflappable, and under different circumstances, we think we would have been friends with her. Though it's true we were never friends with all that many women.

I scan the room for the remote, but I don't see it. On the wheeled table next to Brookie's head is a Styrofoam cup of half-melted ice, the Weekend section of the *Times*. Tuesday is Science, but we don't read that one anymore.

On the television, they are still talking about the shooting. They are always talking about the shooting. It's a slow news summer—a slow news decade, as it goes, depending on your perspective. My following of the story has been tenuous and almost wholly against my will. The shooting is, undeniably, a tragedy. Nevertheless, it's always a little galling to hear talk of other tragedies—to observe the rush to make meaning, discuss policy. The willingness to consider notions of preventability, presumptions of innocence. The reflexive understanding that issues of suffering and death are indeed of general interest. Even the gun fanatics can't get away with explicitly not giving a shit—in fact, they must be seen to seem to give very much of a shit. They have to go on television to twist themselves in self-sealing circles of logic so tight they can only be understood as articles of faith—and who would bother to argue with, would be so audacious as to doubt the sincerity of, one of those? The bottom line is that, whatever one may think of guns, of *course* everyone cares about the dead. The dead were people, after all, and the living are not monsters.

It was all a little much, even before the letter debacle, which launched Matthew's image onto every channel. Now, he is everywhere: they're doing retrospectives of his show, his life, his career in politics. They're doing highlights from his interviews. It all has the feel of an obituary—which I suppose, on a professional level, it is.

Now they're showing clips of him and Alice, standing in the rain.

"Haven't I suffered enough?" I say aloud.

"Probably not," says Brookie. This time I had actually thought he was asleep.

I suppose the wall-to-wall coverage of these letters was inevitable. In a way, *Mattie M* was already the country's major cultural phenomenon—its scapegoat and guilty pleasure, its self-flagellation and original sin. Mattie M is already Jonathan Swift and P. T. Barnum and Andy Kaufman; the Wizard of Oz and the man behind the curtain. He is the person who started the rumor about that scene where the Munchkin commits suicide, and all the people who've ever rewound the tape to try to watch.

"I'm obsessed with this story," whispers Ashley, and I jump about a foot.

"So is Semi," says Brookie. He's speaking in his extra-awake voice now, the one telling us not to write him off just yet.

"I don't know why I care," says Ashley.

"I bet Semi does," says Brookie, and winks one swollen eyelid.

But I am not afraid of him anymore: anything he says about Matthew, I will chalk up to delirium.

"I don't care," I say. "I'm profoundly bored of this, actually."

"You are?" says Ashley mildly, and picks up the remote. Somehow it was right there on the table all along.

TWENTY-THREE
cel

1993

RYAN MULLER'S SUICIDE NOTE IS SIX WORDS LONG: *I DIDN'T KNOW IT WAS REAL.*

Six words: almost nothing, yet more than anyone could have asked for. It's the perfect length for scrolling text boxes, for screenshots, for pull quotes.

I didn't know it was real: a declarative assertion with an unstated antecedent. On TV, they go around and around about the referent: did he not know the gun was real, or did he not know the moral consequences were real? Maybe he didn't know *The Mattie M Show* was real, offers Suzanne Bryanson on CNN. She isn't the first person to conclude this; several more advertisers have dropped out overnight.

"But *The Mattie M Show* is *not* real," says the anchor. "Is it?"

Suzanne Bryanson says she doesn't think that's the point.

I didn't know it was real: a gnomic, sub-grammatical utterance, uniquely suited to wild speculation, divergent suppressed premises. ("Just like the Second Amendment!" says Luke.)

I didn't know it was real: but real in what sense? Perhaps the real here is metaphorical. It could be a reflection of delusion: perhaps Ryan Muller hadn't known *he* was real. Maybe after years of bullying, years of invisibility, he somehow didn't actually believe in his own causal relationship to the world. This interpretation is ventured by a psychologist who works with violent youths. Or perhaps the issue is metaphysical: Ryan Muller didn't register the permanence of death. Or maybe it's epistemological, an issue of theory of mind: he hadn't grasped the reality of the other students' lives, their consciousnesses. These aren't the words commentators are using, but these are the basic issues under discussion: Cel has never seen anything like it on cable TV.

"At least this one's not addressed to Mattie M," says Tod Browning on *Tod Browning in the Morning*.

Over the day, a consensus emerges that Ryan Muller is referring to the skit. Blair McKinney is hauled back on the air, poor kid, to confirm that none of the students had thought that it was real, at first—not only because it was unbelievable, but also because the shooters had been planning to perform a skit on media violence anyway. They'd even workshopped some early ideas in class, he said, and everyone pretty much expected Troy and Ryan to take it way too seriously and do something weird and unsettling for the final version.

"What is going *on* at our public schools?" says Rush Limbaugh. "Is *this* what our taxpayer dollars are funding? That's the real story here, folks, as much as the libtard media wants to make it all about the big bad NRA and your vewy scawy constitutional gun rights. What the hell are they *teaching* our kids? is my question. And why isn't anyone looking at *that*?"

He then launches into a tirade against teachers' unions.

It was true, said Blair McKinney, that Ryan Muller seemed almost surprised at first, that he'd quickly turned away and run. And the ballistics testing has determined that Muller's gun was fired only once, hitting Jacqueline Easton in the arm. But there's of course no way of knowing why Ryan Muller had stopped shooting, or why he'd ever started in the first place.

But if Ryan Muller didn't know the skit was real, says Lee to a nodding Lisa, then he didn't know the gun was real: they are back, over and over, to the gun. Is it remotely possible he did not? Luckily for producers, this interpretation is empirically testable, and uniquely suited to an on-screen stunt. They bring in people to try to guess, though this is probably unnecessary: Cel has never met anyone in the industry who's ever fired a gun—any producer, probably, would do.

"I can't believe they're trying so hard to come up with excuses for this guy," says Nikki. She is sucking a strand of hair in her mouth like a child. Elspeth is seated next to her, green-haired and glazed-eyed. They are splitting a bowl of popcorn, united at last.

"They'd never do that if he wasn't a photogenic white kid," says Elspeth.

"Oh, I don't think we can be so sure about *that*," says Nikki.

"We can, actually," says Elspeth. "They've done studies and every-thing. If a black kid did this, nobody would be searching for ways to forgive him."

She's right about the coverage, Cel thinks, squinting at the television—although she isn't at all sure forgiveness is why they're still watching.

And aren't they all still watching?

CEL'S ANSWERING MACHINE IS FULL ON SATURDAY MORNING. SHE TRIES NOT to let this make her feel important. She still doesn't like this job, but she's starting to see how somebody could—could become addicted to the buzzy adrenaline of crisis, the sense of being chronically in demand. The corresponding right to act harassed all the time, about everything. It occurs to her that Luke probably *loves* this job. The messages are mostly about the note; many are about the letters; a few are about Mattie's gun remarks—coverage of which continues to run in a secondary loop beneath the Ryan Muller thing, like the B plot of a comic opera. One of the messages is from Scott from Sli-go's, saying he knows this weekend must be crazy but if she has any time at all he'd love to buy her a drink. Two messages concern ru-mors about Eddie Marcus—who (according to message one) had been fired from the water commissioner's offices back in the seven-ties under circumstances described as "dubious," bringing disgrace to one of the nation's most prominent packaging families, whatever that could mean. Cel *knew* that guy was rich. The other messages contain insane and/or pointless demands—one of the journalists wants to interview Alice (good luck!), another wants to interview the former intern formerly tasked with sorting Mattie's mail, several want to interview the devil-boy—though it turns out they've been scooped on that one: Cel catches one Damian the Devil-Boy on Channel 5 at lunch, submitting to questioning about Mattie's demeanor the day of the shooting. Cel tries to remember if the devil-boy ever actually met Mattie. Today he is without his makeup, wearing a brand-new Yankees hat over his horns; according to the text box, his name is Ezra Rosenzweig.

Luke has tracked down Mattie's former intern, recovering from mono in Jersey City, and drags him in for interrogation. His name is Jeremy Sampson-Lopez, and he says the same thing the current interns have said: yes, Mattie has access to his mail; no, he never seemed particularly interested in reading it; and the interns themselves don't *read* his letters, exactly, as much as scan them for their central demands. Fans are sent a head shot, whether they ask for one or not; hate mail is cursorily examined for explicit threats. All of it gets recycled afterward and, except in the case of the extraordinarily creepy, no names are written down. Jeremy Sampson-Lopez thinks there might have been some letters like this around the time of Secret Crush, but this was before he worked here and before the time frame of the shooter's letter, anyway.

He looks terrified as he reports on all of this; his swollen lymph nodes are the size of plums. Cel doesn't have the heart to haul him in before Mattie, hoping to shock his conscience. If Mattie still has a conscience, it is certainly unshockable by now.

AT ONE O'CLOCK, CEL HEADS TO MATTIE'S DRESSING ROOM. THROUGH THE door, she can hear some echoey, desolate choral music. She stands outside for a moment, gathering herself.

Inside, the music is much louder—deep voices coiled to a close, hollow-sounding chord. Mattie is faced away from Cel, staring in the mirror.

"Ah," he says. "I see they decided to bring in the big guns."

Cel watches her reflection flinch: is it possible he does not hear the things he says?

"Mattie," she says. "We need to talk."

"We do, do we?"

"We need to talk about this letter."

She is using the singular to be optimistic.

"Do you know how much mail I get in a week?"

"I do, actually. I've spent all morning looking into it." Cel is glad he's still facing away from her; she's beginning to develop a real fondness for the back of his head, relative to its other side. "But you apparently wrote back to this one."

"I write back to a lot of my mail." He flicks his eyes toward her in the mirror. "Believe it or not."

He reaches over to turn up the volume on the cassette player. Cel is somehow surprised to see the music is actually issuing from a modern device. Something about the singing sounds impossibly remote, as though coming from a well or a cavern or an unheated island church in the middle of a dark Balkan lake.

"If you have a memory of this letter, Mattie, you have to tell us," Cel says. "This is the only way we can help you."

"Did I ask for anyone's help?"

A fair point, Cel thinks—which is precisely the sort of thinking that makes her so ill-suited to this moment. Fundamentally, she knows she is an unpersuasive person; she has no real ability to convince anyone of anything—that a particular idea is true, that a specific action should be undertaken. The only parts of her job she's ever been good at involve deflection. She could have been an assistant in a magic show, an accomplice in a long-running con. What she cannot do—what is ludicrous for her to even try to do—is to *exhort*.

"You could get arrested!" she exhorts, and Mattie laughs right at her.

"I don't think so," he says. "But in the unlikely event I should be issued a subpoena, I assure you I will be fully compliant with the law. I promise not to resist arrest on live television. I promise not to pull a Ruby Ridge in our studios. Does that put your mind at ease? Until then, I have a witch hunt to sit out."

"Are you the witch, in this scenario?"

"Maybe there's more than one."

"I would like to know why you are doing this."

"I'm not sure we established I'm *doing* anything."

"I would like to know why you think someone would do this. Why a person in your position would conceal letters from a murderer." She can almost see him stifling an objection. "Fine, an *alleged* murderer."

"I was a defense attorney. I don't do prosecutors' jobs for them. I'm certainly not doing Tod Browning's job for him."

"You *are* doing Tod Browning's job for him! If you don't talk about the letters, that means he gets to talk about them instead."

Mattie rubs his eyes for a long while, then looks at her.

"Well, what about this, then?" His eyes are red and somehow wobbly-looking. "Just as a hypothetical. What about a person who made a promise, and is trying not to break it?"

"A *promise*? To the *shooter*?" *Alleged* shooter, she thinks automatically but will not say. "But—I mean—he's dead. I mean, for one thing."

"Exactly," says Mattie. "So it's too late to ask permission. Or forgiveness."

The music seems to get louder again, even though Mattie hasn't touched the dial. Cel feels as though the space between here and wherever those singers were is amplifying, along with the time between now and whenever they were singing. She pulls her sweater around her; she thinks the music might actually be making her cold.

"You realize that this decision can only do further damage to the show's image," she says.

"I realize that it is likely to further complicate my own," he says. "Yes. But I am further aware that this show will do just fine without me, if it comes to that."

"I don't think that's the network's view."

"Oh, *please*." Mattie sounds a little annoyed, finally: well, good. "I'm sure they've got head shots of a dozen different replacements on file. I'd be surprised if they aren't holding auditions."

Is it possible he has a point? Mattie M is neither the star nor the soul of *The Mattie M Show*—neither its Oprah nor its Lorne. He is a variety-show MC, more or less, and these can outlive their hosts—The *Tonight Show* baton passing from Allen to Paar to Carson to the new guy, Leno. Though really, Mattie's role is less like Carson's than Ed McMahon's—playing the straight man to the show's antics, serving as an onstage proxy for the audience—and though it is certainly not true that *anyone* could do it, it seems likely that a lot of people could. Knowing this makes Cel feel sorry for Mattie all over again—he is an unusual person living an unusual life in which he is largely beside the point. The hardest part of changing is changing back—Cel knows because she's done it—and it's probably too late for Mattie now. Cel is so, so lucky to be young, she realizes. She has never really thought of that before.

"You have a commitment to your employees," says Cel. "A lot of people work here."

"Yes, and a few of them even want to." Cel ignores this. "But my employees aren't the only people I have commitments to."

"You mean the viewers? You hate the viewers."

Mattie never denies this.

"I mean the public," he says quietly.

And now Cel hates him again. The *public*, good *Christ*. Does he think he's Winston fucking *Churchill*? These are the things that Luke would think, and maybe even say out loud.

"Speaking of which." Mattie turns around. "The Gun Control Alliance has invited me to speak at a rally."

"What? Why?" But no, Cel knows the answer to that. Why does anyone want Mattie anywhere? So that people will look in that direction.

"I've accepted their invitation."

"Do you think you're Winston fucking Churchill?"

"Certainly not," he says seriously, which makes Cel want to throw things. Any remotely normal human would be furious at her—how can Mattie just sit there and *listen*? And then more or less agree with her? Relentless rationality is a kind of gaslighting—a form of psychic abuse in the workplace! Maybe she can file a complaint with HR.

"How did this even happen?" she says, and Mattie shrugs. *Don't shrug, don't shrug, don't shrug,* Cel thinks at him, then remembers Mattie is not on TV at the moment.

"They approached Eddie," he tells her.

"I have no idea why you trust his judgment."

"I certainly *consider* his judgment," he says. "I don't regard it as definitive."

Cel grits her teeth; she will not be lured into abstraction.

"I would like to know, please, just *why* you are doing this."

"Would you believe I actually believe in this issue?"

"No." Though Cel still can't quite believe she is talking this way, she is starting to expect that Mattie will let her. She thinks of that character on *MASH,* the one who keeps not being allowed to kill himself. A tragic figure trapped in a comic plot: the ultimate indignity.

"You're a hard person to argue with," she says.

"I've been told I'm hard to agree with."

"That too."

"Well, I'm sorry," Mattie says. "This isn't your fault. I wouldn't want your job."

"I hear that a lot these days."

"Me too."

Something about this strikes Cel as funny, and she begins to laugh. She laughs until she hiccups, and then she says, "This situation is absurd."

"Yes," says Mattie. "But what is faith but a gesture on the strength of the absurd?"

He shrugs like this is something people say regularly, which makes Cel start to laugh again, and this time, Mattie laughs, a little, too.

TWENTY-FOUR
semi

We're left with double consciousness.

Paulie, warbling along with Jean Stapleton to the *All in the Family* theme song. Paulie with a sheet pulled over his face.

The Stonewall today: its arched, little doorway, its gated park leafy and sedate. The Stonewall back then, with its black door and wishing well and many gorgeous extinct taxonomies. Its flame and brownie queens, its screamers and scare drags, its chickenhawks and nellies and little dress-wearing nymphs too lovely for any gender. They are creatures of myth today: but when I was a boy, my boy, dragons and unicorns walked the earth.

We're left with slogans; they snag in our heads like jingles.

Say it clear, say it loud: gay is good, gay is proud.

Death to the Fascist insect that preys upon the life of the people: the way Brookie signed all of his correspondence, for a time.

We're left with the punch lines, the cheap little dramatic ironies.

Anders the bouncer, run out of his career by Fidelifacts, later became an informant for the FBI. There was an article about it after he died. Nick and Peter would have wanted to know.

We're left with fragments of language. "Firn": snow left over from previous season. "Apophatic": knowledge of god obtained through negation. These were written down in a notebook, back when one still groped for metaphors.

We're left with the sound of a ringing telephone. In certain moods, at certain hours, the blinking light of an answering machine can look like a lighthouse observed from sea.

AND WE'RE LEFT, OF COURSE, WITH THE CONSOLATIONS OF *ART*.

After Iceland, I wrote a play in something of a fit. Everyone who was still at it was writing about AIDS, and this is what I did, too— not only is it mostly impossible to be original, there are times you shouldn't even try. In the end, my play was an afterthought: a modestly elegiac retrospective of what had happened, not a voice crying out in the wilderness to warn against what would. It was far too late for anything I wrote to matter; and anyway, Larry Kramer I was not. I'd always been squeamish about art as political communication, back in the years when this was an opinion anyone could afford. Like everyone else, I'd gotten over my objections—abandoned my slavish Nabokovian conception of Art as some exceptional magisterium, existing above and apart from us, its mortal subjects. What was this, in the end, but a form of religious belief? If faith was inescapable, at least let mine be useful: let me lend my dubious talents to a cause!

And so I tried—for months and years, I tried. I tried to write something stirring and morally elevating; I tried to embrace a sort of socio-medico-realist aesthetic. But in the end, I could not. When I tried to pare my art down to its political scaffolding, it seemed there wasn't one; there were only people—ones I'd known, or known better by imagining. I'd spent too many of my formative years absorbing complicating information, maybe: when it came down to it, I did not know how to assert anything in art—even (or perhaps especially) all the things I knew were true and right.

In the end, the play's form reflected these neuroses. Its structure juxtaposed classical conventions—tragic flaws, cathartic crises, a chorus of plague victims offering prophecy and lamentation—with a metafictional shuffling of endings and beginnings, linearity and content. The versions shifted with every performance, and the cast members rotated through the parts. Causality ran backwards some nights and forward on others: the anguished death prompting the tepid political reaction, then the other way around. Scenes were swapped in and out, and I added new material regularly. Start the narrative arc in one snapshot, and the play became a morality tale; moving the ending could change it from redemptive to nihilistic. It matters very much where you end a story: this becomes what you remember, and this becomes the point. The play was called *The Spectators* and was, I knew, the very best work of my life.

Nevertheless, it was a minor project, completely irrelevant politically. I'd imagined it would be received as a thoroughly playwright's play at best—at worst, a loathsome and exploitive gimmick. Instead, it was something of a hit, as these things go; the shuffling made people want to talk about the version they'd seen, and then see it again. Its initial run was extended, and I began to earn a small amount of blood money. It even developed a fan base amongst the artsy teenage girls of one of the city's better public high schools. They came on the weekends and liked to stand around in the lobby afterward, clutching at each other and weeping.

On the show's one-year anniversary, the theater throws a celebratory production.

The evening is appropriately restrained—bookended by sedate preshow cocktails and vigorously earnest postshow discussion. The production turns out to be one of the bleaker versions, though the director claims they had not planned this. Afterward, I am invited onstage for a Q&A with the audience. A man stands and explains that the narrative conception of the play—with its fragmentation and repetition, its endless circling around the central point—is a classic reaction to trauma. Stephen would have liked this, probably. Myself, I have my doubts—I suspect that the really classic reaction to trauma is simply to die, which is why the truly traumatized among us are not here to tell their po-mo stories. Still, I nod politely at the man. Like most Q&A questions, his isn't a question at all.

At the after party, I stand beaming amidst plates of carefully curated cheeses; around me, black-and-white production photos are arrayed on the walls. I'm criminally flattered by all of it, of course, and wish more of my surviving friends were here to see it. Although the theater had offered me a whole big bloc of tickets, in the end I hadn't really invited anyone. Brookie, in an unprecedented expression of interest, keeps vowing to come see it one day—maybe because he knows this is a promise he will not be expected to keep. Although who knows: both he and the show have lasted longer than anyone's projections.

The after-party is winding down when I feel a hand on my shoulder. I can somehow tell it belongs to someone very handsome.

I turn around—and yes, the man is very handsome, as well as very young. Probably too young; certainly too handsome. I am not the androgynously doe-eyed sprite I once was—I have developed a slouch and a bit of a paunch—though it seems petty to complain about aging badly when one is lucky to be aging at all.

"Are you Septimus Caldwell?"

"Semi," I yelp. "Dear *Lord.*"

I can tell he wants to ask what kind of name is Semi. The answer is it isn't one, and neither is fucking *Septimus.*

"I'm Scott Christakous," says the man, offering me a firm, somehow decisively heterosexual handshake. "We've spoken on the phone."

Ah. Yes. The journalist.

"I'm sorry for bothering you here—I know this isn't the time." He scans the room—de-rouged cast members holding flowers, picked-over platter of cheese and fruit. "But I'd really like to talk to you. I'll be at the bar next door, if you'd be willing to meet. No rush—I'll be there all night."

AS IF I DON'T HAVE OTHER PLANS! THOUGH, AS IT HAPPENS, I DO NOT. I wouldn't want to detain any of the crew or, God forbid, the actors—even if I didn't find their ceaseless extroversion tiresome, which increasingly I do. Anyway, any journalist willing to sit through two and a half hours of experimental theater at least deserves a hearing. If I'd had half a clue what he looked like, I might have even called him back.

At the bar, Scott Christakous tells me he has an idea for a journalistic encounter. I ask him what the hell is that. It sounds like something Brookie would have done in the seventies, and these are things generally best avoided.

He tells me it's just a creative way of asking somebody a question.

"I thought this was supposed to be a character study," I say.

"It was."

"And?"

He shrugs. "Mission creep."

"Because of that kid and the letter? You're a regular Bob Woodward." There's probably a Deep Throat joke in here somewhere, but I'm certainly not going to be the one to make it. "Anyway, I don't see how that has anything to do with me."

"Well, that isn't really the point," says Scott. "The point is that there's pretty much insatiable interest in Mattie M at the moment, and he isn't giving a whole lot of interviews. The point is we're looking for a way to get his attention."

"I doubt anything gets his attention these days."

"Well, we have a feeling that this will."

He gives me a shrewd look then, but doesn't ask any questions. He must already know the answers, and that somewhere within them lurks my darker motivations for anything I might agree to do to Matthew Miller. He's gambling that I'll be more susceptible to indulging those impulses if we don't discuss them directly, and in this, he probably is right.

I tell the journalist he's going to have to be a whole lot more specific about what this *this* is, and he takes a jaunty swallow of beer and asks me if I've ever heard of Secret Crush.

"ARE *YOU* SUPPOSED TO HAVE THE CRUSH, IN THIS SCENARIO?" BROOKIE ASKS the next morning. He is having another good day: out of bed and halfway dressed, with enough energy to be bossy.

"Not exactly," I tell him. "It isn't meant to be so literal."

I am quoting Scott verbatim. "It isn't meant to be so literal," he told me the night before. "This is more about surprising Mattie with a person from his past, the way they do on his show. We're hoping your encounter with him will be disarming. A jumping-off point to a broader conversation. You went to school for theater, NYU, is that right?"

"God, you people are creeps."

He laughed and said I didn't know the half of it. Then he launched into the details. The idea, he said, was to send me to *The Mattie M Show* as a VIP Audience Member—a preposterous status which Scott could apparently help me secure through some contact he had at the show. As a ViPAM, in the parlance, I'd be entitled to one (1) Mattie M Meet-and-Greet—this typically meant fifteen minutes of autograph-signing at the studio, but perhaps Mattie would opt for a more private venue once he saw my name on the list. My job, either way, was to record the audio of our encounter. What Scott Christakous and I did with the recording would depend on its content. Anything touching on the Ryan Muller letters could be pitched to news outlets; anything personally revelatory could attract massive sums with tabloids. We could present the recording and transcripts in isolation—with or without my identity obscured—or we could pitch the thing more as a narrative, casting me as the protagonist (he included this, I assume, in case I had ambitions of stardom). But almost anything would probably find a home somewhere, he said, and for quite a bit of money.

"So he's a mercenary," said Brookie.

"I guess that's what you'd call it."

"I think you should do it."

"Of course you do," I say. "You always hated Matthew."

"I didn't hate him *personally*. My objections were strictly structural."

"If someone wanted to pay me to assassinate Matthew Miller, you'd probably think I should consider that, too."

"That would depend on a lot of things," he says. "But I mean, think about it. Here you have a chance to have a conversation about absolutely anything and know that people will listen. You could talk about AIDS funding for an hour and the *National Enquirer* would probably still publish the highlights."

"So what am I going to do—show up with a body bag? Throw some paint on his fur coat?"

"Ask him why he hasn't done more shows on AIDS. Read him a monologue from your play. Show him a picture of Paulie at the end. He'll remember Paulie, right?"

"I think so."

"Or just talk to him like a human being," says Brookie. "*Exactly* what you say isn't the point. The point is to gesture toward something that matters, and know that the entire country will look where you're pointing."

"I just can't see it doing any good," I say. "If this was five years ago—"

"But it isn't."

"Well, right. It isn't. And I'm pretty sure the nation is paying attention by now."

At this, Brookie laughs, and turns up the volume on the TV. On-screen, a concerned-looking matron is speaking very quickly about the Ryan Muller letter. Brookie flips to the next station, which is showing clips from a video game. The third is *Beavis and Butt-Head;* the fourth is a commercial for Alka-Seltzer. The next is Matthew talking to a leather-suited woman with enormous, colorfully be-tasseled breasts. This might be *The Mattie M Show,* or it might be another show running a clip in order to critique *The Mattie M Show:* who can tell anymore?

"It's a *commentary* on the thing," Paulie liked to say, whenever he did something we could not stand.

"It's also the actual thing," we'd tell him.

I turn back to Brookie. "Okay," I say. "Point taken."

I expect Brookie to sum it up for me anyway, but he doesn't. Maybe he's giving me some credit for once, or maybe he's just getting tired. It's been a while since he's talked this much. Selfishly, I want to keep him talking.

"Well, the only thing I know for sure is that awareness-raising is not on this journalist's agenda."

"So hijack the agenda," says Brookie, getting back into bed.

"Secret Crush, though? It's grotesque."

"It isn't more grotesque than parading bodies through a church." Brookie's voice is growing hoarse. "It isn't more grotesque than pleading with Republicans. And anyway, there's no tactic too grotesque for the thing itself."

No argument there. For a moment, we say nothing. On the screen, the leather-clad woman is shaking her breasts with what seems like defiance; the crowd is either yelling or booing or catcalling or laughing.

"I don't want it to seem like blackmail," I say at last.

"Don't think of it as blackmail." Brookie's voice sounds chipped, and I can tell he's going to fall asleep as soon as he gets the last word. "Think of it as a favor he's owed you for a really long time."

DOES MATTHEW OWE ME ANY FAVORS? I CERTAINLY THOUGHT SO, ONCE. THIS is the entitlement of youth—or my entitled youth, at any rate: the belief that suffering is unnatural to the universe, instead of its given state. The question now isn't Matthew's debts, but mine—what I might owe to the ones who got sick, the ones who died. The ones who fought and organized while I chanted along behind, holding signs and half-shouting slogans, because I never did feel totally comfortable with shouting or with slogans. The ones who'd used whatever artistic gifts they had to say something that mattered, *when* it mattered—with zero hope of public adulation, with zero hope of cheese plates. The ones living afterlives as material—as *my* material—whether they would have wanted to or not.

In a mostly conquered land, living is a form of complicity.

Like almost everyone, I'd cared for my friends; I did not fear meeting their wrathful ghosts down darkened hallways. But what had I done in the political sphere, in the world of public action? Besides enjoying the modest prestige of stylishly writing a story that everybody knew, then quietly cashing the royalty checks.

I stare at Brookie: sleeping and still-beautiful, his spatulate chest shifting slowly under the sheets. He is nearly dead and yet not too weak to lecture me until he passes out. The old Brookie would have marched me straight to the studios.

And in the end, I decide that this is who is making the decision—not me, but the once and possibly future Brookie. It's his ghost who is driving: it's his phantom hand upon me, grabbing me by the collar and shoving me out onto the stage.

At the pay phone in the lobby, I call to tell the journalist that I am at his service.

TWENTY-FIVE
cel

"WHAT IS FAITH BUT A GESTURE ON THE STRENGTH OF THE ABSURD?" CEL asks Luke on Monday morning.

"God, he just doesn't quit with these Catholic non sequiturs, does he?"

"It's Kierkegaard."

"How do you know that?"

"I asked."

They are filming the long-delayed juvenile-delinquent episode, finally. The guest list is mediocre. There's the boy who knifed his father—a classic sociopath: empty-eyed and charming. There's the mother of a teenager who'd shot his girlfriend and then himself on the night of their junior prom. There's a compulsive thief whose only notable achievement is being banned for life from every big-box chain department store in the nation. There's a cheerful, stylishly chubby girl with cat-eye glasses and hoop earrings who'd tried to shoot her mother and missed. In the pre-interview, she'd laughed when Cel speculated that, on some level, she hadn't really wanted to kill her mother at all.

"Oh no," she said breezily. She was making a little pagoda out of toothpicks from the craft services table. "I really, really did."

"Mattie also says the letter thing's a witch hunt," says Cel.

"Oh, *that's* the witch hunt?" he says. "Cel, this whole show is a witch hunt!"

"You need to shush, somewhat."

"Why? It *is*! Don't you know who is watching it? The fucking puritans, that's who!" He issues a little shriek-laugh and kicks the doorframe. "A witch hunt! Good God! And he's, what—Joseph Welch?"

"Don't you always tell me that producers need to be invisible?" says Cel, closing the door. "You are being highly visible at the moment. I mean, your voice really *carries* in the hallways."

Also, Cel has a headache. She was out with Scott until four—first dinner, then the Comedy Cellar, which was, unbelievably, his suggestion. When the early show was sold out, Cel agreed it was a great idea to wait for the late one, because she was twenty-four and living in New York and what was any of that for if she didn't do things like this? Also, her job was a joke. Also, she was drunk, which seemed to be happening more often these days. Waiting for the show, they both got drunker; Scott let her complain about her job more than anyone should be allowed to complain about anything on a first date. He was, undeniably, very handsome. Obvious handsomeness tends to make Cel wary—suggesting, as it does, some kind of suspiciously straightforward relationship to life—but then again, Scott laughed at all the right jokes, including her own. The material at the Cellar was solid, aside from the cheesy crowd work—Cel insisted they sit in the back—and an extended exchange between two lounge-lizardy types that reeked of padding. Things tended to get weird at the late show—Cel had been to enough of them to know—though when Scott asked Cel if she'd been here before, she only told him, "Sometimes."

Afterward, they'd made out for a while in the taxi, even though the meter was still running, and Scott kissed in a way suggesting essential soundness and normalcy. This was a relief; you couldn't always tell ahead of time. And instead of assuring Cel that he'd call her, he asked her to call him, which seemed encouragingly progressive—though Cel is too tired to unpack the precise reasoning behind that thought. She does have the worrisome sense that she may have promised Scott VIP tickets to the show, though she truly cannot fathom how such a conversation might have come about.

"You know," Luke is saying now, "in a way, I can almost—*almost*—understand writing that kid back. He was about to become a mass murderer, right? So I'm sure his letter stood out. Why it *cried out* for response is unclear, but hey. Mattie, like the Lord Our God, works in mysterious ways."

Cel crosses herself.

"And as fuckups go, this is huge, and definitely very, very weird—and not in an on-brand sort of way. But there have been worse fuck-ups in the history of the world."

"Hitler, as Mattie himself pointed out."

"Exactly! You might find worse fuckups in the history of entertainment, even, if you really started digging."

"Homicide comes to mind."

"And that's the talking point, right there! Mattie M Did Not Actually Murder Anyone. All he had to do was admit he needed the people on his payroll, who are employed for precisely such occasions, to say so." Luke's voice has downshifted slightly. "And then, not to *tell* us? I mean—I even get that, in a way, as a human. But to conceal it and then try to spin that as some—matter of conscience? After he let us go out there and fall on our swords, take flak for him . . ."

Luke never mixes metaphors; Cel accepts this as another sign of the End Times.

"I knew his ethical preciousness was going to come back to bite us all in the ass!"

"Do you know you're sort of shouting again?"

"I knew it, I knew it, I *knew* it. I kept saying, you'll see, you'll see, you'll see. Well, now they saw."

Cel isn't sure who the "they" is here, but she knows better than to inquire. On the sidewalk below, Cel can see an emaciated figure—gender indeterminate—in a great corvine overcoat. It is ninety-two degrees. The world is full of marvels.

"You know something that *really* bothers me?" says Luke.

"I think I know a lot of them?"

"It's the pointlessness! I mean, if you're Larry Flynt, it makes sense to develop a late-in-life dedication to civil liberties. But this

gun thing—it's not even strategic! It's horrible for the show, alien-
ates the fans, and Mattie's only talking about it so he can pretend he's
actually some completely different person."

"I don't know," says Cel. "Sometimes I think that's what he's
doing the rest of the time."

"Well, that's what *most* people are doing *most* of the time, and
they still have to do their jobs." Luke sighs. "I don't know, Cel. I think
there's something deeply sinister about the guy's crypto-Christianity,
or whatever it is."

"I don't know why you're so sure he's religious."

"I don't know why you're so sure he isn't."

"He was listening to some sort of choral music Saturday."

"Oh, of *course* he was. That poor cultured moral genius, slave to
the common people's id. Forced to interview the great unwashed,
when all he really wants is to be left alone to listen to classical music
in his tower. Poor thwarted statesman, heir to our progressive
dreams! Poor exiled king of Zembla, unrecognized by us all!"

"I have no idea what you're talking about."

"A witch hunt!" Luke barks, sending Cel jumping. "Ha! Have you
no decency, sir, at long last? Have you none?"

"Do *we?*"

"Oh, but we're agnostic about our decency, Cel, which is a kind of
decency in itself." Luke shakes his head; he's finally starting to sound
a little tired. "I mean, who does Mattie think he is to this kid—his
fucking priest?"

Cel shrugs. "I think he sort of thinks that he's his lawyer."

"I DO NOT UNDERSTAND HOW YOU'RE LOSING THIS ARGUMENT," SAYS ELSPETH
on Sunday afternoon. "I don't understand how you're still having it."

She means about the letters. Outside the window, men are playing music—they're there every day in their porkpie hats, strumming
guitars hooked up to portable speakers—though Cel only ever listens from a distance.

"Mattie's just really good at arguing," says Cel. "I mean, he was a
lawyer."

"He *was?*"

"He was a public defender. I've told you that before. I've told you that a million times."

She has, probably.

"Well, that doesn't make hiding those letters any less insane," says Elspeth. "That doesn't change the fact that he has got to turn them over."

Cel stares at her toenails, which are pink; yesterday, she'd submitted to a "mani-pedi" with Nikki, in honor of the date with Scott.

"Why, though?" says Cel.

"Why what?"

"Why are you so sure he has to show me the letters?" Cel realizes she is drumming her fingers against her chin; she hopes she hasn't caught this gesture from Luke. "I mean, why are you so sure that's the right thing?"

"Uh," says Elspeth, with a derision that sounds, frankly, kind of mannish. "Well, the fact that Mattie doesn't want to do it is probably the first clue."

"But that's, like"—Cel gropes—"circular? I think. Like you're saying we know Mattie is bad because he does the wrong thing, and we know this is the wrong thing because Mattie is doing it. . . ."

Is that logic or the opposite of logic? Somewhere along the line, Cel should have been paying closer attention to something.

"Uh, no." Elspeth is staring at Cel uncomprehendingly. "I wouldn't say that is how we know those things."

"Then how do we know them?" How do *you*, is the real question.

"Well, some people use their *consciences*, Cel?" says Elspeth. "They're like a shortcut through these sorts of quandaries? So you don't have to think *quite* so hard all the time."

"I have a conscience."

"I know. I'm reminding you. Why are your *toes* like that?"

"I got them done." She wiggles them. "With Nikki."

"Well, of course you did." Elspeth shakes her head violently; her green hair remains astoundingly still. "Amazing. Next thing we know, you'll be one of those women who cuts out articles about what kind of jeans best fit your body type. One of those women who's, like, earnestly seeking *guidance* about that."

Cel regards her feet, flexing her toes one by one. It's true they don't look like her toes, exactly, but why should that be any sort of criticism?

"You know that doesn't mean anything, right?" she says.

"What doesn't?"

"Being one of those people who does this or that thing. One of those people who cuts out articles about jeans, one of those people who gets a pedicure. I mean, do you really think that kind of stuff matters?"

"I do," says Elspeth, and Cel can tell she's thought about this a lot already. "I think it all matters, sooner or later. Because at the end of the day, what we do is who we are."

"At the end of the day, we *are* our pedicures. Man, you sure know how to catastrophize," says Cel. "That's the word you use when other people do it, right?"

Elspeth shakes her head. "I mean it, Cel. The fingernails, I mean, whatever. But you've got to quit that job."

"I'm trying!"

"No, you're not. That's just a thing you think a person in your position would say."

She reaches out to touch Cel's shoulder, but seems to reconsider; instead, she pretzels her hand into a fist.

"We are who we pretend to be," says Elspeth. "Kurt Vonnegut said that."

"I know that," says Cel. She didn't. "Anyway, if that's true, then maybe you can just pretend to be a decent friend for a while?"

"I *am* being a decent friend." Cel can tell Elspeth believes it, and maybe Cel believes it, too. If goodness is tireless effort on behalf of pure intention, then Elspeth is probably the best person she knows.

What does that make Cel?

"I'm saying this because I care about you," says Elspeth. She is, she is—good Christ, she is. Cel glances at the place on her shoulder where Elspeth decided not to touch her. "That elasticity of yours—I'd watch it if I were you."

"Or even if you weren't, apparently."

"Or don't, then. Whatever." Cel can hear in Elspeth's voice that she's been giving Cel a chance to surprise her, but did not actually expect her to: Cel is behaving exactly as Elspeth knew, deep down, that she would.

"I mean, obviously you know this about yourself." Elspeth has turned to face the window now; she is no longer looking at Cel. "But the thing I'm realizing now is—I think you *like* it."

1983

AT SCHOOL, CEL IS ONE OF THOSE CHILDREN WHO NEVER SEEM QUITE CLEAN, her hair never decisively combed. She is helpless before the physical world, her person and belongings perpetually anarchic—her erasers are always gray, her homework always lost. Nobody believes that she actually does it. The teachers decide stupidity is not the issue; for a while, they explore alternative explanations. Maybe Cel is autistic (after she is observed talking to herself at recess), or hearing-impaired (after not responding to a teacher's fourth question), or attention-deficit-disordered (after her auditory tests come back okay)? For a few weeks the school nurse gives her a pill that makes her heart pound and brings her even further into herself—into her own secret thoughts and plans and memories—which, it seems, is something like the opposite of what's intended. After a while the pills stop coming and everyone seems to conclude that Cel is nothing, really: merely defective and limited in disappointing, subclinical ways, ways that cannot be explained in a single sentence.

Her teachers, at a loss, keep reminding her she is smart—though this, at least, she does not doubt. Cel returns from school each day ever smarter, full of lectures and pedantry.

"You shouldn't stand under the air conditioner," she tells Hal after her first week of life science. "You'll get Legionnaires' disease."

"*What* air conditioner?" says Hal.

"You shouldn't use the dented cans," she declares. "You'll get botulism."

Hal squints into his stew and says, "I'll take my chances."

She learns things from Hal, too—quietly, without her noticing, he teaches her a million little economies. The endless uses for, and surprising durability of, dental floss. How to wipe down her arms and legs while she's still in the shower, so that she can get most of the water off in a hurry. An old army trick, he tells her: it's more important to be dry than warm. They read their way through his *National Geographic*s, memorizing and then reciting their facts. At school Cel announces that tsetse flies are the cause of sleeping sickness, and the teachers look at her like she's Linda Blair. Cel rewards Hal by bragging about him for a week: she brags about his gun, his plumbing expertise, his framed collection of willow-green Nazi stamps, displayed on the wall. They are from the war, Cel tells her classmates, and for the first time she is a little proud of Hal—proud of his part in slaying the dim, vast evil meant by those stamps. Her pride lasts until her teacher pulls her aside and tells her to stop talking about them at school; she adds that, if Cel ever wants to have friends over, she should probably take them down altogether.

"Your *school* wants me to take them down?" says Hal, when Cel reports this.

"Well, *obviously*," says Cel, her voice high and didactic. "The Nazis were very, very bad."

Hal gulps down a laugh she's never heard before. "The Nazis were bad," he says. "Okay, Celeste. If *you* say so."

And then he takes them down. He with the limp they never speak of, the origins of which Cel never does inquire.

She is such a little shit.

"Classic," Elspeth will say later. "Your mother was a victim, so you had to make your grandfather into the oppressor. In order to be an ally. Otherwise you were the oppressor, too."

And Cel will say: "I don't know about that."

"Classic," Elspeth will say, and wink knowingly. "I mean, absolutely textbook."

It's no secret that Cel prefers Ruth, in the seasons when her madness is more like a fairy tale than a nightmare. Hal is just Hal, and is the same in all seasons. He's forever fashioning a fix for some gnawing plumbing problem, eternally handing Cel a sad-looking sandwich that half the time has sawdust inside.

If Hal doesn't fix the house, will it fall down around them in the night? If he doesn't make Cel sawdust sandwiches, will anyone make her anything at all?

Cel does not consider these questions, and Hal never raises them. In this way, she is allowed to be young—which she is, for a very long time.

Hal is an old man by the time Cel remembers him, and he might have even acted like it if he'd ever had the time. But oldness, like a lot of things, turns out to be a sort of luxury—a thing you can resist in small degrees, for a little while, until there is somebody else around to take over.

But who? Cel will wonder years later. Who was Hal counting on to relieve him, and what did he imagine he was waiting for?

And then years after that she will realize that she was the person he was counting on, and what he was waiting for was for her to grow up.

And, in this moment, for a moment, she'll believe that she has.

TWENTY-SIX
semi

I ARRIVE AT THE *MATTIE M* STUDIOS AT NINE ON A TUESDAY. IT IS A WARM, grubby morning; low-hanging clouds are backlit by invisible sun, making the sky look like an egg with illuminated veins. In the lobby, I flash my VIP pass, and am granted access to a special elevator. I head to the fourteenth floor. Like someone planning mass murder, I have studied the layout of the building.

The upstairs offices are bright, incongruously cheerful. The wall above the reception desk exclaims THE MATTIE M SHOW! in bouncy pink letters; the whole place feels like the set of *Sesame Street,* and I begin to suspect that everyone working here is heavily medicated.

At reception, I nearly run headlong into an intern—stupidly young, tepidly attractive, poring over a sheaf of papers while she walks.

"Excuse me?" I say, and the Chi Omega pledge drops her papers. I kneel down to help her.

"Um?" she says, and we both stand up. "Can I help you?" She isn't even trying to sound like she wants to.

"I'm sorry for startling you." I look at her badge. "Celeste." In her picture, she is giving a tight-lipped, secretive little smile.

"You didn't," she says, and frowns. I see now that she isn't quite the second-tier debutante she'd seemed at first. She has a quasi-hooked nose, just shy of witchy, which offsets her slightness and gives her a patina of something else—not danger, exactly, but a sort of flickering puckishness. Something that hints at mischief you aren't sure would be benign. "Are you here to see Sara?"

"Oh, I'm not a guest." I know Sara is their audience coordinator. I hope I sound insulted.

She blinks slowly—is it possible, sarcastically? "Well, what are you then?"

"I get that a lot."

I expect her to laugh at this—I'm good at girlfriend-ing, when I must—but instead, she just stares. I begin to wonder if what I've been taking for coldness is, in fact, a bewildering stupidity.

"It was a joke," I tell her.

"I know. I didn't laugh because I didn't find it surprising." She blinks again—this time forcefully, as though scolding herself.

"I'm here to schedule the VIP Meet-and-Greet," I say. "I think Scott Christakous mentioned I was coming?"

"Oh." Now she just looks terrified. "Yes. Remind me your name?"

"Semi Caldwell."

"Semi like the truck?"

"Sure," I say. "I'm such a big fan of Matthew's show."

The "Matthew" just slips out, and I can see it makes her curious—suggesting, as it does, some particular knowledge of a different life, a truer self. Now, of course, I know that the distinction between "Mattie" and "Matthew" is as significant as the distinction between "Bigfoot" and "Yeti": at the end of the day, the ontological problem lies elsewhere.

"Well, he usually likes to do these things after the taping." The girl frowns again. "But I'll tell him that you're here."

She leads me to a waiting room. There's a pretty interesting crew in there already: enormous-breasted woman; a tiny man with webbed, nearly flippered hands; a person who seems to be either at the very beginning or the very end of a serious relationship with methamphetamine. They glance at me, briefly bored, then away again. They're here for auditions, I guess, if that's the way it works around here. The sorority girl gives me a sharp, inquisitive look on her way out the door, and I wonder what she's wondering. Well, let her wonder. Let her gossip, even, if she's the type! The space between Matthew and me contains several lifetimes of trouble: high-stakes professional blackmail; garden-variety soul-annihilating heartbreak; personal disgrace, divorce, the exciting possibility of national scandal—not to mention the twin hypotheticals of our deaths: since, strictly as a matter of statistics, we should certainly not *both* be alive. Next to all of this, what I'm doing amounts to nothing. It is, essentially, a prank—a whoopee cushion on a chair, a water balloon dropped from no great height. A decade of watching lives fall to pieces will really blunt one's appetite for blood sport. I have no interest in ruining Matthew's life at this late date.

Then again, I remind myself, times have changed. Queers don't die from rumors anymore, only from absolutely everything else. Death has been outsourced to a more efficient entity; it is now being ruthlessly mass-produced—blame globalization! What a relief that would be—to be able to lay the blame on an insensate historical force, rather than the callousness of actual humans. I realize I've begun jotting notes; I laugh and throw my pen against the wall. Now a few of the other unfortunates are staring: well, who cares! The bottom line is that I don't mind if I leave my visit with a few people scratching their heads and wondering, *What the hell?* What the hell, indeed, kids—you tell me!

The sorority girl returns and pulls me into the hallway. Across the hall, a tiny man in a leotard is bellowing into a pay phone.

"He wants to meet you for *lunch*," she says. "Gabriel's on Columbus Circle. Noon tomorrow."

"I do not wanna see any of your animal-nosed friends running around dressed as fairies!" exclaims the man across the hall.

The intern is staring at me patiently, awaiting explanation.

"I knew Matthew a little," I say. It seems I still cannot say his name without a slight, nearly subliminal tenderness in my voice. "Back in the seventies."

"Oh great," she says.

"Well, there's a reason Steven Ortiz doesn't *dance* on the stage," says the leotarded man. "I wouldn't start anything till you start hitting the gym."

"You're not going to ask to be on the show, are you?" says the intern.

"What?" I scan the hall again—with its manic chromatics, its exuberant promotional posters, its coyly arranged head shots—all of it seeming to screech in unison: *We are having fun here: aren't we?!*

"Because he really hates when people do that, and it isn't even up to him," she says.

". . . You know what happens if you take steroids without going to the gym?" says Leotard. "You get fat."

"Why would anyone want to be on this show?" I say.

"You'd be surprised." She looks so serious that I want to laugh at her. "He gets it all the time."

"Well, I'm just here as a spectator," I say. "Believe it or not."

"I'm just letting you know," she says. "We've seen it all around here."

". . . No, your job is just to stand there as a tree and look pretty," says Leotard.

"I doubt that very much," I say, offering her my hand.

A PAGE LEADS ME BACK DOWN TO THE LINE OUTSIDE THE AUDITORIUM, WHERE I wait with an army of polo-shirted out-of-towners, already starting to sweat into their fanny packs. A different page walks down the line, distributing nondisclosure agreements. A hush falls over us as we enter into this new, more formal understanding with the show— although if I've learned one thing from my time with Matthew, and it may indeed be only one, it's that these sorts of things aren't legally binding. They are psychological maneuvers, not unlike the things hospitals get you to sign to make you think you've forfeited your right to sue them.

In front of me, a couple is discussing the Ryan Muller suicide note. At this point, the story of Matthew and the shooter seems to be running on its own inertia—though the two stories are both so dense, the gravitational pull between them so massive, that it's hard to parse its mechanics: What exactly are we saying happened here, and what exactly are we deciding that it meant? At the end of the day, which of these two black holes is being subsumed into the other? And how many of us will be sucked in, too, before all of this is over?

Not me, I decide. Not me.

After a while, a cheer goes up: we are being ushered into the studios. Inside, the walls are lined with posters of Matthew—looking amused and intelligently handsome, in a nice-dad sort of way. One can nearly imagine him as the sitcom straight man, playing opposite the antics of all of fucked-up America. I remember a book Matthew had had, about the theory of the changing American character; I wish, for the thousandth time, that I could remember who wrote it. My mouth, I am noticing, is very dry.

Inside the auditorium, beaming pages direct us to our seats. I am in the fourth row. Next to me is an enormous woman wearing a confusing amount of paisley. A man behind me comments that we are lucky to be here: they usually film three shows at once, but today it's only one. A real scholar of the form, this guy. And all at once the house lights dim, a jazzed-up version of the *Mattie M* theme music commences, and an unseen announcer declares that the man himself will be imminently upon us.

And then, as prophesied, he is.

Matthew jogs onto the stage, clapping along with the crowd. He is, naturally, much older. But his aging is somehow abstracted—lacquered beneath something more than money, or stage makeup, or fame. He is half-dancing in a way that makes me almost glad I could never take him anywhere, back when I wanted to.

"Rumors of my death have been greatly exaggerated," he says. So his nerdiness, at least, remains intact. You never know what will be the last to go: I've learned this from watching a lot of dementia. "I'm not ready to give up the ghost quite yet."

The crowd squeals, and Matthew flashes them a smile. It's as though he isn't really here—as though he has, in some fundamental way, absented himself from these proceedings. Perhaps his real self is shut up in an attic somewhere, decaying in a portrait. I try to remember what his real smile looked like; I'm pulling a blank, which is too bad. But this is the way of memories, I've found: you can't make any assumptions about which ones will stick around.

And now Matthew is leaving again, promising to return in mere moments with an absolutely fantastic show. And are we ready for an absolutely fantastic show? We aver as a chorus that we are. I remind myself that most people take pleasure in affirming their agreements in unison. Sports fans, religious believers. The paisley-shirted woman is staring at me; I am, it seems, forgetting to clap. I clap, obediently. I absolutely will not hoot.

After Mattie exits, the paisleyed woman leans in and asks me where I'm from. Iowa, I tell her. She beams and says that they're from Indiana. How about that, I say. And you're here all alone? I tell her that I am. You poor thing, she says. She looks actually sorry, and I wonder darkly who she voted for. I take solace in the idea that she doesn't know to whom she's extending her pity, or to what deviant purposes it might be used.

And then the cycle starts anew: Matthew is bounding out all over again, a kicky Astaire-ish spring in his step. This is nothing like the beleaguered shuffle he'd once used to traverse county courtrooms, prison hallways, the trash-strewn streets of a city given up for dead. He stops at center stage, waving with fresh enthusiasm. Somewhere far out beyond me, the crowd is going crazy. This is the stamina of the campaign trail, I realize—to do and say the same things over and over, to make them feel personal and necessary and new, every time. Mattie is making modest *now-now* motions, and I feel the audience understand collectively that there's a preordained shape to this ritual—something like haggling, or a mating dance—and that we will know by instinct when it is time to end.

We do; it ends; we sit. Mattie welcomes us once again to the show, although I somehow feel I cannot hear him—or maybe I'm hearing the countless other times I've heard him deploy this exact same phrase on TV. It's possible I've seen it more than I think—it's one of those shows, like *Seinfeld* or *The Simpsons,* whose entire canon you could internalize more or less by accident. Today's guests are about what a person might expect. There's a monosyllabic kleptomaniac, a sullen Oedipus who killed his father with a hunting knife. He has an ellipsoid of sebaceous acne across his cheek; he keeps tilting his head to get it out of the direct line of the cameras, which he alone seems to understand intuitively. There's the shattered mother of a young man who'd killed his girlfriend, then himself, on their prom night. She speaks of her son—emphatically and exclusively—as a suicide; she refuses to look the pimply patricide in the eyes. Finally there's a beaming, scrub-faced adolescent and the equally beaming mother she'd tried, and failed, to kill. Their dynamic suggests a duo whose harebrained scheme has launched them farther than they'd ever dared to dream: they both seem absolutely delighted to be on television.

Matthew listens to their stories kindly, murmuring his sympathies. He ventures the most obvious speculations—you must have been so frightened/angry/sad—and they nod, astonished at his perception. He asks straightforward questions, then turns to offer reassuring declarative statements to the audience. The whole thing reminds me of the way he'd talk to people outside subway stops, as a campaigner and then a public servant. He had a habit of aggressively empathizing with every complainant; they all walked away with the sense some tacit promise had been made, and maybe half the time, this was true. But you could never tell from the conversation, because he sounded sorry for everyone. Once, this had seemed compassionate; later, it looked sinister. To see it again now, here, is just confusing.

The commercial break is a ninety-second interstice of dead-aired flurry. Matthew doesn't look at us. He doesn't look at the guests, either, when they try to glance at him for encouragement. They smile at each other instead, in nervous solidarity: some of them are victims and some of them are murderers, but they are all on TV. All distinctions pale in comparison to this fundamental fact.

When we return from the break, Matthew moves into the audience. There's a kind of clunkiness to this, a sense of community-theater-type blocking. It's finally registering with me that, in this moment, I have some tremendous power over Matthew. I could vault over the three rows separating me from Matthew Miller. I could touch his hand, or kiss him in a way that would tell everyone the truth of what had passed between us once. I could sneak up behind him and punch him right in the kidney. Isn't this why I'm here? To remind him that sometimes ghosts turn into poltergeists? I wonder how long it would take the security guards to tackle me. The steroidally burly men hovering just offstage are fake, of course, but I wonder if they are also real. Or would others be summoned—some secret, untelegenic army emerging from behind the curtains?

Matthew's questions are taking a turn toward old-school *Comment:* what sorts of mental health services had been available to the families, whether they'd been able to access any support or funding, what their insurance and educational systems had afforded them. Even the planted audience questions are starting to feel a little wonky, as though everyone here has been tasked with conducting some kind of dreary social survey. One such querent emerges from my row, and Mattie comes right over to hand her the microphone. His head turns in my direction; I gulp down one breath, two; his eyes look through me.

At this, I feel a perverse satisfaction—something reminiscent of the way I'd feel when I'd come back from some epic walk, in the months after Matthew left, and find my feet were bleeding.

Matthew's line of questioning has turned toward guns. He wants to know how everyone who'd used one got it; of the ones who didn't use guns, he wants to know why not. The mood in the audience has settled into determined politeness; the headphoned producer to the left of me looks concerned. My own boredom is tinged with nostalgia, and I stare at Matthew, for the first time, with something like fondness. It is possible, even now, to imagine him serving on some kind of congressional committee—from a certain perspective, it isn't hard to imagine him as a senator. But then, it isn't that hard, either, to imagine him as a pratfalling saltimbanque, doomed to wander the world, playing whatever kind of fool is in fashion. Condemned to use his gifts to parody his ambitions. From a certain angle, one could be tempted to view this as sort of the point: *The Mattie M Show* as an act of vengeance against the world that thwarted him.

But real people do not live lives to prove points. That's a mistake I used to make all the time in my writing.

"Kind of a weird episode," whispers the paisleyed woman; we have arrived at our final commercial break, somehow. I allow as how the episode *was* weird. Inside, I congratulate myself for not being this woman. For I had seen some of the world's true strangeness in my time upon this earth; I'd seen things that this woman did not understand and could not fathom and would no doubt be obliterated by the knowledge of, like Lot's unimaginative wife. For the first time, I look the woman square in the face, the better to take stock of our difference.

But when I do, I find that something has changed; I know her less, somehow, than I did before. I look again, and something flashes before my eyes—not this woman's life, but something like its opposite. For a moment, I feel the negative space that might enclose it, I feel the possibilities it might contain. There's a disorienting vertigo—like déjà vu, or that pre-somnolent sense of dropping through fathomless floors. I can feel Paisley resisting the urge to ask me if I'm okay: just the sort of pointless Midwestern discretion my grandmother would have approved of. I nod once to tell her that yes, I am, so she doesn't have to ask. I do not want to look at her again just yet. I let my eyes drift to Matthew, and feel Paisley's gaze following my own.

"He's shorter than I thought he'd be," she remarks. I study Matthew's face in the monitor. Is it possible that if I look hard enough, some secret knowledge will come back to me? I know he had a scar dashing out from his left eyelid. I know he had thick white crescents on his fingernails. I don't know what his smile looks like, or if I did, I have forgotten.

"But I guess celebrities are never really what you think they'll be," she says.

A woman rushes out to dust Mattie's cheeks; he does not thank her, and he does not smile. Around him, be-khakied, be-walkie-talkied young people direct the administration of hair gel and bottled water.

"Hardly ever," I say.

He *didn't* really smile, I'm remembering now. He didn't smile much, or laugh. Instead, he'd make his eyes pulse in a billion different ways—amusement or desire or skepticism or rage—an infinity of micro-expressions, so many that it was easy to believe he conjured each one only once: that it belonged only to the moment you were in with him, and that it would never come again.

"It's always kind of hard to remember that you don't actually know them," says Paisley.

I turn to Paisley again, and this time I make it a point to look right at her.

"Some people make it really easy to forget."

TWENTY-SEVEN
cel

ON TUESDAY AFTERNOON, CERTAIN FACTS EMERGE.

1. The studio is unhappy with Mattie's "politicized" handling of the juvie show.
2. They are threatening to can it and force everyone to work overtime.
3. It is rumored that a "You're Too Fat for Porn!" episode is being considered, because those guests are always easy to come up with on short notice—however:
4. The unions have objections.

The day had begun promisingly enough, with a pep talk from Eddie Marcus.

"Hi there!" he'd chirped at Cel when she walked into the greenroom. He sounded cheerfully noncommittal, as though he wasn't sure if he was supposed to know who Cel was but was happy to extend his graciousness to all people of the world, regardless.

"Have a muffin!" he added, gesturing toward the craft services table as though he'd arranged it for Cel personally. Obediently, she took one. She felt detached, nearly relaxed, as she nibbled it, watching the sound guy retape Mattie's mic.

When Luke appeared, Cel said, "Have a muffin!" He gave her a look like *Fuck off*. Cel smiled at him serenely. I am here only in an observational capacity, she told herself. I am the United Nations.

This peace, however, was short-lived. Cel watched Eddie's face turn pale in the first segment, positively pearlescent in the second, when Mattie went full C-SPAN. His neck still radiated a hearty tan; Cel wondered about bronzer. The mood in the room darkened, then erupted, with Luke shouting "What the hell!" He whirled at Eddie Marcus—flew at him, as they do in Russian novels. Cel was glad Luke had somebody else to fly at, these days. "Did *you* tell him to do this?"

"Why the hell would I do that?" shouted Eddie. Cel wasn't sure she'd ever heard such a rich person yell before—it thrilled her, a little, obscurely—though she didn't think she believed him then, and certainly did not now, as it has further emerged that:

5. Eddie Marcus had helped arrange Mattie's speech at the gun control rally (Cel knew that part already), which

6. Mattie fully intends to go ahead with.

There is apparently nothing in his contract that explicitly prevented him from doing the rally—a fact helpfully pointed out by Mattie himself, when Cel dropped by his office to arrange the VIP Meet-and-Greet. His face had turned a strange color when he'd seen the guy's business card—it was as though his skin curdled, somehow, right before her very eyes—and Cel wondered if he somehow knew him already. Scott probably would have mentioned that. Though then again, maybe he did—the whole conversation was so dim and hallucinatory she hadn't even been sure it was real until Scott called to follow up, and at that point it was too late to ask questions.

At a loss, Cel listens to her voicemails—which are, she is pretty sure, getting more unhinged. There are messages from Christians threatening to pray for Mattie, paranoiacs threatening to kill him. There's a crackpot claiming to have seen Mattie and the shooter on a road trip and demanding payment for the details; he goes so far as to spell out his mailing address—at a P.O. box: where else?—and call back when the tape cuts him off. Cel imagines Mattie and Ryan

Muller toodling around the country together—like Thelma and Louise, or like Humbert and Lolita? Cel has no idea.

Cel heads to Luke's office to complain. Sanjith and Jessica are there already, looking put upon; Luke looks exactly as put upon as usual. Cel wants to whine about her messages—she is put upon, too!—but everyone, it seems, has the same problem. There are journalists calling Luke about rumors that Mattie was himself a gun owner (Jessica rolls her eyes), journalists calling about rumors that Mattie might be gay (Sanjith yawns). There are journalists calling Sanjith wanting to rehash the Secret Crush debacle, journalists calling Jessica to try to resurrect some scandal from his moribund political career.

"But why?" says Cel. "Isn't the homicidal teenager fanboy enough?"

"Nothing like some twenty-year-old low-level municipal shenanigans to really move copy," says Luke.

"I mean, what are they hoping to find—the Lindbergh baby?" says Cel. "Are they hoping he's got a dead girl in his dressing room? Or a live boy?"

She expects laughter, but all she gets is a snort from Luke. Sanjith looks stony; Jessica, frankly alarmed.

"That's a joke," she says, and cringes. This is exactly what the VIP guy had said to her that morning, while making a bad one. "And it's not even my joke, anyway. Some senator said it first."

At two, word goes out that Mattie and Eddie Marcus have been called into a meeting with net executives. This is a cause for rejoicing amongst the underlings—they may all be about to lose their jobs, but they are also, it seems, off the hook. They order pizza and scan the classifieds. There's an emergent sense of camaraderie among them, now that it's nearly over; one day, perhaps, Cel will remember all these people fondly—Sanjith and Jessica and even poor old Donald Kliegerman, that goon—as fellow veterans of a very strange, very dubious war. The invasion of the Falkland Islands. She can't quite summon this feeling about Luke, because she has the suspicion he'll find cause to call and berate her routinely throughout her life.

Luke has recently arrived at a grand unified theory of Mattie's behavior, which is that he's trying to get out of his contract so that he can go back into politics. This, Luke says, explains everything—Mattie's insane behavior the last few months, his total unconcern with the network's wrath. A few months back, a journalist had called about a focus group held in midtown, in which participants were asked to consider the potential Senate run of a daytime TV host, and under what circumstances they might be willing to entertain voting for such a candidate. But the journalist didn't seem to really think that this was Mattie—almost anybody else on television would make more sense—and Luke had mostly forgotten about it, until the announcement about the gun control rally.

"Think about it," Luke says now. "Mattie can't quit, right? His only hope is to get fired. So he hatches a plot to lose the show as much money as he possibly can. When the show experiences a PR crisis, he makes it worse at every turn. That Hitler thing? Come on. He used to be a politician: you think he really doesn't know how to not say the word 'Hitler' on TV? When the network tells him he needs a minder, he negotiates to bring in the *very* guy who ran his mayoral campaign. And suddenly he's using every chance he gets to talk about guns. Why? Well, it's not to help the show. It's not to connect with our viewers. It's not because he's spent years talking about guns with the voters of New York City. It's because he's talking to the voters of New York *State*—because he knows that they, like everyone else, are paying attention."

"Luke," says Jessica. "You sound like a crackpot right now. You sound even more insane than Mattie, and even Mattie's not insane enough to do this."

"You are sounding a little New World Order, man," says Sanjith.

"I really think it could be true," says Luke, and he actually sounds a little hurt.

"Well, *fantastic*," says Cel. "This is just what we need. And here I've already stuck my head in the oven once today!"

Jessica and Sanjith stare as though she might do it again, right in front of them, and Luke declares the meeting adjourned.

———

"TOUGH CROWD," SAYS LUKE, WHEN THE OTHER TWO HAVE LEFT.

"You're telling me," says Cel. "I mean, I know the oven joke was dark, but you can't tell me it's too dark for them. They work here, for Christ's sake."

"It isn't that the joke is too dark." Luke crouches over his mini-fridge and produces two Cokes. "It's that they don't totally believe it's a joke."

"Oh *thanks*," says Cel. "So everyone really thinks I should want to kill myself?"

"Certain kinds of people get to make certain kinds of jokes." He hands her a straw. "That's all."

"Oh. So who should I have been to make that joke?"

"Well, a man, for one thing."

Cel rubs her eyes. "Well, thanks. I'll get right on that."

"A white man, ideally. You want to start with a lot of authority, so that we can laugh when you squander some of it. So that we can consider the possibility of your wounds without getting too uncom-fortable. With women, it's like you're walking around all the time with a life-threatening injury. And when you make a joke about it, it's like you're pointing right at it."

Cel blinks a few times. She isn't sure she's ever heard Luke say two totally sincere sentences in a row; she's certainly never heard him issue a dissertation.

"Jesus, Luke. Is this the kind of stuff you say on dates?"

"I just—you know what? Never mind. Forget it."

He spins his chair around; sighs through his nose; spins back.

"I just mean—like, you know when a pudgy male comic talks about his body, and how unattractive it is, ha-ha? That's the sort of thing that would seem really confusing from a woman. A man can point out how gross he is, and we don't think he's trading on some-thing he actually needs to survive. So we laugh."

"We do?"

"But we think a woman's attractiveness is really, really impor-tant."

"You are a gentleman and a visionary."

"I'm using the societal 'we'! Jesus. It's fucking rhetorical, *obvi-*

ously. What I mean is, we *as a society* think attractiveness or what-ever is so vital to a woman that it's basically beyond irreverence. Or beyond *her* irreverence—for everyone else, it's always open sea-son."

Cel is aware that she is goggling now, gnawing rabbitishly on her straw. She has thought about this problem her entire life, but never articulated it so fiercely; she can't believe Luke has thought about it at all, let alone developed a whole big thesis. It's almost like listening to Elspeth and her theories, except that Cel never recog-nizes her life in those. She wonders what else Luke has theories about.

"Jesus, Luke," says Cel. "Were you a Women's Studies major or something?"

"I took a class," he says, and Cel tries not to fall right over. "The point I'm trying to make is—you say the oven thing, a guy says the oven thing—they don't think either of you are going to do it. They're not, like, dialing a hotline. But when a white man makes a joke like that, we think he's picking on someone who can take it. When you do it, we think we're watching someone get bullied."

"Therefore women aren't funny. QED."

"Yeah," he says. "I mean, obviously nobody is actually thinking about any of this on a conscious level."

"Well, but you are." Cel realizes she's chewed her straw nearly into sludge. "I mean, you've thought about this a lot."

Luke flinches a little.

"I think about everything a lot," he says.

1975

IT IS ALMOST MIDNIGHT AND CEL IS STILL AWAKE, WATCHING RUTH BANG ON the television with her shoe. Their TV is black-and-white, rabbit-eared, alternately high-strung and stupidly insensate—like an actual rabbit, Cel says, and Ruth laughs. Cel is five. Ruth bangs a final time and then, through the mizzle of bullet-colored static, an image ap-pears: a man with pale, jumping eyes, standing anxiously beside the record player.

The *Mighty Mouse* theme song is playing; the man on television is waiting for its chorus. Cel and Ruth laugh and laugh—at the solemn lip-synching, the earnest urgency of his gearing up to do it, and at something else Cel can't put a name on yet and maybe never will. She loves *Saturday Night Live* because if they're watching it at all it means they're already breaking half of Hal's rules. For the rest of her life, *Live from New York it's Saturday night!* will give Cel a sense of promise and thrilling subversion: one day she will follow this feeling all the way to New York City.

Around them, the house is dark. Ruth likes to turn out all the lights that aren't already burned out whenever they watch TV, letting its reflection play out in the picture window. The images loom above the dark woods like an animatronic meteor; looking at it makes Cel shiver. She huddles deeper into Ruth, ready to laugh again when she does. They laugh at Mighty Mouse until they're sick; Ruth laughs until she cries and then keeps laughing beyond that, until things start to get tangled and some critical switch flips and she is sobbing instead of laughing. This happens sometimes, and Cel has learned to fall into her own sort of fit when it does, growing hysterical and wild. This time, she throws a frenzy—she carouses and shrieks and, in a fit of inspiration, even meows—and something about this pushes Ruth back to laughing. Sometimes Cel cannot stand how much she loves her mother. She celebrates by falling off the sofa. And then Ruth falls off the sofa after her, cry-laugh-crying, her eyelashes clumping prettily from her tears.

Cel lives her real life outdoors. She spends the summers in shorts, usually shirtless, the phragmites whisking against her legs. She stations herself in the stream, hypnotized by the rippling water, fleeing only when the humid afternoon susurrus grows thick and coiling all around her. She runs inside to listen to the thunder, so fierce sometimes she feels like a marble being shaken in a palm.

In the stream, Cel is predatory and alert. On the beach, sycophantic squads of ants go fanning across the sand. The sight of a blue crayfish claw in the mud sends a feral thrill down her spine; she tried to cook one once, but its meat was so stringy and soapy that even Hal spit it out. The fish she regards as her allies, and with them it is strictly catch-and-release. Cel scorns the pale little sucker-fish—so easy to spot, so easy to catch; she covets instead the dark and darting minnows, some as fat as her thumb. Bigger fish are slow but rare; she might spot a trout once a year, if she's lucky, and stalk it unsuccessfully all summer. The only one she ever gets to touch is already dead: pinned under a plastic bag, eddying around a pool beneath a little waterfall. Up close, its colors are almost luridly bright, like a clown with melting makeup, and seeing it this way feels wrong. It is, after all, just a very small unimpressive thing, when alive in the water it had seemed lordly and strange.

Best of all are the real animals and their clues: the iridescent clamshells, chipped from where the raccoons had broken them open. In the wet sand, delicate footprints in the shape of tiny human hands. Bears make dusky semicircles in the grass, and leave a sharp, cautionary scent if you've only just missed them. Cel sees them sometimes, too—she sees bobcats, and coyotes, and an inexplicable red thing in a tree. She looks it up later with Hal: it is a marten, apparently, which Cel has never heard of. What she really wants to see is a mountain lion. Ruth claims to have seen one, though Hal doesn't think it's true. Cel makes her tell the story over and over—how the tawny cat with the long, long tail had once come down over the hill—and Cel decides that she believes it. She watches the woods obsessively, waiting for her faith to be rewarded.

The forest has its own mythology, complex and self-referential, marked by omens and touchstones. The enduring, talismanic mysteries posed by the forest: the ski pole stuck in the ground halfway up the hill; the red truck she discovers near the top, half-obscured by vegetation, that she swears was never there before. The wiry half-dead grapevines, tangling amidst the hemlocks. The sagging stone wall that Hal says is from the olden days, before all the farmers gave up on the shallow soil and moved west.

Then there are the great mysterious events, totemic and elevating and defining of eras. The time nudists come walking down the river. Another time it's a family with children—like something summoned directly from Cel's dreams—though they only stay through one summer and a divorce. Anything, it seems, can come crashing through the forest; anything could be given, and anything taken away.

The darkest portent—the one that can only be called a curse—is the night the giant white pine tree is hit by lightning. It was a catastrophe of literally nightmarish dimensions—Cel has many times dreamed of this loss—and something about the combination of prophecy and grief renders her inconsolable. Only Ruth understands the extent of her sadness, just as only Ruth understood her hysteric hilarity when, years after adopting a tiny tree—Cel wreathing it with stones for protection, Ruth cooing at it with a singsong, hypocoristic lilt, both of them devoting themselves with an ardor that Cel hadn't recognized at the time as, essentially, maternal—they finally realized it was a bush. They laughed over this with the same intensity they later extended toward the pine, while Hal muttered darkly over boys he'd known in the war who were mourned less than this goddamn shrub.

But in the woods, things matter, both differently and more. Home is where things are said and done that might later reveal themselves to never have happened at all. Trying to decipher Ruth is like trying to learn a language that keeps changing its alphabet, and sometimes insists it has no written tradition at all. In the woods, everything is real and also more than real: all stones are arrowheads, all rustles are bears. Though Cel isn't greedy: she rejoices every day over the more quotidian revelations. The stubborn handful of beech trees amidst the conifers; the place deep in the forest where a stand of chartreuse ferns grow in a shaft of narrow light. A dark panicle of deer scat in the snow.

The seasons comprise a liturgical year, complete with rituals and rites. Cel marks time from the icing of the stream in the winter; to the blooming of the mountain laurel, the color and shape of cumulus clouds; to the resurrection of the tiger lilies every Fourth of July; to the springtime emergence of the painted trillium—so intricate it seems to belong in a museum, so beautiful it seemed impossible that it would have really been there if Cel hadn't come along to see it.

And maybe, just maybe, it hadn't: after all, who can say that it had?

semi

I AM BESIEGED BY HUMIDITY AS I EMERGE FROM THE FIFTY-NINTH STREET STA-
tion; the air is so thick it feels like an impostor. This is why I'm bent
at the waist, why I need a moment to catch my breath, as I straggle
along Columbus Circle.

Matthew is at the restaurant already. He probably makes a habit
of having his girl misstate the time. Must be nice to have *staff*—
maybe this could be my opening line? But no, this makes no
sense—it is not a rejoinder, only the eruption of a mind in dialogue
with itself. Which is what this whole thing always was, in fact.

"Hello." I seem to have sat down already.

Matthew looks at me and says, "Oh." This *Oh* is part laughter,
part harrowing sadness: it sounds like the exclamation of a person in
an absurd freak accident the moment they understand that this
(this!) is what is actually going to kill them.

There is a long, drowning pause.

"You look well," he says.

"Ha."

His mouth opens, closes. He looks like a lamprey.

"You look like a lamprey." His mouth closes more decisively, and
then he laughs. He has one of the sadder laughs I've ever heard—

though the competition in this area is stiff—and it relumes something within me. I tell myself this is not recognition, but déjà vu: a skipped beat in the brain.

"It's been a while."

"An age!" There's an unhinged merriment in my voice. "Since '79, I think it was?"

"That sounds right." It seems just possible he isn't sure. I tell myself that these preliminaries are important; once they're dispensed with, once I can be sure of the steadiness of my own hand—then, then, I will turn on the recording device in my pocket.

"Well, here you are," he says.

"Alive and kicking." I'd like to pour myself some water, but this seems inadvisable. "Maybe you wondered."

"I'm so glad," he says. Then: "I was sorry to hear about your friends."

I suppose he means this in a general way; I can't imagine he's been scanning the obituaries.

"Oh, did some of them still owe you money?"

I was hoping we could negotiate our way to some mutually acceptable level of hostility—but all of a sudden the waiter is upon us, imperiously listing the specials. I remember why I hate going to restaurants: I can no longer bear being a supplicant on my own time.

When he finally leaves, Matthew asks: "Are you still writing?"

His voice has fallen into its familiar tessitura, which is how I realize he's been using his TV voice until now. This certainly means it is time to turn on the recorder. I drop a napkin, retrieve it, and do.

"Oh *yes*," I say, emerging. "I've had a play about AIDS running at the Underground for a year. It's been a huge sensation. I'm surprised you haven't heard."

None of this will sound great on the tape, I realize.

"I live a pretty cloistered life these days," says Matthew.

"Positively priestly, I'm sure."

"I'll have to come to see your show."

"I could probably comp you a couple tickets," I say. "No guarantees."

"Are you working on anything new?"

"Oh, always." This is a lie. All my new ideas keep getting sub-sumed into *The Spectators:* more and more, I have the sense I will be writing it for the rest of my life. "My new project is about the Mat-tachine. That was the group that—"

"I know."

"You know. Okay. So it's about, you know. Fools speaking truth to power."

I've invented this project strictly for the thematic purposes of this conversation.

"Well, you always did like an allegory."

"These days all anyone writes is allegory. Or autobiography. Which are embarrassing in different ways, but what can you do? Anyone who's still getting to pick their humiliations at this point is very, very lucky."

"My guests must be the luckiest people in the world, then."

"I'd say they *are* relatively lucky, yes. You know, in the scheme of things? I mean, none of your guests are AIDS patients, are they?"

"No," says Matthew quietly. "Not since *Comment*."

"Not since more than four people have been watching, you mean."

"I didn't think it would be the right fit," he says carefully, "for this version of the show."

"Totally. I mean, what a drag, right? Best avoid the topic entirely! There's some precedent for that, you know. Not only the more glar-ing examples—your federal government, your mainstream media. Even some of us in the *gay community* prefer not to discuss it."

"I believe it," he says.

"For example, there's this photographer—you wouldn't know his work—who spent years taking picture of AIDS patients? Now he photographs llamas."

"Sounds like a familiar trajectory."

"Upper-class llamas, at that."

"Is there any other kind?"

"Or Robert Ferro—another unfamiliar name, I'm sure. He just wouldn't put the word 'AIDS' in his last novel. Just wouldn't do it. It's one of those words that if you let it be one word, it sort of becomes the only word, you know? And who wants to be summed up like that? Still, *entre nous,* I think it was bad form of him. I mean, there's a war on. Even Hemingway had to drive ambulances."

Matthew, I notice, is twirling some spaghetti around on his fork. Its presence makes the entire scene feel abruptly dreamlike—*and then I was sitting with Matthew Miller in midtown, and then he was eating spaghetti!*—but a scan of the minutes preceding does reveal a dim memory of ordering food. I look down and notice a plate of mussels.

"But enough about me!" I say, cracking one open. These must be expensive; some part of my brain, clearly, was operative. "I want to hear about *you.* Do you still watch wrestling?"

"No." Matthew laughs again, that rueful dammed-up laugh, and I hate him for it—what does he know of sorrow, and how dare he parade it around like that, where anyone at all can hear? Over the years, I've come to understand that the truest grief is often undetectable; this creates the suspicion that casually demonstrated pain is inauthentic. Or maybe I'm only turning into my grandmother, and am finally just embarrassed by *displays.* "I suppose I don't need to anymore."

"You've got your day job for that."

"It's a similar idea. Different participants, slightly different skill set."

"It seems to keep you busy."

"Yes," he says tiredly. "That is exactly what it does."

"Your staff seem awfully peppy, anyway. That little cheerleader producer is just a doll."

His eyes flash. This is some distant descendant of an expression I once knew—there's that sense of an urgent awakening that you alone have summoned—and I remember how it stirred me, how it stunned me, once.

"You don't have everyone's number, you know," he says.

"I *do* know." I knew it just yesterday, for example, while looking at that paisley-shirted woman. But knowing this isn't the hard part. It's the remembering. "I don't think I need to remind you who first taught me that."

He issues a flinch that somehow apologizes for itself; he seems to realize he hasn't any right. I've read about a cognitive disorder in which the sufferer becomes convinced that everyone around them has been replaced by simulacra—that they are surrounded by identical, sinister doubles. I can imagine this experience, I think, by multiplying Matthew Miller by everyone.

"So what's the story with the kid-murderer's letters?" I am trying to sound conversational.

Matthew puts down his fork.

"Is that why you're here?"

I hunch over my mussels. "Not exactly."

"Are you working for someone?"

"I'm just curious."

He sighs, and I know he doesn't believe me. To prove to myself I was going to do it anyway, I turn off the device in my pocket.

"I just think it's interesting," I say. Although I don't. As a politician, Matthew wrote back to all his letters, and some of those were from people who'd already committed murder; to me, his writing back to that shooter is one of the least surprising things he's done in decades. "Although you always did like to side with the underdog."

"I like to withhold judgment," he says.

"Don't you think that's cowardly?"

"I think it depends on the circumstance."

"Well, you always liked to let things depend on the circumstance."

How this had impressed me, how it thrilled me, once—Matthew's ability to understand opposing arguments, to articulate them better than their own best champions ever did. I'd never wanted Matthew to succeed in politics, but he did, for a time, make me believe in them. He made me believe, anyway, that an acknowledgment of reality's ambiguities was not a useless dithering, but a righteous first step toward action. We all know better now, of course—the political sphere has long ago exposed itself as a self-sealing pageant, immune to decency or data. But my disillusionment really began, I'm understanding now, with Matthew. His ludicrous post-politics career wasn't even the half of it.

"You aren't who I thought you were," I find myself saying now.

Brookie said this to me once, back when we were little children and thought we were breaking each other's hearts. *You aren't who I thought you were:* I'd found it very hurtful. It seems a peculiar kind of loss, coming, as it does, alongside a retroactive blessing—leaving you with the unbearable knowledge that you'd had someone's regard, once, before you squandered it.

For a long while, Matthew studies a spot above my forehead.

"When you and I knew each other," he says finally, "I *thought* a great deal. I spent a lot of time thinking about what was right, and I spent a lot of time wondering where I had it wrong."

I don't get where this is going; I hope to God it isn't turning into a case of Matthew getting things off his chest. Whatever he's got in there can stay right where it is.

"I wasn't arrogant, you know." He says this forcefully, as though rebutting some long-standing accusation.

"I never thought you were arrogant." Though I don't remember, precisely, whether I did or not. The light around us has a dense, waterlogged feel. "I think I mostly thought you were delusional."

"Well, you turned out to be right about that," he says. "Because the only thing I never thought about was whether it would ever matter what I thought. I only cared about my beliefs because I assumed my life would be full of opportunities to act on them. I felt that even after I dropped out of the race, you know. Even when I worked on *Comment.* I still believed my life would be some sort of, you know. Some sort of moral canvass." He shakes his head. "I don't get the sense you were ever under that impression."

"I'm an artist," I say. "I was born to be inconsequential."

"So is everyone," says Matthew. "If you're really lucky, you might have a handful of chances not to be. And if you miss them, then your convictions will be of interest only to you. They'll amount to a form of solipsism."

"But you're on television," I say. "Everything you do matters."

"God, I hope you're wrong about that."

"So make some new chances, then." I am getting fed up with this. "You're rich. You're healthy. You're alive, which is more than a lot of people can say."

"Make some new chances," he says. "Yes. I am trying."

"With the gun stuff?"

"Partly that."

"Well, why stop there? You should go back into politics!" I laugh. "You should run for president! You'd probably be elected in a land-slide."

Matthew frowns as though I've said something cruel, and I won-der if this is a thought he's actually considered. A woman on the sidewalk pauses to goggle at Matthew through the window; her wispy-haired baby is goggling at me. I goggle back.

"It isn't always clear, what it means to do the right thing," says Matthew. "But we never get to know when it's our last chance to try. And eventually, there comes a point when you're grateful for the chance to make small gestures."

"Is this what this letter thing is, then?" I say. "A gesture?"

"No," he says. "As usual, I mean something else entirely."

"Well," I say. "I'm still listening."

This moment feels magnified and strangely remote: I feel I'm staring it down through a loupe. At the window, the woman is still staring; Matthew turns to wave at her and she scurries away, morti-fied. He looks relieved when he turns around—because she didn't want his autograph, I suppose.

"What do you want from me?" he asks.

"Nothing." And maybe, in this moment, it begins to be true.

"Then why are you here?" he says. "I mean, really."

The feeling in the room teeters for a moment—something like the suspense that spears through a subway station when somebody gets too close to the tracks.

And then I say: "I'm still deciding."

AFTERWARD, I HEAD TO THE RAWHIDE.

I am searching, I think, for a dose of the invisibility I felt in the *Mattie M* waiting room. It's not so easy to come by, even in New York. There are always looks: that flick of curiosity, that momentary advance-and-retreat of speculation. The partial uprising of an eye-brow followed by its brutal suppression. It's been a while since I've been there, though in the old days we went all the time—usually as a last resort, like anything right around the corner. I wonder if the Puerto Rican guys still play dominoes outside on Saturday nights. We started going in '79, I think: now *this* is a place that's seen it all.

I push the curtains aside and enter caliginous depths: inside, it is always dark, and never the wrong time for a cocktail. Once, Matthew had told me long ago, this place had been a candy store. I order one drink, then another, and then I notice someone staring at me. He has bright, watchful eyes and a nose the right kind of crooked, and for old times' sake, I follow him into the bathroom. We clutch at each other for some incalculable while until I drop to my knees. We wordlessly negotiate: no condom, and no further. We are mortal again, for a moment, as I unzip his jeans. And then, for another moment, we are not.

TEN YEARS INTO THE PLAGUE, AND WHAT ARE WE LEFT WITH?

We are left with images.

The shadowy men in the lots near the pier, the piano patterning of lights on the buildings just beyond.

The shivering, astral sheen of headlights on the East River.

Paulie taking an unabashed chomp of cheese in the park, a strand dribbling down his chin.

Paulie's scarred saurian hands, his strangely unblemished face, as he lay, finally quiet, in his casket.

The countless times we'd asked him to be quiet—how we'd demanded, shouted, issued toothless ultimatums.

That single spoiled orchid he used to keep above the mantel.

The rust smell of the jail cell, that night we got arrested and first met Matthew Miller.

The way Matthew bent over Stephen, an expression of impersonal, unsurprised tenderness on his face.

The way he said, "I don't think you're ready to give up the ghost quite yet."

The day nineteen years later when Stephen finally was ready, and finally did.

The way Stephen's eyes dimmed and waned that night; the way they still wanted to come back to us.

The smell of Stephen's Penhaligon cologne, back at the very beginning.

The bleach burn of the stranger in my throat—right now, right this very second—as I walk down Eighth Avenue.

I'll never see him again, but that's not saying much: to think that once it was a thrill, to lose a man you'd fucked to New York City.

MOST OF ALL, WE ARE LEFT WITH THE COUNTERFACTUALS. THEY COME TO US late at night, every night: the question of the iceberg, the question of the lifeboats.

If they had shuttered the bathhouses.

If they hadn't shuttered the TB clinics.

If Rock Hudson had declared himself sooner.

If Jimmy Carter had still been president.

If Gerald fucking *Ford* had still been president.

If Matthew Miller had been the mayor of New York.

Though it's easy to overestimate this one. Matthew Miller would have confronted the same lack of federal funding and national public health infrastructure; he would have been bullied and bludgeoned by the same political forces, seen and unseen. It is unclear what a man of courage might have done in this context, and it is unclear whether Matthew Miller would have ever become one.

Still: one suspects he would have mentioned it. At the time, this would have been no small matter.

In politics, as in theater, timing is everything.

cel

EVERY NIGHT, STILL, CEL DREAMS OF THE WOODS. SO IT CANNOT BE ENTIRELY right to say that it has been years since she's been home. On a literal level it is true: the last time she went back was in November of '89, right after Ruth died, and not long before Hal, his thankless missions finally completed, allowed himself to die as well. Cel was irrationally surprised by this. She had perhaps not entirely believed old Hal had it in him—death being the sort of enforced idleness of which he seemed congenitally, permanently incapable. But then, there was the matter of Hal's death certificate, followed by the amphora of his alleged ashes once the UNH forensics students were done with him. Cel had to accept the truth of these things; she had not gone to see Hal's body. She told herself he wouldn't have wanted her to. More likely: he wouldn't have cared. But there was no one to watch her bravely appear, no one to notice if she did not. And hadn't she been through enough for one year? Elspeth assured her that she had, as she wept on a stool in the common room. She'd been through enough for one *lifetime,* said Elspeth, and Cel felt a secret, sequestered relief: an ignoble hope that she might, from here on out, be off the hook.

And so the last time she saw Hal turned out to be the last time she saw everything: the house, and the woods, and Ruth—looking strange but not dreadful in the casket. They'd left it open, so that people couldn't imagine things were worse than they were. Afterward, Cel and Hal moved through the house sorting bric-a-brac, aeons of detritus, with an abstract, half-feigned sense of urgency. What is this impulse to start moving things around when someone dies—to disrupt items that had sat in the same place, demanding nothing, bothering no one, for decades? A Whip Inflation Now pin, a rusted bottle of Brylcreem. There was not necessarily a point. And yet this was what was done, it seemed, and Ruth had always had a strange, intermittent regard for what was done. The way one organizes a bridal shower, the way one lays out a table—Ruth spoke of these rituals as ongoing, part of a pageant that continued somewhere without her and that she might, at any moment, rejoin. She had her fussy little flourishes, her inscrutable points of judgment. She'd hated the blue mohair couch Hal brought home, in a fit of what he'd hoped would be upward mobility. Though in fact they'd been aggressively downwardly mobile—even during a time (and really, it was the only time) when a lot of people were going the other way. It took years for Cel to realize this part: that where Ruth wound up was nothing like where she started.

But here, sorting through the house, is the evidence. Ruth's teetering old piano, for one, which Hal will sell for lumber at a price gauged artificially high by pity. There are the prissy little things Cel finds in Ruth's drawers: heavy, high-quality stationery; frilled linen with tiny blue flowers—these, it seems, are relics of something more than money. At the bottom of the drawer, she finds a collection of porcelain miniatures she remembers from her childhood. According to the lawyer, they would have been worth a lot, if there'd been a whole lot more of them.

"Well, you could say that about anything, couldn't you?" says Hal. "You could say that about a wheat penny."

"Not anymore," says Cel. She is using what they both regard as her college voice. "They're out of circulation."

One of the figurines shows a little girl pulling a sled across a snowy field; another has a boy in a straw hat painting a fence—and this, she understands without even thinking, is Tom Sawyer. She stares as signifier merges violently, permanently, with signified. One of the figures depicts a tiny park done in crisp, crayon-bright colors: green landscape, blue river, red bridge. In the stream are boats shaped like swans: this, she'd always known, was the Boston Public Garden. Her mother had always promised to take her there, to see them. She stares at the little park in her hands. She admires the intricacy of the swans—their black beaks, their bowed necks. As a child, Cel had never really understood what a swan boat was, had always been a bit apprehensive about finding out. But now she sees what a child might have seen—the charming, fairy-tale quality of the park, those swans like cumulus chariots—and she understands finally that someone must have taken Ruth there as a child, and that she must have loved it very much, and that this hadn't stopped her from throwing herself off a bridge thirty-one years later.

"Anyway," says Cel. "That isn't really what he means."

"Oh no, Celeste?" says Hal. "Then educate me."

Cel puts the figurine down. She doesn't think she wants to take it with her.

"You wouldn't understand," she says. "He's talking about something else entirely."

ON FRIDAY MORNING, THE VIP IS BACK.

"You're back," Cel says, when she meets him halfway down the hallway.

"I came to drop this off for Matthew." He is holding a package under his arm; Cel wonders idly if it's a bomb.

"Oh," says Cel. "Is this something you want him to sign?"

He shakes his head and hands Cel an envelope containing an object the size of an ear. Hopefully not an actual ear.

"Seems like you guys are in a bit of trouble around here," says the VIP.

"I guess." He means the letter, she figures. "I mean, the thing about Mattie is that there's no one he won't talk to." She eyes him. "Or maybe you know that."

"I like that line of defense," says the man. "It's very classical. Retroactively casts a flaw as a strength."

Cel squints at him. He is slight and a little paunchy—nervous-seeming energy, receding hairline. Smart, strangely soulful eyes. Not, she thinks, the usual viewer. "I guess you're probably a writer," she says.

"Is that what you're trying to be?"

"No."

"Not the *stage*, I hope."

"I'm not really trying to be anything."

He scoffs. "Of course you are. You're, what, twenty-four? And you live in New York City."

"I might move," she says.

"Don't tell me. California."

Behind the VIP, a giant red promo poster is approaching on a lorry. Cel wonders where it's going and if the man wheeling it even works here—he's wearing overalls, so she's going to assume that he does.

"Well, nobody's trying to *be* anything out in *California*," says the VIP. "So you will fit right in."

Cel says nothing. She can hear a different sort of silence start to bleed, then clot, into the pause between them, and then the man laughs.

"Well, good luck out there," he says. "And don't let anyone tell you the golden age of cinema is over! Remember the golden age of anything is always right before you got there."

"I hear that a lot around here."

"I bet you do."

There's a lateritic turn to the light: can it possibly be evening already? But no, it's only the bright red promo poster blocking a window while it's wheeled off to wherever. The VIP, Cel notices, is turning and walking away.

"Hey," she says, and he stops.

"Yes?"

"Was Mattie a good lawyer?"

He laughs again. "Was Mattie a good lawyer," he says. "I can tell you I had zero complaints about his lawyering."

"I can't imagine Mattie as a lawyer. Or a politician."

"He was highly regarded as both, if you can believe it. Some people thought he was a sort of political genius. A real working-class Kennedy. He even had the crypto-Catholicism down."

"Isn't everybody the Kennedy of something, though?"

"No."

"Just like everywhere is the Paris of somewhere?"

"No, not remotely."

"We read his mail, you know," says Cel. "Ever since the—well, recently."

The man shrugs. "There's nothing in there to read. It's just a recording of our conversation. I thought he might be interested."

Cel nods. The promo poster, she sees, has been abandoned by its minder. It leans against a wall, an enormous sideways Mattie giving a perfectly horizontal thumbs-up.

"Mattie as a Catholic!" she says. "It's impossible."

"I didn't say he *is* anything." The VIP puts the *is* in quotes. "And impossible isn't saying much, these days."

"I guess not," says Cel. "The other day someone told me that there are more people alive right now than have ever died."

Was that really just the other day?

"I don't think that can be right," says the man. "Everyone I know is dead."

CEL LISTENS TO THE TAPE RIGHT AWAY, OF COURSE, AS THE MAN MUST HAVE expected that she would. The conversation is muffled and confusing, but several things are evident. First, it is clear that Mattie has no idea he is being recorded. Second, it is clear that the man thinks he's engaged in some sort of aggression, though its precise nature is unclear. In terms of what is literally said, it could be worse. Mattie's contempt for the show comes through, which isn't great, but there's no mention of Ryan Muller or the letters. What mostly emerges is a sort of oblique lecture about AIDS—anfractuous, high-minded, fairly one-sided, and not at all unlike the kind of thing Mattie used to do on *Comment:* this means no one will pay attention. More ominous is the conversation's subtext: it is screechingly obvious to Cel that Mattie and the VIP were lovers once, though it's equally obvious that they currently are not. Though there have been rumors about Mattie for years, an actual outing would be another matter—likely to be a fatal blow to the show at any time, and right now, of course, forget it. The problem isn't so much that the cultural conservatives would go off the deep end—when it comes to Mattie, they're pretty much already there. And the show's viewership is obviously not exactly squeamish about nontraditional lifestyles. But evidence of Mattie being gay would make him one of the *guests;* viewers would no longer trust him to navigate them through the underworld, or to bring them back again safely. So yes, Cel thinks: documentation of Mattie's sexuality would be a very, very big deal. It would certainly be highly lucrative, as blackmail or as news. But if this is blackmail, why does the man leave their past together implied? And if this is an item he's trying to sell to a tabloid, why did he bother giving them a heads-up? And if it's meant to be a public service announcement, some kind of arty comment or critique—well, it just isn't. Or if it is, Cel doesn't get it.

She plays the recording again, trying to listen for what the man wants. Mostly, he just seems to want to talk to Mattie—to let him know he's angry at him, still, after however many years. This is his agenda; the interview is the pretext. If there's another scheme he's meant to be prosecuting here, he is clearly very bad at it, and it is very likely not his own. So who is really behind this conversation?

Scott.

Scott. Well, sure.

Cel mourns, briefly, for all the jokes she'd thought he'd laughed at.

CEL GETS DRUNK, THEN TELLS ELSPETH.

"This is entirely absurd," says Elspeth, correctly.

"Faith is an attempt made on the strength of absurdity," says Cel, and hiccups. "*Kierkegaard* said that."

"That sounds—out of context."

"Faith is an attempt made on the strength of things taken out of context."

"You're drunk."

Another on-point observation from Elspeth!—who, Cel sees, is staring at her sadly.

"Why did you ever even take this job?" she says.

Cel considers: she must have had an answer to this once.

"I have a degree in English," she says finally. "I wanted to do something with words."

"Words, Cel? *Any* words? Like the way Leni Riefenstahl wanted to do something with images?"

"Come on."

"I'm sorry. I just never could have imagined you devoting your life to making fun of the poor."

"Making *fun* of the poor? Who the hell do you think watches this show?" Cel realizes she is somewhat shouting; she needs to start spending less time with Luke. "It isn't rich psych students, I'll tell you that. It's not the staff of *The New Yorker*. They're the ones wringing their hands over this thing. Poor people, believe it or not, have real problems."

"Jesus, Cel."

"Anyone who thinks the show is making fun of poor people has to think poor people are actually like that. That they're *actually* fucking their goats."

"Well," says Elspeth. "It's finally happened. You've finally started to believe your own bullshit."

"Go fifty miles outside any college town and it's wall-to-wall goat-fucking, as far as the eye can see."

"You've *definitely* started to believe your own bullshit, Cel. You're, like, converted."

"You know why rich people hate the show so much?" says Cel. "Because they're afraid of how much it disgusts them. Because it makes it so much harder for them to feel so tolerant and great about themselves. Because they need poor people to be these exalted endangered panda bears—or lazy wretches, you know, depending on their politics. But maybe those are equally fucked up."

Cel is crying, apparently. She goes to the window to hide.

"I thought you cared about me," she says dramatically. Like everything she really means, it comes out sounding false: maybe Elspeth thinks so, too.

"Cared about *you?*" says Elspeth. Cel is blinking through her tears. In the distance, some building's swordfish-nosed antenna is blinking at her right back. "And who would that be, exactly?"

LEANING ON MATTIE'S DOORBELL, CEL REALIZES SHE PROBABLY SHOULD HAVE called ahead. She'd been galvanized on the way over—stirred by alcohol and insult and the newfound conviction that, no matter what Elspeth said, she *did,* once in a while, know how to do the right thing. She sobered up somewhere along West Houston and now the principles in play seem murkier, as does the logic of showing up unannounced. And yet, is this not a matter of professional urgency? Luke would certainly argue that it is. She should probably have called him, too, now that she thinks of it.

Mattie seems surprised to see her, though not as surprised as he should be.

"Oh," he says, his eyebrows arcing into vortices. "I thought you might be someone else."

She apologizes for bothering him and he says not to worry and then Cel is inside Mattie's apartment, sitting on a surprisingly frayed sofa, while he fetches her a glass of water she didn't ask for. The apartment is spare, nearly parsonic—more damning evidence of Christianity: she'll have to tell Luke about *that* before she leaves. Because she is leaving, she realizes, even if no one is going to make her.

"I came to bring you this," says Cel, handing him the envelope. "It's a recording of your conversation with that VIP guy."

Mattie mouths the word *Oh* before he says it.

"I thought you'd probably want to have it," says Cel.

"Yes," says Mattie. "Yes, certainly I do."

He looks at the envelope intently, though he does not open it. Probably he's waiting for Cel to leave. She begins to stand.

"Did you listen to it?" says Mattie.

"Oh." She sits again. "Yes. Yes, I did. I'm sorry."

Though she doesn't know why she should be, she somehow actually is.

"I don't know what it means," she tells him. "I mean, I don't know what he means *by* it."

"I might have an idea."

"That's, well. That's good. But you'll actually probably want to be discussing that with Luke, mostly, because actually I guess I'm quitting?" Should she say this so baldly? And shouldn't she be saying it to Luke, come to think of it? "I'm giving my notice, I mean."

"Ah. Well. Good for you." Mattie drops the envelope on the coffee table and leans back. "What's next?"

"I think I'm going to go to California."

"California, huh? Well, that shouldn't be hard for you. Most Changed, and all."

Cel is surprised he remembers this about her. Then she remembers that he remembers everything. Then she remembers, very faintly, that it isn't even true.

"Well. I'd tell you a secret about that, but."

"But people really need to stop telling me their secrets."

"This one's pretty mediocre. You could probably even guess."

"You were voted something else, then," says Mattie. "Most Likely to be Reluctantly Employed by a Tabloid Television Show. You were never voted Most Changed at all."

"I was." She pauses for what she hopes is clearly comical suspense. "It's just I didn't."

"Oh?" Mattie looks her up and down, as though it's possible Cel has been a twelve-year-old all along. "You stayed the same, you mean?"

"I mean I wasn't really any way at all."

"So you *were* born for PR!" Mattie rolls his neck; she can hear it cracking. "Tell me this: did you lie a lot as a kid?"

"Did I *lie* a lot?"

"Withdrawn."

"I mean—what's a lie? What's a lot? I mean, I guess. Doesn't everyone?"

"What did you lie about?"

"I don't remember."

He smirks, like, has she forgotten the subject under discussion?

"Well, little things, mostly," she says. "Or—they weren't really lies, more like stories? I had this long con involving four-leaf clovers."

"And here I thought the real money was in network TV."

"It was spectacularly stupid. I'd pick two clovers and pull two leaves off one of them and braid the stems around and then go running to the other kids and say I'd found a four-leaf clover. They didn't understand why I was so much better at finding them. I told them it was because I lived in the woods. But it was weird they believed me, because we pretty much all lived in the woods."

Cel is sure she's never discussed this with anybody, and she can't believe she's discussing it with Mattie, at midnight, in his own apartment. She can't believe this is his apartment—it looks like a student loft, the crash pad of an underpaid commuter. It poses the corollary mystery of the one Cel encountered in her own apartment: Nikki's clothes, her concerts, her juicer. How had Cel thought *these* fit into the equation—the unforgiving calculus of income versus expenditures?

The answer was, they didn't, and neither does this place.

"Anyway," she says, "this went on for years. I was actually kind of known for it. I'd do it sometimes in high school, even, just to maintain my cover retroactively."

"That isn't really a lie, though, is it?" says Mattie. "More like a really bad party trick."

"That's exactly how I thought of it!"

"And then you learned your lesson and you never lied again."

"Well, not exactly."

"No?"

"Once I told a girl I'd had a bunch of horses that had died," says Cel. "The horses part was to make her think I was secretly rich, even if she'd maybe heard other things. The dying part was to account for the fact that there were no horses."

"Lying for personal gain," says Mattie. "You were born for sales."

"But it backfired—because she wasn't impressed at all, she was just sad!" Cel laughs. "I think in another life I probably would have been a town gossip. I just happened not to know any, so I had to make things up."

Cel likes this sentiment as a sentence, as a jokey thing to say—it sounds like it could be true, and surely it is true of someone, and who's to say this someone isn't her? But even as she says this she knows, with unusual conviction, that it is not. And she is seized by the realization that nobody besides her knows this, and that if she doesn't say it out loud to Mattie M right this instant, then nobody ever will.

"No," she says. "I guess that's not it, either."

"No?" says Mattie. Even though he doesn't ask her to elaborate, Cel somehow believes he wants to listen: is this the sorcery he uses on his guests? She has never for one moment thought that Mattie actually cares about them—but right now, she can see why some of them seem to think he does.

"My first lie I remember," says Cel. "I was maybe four or five. I spent all of recess making this really elaborate monster footprint in the mud. I wanted to show it to these other girls to scare them."

Cel realizes that even if she can articulate this thing, the only two people who know it will be her and Mattie M, and that this is quite possibly worse than no one knowing it at all.

"And I showed it to them and they were terrified, and I was very pleased. But then this little boy came over and told the girls *he'd* made the footprint, even though I could tell he was kind of scared of it, too. And I remember thinking how brave he was to do that. It really blew my mind that he was lying to be good, and that there were things that could be kindnesses only if nobody knew that's what they were. And that I, the villain of this story, was the only one who knew what he was doing, and to tell anyone about it would be undoing his kindness. There was this thrill and shame and secret amazement in that, I think." She laughs and shakes herself a little. "The moral of the story being that truth is complicated."

"You should have been in intelligence work," says Mattie. "Or fiction writing. Some kind of intellectual retail."

"I should have been a missionary, maybe."

"Probably not that," says Mattie dryly. Then: "You want to know what sold C. S. Lewis on Christianity?"

"C. S. Lewis?" What she really means is: *Christianity?* Cel isn't even sure if this conversation is legal: does this apartment count as the workplace?

"J. R. R. Tolkien—you know, the Hobbit guy?—told him that the whole thing, Christianity, was a true myth. A true myth, you know? I've always liked that."

"So you *are* a Catholic!"

"Who told you that?" says Mattie. "Never mind, I know who told you that."

He goes to the window and places his hands against the glass. Above him, a smeared, greasy-looking moon hovers over the skyline.

"What's that thing that Mencken said?" he says, as though this were something they were only just discussing. "Something like, a philosopher is a blind man in a dark room looking for a black cat that isn't really there—a theologian is the man who finds it?"

"Is that a true myth?" says Cel. "Maybe he just *says* he finds it."

"Well, exactly."

"Promise me you'll never say any of *that* on television," says Cel. "It'll give poor old Luke a grand mal seizure."

"I won't."

"He's been trying to tell me for *years* you were religious."

"I'm not."

"Good," says Cel. "Because it is way too late to be useful."

Mattie comes back to the couch and sits beside her. He's so close she can see the calcium deposits on his fingernails. Is it possible he was really living here all along—coming back night after night to this apartment, with its Nixon-era furniture and its fragile, assertively middle-class lighting? What would Cel have done if somebody had told her this? The same thing anyone else would do: she would not have believed it.

"Why do you think Ryan Muller wrote to you?" she says.

"I really don't know," says Mattie. "I've thought about it a lot. And all I can come up with is this: I think he knew he couldn't shock me.

I think he figured that, whatever he could say, I'd probably heard worse."

Cel isn't going to ask if this turned out to be true. She still doesn't give a shit about Ryan Muller's privacy, but she is beginning to give something of a shit about Mattie's. It's this apartment that is doing it—it's wearing her down, with its teetering bookshelf and its dusty tomes of political theory. She somehow feels she knows too much already.

"Did you ever think of going back to politics?" she says. "Before all of this, I mean."

"Quite a bit, actually."

"Why didn't you?"

He looks at her and mouths the word *Contract.*

Oh, Cel mouths back, then says aloud: "Of course." She looks away from him, toward his little window. Broadway is out there somewhere, she supposes. All Cel sees is her own pale reflection, the definitive darkness beyond.

"You know what *I* wanted to do?" she says.

"This, obviously."

"Never mind. I mean, it's ridiculous."

"Would you believe I have an extremely high tolerance for the ridiculous?"

"I sort of wanted to do stand-up," she says. "You know, comedy?"

"Why not. You're funny."

"You never laugh at my jokes."

"Don't I?" he says mildly. "I always mean to."

So now Cel knows he doesn't think she's funny. She waits to start holding this against him, but it isn't happening. This is another entirely novel mental state: she wonders how many of these constitute some sort of neurological emergency.

"Jokes are true myths, too, aren't they?" Mattie is saying. "Stop me if you've heard this one! Man on a sinking ship frees his pet gull from its cage. There's a joke. Or a true myth. I mean, in this case it's actually true. Whatever made the guy do that is the thing I want to believe in. They should make *that* into a religion."

"I'm sure someone has," says Cel. "If there's one thing your show has taught me, it's that someone out there has done absolutely every-thing."

"That's the worldview of an extremely old person. You're much too young to say things like that."

"I was raised by my grandfather," says Cel. "More or less."

"I knew someone who used to say that sort of thing about every-thing," says Mattie. "Though I guess he was young then, too."

Cel nods respectfully, trying to look as though she really does believe that she, too, will get old. Privately, she has her doubts.

"You know what I think?" says Mattie. "I think you're the kind of person that in another life could have been absolutely anything."

"But here we are," says Cel. "In this one."

"*Exactly,*" he says, holding his palms up to the sky.

THIRTY
semi

TEN YEARS INTO THE PLAGUE, AND WHAT ARE WE LEFT WITH?

We are left, occasionally, with miracles: tonight they're letting Brookie out to see my play.

I usually skulk in the back—embarrassed to be seen attending at all—but Brookie's wheelchair means automatic front-row seats. It's a novelty to see the thing up close—the actors' makeup ghoulishly mimetic; their bodies starved, with Method lunacy, into emaciation. The curtain goes up on such a figure—supine and shrouded, way up in the hinterlands of stage left. The spotlight is aimed several feet downstage from him, casting a circle the actor does not reach, conjuring a sense of loudly *cosmic* exile that strikes me, frankly, as unfortunate. But then, if I wanted to be a control freak, I should have written a different play.

The figure is draped over a grate, shivering in a way that makes us understand both that this is a floor heater, and that it isn't actually the winter. Actors terrify me: I hope to never understand what they do. For a moment, we listen to him pant. Then he painfully rolls over and begins crawling toward the light.

And even though they know what's coming, the crowd gasps when they see his face: this time, this is the beginning.

NARRATOR:

It was during the Black Plague that they began marking the dead. Someone told us this, once upon a time, and for all we know it could be true.

For a while, we kept a tally of our own—the faces all done in the same bad makeup, the bodies all posed with the same uncharacteristic formality. Or maybe not all, but who can remember now? The scale of loss will come to rob each death of its particularity. One day we'll come to be jealous of our early miseries—those losses that still felt singular.

There are ways only young hearts can break. In the end, even grief turns out to be finite: a resource we can squander just like time, and in ways we'll never stop regretting.

CHORUS:

We went to Tina Turner–themed drag shows. We went to support groups for the worried well.

We still went cruising, sometimes, and pretended we were new in town. We pretended we were still pretending to be straight.

We went to therapy, to address the childhood emotional emergency that might cause the disease to psychointubate within us.

We went to a snuffling Hungarian doctor on Clinton Street. He gave us brutalizing, old-world massages and sent us home with a tincture that looked like and probably was paprika.

We took it anyway.

COMPANY:

It was said that you could get it through household contact.

SIMON: "I guess that depends on what kind of *contact* is going on in your household."

It was said the employees of a London switchboard had quit the phones en masse: they were afraid of catching it from the wiring.

It was said that when a PWA had gotten into a fender-bender in midtown, they'd called in an actual hazmat team.

It was said to have spread to a grandmother in Long Island, a housekeeper at Bellevue.

It was said, by SIMON: "The infectious disease of the people!"

It was said, by JOHNNY: "Just like *La Traviata!*"

(*He starts to sing an aria. Tonight, the actor playing Paulie sounds so freakily like him that Brookie and I both begin to cry.*)

CHORUS:

We watched PSAs.

We watched a tumorous burl grow to the size of an eggplant on a human face.

We watched a special where Barbara Walters told a man that he was positive.

We all agreed this made for great TV.

We wore tortoiseshell glasses over eye patches, stage makeup over KS lesions.

We wore pins proclaiming We Would Survive.

We wore Jeane Kirkpatrick masks for Halloween.

(*Actor appears in mask, stilettos, and nothing else. Though the script calls for all roles to rotate, they have a very good reason to use the same guy for this one: the audience whistles and claps and hoots for a full min-ute.*)

We went to fund raisers at the Saint; we went to the St. Vincent's ER. We went to see *Amadeus,* and held forth about the superior-ity of the stage version.

(*Knowing laughter, here, from the audience.*)

We still went walking, sometimes. We walked past turquoise buildings in SoHo; we walked past doormen watching portable TVs. We walked across the Manhattan Bridge, where someone else was walking in the distance: for a long time it was not clear if the figure was moving toward us or away.

IT'S ALWAYS STRANGE TO WATCH THIS PLAY: I KNOW EVERY WORD, AND STILL never know what I will see. Up close, the set's resurrections are un-canny: the boat to Fire Island, the flickering candles on what's meant to be a distant beach. The abattoir of the St. Luke's–Roosevelt ER, circa 1984. I don't know how the design people do this stuff. They manage to conjure many things that I've forgotten: the way, for a while, almost every couple looked like some kind of outrageous May–December romance. The pump-top dispensers of lubricant at St. Mark's. The way the sick faces looked strange in the beginning, until there were so many that the healthy faces started to look strange, too. How *I* must have looked strange, with my pretty un-blemished face, as I moved through certain circles. I knew it, of course, but I'd never seen it: now that I have, I know it differently. I'm lost in this for a while, ghosts and memories on the stage and off, and when I tune back in, the show is nearly over.

Every night begins with a big cast and ends with a small one. This is true even when time within the play is moving backwards, as an acknowledgment that real time is not—a fact also reflected in the high turnover of the cast.

There are four actors on the stage now, doing another section about spectacles.

COMPANY:
We watched intubation and agonal breathing.

We watched freezing feet turn purple; we watched last rites of every kind.

We watched the massacre of the innocents: the hemophiliac children, the family whose house burned down in Florida.

RIVER: "What a shame. The first civilian casualties."

("You gave me one of the last lines!" Brookie whispers. "It isn't you," I say. "It's the character. And anyway, this isn't the ending every night.")

We watched the McMartin Preschool trial on *Rivera*.

We watched the baby in the well on CNN.

We watched the dying stare into the darkness and see their parents and their partners, their gods and their dogs.

We watched the dying stare into the darkness—

And stare—

And stare—

And, finally, see nothing at all.

THE SHOW ENDS TONIGHT WITH A TABLEAU: THE SILHOUETTE OF REAGAN, PARalyzed at the podium, with the entire resurrected cast sitting cross-legged before him. I'm always squeamish about beginning or ending with Reagan—it seems too dramatically stark for a story about how there are many ways to tell a story. But then, this is why there have been other versions before tonight, and why there will, for at least a while longer, be more. And I do like the elegant recursiveness of the image—the audience watching an audience watching just another audience.

And so tonight, ten years into the plague, this is what we are left with: the freeze-frame of a man who could have acted, but did not.

And Brookie, staggering unbelievably up from his wheelchair, to start a standing ovation.

AFTERWARD, IT SEEMS, MATTHEW MILLER IS STANDING IN THE LOBBY.

When I see him, I do a double take. It seems I'm not the only one: the lobby is a mass pantomime of ignorance—no one in this room wants to admit to knowing who he is. This is how he's managed to get away with standing there, in plain sight, while he waits, presumably, for me. This is the kind of tactical thinking that might have been useful in a politician: in a person without a cause, it just seems sneaky.

"You came," I observe, when I finally reach him.

"I said I would."

"Did you? I find a lot of people say a lot of things."

"Well, you don't have to take my word for it, do you?" he says. "We've got it all on tape."

I lower my head. Matthew Miller is here—again and finally—and in any other life, I think I'd be too amazed to stand it. But the weir defending reality from possibility has collapsed long ago, and I accept this as one of the many ways things can go.

"It's a beautiful play," he says.

"It's about ten years too late."

"You wonder if you'd written it earlier."

"I wonder a lot of things."

"If, if, if," says Matthew softly. "Don't start counting or they'll drown you."

I remind myself he is not hurting me; that there are no wounds that he can open. Or maybe it's that there are only wounds, all cauterized long ago.

"Sometimes I think none of it would have mattered," I say.

"Sometimes I think we've just entered an age of nihilism. Sometimes I think your show is actually helping us acknowledge that. To that extent—well, it's honest, anyway, which is more than I thought I'd ever say about you."

"You sound like Suzanne Bryanson."

"Who's that?"

"My nemesis, apparently."

I wonder where Brookie has gone; I wonder dimly if someone thought to wheel him home.

"Speaking of which," I say. "How's Alice?"

"She's well. I hear."

"You split up."

"It took a little while."

"Amazing," I say, and shake my head. "How did you ever manage to hang on to that woman?"

Matthew says nothing for a moment, and I realize he's decided, for his own inscrutable reasons, to take this question seriously. An isosceles of failing light has insinuated itself onto his face: why does it keep having to stay so light, for so long, regardless of the circumstances?

"I think she decided that she could look at our life as a kind of truth, or else a kind of lie," he says. "She knew she was still going to have to decide which one to believe in."

Have I ever dared to dream of a life where I knew anything for certain? Would I even want to, anymore?

"Or *behave* as though she believed, was how I think actually she put it. I suppose that's when I should have left."

"Oh, *that* was when?"

"But I didn't, and so we lived in one version of the story."

"Until she stopped believing you."

"Not exactly." That voice: I can still remember its precise sonority through a rib cage. "I think she never believed me any more or less than she did on that first day, when I first told her about you. She knew then—she probably knew already—that a life with me could only take place in some strange space, between two incompatible realities. She knew that one of those realities was happy. And she said when she was young, this was the version that felt—not necessarily likelier, but more alive to her. She said she wanted my love more than she feared my contempt."

"But then, one's calculus shifts."

"Hers did. She found she wanted to know she was not pitied more than she wanted to hope she was loved. She said she wanted to face the second half of her life with all of her premises clarified."

Alice: oh, poor Alice. For the longest time I'd assumed—no: also? I had hoped—that she was very, very stupid.

"Or maybe it just took her that long to figure out I wasn't worth the trouble," says Matthew.

Was he worth the trouble? This is a question asked only of the young, by people who think they're already old. But the truly ancient know that everything is trouble, that the opposite of trouble is death. And so in the end, we make our peace with trouble, as a sign of having lived a little while upon this earth.

"I have something I'd like you to have," says Matthew.

"Not *roses*, I hope."

Matthew doesn't laugh. He seems driven by a strange impulsion and—for one sweet, atavistic moment—it feels like absolutely anything might happen. Then he opens his briefcase. It looks exactly like the one from the seventies, though it cannot possibly be the same one. Then, he pulls out an envelope: this he handles with the delicacy of a breviary.

"What is this?" I say.

"A letter." He hands it to me.

"For me?"

"No," he says. "But I think that you should have it."

A beat passes between us, and I begin to understand.

"I think you'll find it interesting," says Matthew.

I laugh. "I bet I'm not the only one."

"No," says Matthew. "But you're an artist. I think you'll know what to do with it."

```
Dear Mattie,

    I don't really know why I'm writing to you. Well, I
do, sort of. I guess it's kind of a joke, though I don't
```

know who's going to be laughing. Not you, because you won't ever read this. Not me either, because I don't really laugh anymore. But it started when kids at school started calling me a Mattie M guest. Because I'm Goth and into death metal and wear cat ears. Before the Mattie M thing they sometimes called me Bilbo (like Baggins—I'm not that short anymore but Blair McKinney told everyone I have hairy feet), Muller the Goriller, which is AT BEST what Ms. Stinson would call a slant rhyme; Lurch (from the Addams Family), or freakazoid, fag, or Fatty (because everyone here is a genius). They started the Mattie M thing a couple years back. I actually hadn't seen your show too much then—another point for freakazoid!—but I guess I knew what they meant, especially when they started saying things like "On today's episode, Mattie M talks to Ryan about his sex change operation/900-pound scrotal abnormality/losing his virginity to a VCR/having man-titties we can all see right now through that terrible T-shirt!!" whenever they passed me in the halls.

So that's when I started watching, I guess partly to see if there actually WAS someone like me on your show—like someone into death metal or wearing cat ears or whatever—even though I didn't think there would be because I sort of knew that someone like me wasn't actually freaky enough to make national TV. Even if the geniuses at my school think so because they have absolutely no imagination whatsoever.

So I tuned in one day and it was a show, sure enough, about this brother and sister who were also boyfriend and girlfriend. And at first, I felt, like, I don't know. Mostly grossed out? But in a way that made me kind of want to keep watching. And I think maybe there was a little bit of relief, too. Like if I'd tuned in and immediately seen a kid like me, some fat boy in all-black and ears, with you asking him questions in this really sympathetic way about his awful life—I guess in a way that would've been nice. But in another way it would've been terrible, because it would've been confirmation that I'm the weirdest sort of person in the world, and that would have been so depressing, not because I'm scared of being that weird but because I'm scared of the world being that boring.

So I guess I was kind of glad that they were weirder, and I was sort of interested in the way they were weird, and then I realized that those feelings were getting tangled up in this sort of angry way—like I was looking down on them. I was thinking, like, "I can't believe these people!!" and "how can they BE this way??" and "I would never, never, NEVER do what they do!!!"

You can probably tell from reading this that I was thinking they were FREAKS (ha ha), though I didn't real- ize it at the time. It's like a dramatic irony, I think, looking back?

At the time, though, I was just sort of absorbed in the show, and this brother and sister. You were asking them some pretty good questions, I thought, about their lives and this whole weird thing they had, and the way you were asking was different than how I was expecting. I guess I imagined it would be really judgmental or fake- concerned, like saying a lot of things meant to show them how wrong they were and show us how wrong you knew they were while pretending that you were saying those things BECAUSE YOU CARED. Like if my guidance counselor had to talk to these people, that's how she would talk. Or I guess on the other hand you might have been really weirdly solicitous (SAT prep word!), like how TV anchors are when real people come on their shows to TELL THEIR STORY. But you weren't like that, either. Instead you were just sort of calm and thoughtful and you let them talk, and you were polite to them without seeming like you were saying what they were doing was either OK or not OK—it was like you weren't weighing in on that, like that wasn't what your job was about to you.

But then meanwhile through all this, the crowd is starting to go nuts. The brother and sister are talking about the first time they did it, and the jeering starts—first a little but then more and more, like the wave or something at a fucking pep rally—and maybe it was that, the way it started to feel like sports, that made me snap out of it and realize that, wait a minute, this whole time I'd been going along with the crowd. I was just doing in my head what they were doing out loud. And that made me sort of sick and mad and all of a sudden I was feeling VERY on the side of the brother and sister. Not because what they were doing seemed so great or even particularly OK—I don't even know what I think of it, still, to be honest, I mean it definitely gives me the profound heebie-jeebies and almost nothing makes me feel that way, but I'm not sure how important that is, because I know I give everyone the heebie-jeebies too, and anyway this is sort of a victimless crime? But anyhow I could see that they were the kind of people who will always make everyone around them feel like they are somehow REQUIRED to take a side about them, and then have a big parade about which side they picked, and obviously everyone was going to pick against them, always.

And so I could sort of feel myself changing sides, and all my anger and grossed-outness was going in the other direction—toward the audience, not the guests. And by the time things settled down and the brother and sister started talking again, I was thinking like, yeah, they're total fucking freakazoids, but in a choice between the freakazoids and the people whose idea of a good time is laughing at freakazoids, I'll take the freakazoids any day, thanks.

I don't know if that's part of the point of your show, but I think maybe it is.

In conclusion, I guess I could say that the good thing about all this was that it made me understand a little about how those kids at school feel about me, how easy it is for people to feel that way in general. But that's also the bad thing. Because you know how it feels to be treated badly but I guess you don't think about how it feels to do it, and this made me think about that—and it was such an ugly feeling, I was embarrassed afterward for having felt it, even for like five minutes while watching a television show when it didn't matter at all anyway. And I know that I have ugly feelings too, but I also know that I'm trying to get AWAY from them (counselor-suggested letter-writing, case in point!!). And so this made me think about how the kids at school must LIKE living in those feelings—I think maybe most people do. And knowing that didn't make me hate the kids at school less, it kind of just made me hate people in general even more.

But one good thing is that now when they tell me I'm like a Mattie M guest I say, yeah? You're like a Mattie M AUDIENCE MEMBER. And that usually shuts them up while they think about it, because as always they have no fucking idea what I mean.

> Sincerely,
> Ryan Muller

YOU'LL KNOW WHAT TO DO WITH IT: THIS WAS, OF COURSE, A BLUFF. I DO NOT know what to do with it. But I know what not to do. And I know that Matthew is either baiting me or trusting me.

Are these somewhat the same things, in the end?

Or maybe the whole thing's a sort of trap. Here's my radical vulnerability, Matthew is saying: you may choose vengeance or simpering Christian mercy; turning the other cheek or biting me right in the ass. Well, I choose neither, pal! I choose inertia!

Maybe character is destiny, I think, as I read the letter again and again, back in my apartment. And maybe, after all, Matthew Miller knew my own.

cel

ON MONDAY AFTERNOON, CEL HAILS A TAXI OUTSIDE THE STUDIOS.

"Do you work there?" asks the driver. Cel thinks maybe he's Punjabi.

"I did."

"Did you make a lot of money?" He sounds like he might be considering a change of career.

Cel gulps. "I did."

At Grand Central, they're restoring the constellations on the ceiling. The constellations are partially backwards, she's read, though that's not what they're fixing—they're only peeling off the layers of tobacco smoke they used to think were soot. Cel can see patches where the original glowing pale green is emerging, reminding her of the aurora borealis. She saw that once, because of Ruth. "Get up, get up, get up," she'd said, as though it was some kind of emergency—which, after all, it was.

She takes a train to New Haven, another train to Springfield. A bus all the way to Hanover; an even smaller bus after that one. From the station, she hitchhikes for a while: she keeps expecting someone to ask her what the hell she's doing, but no one ever does. Her shirt is ripped from changing in the Greyhound bathroom; on the road, she ruins her shoes. She takes a pleasure in the irrevocability of this: the only thing she knows for certain is that she will never have shoes like these again.

At the house, Hal's NO TRESPASSING sign is still posted. It is rightly being ignored—a trail of trampled-down grass leads from road to stream. Cel likes the thought of rogue fishermen being lured here, so tempted by her stream's magic they cannot bear to stay away. She takes down the sign, clutches it to her chest, and begins to trespass.

The house, she'll leave alone. Her business, now as ever, is with the woods. With the stream. With the tiny matter-of-fact plants she can no longer name. With the deep ocher water, muddied from rain. With the trees casting shadows that look like scaffolding to her now—she doesn't remember what they used to look like. With the tiny white flower clinging ferociously to the very edge of the bank—so precisely what Ruth would have liked that Cel can't help but scan the stream for other signs: of glass or toys or treasures. There is nothing in the water right now, it seems—but this, like everything else, could change.

Cel pulls off her jeans and sits down in the stream. She pulls off her shirt and hikes into the woods. Why? Is she trying to commit suicide by redneck? In the forest, many things besiege her; she remembers them all at once, pulling literal cobwebs from her eyes. She scrambles over rocks with a competence that surprises her, then makes her smug, in the exact same place it used to. She hadn't even known that place was still there. She is startled by the number of upended tree roots—ominous and stark, like the warnings of vanished civilizations.

There must have been a hell of a storm here since she left, and the part of her that will always be a baby is sorry that she missed it.

She reaches the top in an hour: but wasn't this a pilgrimage once? She sits on a rock and awaits visitation.

IN WESTERN CLEVELAND, CEL BUYS HER FIRST AND ONLY CAR.

This, she has heard, is the official start of the Midwest; she feels that Hal would have advised her that the prices here would be more reasonable. It is Hal who taught her to drive stick shift; Hal who taught her to drive at all—in tiny circles around the Big Y parking lot, years before it was legal.

She selects a jaunty little teal Geo Metro, which she begins to hate before she's even out of Indiana.

But before that, she buys a train ticket. A man asks her about the beautiful concourse he's seen in all the pictures, and she has to tell him that's the other one. And for once in her life—and it will be only once—she'll feel like a New Yorker.

But before that, she takes a taxi to Penn Station. On the radio, they're discussing Ryan Muller; she's relieved when the tunnel scrambles the signal.

But before that, she goes inside the studios one last time. She has a badge to turn in, a desk to clean out. Luke comes by to supervise. He leans over her to ask if she's been stealing straws from craft services the *entire* time she's worked here, and then she kisses him. It's a joke, then it isn't, then it is again.

She pulls away and he blinks at her.

"What?" he says.

"Nothing!" she tells him, and runs laughing down the hall.

SHE WILL END UP IN SAN FRANCISCO, WHICH IS AS FAR AS SHE CAN GO WITH-out a passport. The wind from the Pacific is unruly, unmitigated by any serious buildings. She walks along the Embarcadero; the Golden Gate Bridge prickles in the distance, like a glowing spine. In North Beach, the streets go up at vertical angles; Cel hunches, nearly crawls. She feels like she could actually fall off the sidewalk and into the bay—this is not dissimilar to the way she'd felt the first time she saw a Broadway show: that vertiginous sense she might drop into the orchestra pit ("Not possible," said Nikki, through cheerful bites of popcorn).

On Kearny Street, she notices a sign announcing an open mic night in front of a place called the Purple Onion.

She'll peer into the doorway, trying to glean a sense of the place, but the only way to see it is, it seems, to enter. She goes in and, on a savage impulse, adds herself to the list. She'll down a whiskey and a half before her body catches up to what her brain has decided and her hands begin to shake.

She does not listen to any of the others; on a napkin she is preparing to burn all her life's material. Everything she's ever used at parties; a few she's been too afraid to even try.

The cutest vintage accessory of all is the Lindbergh baby!

(What is it with her and the Lindbergh baby?)

Thyroid cancer is like the dogfish of cancers.

(A high-concept head-scratcher, at best.)

A bit about Curious George's keeper, speculating about what might be under that yellow hat of his.

(*The skeletons of Georges I–IV?* Cel has always felt that everyone will understand this joke, but these are not the things you know for sure until right now.)

She trips a little on her way up to the stage; for a moment, she can't see anything at all. She wonders if this is what it's like for Mattie, every time he stares out at the audience. When you gaze into the void, the void gazes back into you: pick your voids, then, very carefully. Cel feels a sense of pulsing all around her; she can hear the clinks of glasses, the muffled skeptical murmurs.

"You just never know about people," she begins. "You never, never know."

AND SO THIS IS WHERE SHE'LL BE: MONKEYING ABOUT ON A STAGE IN SAN Francisco, having the hands-down time of her life, so buzzed on joy that when she walks off the stage and hears someone say *Holy shit, Mattie M's been shot!* she'll smile and get ready to laugh, waiting for the punch line.

THIRTY-TWO

BY THE TIME SHE REACHES LUKE, CEL ALREADY KNOWS WHAT HE WILL TELL her. She's learned it all from CNN, which she watches for several hours at a strip club called Big Al's. This is the first place she finds that will admit to having a television, after she goes tearing out of the Purple Onion, weeping. A man in the doorway sees her and says, "Hey, sweetheart, you were fine! How 'bout a smile?"—and Cel somehow has room to feel pleased, then insulted, then disgusted with herself, all while crying and running, inexplicably, up a hill.

At Big Al's, she explains herself to the manager. He is balding and, she somehow understands, kind. He's already heard the basics: that Mattie M was shot, that the shooter was that guest who'd gone bananas on that other guy with a tire iron a while back, that he'd turned himself in immediately.

What he does not know is whether Mattie is dead: this seems to him a secondary matter. Nevertheless, he lets Cel into his office to watch TV, and even watches with her, for a while. She finds it oddly comforting, to be watching along with someone.

From CNN she learns that Mattie is in critical condition at a New York hospital. She does not learn which one. She learns the shooting occurred at the end of the rally, just as Mattie was leaving the stage.

She learns from an extremely pale eyewitness that "it did not look good."

She learns that Mattie's speech was a great success, in the view of the same eyewitness.

She learns that the shooter was calm while being taken into custody. "I did what had to be done," he reportedly had said.

She learns there are no updates on Mattie's condition.

She learns several eyewitnesses believed he had died at the scene; some are skeptical to learn that he had not.

"It really didn't look like something someone could survive," says one of them.

At some point, the manager brings her a sandwich. Then he brings her a drink. The sandwich is very good, the drink much better. She's begun thinking of the manager as Big Al, though that probably isn't his name. He seems unfazed by the fact of a weeping young woman in his office; maybe this is something of an occupational hazard, at a strip club.

"Was he a good boss?" he asks at some point.

"No!" says Cel. "He was horrible!"

She laugh-cries in a way that sounds too much like Ruth: then she just cries, for a while.

Big Al lets her use his phone, even though it's long-distance, and he won't take any cash, not even for the sandwich. His patience seems extraordinary; as the hours pass, Cel begins to consider ulterior motives. Her situation is a spectacle, after all, and will be an interesting story to tell at parties.

Cel will tell it many times herself, in fact, and in many different ways, and after a while she'll start telling it as a joke, first at bars and then on stages: the story of Big Al and his creepily delicious roast beef sandwich and how when *this* is what happens the first time you try stand-up, it's hard to ever be too afraid of any kind of bombing that's not a literal act of political violence. She'll use the story to remind lackluster audiences that it could be so much worse; she'll use it to remind hecklers that, unless they've got some really top-notch zingers, the worst day of her comedy career is already behind her. It will become useful, this story, and maybe Cel senses the use of it even now, in Big Al's office. Maybe he does, too, and is being kind because he's curious.

But no, she eventually concludes: he is being curious because he's kind. He's probably some kind of modern saint, she decides, as she calls Luke then Sanjith then Luke then Jessica then Luke then Elspeth then Luke then Elspeth then Luke then Luke then Luke.

From CNN, she learns that the CPA has released a statement; she changes the channel before they read it aloud. She wonders what Tod Browning or Lee or Lisa will be saying about this tomorrow; she wishes she could watch New York TV.

She learns that the NRA has not released a statement. They never will, in fact, though this is something she learns much later. She'll learn other things, too, in the days and years ahead. She'll learn that Mattie was shot four times with a legally obtained ten-millimeter pistol, sustaining a head injury that was "not compatible with life," in the words of the autistic infant doctor tasked with delivering the news conference. She'll learn that when the gunfire began, some people thought it might be part of the demonstration—a part of Mattie's speech or maybe even his *show*—and that a few of them had lingered near the podium, declining to run, hoping to be on TV. She'll learn that a lot of them *did* get to be on TV, because they were the only ones still hanging around when the press showed up ten minutes later.

Later, Cel will learn the text of the speech Mattie gave before he died; she will, along with many other people, be surprised at how good it was. She'll learn there is hope among activists that Mattie's speech and death, alongside the Ohio shootings, could be a significant catalyst for gun reform.

Later still, she'll learn this hope has been abandoned.

At Mattie's funeral, she'll learn he'd been a hatcheck attendant as a child. She will not learn what a hatcheck attendant actually is. She will learn that Mattie's ex-wife is small and sort of ugly and that whatever Mattie did to her wasn't bad enough to keep her from showing up at the service, where she'll cry and cry and speak not a single word to reporters.

Cel herself has stopped crying by the time CNN makes Mattie's death official. She tries to start again, but can't. She says this to Luke when she finally reaches him—after she calls one last time, for absolutely no reason, as there is nothing left to ask.

"That's how I feel all the time," he says. "Crying for me is like trying to come on coke."

"*What?*" Cel hiccups a little. "Are you—are you trying to make a joke right now?"

"I get really close, you know, I *want* to, but—"

And then, unbelievably, they are laughing.

BROOKIE COMES HOME FROM THE HOSPITAL THE DAY THEY BURY MATTHEW. Together, we watch the coverage of his funeral. Outside the church, the press is interviewing protesters.

"Well, *that* looks familiar," says Brookie. He is having another good day: a couple more of these, and we might just start calling them "days." The doctors don't know why he's still alive; his death remains, as the doctors stress, a statistical certainty. But even they admit that, from a purely medical standpoint, Brookie is not dead yet. From a medical standpoint, there's no reason he can't squander his remaining minutes on this earth gawking at a funeral for a man he'd despised long before it was fashionable, while holding the hand of the only living person who has loved him, unbelievably, for even longer.

The protesters, it's becoming clear, are not establishment-type loonies; the professional talking heads' crusade against Matthew has abruptly ended, though no one's claimed a victory. It seems inevitable that syndicated episodes of *Mattie M* will be quietly un-boycotted, and can be expected to run relentlessly until the end of time. Forget the cockroaches: this is what will outlast us all. A dubious legacy for everyone, not only Matthew Miller.

"You should have gone to the funeral," says Brookie.

"I wanted to be here today," I tell him.

It is true. I do not need another funeral. That is not where grief happens anymore.

It will happen in other ways, I suppose, in the months and years ahead. I am coming to understand that mourning will be the work of my lifetime; I will go to my grave without seeing it complete. But some of my grieving for Matthew, I find I have already done. Not all of it—hardly all—but enough to feel the difference. It must have happened years ago, while I was wandering the city and gnashing my teeth and believing I had come to know true sorrow.

This was a delusion that became a mercy: these days, I'll take them both.

AFTER MATTHEW MILLER LEFT THE FIRST TIME, I TOLD EVERYONE HE NEVER wrote me. But the truth is I did receive a letter, once—typed, unsigned, mailed from Staten Island.

I know no one on Staten Island and have no idea why anyone would go there—though it's true that Matthew Miller went everywhere, in those days when he still went anywhere at all.

Through the years, I've kept the letter—though let it be said I've kept a lot of things: Brookie has reminded me of the high incidence of hoarding among eccentrics in their middle age. When his jokes get meaner, I can tell he's feeling better, and feel entitled to ignore him.

I wait to reread my letter until Brookie goes to bed. This happens at seven o'clock precisely; he has a thing about making it past the *Nightly News.* The letter lives in the box under my bed, along with a bunch of play programs and old issues of *The AIDS Newsletter* and the letter from Ryan Muller and some scattered Polaroids Paulie took a million years ago. Those photos were annoyances once, objects of intense sentiment later. Now, for the first time, I see they might be pretty good pictures. Would Paulie have been a photographer in another life? In any life that he deserved, he would have had a lot of lives.

In my room, I sit staring at the letter; outside, it isn't even thinking of getting dark yet. I do not know who wrote it or who it was meant for; the window for certainty now is past. But for tonight, I will decide to imagine Matthew—standing on the deck of the Staten Island ferry, letting the air slam into his lungs, clutching the letter I am holding in my hands, imagining the day, or perhaps the many days, that I will read it.

After I went back, alongside my devastating guilt would be an almost tactile desire to stop time, to step outside of my life, for just a single moment. And once, I finally did: I fell asleep on a flight from New York and dreamt a lucid dream about you. We were moving around weightless in a room. It is still embarrassing to remember the intensity of my relief in that moment—not because it was finally happening, but because it finally wasn't. I was being given the gift of a conscious moment alone with you—not just physically, but morally, temporally alone, a moment recused from any causal relationship to reality. And so in that moment—excused from all gazes, mine and yours, both—I did it: I kissed you, and you didn't feel like an apparition, maybe because we both were. It didn't feel like the first time, or the last, because it wasn't any time at all. And you seemed to know and understand this, too—that none of it was real, that none of it would count.

But even all these years later, I have this lingering hope that perhaps it did—that on some other plane it happened, that in some footnote to time it was noted, and somehow I was not the only one of us left with its memory. In this life I cannot have this moment—I cannot even dream of speaking of this dream—and perhaps, after all, I never even dreamed it: for who is to say who is reading this letter, and who is to say who has sent it? But if the string theorists are right, then in some universe I am signing this letter, and in another we are moving weightless through that room.

I am not saying I wish that it were otherwise. Sometimes a choice becomes right in its making. How long we gaze behind us, at least, is something we decide. And whatever the myths tell us, it's ourselves we destroy with our looking: Orpheus has that part wrong.

But I am also saying this: were I granted another moment of that phantom present—a single now that was only now, and not the future plunging to the past—it is that room I would go back to, and it is you I would hope to find there.

FOR SEVERAL YEARS, AND SEVERAL REASONS, THE BEST DAY OF CEL'S LIFE will be the day Mattie M was murdered. She will find this awkward, always. It will bother her that she was onstage, deliriously happy and more than a little drunk, while Mattie was dying on a scratchy patch of grass somewhere, observed by every single person who'd go on to talk about it on television. One of them will even write a book about it—an entire fucking book! It seems callous, somehow unseemly, that Cel hadn't known. She'll feel she should have felt it, somewhere out there in the universe; in darker moments she'll fear she would have, if she hadn't been standing before an audience.

But what would she have done if she had known, in the moments right before she went onstage? The audience wouldn't have believed her if she'd told them; they would have laughed and thought it was a joke. And even if they knew it was not a joke, they might have laughed at it anyway.

Because that moment on the stage will always be distorted in this way—bracketed by a corrupting dramatic irony—it's the trip to California Cel will come to cherish most. Driving underneath that powder-blue sky, dodging shuddering rigs, reading billboards out of something that—she realized halfway across the country—was less like boredom than like curiosity. She knows that somewhere on that drive, Matthew's fate was sealed—the shooter was packing his van, double-checking the appearance schedule, beginning a drive of his own. But Cel will never know exactly when—the moments are equal in their almost-guilt: the tenuous absolution of riflemen in a firing squad—and this allows her to recall them all with almost-tenderness.

The pocked landscape dimming into sky; the grass crumbling to caliche when she reached New Mexico. The grotesquely enormous crosses dotting the roadsides, like relics from the Appian Way. The eerily lunar geometry of Carlsbad Caverns: its filigreed grottoes, its preposterously priapic columns; her own footsteps sounding icy and very far away—farther and farther, somehow, with every step she took.

For some of the same reasons, she'll come to cherish her memories of New York: in later years, there will be other reasons, too. The thing about memories is you forget them all: almost all of a city, almost all of a woods and little stream. One day Cel will forget trying to eat the scrawny almost-carrots underneath the Queen Anne's lace, though she'll remember nibbling tiny red bead-like berries from a bush, and how she knew right away that she should not have. She'll remember the wild blackberries, as fat and shiny as the flies that hid on them; the flies themselves she will forget. She'll forget the tang of lemongrass on her tongue. She'll forget the rickety roller-coaster feel of the pedestrian walkway on the Brooklyn Bridge. But she'll remember walking over it one random day in May, feeling truly end-credit levels of happiness, though this wasn't actually the end of anything. She will remember the way the shadows of traffic moved like schools of fish in the East River. She'll remember roving summer sunlight on the water. And she'll remember a little nothing moment from the day before she left New York. She's running some nameless errand on the Bowery, wearing that ridiculous yellow raincoat—which for reasons no one ever understands, she'll keep for years—and she catches a glimpse of a girl in a storefront window.

And in spite of the raincoat, and for a single moment, she does not recognize this person.

And in something that's both less and more than a moment, she wonders: *Who is that girl?*

And she thinks: *Oh, she could be anyone!*

BROOKIE'S BEEN IN BED FOR HOURS, AND IT STILL ISN'T QUITE AS DARK AS IT should be. I pull down the blinds and hit the lights and let the television make the room feel darker.

Matthew is still today's top story. Even in death he's a ratings wizard—though otherwise he's become a different person overnight. Today, according to the television and depending on the channel, he's a nationally beloved rapscallion, a puckishly provocative entertainer, a sincere progressive idealist, a once-thoughtful journalist and once-serious politician. And maybe he would have been again! Maybe Matthew Miller could have been a senator! Stranger things have happened, after all: we know because we saw them on his show.

They are trotting out lost tidbits from his political career—the unimpeachable platform, the pro bono civil liberties defenses, the trip to register voters in Mississippi. These were the same resume gems I'd once used to harass Brookie, and now they were boring all of America! Including me, a little, in much the same way Matthew used to. I had no idea this stuff was even public knowledge; I have the sense quite a bit of it is news to the anchors. Who has time for investigative journalism in a twenty-four-hour news cycle? Answer: whoever pre-writes the obituaries.

They handle his scandal tastefully—really, they hardly handle it at all. A lesson in decorum, I guess, for any budding Matties who may be watching. There is no mention of me, thank God, or any surfacing of those ill-gotten photos. Those were the only images of us there were or ever will be: we never took any ourselves. They would have been a liability for Matthew, I suppose. And I was always the kind of person who let other people take the pictures.

They have a million photos of Matthew and Alice, though, and maybe this is why they hardly mention their divorce. There are pictures of the two of them at his law school graduation, on their wedding day—Alice wasn't photogenic even then, though I guess I never did see her in person. There are pictures of the two of them at some gala I never heard about—during my time, I suppose, since it could be no other decade than the seventies. In this photograph is an answer to a question I must have cared about desperately once; now it doesn't even seem like a question at all.

Others are coming back, as I watch the television montage. *Did he ever love me? Did he ever love Alice? But did he ever really love me?*

To a child, any answer longer than a word feels like a deceit. Sometimes I still think that it is. But for now, for just tonight, let us call it a duality.

On TV, Matthew and Alice are standing united at one of many dreadful conferences; they are dancing at a wedding I can only assume is not their own. They are the smiling high school valedictorian and salutatorian—not in the respective order you'd expect—being heartily congratulated by their local newspaper. In this photo, they are nearly cute together, in a certain cerebral, sub-erotic way: I almost catch myself wondering what could have ever gone so wrong between them.

And this is the other part of why I did not go to the funeral. It wasn't only that Brookie came home today: he will, after all, be here tomorrow. Yet in the story that I tell myself in later years, today could be a beginning or an end. In real life, it is both: this is the nature of reality. But in memories, like all works of fiction, we need to make some choices.

I turn down the volume on the television. It is saying nothing I haven't heard before, or ever need to hear again. They're showing shots from Matthew's mayoral campaign, then State Assembly campaign, then inscrutable political activities from even earlier than that. They zoom in on an image of him as a young man—far younger than I ever knew him. He is speaking at a podium somewhere—perhaps at a gymnasium, perhaps to a union—and his mild features are sharp and fervent. And though I have no idea what he's saying, I have the sudden certainty that he means it.

I close my eyes and hold this image in my mind. Slowly, I begin inching toward the television. I fumble with the buttons until I find the one that makes it stop. In the darker darkness behind my eyelids, I see this Matthew more clearly: the furrowed vertices of his eyebrows; the lashing, semi-submerged intensity of his gaze. For a moment, I let this image eclipse the others—the other memories, other possibilities, kaleidoscopically arraying themselves around and among and above the moment I hold in my mind. I know they'll be back, as ghosts always are: haunting being a treatable but not yet curable condition. But for now, there is only this. The only me is in this moment, the only Matthew is in that one—that moment when he believes something he is also saying out loud. When he believes that he will do this for the rest of his life. When it is still possible he is right.

It is then that I decide: this is the one I will remember.

ACKNOWLEDGMENTS

THANKS TO MY SINGULAR AGENT, HENRY DUNOW, AND MY DAUNTLESS EDITOR, Andrea Walker. Thanks to everyone at Penguin Random House, especially Emma Caruso and the much-missed David Ebershoff.

I am grateful for the following works: *Stonewall: The Riots That Sparked a Gay Revolution*, David Carter; *Geography of the Heart*, Fenton Johnston; *Chronicle of a Plague, Revisited*, Andrew Holleran; "Poor Teeth," Sarah Smarsh; *Ed Koch and the Rebuilding of New York City*, Jonathan Soffer; *And the Band Played On*, Randy Shilts.

Thanks to everyone at Texas State University. I am especially grateful to my astonishing MFA students, and to Tom Grimes, who first lured me to Texas to teach them.

Thanks to my families: the boundlessly good Perrys and Martins, the cantankerously resilient Fletchers and Selbys and Joneses and Birdgenaws—and most of all Carolyn du Bois, who gave me everything except a totally solid understanding of how to spell my last name.

Thanks to Dalia Azim, Adam Krause, Keija Kaarina Parssinen, Kate Sachs, and Mary Helen Specht, for the feedback. Thanks to T. Geronimo Johnson, Karan Mahajan, and Tony Tulathimutte, for the advice. Thanks to Roman Butvin, for the Russian. Thanks to the staff and clients of Front Steps, for the perspective. Thanks to Angie Besharra, John Greenman, Becka Oliver, Stacey Swann, and Mike Yang, for the blood sport. Thanks to Stephanie Noll and Stacey (again), for their kindness in New Mexico.

Thanks to Jen Ballesteros, Prerna Bhardwaj, Will Boast, Dave Byron, Katie Chase, Callie Collins, Lydia Conklin, Morgan Gliedman, Louisa Hall, Akemi Johnson, Matt Lavin, Chris Leslie-Hynan, James Han Mattson, Kate Medow, Jill Meyers, Ilana Panich-Linsman, Maya Perez, Adeena Reitberger, Kirstin Valdez Quade, Justin Race, Cassie Ramos, Nina Schloesser, Maggie Shipstead, Tyler Stoddard Smith, Becca Sripada, Patrice Taddonio, and Laura Vert: for pretty much everything else.

The parts about Northampton are for Aislinn. The parts about the woods are for my father.

The rest is for Justin Perry: I will never know what I did in my last life to deserve you in this one. Whatever it was, I say to the universe: you're welcome!

acknowledgments

ABOUT THE AUTHOR

JENNIFER DUBOIS is the author of *A Partial History of Lost Causes,* a finalist for the PEN/Hemingway Prize for Debut Fiction. The National Book Foundation named her one of its 5 Under 35 authors. Her second novel, *Cartwheel,* was a finalist for the New York Public Library's Young Lions Award. An alumna of the Iowa Writers' Workshop and Stanford University's Stegner Fellowship, duBois is the recipient of a Whiting Award and a National Endowment for the Arts Creative Writing grant. She teaches in the MFA program at Texas State University.

jennifer-dubois.com

Twitter: @jennifer_dubois

ABOUT THE TYPE

This book was set in Scala, a typeface designed by Martin Majoor in 1991. It was originally designed for a music company in the Netherlands and then was published by the international type house FSI FontShop. Its distinctive extended serifs add to the articulation of the letterforms to make it a very readable typeface.